Don't Look Back

S. E. GILCHRIST

Don't Look Back © 2015 S. E. Gilchrist

Published by Suzanne Hamilton

ISBN-13: 978-0-9925266-3-4

Cover Art: Damonza

Edited: Cathleen Ross

DEDICATION

To my wonderful CP and friends, Erin Moira O'Hara,
Cathleen Ross and Stacey Nash.
For Kerstie, Kyle & Blake and their endless support.

CONTENTS

ACKNOWLEDGMENTS

I would never have realized my dreams of being a writer without the motivation and support of my loving family and friends and the wonderful writing communities of: Romance Writers of Australia, Romance Writers of America and Romance Writers of New Zealand.
Special thanks to my face-to-face writing group, Hunter Romance Writers.
You ladies rock.

CHAPTER 1 - PREPARE

In the not too distant future.

I reckon hell couldn't get any hotter. Forty degrees in the shade and still rising and here I was stuck inside the Adults Literacy classroom enduring another day of torment. The air conditioner jammed in the window, rattled and wheezed, intermittently puffing hot, dusty air into my face. My nose tickled while I fisted my hands and stared so hard at the projected image on the whiteboard my eyes watered.

Judging from the loud sucking noise coming from Phil Johnson, my lecturer, he was shifting those disgusting false teeth of his around his mouth.

He raised a hand to smooth a few strands of greasy hair covering the bald patch on the top of his head. Beneath his arm-pits, sweat stained his puce business shirt.

This guy had a serious hygiene problem.

But at least I was out of smelling range.

From the corner of my eye, I caught the Sudanese boy picking his nose then inspecting his finger, a look of utter boredom on his face.

My stomach rolled. *Eeuw.*

Another classmate, a turbaned man in his mid-thirties and who'd hit the shores twelve months ago, had his head on the desk and snored like a snuffling pig. I'd heard the shifts out at the local abattoirs were killers.

The rest of the class didn't look any more enthusiastic and as a teacher, Phil was just as depressing. Unless I passed this exam I could be doomed to spend the rest of my life in this room. If I did pass I'd be accepted into the local college and I wanted that land-care apprenticeship so bad, I could taste it.

Talk about pressure.

In a month's time, I'd be nineteen and I had to find some direction in my life. There weren't a lot of options for me. I'd failed my Higher School Certificate last year, not that I'd ever thought I'd do otherwise, given my disability.

I guess it could be worse.

At least, I don't see dead people.

Phil finally clicked his teeth into place. "Well, Tara?"

Think. It could be a trick. But if I'm wrong....

A lone bead of sweat trickled between my breasts making me itch. My heart jolted and hiccupped like a deranged circus clown as desperation clawed its way up my throat. *Please. Please. Please.*

Focusing so hard, pain sliced through my brain, I mumbled the first line of the first verse in the Australian National Anthem.

"Excellent." Phil beamed.

Am I awesome or what? Although it wasn't too hard a guess. Phil had been humming the song while he set up the data projector.

Placing one hand behind his back, Phil paced to the desk and pointed to another classmate, a thirty-something single-mother. She had an awesome tat of an eagle on the top of her shaved head. "Gloria, read the third line of the second paragraph."

"Huh? Who me? I don't read this shit man," drawled Gloria.

I collapsed onto the hard, plastic chair. *Whew.* That was

2

close. I slunk lower in my chair, breathing deep to try and steady my racing heart. But it didn't work.

I had to look.

I had to see if it was still there.

With the attention deflected off me for a few minutes while Gloria and Phil entered into a feisty argument at the front of the classroom, I stared at the whiteboard.

That's it. I really am crazy.

I squinted.

I blinked.

I rubbed my eyes.

It did no good. Four paragraphs but to me, as usual, it was a bizarre jumble of letters and spaces that would take me like forever to decipher.

Apart from a message that stood out in bold, double-sized font:

GM#9 Prepare.

Like huh? What was GM#9? Or maybe it didn't mean anything at all. Maybe it was my stupid brain playing its usual games.

I rubbed a hand across my forehead that throbbed like I'd indulged in a two day drinking binge. Problem was, this wasn't the first time I'd read something that couldn't possibly exist.

But I'd learned the hard way over the years to keep my mouth shut and my head down.

"Very well," snapped Phil, obviously giving up the battle with Gloria. He swung round to glare at the class. He stomped over to the data projector and changed the screen. His gaze swept the room and alighted on me.

Seriously, why me?

Do I have some kind of red target painted on my chest?

"Tara, you will show your classmates the correct way to behave in a room of learning. Read the third line of the second paragraph."

There was no way it could be the same answer a second

time round.

What could I do?

I straightened and focused on the board. Another mad jumble of letters, numbers and spaces taken from some blog – a favorite trick of our teacher to test the extent of the classes' reading skills which were pretty pitiful to say the least.

Nothing made sense but at least there was no longer any weird message amongst the mess. Plucking my glasses from the case on the desk, I perched them on my nose. Playing for time. *Nope.* Didn't do a thing. My mind raced over various possibilities.

I could fall to the floor in a fit, yell *fire*, attempt another bluff in the certain knowledge I'd fail.

Why did everything have to be so hard?

Voices sounded from outside the corridor. The next moment the door opened and in trooped a bunch of people.

Another reprieve.

The district mayor, with two self-important PAs in pencil-tight skirts either side of him and, god forbid, three suits who looked like they'd come off the set of an old gangster movie. They sported shades darker than midnight and jerked their heads as if scanning every nook and cranny of the classroom.

As if they suspected there was a terrorist in here masquerading as an English student.

I sniggered then stopped as my gaze landed on the last incomer; Crystal Chambers, the mayor's pampered brat. The same Crystal who'd played every 'mean girl' trick possible on me, from the moment I'd arrived in this hick town. I was positive the term, snitch bitch, had been specially invented for this chick.

Wow. This day could not get any worse.

Dressed in a trendy linen skirt suit, model-perfect makeup and with not one hair out of place, she was such a wannabe.

Leaning over my desk to get a better look, I sucked in a sharp breath as her unnaturally firm chest caught my eyes. *OMG, Crystal's had a boob job!*

"Tara Ferguson! What are you doing here?" Crystal called out in that clear, carrying, high voice of hers making me slink lower in my seat.

Cow. She knew full well what I was doing here, since she'd made several snide comments on my Facebook page three weeks ago when I'd posted my news.

"Daddy, look it's Tara; you remember, from high school." Crystal struck a pose on her six-inch fire-engine red stilettos that I instantly lusted after and soothed a manicured hand down her short ice-blue skirt. From under her broom-sized false lashes, she snaked a look at me and cooed, "Still can't read, Tara? Oh you poor thing."

The group of officials turned to look. Now the entire classroom had roused from their heat-induced stupor and stared at me too.

If only I had a gun.

Glaring at Crystal, I crossed my arms over my practically non-existent boobs.

The next instant, my beeper went off. (And yeah, I know, so old tech but it was courtesy of my mother and seriously not worth the grief she'd direct at me if I dared move without it.)

Yes! Thank you God. I was so outta there.

With the speed of a bullet, I shot to my feet, shoved books, iPad and a water bottle into my back pack and hustled to the door. "Sorry, Phil. I have to go."

"Must we go through this every lesson, Tara?" bleated Phil, sucking loudly on his teeth. "Or is your mother determined to persecute me?"

The mayor stuffed his hands in his pocket and puffed up his chest to an enormous size. Any minute now and a button would pop off his vest. Possibly blinding someone for life. "What exactly is going on here? This is an official visit. I have the media lined up in the cafeteria."

"Mister Mayor, your honor...." bleated Phil, an oily smile spreading over his face. He was such a brown nose.

"Still at your mummy's beck and call, Tara," sniped Crystal.

Shrugging the backpack over my shoulders I pushed past, sending Crystal teetering on those gorgeous heels of hers. "Still at your Daddy's beck and call, Crystal?"

"Oooh! Just you wait!" screeched Crystal slamming the door behind me and missing my heels by an inch.

The classroom erupted into a muted roar of jeers, whistles and catcalls.

Mister Johnson's squeaky voice called the class to order. The thumping noises signified he pounded on his desk but as I passed down the corridor the sounds died until all I could hear was the slapping of my canvas shoes against the scuffed linoleum covered floor.

I signed out and left the five-roomed building that passed as Wallaby Creek's technical learning centre and jogged to the bicycle rack. Another pain in the arse. Because I couldn't interpret road signs, I was unable to apply for my license although I could drive a car as good as anyone. Plus I had the memory of an elephant and a pretty good sense of direction. Still, none of those skills counted when you fronted for a driving test.

If you didn't tick all the boxes, you never fitted in.

Sometimes, life totally sucks.

I yanked my bike out of the rack and jumped on. Pointless to keep the thing chained. It was so old, if anyone was desperate enough to steal it, they were welcome to it.

Pumping the pedals, I shot down the drive and onto the main road. It was a considerable ride to the other side of the small country town where I lived with my mother and younger brother. But not for much longer. Everything hinged on obtaining that apprenticeship. Soon I'd be living and working on a farm and only returning home for a weekend every so often.

That was my dream.

It didn't sound like much, but shit yeah, I wanted it bad. I only hoped it wouldn't be forever out of my reach.

The afternoon sun beat down on my head burning my scalp along the line where my hair parted. Sighing, I braked and rummaged through my backpack until I found my battered Akubra. The last thing I needed was a lecture on the dangers of skin cancer when I got home.

Using my pent up frustration as fuel, I pedaled as if going for gold, weaving my way along the dusty streets. A few straggly gum trees raised their arms in mute supplication to the sky, begging for relief from the dry heat.

I could feel their pain.

The shade they cast over the gravel road was sparse. Sweat beaded my forehead and trickled uncomfortably down my spine. My cotton tee-shirt and cut-off jeans felt sticky against my warm skin.

My knees wobbling like jelly I swerved onto the verge before bumping my way down a rutted path running along one side of our house.

Finally.

At the sight of a boy's bicycle propped up against the old weatherboard and iron-roofed house with grills over every window, I gritted my teeth. Looked like my brother Dan had also been 'summoned' home.

This has got to stop. The chances of the alarm being for a real emergency were about a billion in one. Angry thoughts swirled through my head, as I rode past the sagging door and into the shed where I left my bike. But boiling under my anger and embarrassment was genuine worry.

Mum was getting worse.

Somehow I had to talk her into seeking the help she needed.

Trudging up the back steps, I yanked open the screen door and strode into the kitchen. I threw my backpack onto the old timber table and tossed my hat after it. The bag skidded across the surface, knocked over a vase of bush flowers and sent everything crashing to the floor. This really wasn't my day.

I looked up from the mess, to see my mother standing on the threshold and shaking her head and marveled at how normal she appeared. Nut-brown hair, the same color as mine apart from the glints of grey, but she wore hers to her shoulders and held back from her face by one of those flowery headbands she loved so much. She already had on her exercise outfit; off-white, baggy cotton pants to her shins and a loose, short-sleeve, cotton tunic in butter-yellow.

She looked just like any other mum; except for the stopwatch she held in her hand.

I planted my hands on my hips and resentment welled as I remembered the number of times she'd embarrassed me. Problem was I still couldn't figure out whether my mother was crazy as a fox or just plain bat-shit crazy.

Mum clicked the stopwatch she held in her hands. "Sixteen minutes. I don't think that's fast enough. You really will have to try harder next time, Tara."

"Mum! There can't be a next time. You have to stop doing this odd behavior. There were complaints last time. Mister Johnson talked about placing a restraining order on you."

My mother waved a hand in the air as if she was royalty. "Nonsense. I spoke to Phil and we sorted it out. In fact, he was quite interested in my theories."

Repressing a shudder at the image of my slimy teacher and my poor deluded but naive mother having a cosy chat over a pot of tea, I turned the tap with a vicious twist. The pipes shuddered and groaned until a stream of water spurted into my glass.

"This place is the pits. We really need to get someone in to look at the plumbing."

"Details." She placed the stopwatch on the side-table. "How did you go today?"

I buried my nose in my glass. Anything to avoid the concern in my mother's eyes. I shrugged. "Fine, Mum, don't stress."

"Mmm. I wish you'd give up this idea of applying for an apprenticeship. You already have a job."

I sighed. "A casual bar-tending job is not going to see me clothed and fed in my old age. I need to complete my training, get experience in working on the land."

"I've told you before there is no need to worry about such matters. The important thing is to keep off their radar. Daniel made it home in eight minutes," my mother prattled on.

Maybe she was trying to drive me crazy?

I placed the glass in the sink. "The high school is closer than the community college," I pointed out feeling suddenly overwhelmed.

"If this had been a real situation, Tara, you wouldn't be standing there looking so irritated."

Totally pissed off and running out of options is more like it. "There is *not* going to be an Armageddon. There is *no* secret society watching our every move."

"How can you say such things, Tara? We've discussed this so many times."

I rolled my eyes, groaning at my mother's obvious bewilderment at my lack of belief. Drawing in a steadying breath, I tried for reason for the umpteenth time. "How about we concentrate on what we can fix; like say, the house? It's falling down around our ears."

"No. We need more focus on our survivalist skills. We have to be prepared."

"Crap," I mumbled, resisting the urge to rub the bristling hairs on the back of my neck at my mother's use of that word, *prepared*.

A coincidence. It had to be.

"There is no need for that language, young lady, regardless of how old you are."

"There is no conspiracy, no terrorist cell living in the

house next door, no imminent death, doom or disaster about to crash into our lives."

"We have to be prepared," she repeated. "Why only yesterday I was positive I served a *Warder* at the supermarket. If they're here then the time is close."

Pain spiked over the top of my head. This *'warder'* thing was something new. Mum was getting worse.

"He's our new sensei. If only I knew whether the Warders can be trusted," Mum continued to speak. "They were made differently, you know. They're not like you and if they're here, the others could turn up at any moment. You have to be strong and trained to survive. You're one of the special ones. The ones who will lead us into our future."

"Right." I rubbed my head. My fatigue fled as frustration rose and my headache gained momentum. What I wouldn't do to be out of here. Let someone else deal with this problem. But if I left who would look after her? Dan at barely sixteen was too young to hold any influence over her.

I'm trapped.

And that realization made it even more imperative that I gained legit qualifications. Once I had some decent money coming in I could pay for a carer to 'baby-sit' her. Take her somewhere better than this one-horse town, a town where she'd have access to proper medical treatment. Maybe even some kind of live-in, half-way house where she could be both treated and looked after.

Maybe, I'd be free to live my life.

A dull pain pounded at the base of my temple. Shame swept over me. *I'm so selfish.* It wasn't that I didn't love my family; I did. But freedom tempted me. Freedom and fun. Clubbing, parties, dances, dating; all those and more lured me stronger than any addiction.

And it wasn't as if I'd be gone forever. I just wanted a taste of the life normal girls lived.

I ducked my gaze and drew another glass of water then

sculled it.

And all the while, my mother stood in the doorway smiling serenely as if there was nothing wrong.

"Where's Dan?" I asked, setting the glass down again.

"Setting up for our tai chi session and I intend to do some deep meditation this afternoon. Why don't you join us, honey?"

"I've got work plus I need to study."

"Tara, please, forget this schooling business." Mum threw her hands in the air, clearly exasperated.

I know exactly how she feels. I leaned back against the kitchen sink and glared across the room.

"Well, if you don't intend to join us, you may as well clean up that mess. Oh and by the way?" About to leave the room, my mother turned and added, "I'm pulling Daniel out of school."

"What?"

Mum nodded.

"Are you serious? He's brilliant. No, he's more than brilliant. He'll probably be the best astro physicist on the planet and you want him to leave school?"

"Exactly, that's the reason why he must leave. He'll continue his studies from home from now on. Now, Tara, I expect you to respect my decision." My mother's pale blue eyes turned to steel. "He's my son and I need him here."

If only I knew the right words to say, how to handle her strange ideas, how to make her better. I tried again for reason. "I understand you believe that, Mum, but nothing is going to happen. You've got to get your paranoia under control."

"If only that were true. Too many events lately have indicated to me that matters are more serious than I first thought. At any moment, we could be faced with an event that will signal the end of all life as we know it."

"Seriously? Do you really believe a bunch of terrorists are going to stalk into our town? Out here, in the middle of nowhere?"

"I realize that there are no shopping centers within a reasonable travelling distance that constitutes your idea of civilization, Tara, but we only live two hours drive from Canberra. And surely you're not forgetting that our town is home to a large air-force base plus the new Airborne Early Warning System scheduled for completion in three month's time? A logical target wouldn't you agree? If it ends up being as simple as terrorists, I, for one, will be thankful."

I flicked my fringe out of my eyes. "I think you're talking a load of rubbish."

"I'm only concerned for both of you. Do stop arguing, Tara. If you don't hurry, you'll be late for work."

The next moment, I found myself staring at the empty doorway listening to the sound of my mother humming as she walked down the hall.

Jaw clenched, I rinsed the floor cloth under the tap and gazed out the window. Oh, if only I had a normal family. Normal parents who actually lived together, a decent house, better clothes, a brain that worked like other people's.

I'd always dismissed my mother's wild flights of fancy as crackpot, paranoia, the product of an illness that appeared to grow stronger with each passing year.

Or perhaps caused by my parents' divorce when I was sixteen, two years after we moved to this town. I'd always considered Dan and myself to be lucky; there hadn't been any major fighting or any lasting bitterness. Although, when our parents did spend time together it seemed all they could do was bicker or conduct heated discussions in whispers when they thought there was no one listening.

Soon after our parents split, the knowledge had filtered through that Dad suffered from depression and had turned to drugs to combat his illness, consequently losing his job.

My stomach cramped. Another set of problems I had no idea how to fix. I'd never taken sides, never considered the divorce was anyone's fault in particular. In fact, I'd often felt guilty that I'd been unable to give Dad the help he'd needed, that I rarely saw him now.

If I'd noticed his illness earlier, if I'd been more supportive, maybe my parents would still be together.

At first, we'd struggled as a family trying to cope and give support to Dad but it hadn't worked. It was as if he didn't want our help or was too ashamed. The next thing we knew he'd joined a bikie gang and moved to another town. He'd grown his hair, embraced body piercing, and now survived on what he earned scrubbing the same floors he'd once walked as a scientist.

Mum had filled her days and nights with drilling Dan and me on survivalist training, enrolling us in more self-defense classes and seemed obsessed with prophesies of doom.

Some days it just felt so hard.

Better to day-dream of a job in the city, by the ocean, complete with lots of trendy bars and heaps of clothing stores, the opportunity to meet guys who could talk of something other than the drought and sheep.

A girl needs her dreams even if they were impossible to achieve.

Take it one step at a time, a favorite saying of Dad's.

I plucked two paracetamol tablets from their packet and chased them down with another glass of water. From the living room, came the chiming of recorded bells, as Mum and Dan practiced their ritual stretching before beginning an hour of meditation.

Closing my ears to the sound, I ran a hand over my straight hair. I was glad now that Mum had suggested a few years ago, I try a short haircut. The bob was so easy to look after. No more braiding or spending hours drying it.

Although Mum's attitude had been more towards *easier to take care of once the shit hits the fan and we had to forage to survive.*

Despite my concern, I couldn't help grinning as I

picked up my backpack and went to my room. I had to admit, my mother never backed down. I threw my bag onto my bed and hurried to the bathroom where I had a super quick shower. Returning to my room I dressed in another loose tee-shirt, this one bright orange, and fresh denim jeans and hauled on clean socks. I ran a brush through my hair, applied some dark-brown mascara and a swipe of coral lipstick. One last quick glance in the mottled mirror on my dresser and I was ready.

My room was stifling. I flapped a hand uselessly in front of my face while I cast a critical eye over my bedroom. No breeze shifted the thin lace curtains of the open window. The lack of furnishings made my room feel over-large but I liked it that way. I took a moment to admire the opulent purple walls, the second-hand double bed covered with a crocheted throw rug of multiple sapphire blue, emerald green, crimson and gold squares. I'd made the rug myself last winter and was pleased with the exotic slant it gave off. The furniture may have been old and battered but it gleamed from regular polishing.

And better still, Mum owned our home outright.

It should have given me a sense of security but it didn't; where had she found the money?

Pinching the bridge of my nose where the pressure had eased to a dull throb, I sighed. What I wouldn't give to have a normal life.

Sitting on the edge of my bed, I pulled on my just-purchased-last-week, knee high, four-inch heel, black leather boots (and hell to walk in but what girl in her right mind could resist?). They'd cost me my entire pay packet but they were worth it. Wearing them, made me feel I could take on the world.

Hurrying along the hallway to the back of the house I pushed open the screen-door that led onto a small porch with three steps down into the massive back-yard. Grabbing the rail with one hand, I swung over and jumped to the ground. So much quicker than walking down some stupid steps. Lengthening my stride, I crossed the short patch of grass so dry, it crackled beneath my feet. A stark reminder of how long the current drought had lasted.

At the very end of the quarter acre allotment lay the vegetable gardens in rough regimented rows. For like, forever, Mum had insisted we grow as much of our food as possible. Every seed was retained and carefully packed away in row after row of airtight containers (mainly used jam jars or old cookie tins) and stored under the house. Beneath the shade of a mature mulberry tree, a rickety structure of corrugated iron and wire in one corner sheltered the hens from roving foxes at night. Their contented clucking as they pecked over the ground soothed some of the tension stiffening my shoulders.

Heat from the sun belted down; the air thick with no breeze to bring any relief. Rays from the late afternoon sun burnt through the thin cotton of my tee-shirt stinging my shoulders and bare skin as I strode down the gravel path beside the house and out the back gate. A short cut, which would delete an entire block from my walk and make the trip to the main street so much faster.

I hastened down another residential street, crossed a tarred road and hit the concrete pavement almost at a run. I checked the time on my mobile. *Shit, I should have been there by now.*

I started to jog while my mind zeroed onto the subject that worried me every day. What I couldn't understand was how Mum could function fine with everyday life and still go off on her wild tangents. She worked at the new supermarket on the check-outs most days and often sat up until the early hours of the morning writing articles for ezines on self-sufficiency, herbal treatments and remedies. It made it difficult to understand why she was so fixated on her crazy ideas and paranoia.

If it were anyone else but Mum, I'd be looking into drugs or heavy drinking but Mum never touched either.

One more corner and I hit Main Street which hummed

and buzzed with life.

Kids on scooters shrieked and sped down the footpath. Harassed mothers pushed prams or bustled past with bulging carry bags in their hands. A ute cruised past, an excited blue heeler barking hysterically from where the dog sat on top of bales of hay in the back.

Quite a few of the shops were boarded up since the advent of the one and only supermarket, which had been built on a vacant block on the edge of town. But a few die-hard determined folk clung to their livelihood eking out a living from loyal customers.

On the next corner squatted the pub. The triple-story building towered over its neighboring shops and even though times were hard in small rural communities it did a roaring trade.

Glad to be out of the heat, I stepped into the shade provided by the wide verandah that extended the width of the footpath and wrapped around two sides of the hotel. Wine barrels filled with flowering hibiscus shrubs were lined up against the walls and provided a softening effect against the old bricks.

I made a mental note to water the plants before I left that night as I pushed through the batwing doors and into the main bar. The clinks and bells of the pinball machines and the ribaldry of a group of men playing pool greeted me. The stink of stale beer combined with frying food filled my nostrils. My stomach growled. No time to grab something to eat. My shift had started ten minutes ago. No one paid any attention as I hauled my arse up onto the bar that spanned the length of the room. I swung my legs over and jumped down to the other side.

A grime-stained farmer in a dusty Akubra and sun-faded clothes shambled up to the bar.

"What'll it be?" I smiled. Time to earn my pay.

CHAPTER 2: WARDER

Several hours later, I cast a swift glance at the old railway clock nailed to the opposite wall. A quarter to ten. Thank heavens, fifteen minutes to closing time. I flexed my aching feet inside my boots that felt as if they'd shrunk at least one size from all my running up and down fixing drinks, serving food, removing glasses and used dinner plates and picking up chairs. I was knackered. And those boots were definitely not work material.

Yawning, my gaze tracked to the door when a group of laughing people strolled inside. I froze. I knew most of this lot. Several were from my old high school and who should push to the forefront to sashay up to the bar a big Cheshire cat smile on her face, but Crystal.

Wait for it.

After pausing to eye me up and down, Crystal indicated her equally well-dressed friends. "Drinks all round, Tara. We'll have martinis. That is of course, if you know how to make them. Oh, and make sure you use clean glasses. We wouldn't want to catch anything."

Longing to flick the tea towel I'd draped over one shoulder into Crystal's face, I snapped my mouth shut and reached for the glasses under the counter.

"Make mine a beer thanks."

Quiet even tones, distinctly male.

The hairs at the back of my neck prickled. I glanced up to meet a pair of ice grey eyes in a smoothly handsome face. My mouth dried.

His bad-boy aura made him appear older than what I suspected him to be; maybe four years older than me. Five tops.

He leaned on the counter, hands clasped lightly together, his posture beautifully showcasing bulging forearms and wide shoulders. Even better, he wasn't overly tall, maybe five foot ten or a tad over. I'd briefly dated a basketball player in High School and had suffered cricks in my neck from looking up at him the whole two weeks we'd been together.

There was a tattoo on his upper left arm but it was hard for me to make out the pattern in the dim lighting. (I had a weakness for tattoos, they were on my 'bucket' list.) Anyway, I was too busy checking out the rest of him to care. Dressed in a tight black, v-neck tee and faded blue jeans and with slicked back blond hair and a day-old stubble lining a jaw any model would have given their left lung for, he looked like every girl's dream come true.

Lean, mean and screaming city-tough, I wondered what on earth had brought him to a place so obviously way off his radar.

The expression in his eyes was cool, considering, as he locked glances with me for a long sixty seconds.

Words tangled in my throat.

He broke contact, straightened and half-turned to send a slow smile at Crystal who had plastered her bone-thin body clad in a white micro dress up against his back.

"Gorgeous, isn't he?" Crystal purred, rubbing against him and tossing back her long, salon-blonde hair.

Clamping my lips together so I wouldn't give into my longing to cut her down, I quickly attended to the drinks order. I poured the beer last and pushed the laden tray towards them.

"Card or cash?" I held out my hand.

Crystal rolled her eyes. "Plastic of course." In a theatrical gesture she proffered her credit card.

"Keep it, this one's on me," said the stranger digging into his pants pocket to retrieve his wallet which he flipped open and picked out a fifty dollar bill.

"Isn't Alex wonderful? We met on the station platform this morning when I was waiting for a package for Daddy. We hit it off immediately." Crystal returned her card to her eensy clutch, closing it with a snap.

"Good on ya, mate. Cheers." Kevin Brewster grabbed a glass off the tray.

Oh wonderful. Kevin and I had had a brief 'thing' last winter until I'd broken it off. The guy did nothing but smoke weed.

He raised his glass high. Liquid sloshed over the side. A few drops splattered onto Crystal's bare skin and she squealed.

Ignoring Crystal, Kevin added, "Hey, Tara, how's it going? Haven't seen ya since school."

"I've been busy." Avoiding Kevin's spaced-out, red-rimmed eyes, I opened the cash register and placed the change onto the counter. I couldn't *'read'* maths sums and equations but I was a wizard at arithmetic in my head and provided I didn't have to write anything down. Picking up an already clean glass, I polished it with the tea towel.

"Yes, growing vegetables and pouring drinks makes for such a hectic life," Crystal snickered. She ran a hand down the newcomer's arm and fluttering her lashes, cooed, "Alex and his father have moved here from the city. I intend to make certain they receive the best possible welcome."

"I bet," I smirked.

The guy, Alex, swept that calm appraisal over me once more.

I raised my chin and stared back.

His lips tilted at the corner in a mocking smile and he

turned his back, leaning against the bar while he lowered his head to murmur something in a low voice to Crystal.

My gaze immediately zeroed onto the tattoo on the back of his neck, easily seen since the guy wore his hair cut military short.

My heart hiccupped.

Goose-bumps rose on my skin as coldness flashed like an icy wind over me.

What to others might appear as a random squiggle of lines and squares in something that resembled an Aztec drawing, I saw a word;

WARDER.

Mum had mentioned the word, *Warder*.

Another coincidence?

The glass slipped from my hand and smashed onto the floor, showering splinters over the sticky tiles.

The guy spun round, narrowed eyed and pinned me where I stood with the intensity of his stare.

Move.

Act natural.

The words hammered into my brain. Feeling as if I lacked control over my muscles, I forced myself to crouch and retrieve the glass fragments. Hands trembling I cleaned up the mess and placed the remains into a bin.

Holding my breath, I straightened.

Looked around.

But the guy was gone.

***

Alex

Changing down to second gear, I turned off the road and my car glided to a stop in the wide concrete parking lot outside the new mechanic's shop. I switched off the engine. In the sudden silence, the sounds of the night floated through the open window, the soft rustling of leaves and the creak of branches as a light breeze sighed across the land.

The muscle at the corner of my right eye twitched. A

soldier had no right feeling lonely; not when the stakes were so staggeringly high. I had a job to do.

And not just any job.

This was the job of my life.

My defining moment.

What I'd trained, walked, talked and breathed for every moment since I could remember.

Before hauling my arse out of the car, I concentrated, filtering out the muted indistinguishable babble of the neighbor's television, the screech of fruit bats fighting over the seeds in a nearby cocas palm tree, the barking of a lone dog further down the street.

All clear.

Satisfied, I climbed out and locked the door, giving my 'baby' an affectionate slap on its neon paint work as I passed.

Striding around the side of the concrete-block building I went through the gate then on into the narrow yard separating the business from the house. No welcoming lights blazed from the darkened windows. The air between the two buildings was stuffy. I took a deep breath, sucking down heat, the stink of garbage overlaid with the sweet scent of a scraggly rose bush that somehow managed to survive in rock hard ground and pitiful rainfall. A cat shot out from its hiding place under the building and took off down the street, setting the dogs further along the road into a frenzy of barking.

Small towns.

All so similar.

I'd lost count of the number of places I'd scoured over the years searching for my mark. But now? Now we were close.

The knowledge sat satisfyingly deep in my bones.

And with what I knew was coming, in a matter of days I'd achieve my life's purpose.

Or I'd be dead.

Nothing like no options to spur a man onto his goal. I

grinned wryly.

The screen door was unlocked. I pushed it open and entered straight into a cramped living and dining area combined where a lone lamp radiated a dim light revealing the sparse furnishings. Tossing my keys onto the sideboard, I headed for the couch where I sank down onto the spongy cushions, wriggling my butt and enjoying the softness.

With my legs stretched out, I closed my eyes and took a moment to re-examine the events of the past few hours. Step by step I re-lived my every action, paying attention to the most minute of detail, looking for the slightest hint of a mistake.

There was no room for error in this mission.

A coolness trickled down my spine.

I knew without opening my eyes, my father had entered the room. Not pop. Not Dad. Occasionally I might get away with calling him, father. Nah, mostly it was 'Sir'. Like any other soldier.

But, hey this was my life, I'd never known any other, never wanted any other.

I stayed where I was, not bothering to heave to my feet like I normally did. I frowned at my first ever whiff of rebellion wondering where the hell *that* had come from, what had triggered it.

My eyes snapped open to find him standing as if on parade in the doorway, his gaze cool and considering.

"Report," ordered my father, Colonel Bob Garroway of a secret army.

We'd been bred specifically for a dual purpose; to stand between our marks and those who would annihilate them until the alien armada arrived. Secondly, we'd be the conduit between our marks and the aliens who we'd termed 'friends.'

Our alien 'friends' had named us *Warders of Earth*.

"There are a few possibilities. I've eliminated most of them. It now comes down to Crystal Chambers, Emma

Andrews, Marnie Tolini." I paused, thinking about my encounter with the babe behind the bar. My left hand curled into a fist.

My father's stare dropped then zeroed back onto my face. "Good work. Do they suspect anything?"

"As far as I can tell at the moment, no. What about you? How are you going with your assimilation into the community?"

My father lowered himself into the armchair opposite. "So far, everything is going according to plan. You need to work faster, Alex. Our time is running out."

"I know. I've sent word for Shay to lend a hand. One of the marks lives in Sydney. Shay will do a snatch and grab of her computer and phone. I realize its a risky move and one that may reveal our presence to the authorities but I felt it was necessary. When he hacked into her social networking links he found nothing. With luck this way, we'll get access to a reasonable amount of data about her background and an insight into anything she may be hiding."

"I find it interesting we were unable to identify who sent the anonymous message we received pointing us to this location. Wallaby Creek would never have entered my radar otherwise." My father's voice was dry.

"Whoever it was must have exceptional IT skills."

"Yes. I suspect we're not alone in this town, Alex, although I've received no intel to verify my suspicions. They're close. I can smell them." His eyes fierce, my father held me with his gaze.

By 'they', I knew he referred to our enemy, the Mundos Novus force; a zealous army with a single agenda – eliminate us and our marks. Why? I had no idea but I thought it had a lot to do with greed and power.

"Yeah, I've sensed their presence here too," I muttered then fell silent for a few seconds.

A strange reluctance gripped me until I shook off the unusual feeling with a twitch of my shoulders. The words felt as if I had to force them from my mouth. *What was going on here?* "There is another possible GMU."

"Oh?" My father bored his eyes into mine as if he was peeling away my skin to probe inside my brain.

One tiny bead of sweat formed on my upper lip. Resisting the urge to squirm beneath that all-knowing, all-judging stare, I fought to keep my face impassive. "A chick called, Tara Ferguson."

A girl not like any other I'd ever met.

There'd been something in her wide, brown eyes and the curve of her smile, that called to me, made me want to leap over that bar and scoop her into my arms. And that *was* scary. I definitely was not the *'forever'* type. I was more the one-night stand type of guy on the rare occasions I sought out female company.

Pointless looking for anything more, when the next day I'd be on the move again. But I was always honest. No way did I want to leave some grieving chick behind.

But this one was different.

I could sense it.

Not that I intended to follow through on my interest. I'd play it cool, keep my distance, protect myself.

CHAPTER 3: FRIENDSHIP

Tara

"I tell you, Em, it was the weirdest thing," I said into my mobile. With a gentle nudge of my toe against the tree trunk, I set the hammock swinging lazily.

Through the tangle of branches and leaves above peeped twinkling stars. Still hot from the scorching day, the air sweet with the scent of dusty eucalypt and lemon, pressed in around me. But out here in the backyard, was at least three degrees cooler than my bedroom. The summer had been long and hot. Australia still baked in temperatures six degrees above average, even though the year had ticked past to mid April. Everyone spoke of nothing but the hope of rain to break one of the longest droughts in history.

"Uh huh." A massive yawn sounded from the other end of the phone.

"You can't sleep, this is important."

"Sorry, it's just that I've been cramming for a uni exam and I'm beat. I know it's only early in the year but I'm keen to get good marks to maintain my overall grade."

I repressed the surge of instant envy at the word *'uni'* and muttered, "Yeah, well, I've got an exam on my plate too."

"How's the reading program going?" Warm sympathy laced my friend's words and my brief moment evaporated.

"Okay, I think. I'm mostly guessing and bluffing my way through it though. Nothing has changed. In fact, I think my problem is getting worse." I quickly walked my friend through the episode (as I called it) I'd had earlier in the day at the college.

"Wow! And you saw that message later today?" squeaked Em in her high pitched voice. "This is so fascinating. Maybe there's something in your Mum's beliefs."

"What are you, like four? This isn't a bedtime story, Em!"

"I know, but if your mum is right we need to be prepared, too."

I repressed a shudder at that repeated word *'prepared'*. Was the entire world trying to send me crazy? "Please try and be sensible, Em."

Too late.

My best friend was already off and running in a quickly voiced rattle of words that made my head ache until I had to interrupt.

"There's no need to shout at me," huffed Em. "I don't really believe it but just in case. You know, like insurance. Dad says one must always be prepared and it's better to be safe than sorry. And you can't deny the media attention lately about mankind being poised on the brink of a new threshold."

She sounded like she was quoting a prophet.

"I'm fairly sure they're talking about some new computer chip that's going to revolutionize all technology. You know; talking cars, computers, TV's, hell probably even dish washers and toasters," I quipped.

"Well, I intend to discuss it with my parents. I'll come over on the weekend. Oh wait! Better yet, if you're working at the pub on Friday night, I'll meet you there for a drink or two before closing time."

"All right."

"I'll text Marnie and see if she'll come home. It'll be fun for us all to be together again."

Suddenly, life didn't seem such a grind.

I felt lighter and grinned. "That sounds great. Thanks, Em. I'll see you soon."

***

The next day dawned hot and still. After my six kilometer run in the morning, I headed off to another day of study feeling distinctly anxious.

This was it.

The final exam.

The one that could well determine the course of my future.

It was enough to make me want to throw up. My stomach quivered in a knot of nerves as if I'd spent the night on some dodgy carnival ride.

By the time I reached the community college, I could have done with another shower.

But my lecturer appeared to have caved in the face of the crushing heat inside the room after we'd completed the multiple-choice questionnaire. After mumbling a few instructions, he gave us an essay to write on any subject of our choice while he played on the internet with his laptop.

The abattoir man slumped in his chair, snored, head lolling to one side. The Sudenese boy scratched his name into the desk with a pocketknife. Gloria...Gloria actually looked as if she was writing something. The other students either dozed, played games on their laptops or listened to music on their iPods.

By using a piece of cardboard with a rectangle hole cut in the middle, which I placed over my paper so I could write one word at a time, I scribbled down a page on the value of chook poo as fertilizer. I'd found this method of writing stopped the words written on the lines above from jumbling up into a pile of scrabble letters.

That small effort though cost me dearly because by the time I'd finished my head throbbed so badly I thought my brain was going to ram its way out of my skull.

But I was happy with what I'd achieved. Surely the essay would help lift my grade?

I packed up and wearily made my way home. The streets were practically empty as I pedaled along. No doubt everyone was either cooling off at the pub or the local swimming pool or lolling in front of their air-conditioners.

I wished I could join them.

The heat bouncing off the tarred road was so intense, I worried my tires might burst. But I made it home without incident.

I spent the remainder of the afternoon working in our garden and it wasn't long before my headache vanished. Gardening always had this effect on me, easing away my worries and giving me a sense of satisfaction I didn't find anywhere else. Using the shovel, I dug and heaved until the rambling pumpkin vine had been removed. I made several trips back and forth to the old tin shed where I laid the pumpkins on the roof to dry out.

I stepped back and admired my efforts. Pulling out a few stray weeds, I tossed them over onto a pile of rubbish and picked a handful of peas to eat.

When my mobile pinged a message, I retrieved it from my pants pocket and slowly read the one line text from Em. Awesome. Looked like a girly weekend was on the cards.

"Tara!" called Mum from the back steps.

"Yeah, I'm finished." I put away the garden tools inside the shed and locked the chooks up for the night. Wiping dirt from my hands I wandered toward the house, yawning and flexing my sore shoulders.

"Are you coming with us tonight?" Mum opened the back screen door and walked down the steps. She reached out and enfolded me in a hug that made my eyes sting. If only she could be like this all the time; normal, like everyone else.

"Yeah, I guess so." I hugged her back, my chest swelling with a mixture of love and baffled resentment.

"The discipline of Martial Arts is a wonderful way of improving self-control. Now, I've laid out your uniform on your bed, so all you have to do is change your clothes."

"Thanks, Mum." I decided against commenting about her *'self-control'* jibe and pulled away before running up the steps. "I need a shower first. I stink."

"Be quick or we'll be late."

"Hey guys, listen to this!" Dan popped his head out into the hallway and gestured us into the lounge room.

"What's up, Dan? I need a bath." I leaned against the wall and not bothering to cover my mouth, gave a mighty yawn that nearly cracked my jaw.

"Shush, Sis! Listen! It's an emergency broadcast." My brother fiddled with the remote and raised the volume.

I hugged my waist. My tiredness fell from me as horror mounted at the advice just to hand. A pharmaceutical facility in Germany had been bombed; timed with a suspicious explosion that had decimated a munitions factory in the US.

"It has begun," said Mum, her eyes wide with fear.

Could Mum be right after all?

***

It didn't take long to drive to the local community hall.

"Don't you think we should stay home?" I asked as I climbed out of the car.

"I know this is dreadful news but we have such little time. You must continue your training."

"Mum," I groaned.

Shadows from the setting sun fell over my mother's face. Suddenly, she looked older and I pushed back the snappy words I'd intended to spew, saying instead, "The new instructor starts tonight."

Mum smiled. "I hope he's a good teacher. Don't bother to lock up, Daniel."

"Yeah, as if anyone would want this old heap anyway!" I poked my brother in the ribs.

Dan tossed the keys in the air, and caught them from behind.

Smart arse. But his antics made both Mum and me smile. Although in reality he was too young to apply for his 'L' plates, Mum insisted he learned how to drive. I often polished my driving skills by taking the car out in the dead of night when the only policeman this small town boasted was usually out for the count at his girlfriend's house.

Mum tossed a *'hurry up'* over her shoulders, tightened her yellow belt over her white *gi* and disappeared through the door. I rolled my eyes at my grinning brother before linking my arm in his. Together, we sauntered into the hall. The class had begun and at the front stood our new sensei.

I checked him out.

"He doesn't look too bad, I guess. Look how short his hair is, Dan. It's almost a number one."

"Yeah, I bet he's an ex-army guy or an ex-cop. He looks really fit. He'll probably run us ragged, Sis. We had better get into our places quickly. I don't feel like doing an extra twenty push-ups in this heat." Dan whacked me on the shoulder.

Usually, I wouldn't put up with his crap and would have challenged him to a scuffle. But tonight I didn't have the energy.

I sighed and positioned myself in the fourth row and bowed. Mum, as usual, was in the front row. The ceiling fans spun at a rapid pace, doing little to relieve the heat. All the fans seemed to do was blow hot air into my face. I looked longingly at the open windows, vaguely aware the new sensei was speaking. I fantasized I was sitting on golden sands with waves crashing near my feet. I brushed my fringe off my forehead and looked to the side, expecting to see Nick Tate, a boy the same age as my brother and who lived down the street from us.

But instead my startled gaze met the eyes of the

stranger from the pub.

I nodded jerkily.

What was he doing here? Was he following me? A tingle of heat that had nothing to do with our Indian summer teased my skin.

He smirked as if he heard my thoughts. His mocking smile did little to warm his ice-grey eyes and he gave no indication he recognized me. He sure as hell, didn't bother to return my mumbled *'hello'*.

Right. If there was one thing I couldn't stand, it was arrogance. This guy obviously had it by the bucket load.

Nose in the air and wishing I'd kept my mouth shut, I swung around to find everyone staring. At the front of the class, the sensei tapped the floor with his foot impatiently.

"Introduce yourself, Tara," hissed Dan.

And if there was another thing I hated, it was people staring at me. Wanting to sink through the floor, I mumbled my name, my knees sagging with relief when that stern gaze passed onto someone else.

The lesson began and there was no time to think. The warm up exercises were more rigorous than any I'd done before and that was just the beginning.

Over and over the new sensei pushed us; testing our techniques, barking commands, and soon I wasn't the only one red-faced and wheezing.

"This guy is a nightmare," I said to my brother, wincing as I pressed my hand to the stitch in my side. What I wouldn't give to lie down on the floor and not move for a week. Even Dan was puffing like a steam train. The new sensei certainly believed in making us work hard. "I feel like I'm at boot camp. I'm not going to be able to move tomorrow."

Dan wiped sweat from his forehead with the back of his hand. His elbow jabbed me in the ribs.

"Yeow, what was that for?"

"Jeez, Sis. Not so loud. I think the guy standing next to you is Alex, his son."

I-think-I'm-so-awesome, was the sensei's son?

I planted my fists on my hips and glared at *'I'm-so-awesome'*.

"Who cares?" My heart seemed to fill every part of my chest and I was positive my face was on fire. Would this lesson never end?

"Next, fifteen minutes free-style sparing," barked the sensei.

I groaned, rolling my eyes. Still I turned towards my brother obediently. Dan grinned and muttered, "I'm gonna whip your arse, Sis."

"I'd like to see you try," I joked back.

But sensei hadn't finished.

"I have arranged a system, whereby each week you will have a different partner to spar against. This will ensure that you will develop an ability to cope with different techniques. I will call out your name in pairs."

Now wasn't that just perfect, I thought as the sensei barked out my name and partnered me with his son. With one quick snap, I tightened the blue cloth belt about my waist.

My brother stepped closer and whispered, "Be careful. Alex might have heard you bad-mouthing his father and he's a black belt. I wish sensei had placed me against him."

Although younger than me, my brother already topped me by a few inches and this past year, he'd begun to muscle up what used to be his thin, boyish frame.

Dan frowned as he pushed his hair back from his face. His eyes had that wide, puppy-dog stare that told me louder than words that his anxiety was kicking in.

I reached over and squeezed his hand, scoffing, "I'll be fine. I'm not a master of kick butts yet, but I can handle this guy. Just you watch me."

"Be careful, Sis."

I took up my fighting stance. Mister *I'm-so-awesome* was taller than me, his broad shoulders filled the white *gi* he wore in a way I shouldn't have found impressive but I did.

He certainly looked more formidable than my easy-going, younger brother. The speculative expression in his grey eyes and the straight line of his mouth sent a scurry of shivers down my spine.

Maybe Dan was right. Maybe I should learn to keep my mouth shut.

There was no time for further thought, as sensei barked out, "Begin".

The first few moves told me everything I needed to know.

I was out-skilled by a very well-trained opponent; one who appeared determined to beat me and probably humiliate me into the bargain.

Yeah, I definitely needed to keep my opinions to myself.

A sudden grin appeared on Alex's face as he nimbly side-stepped my punch. He grabbed my wrist and swung around, throwing me over his hip.

I landed heavily on the hard wooden floor, gasping. Anger flooded me. I wasn't going down without a fight.

I swept my left foot sideways, connected with his ankle. He stumbled. Taking advantage of his momentary weakness, I leapt to my feet and rammed him in a classic shoulder charge. It sent both of us tumbling to the floor.

We rolled over and over.

He blocked every punch, my every sneaky move until he managed to grasp both my wrists and hold them over my head. His body hard and hot pinned me to the ground. His eyes blazed into mine.

"Say it," he demanded.

I'd be dammed first.

Instead I mouthed, *"Fuck you."*

To my intense surprise, he laughed and immediately released me. He sprang to his feet and tugged his jacket in place. Next he bowed in my direction before sauntering off.

Cocky bastard.

33

"Are you okay, Tara?" Dan asked holding out a hand towards me.

Flushing, I accepted his help and scrambled to my feet. One quick look around revealed the rest of our group had all stopped and were gaping at me.

Oh wonderful. Now, I'm tonight's entertainment. Tomorrow, I'll probably be headlines in every social media platform in the country.

"No worries," I said and gave a reassuring smile.

The lesson concluded after the free-spar.

Relieved, I jerked a bow to sensei. Before I could stop myself, I looked round the hall for Alex but all I caught a glimpse of his back as he disappeared through the side door with his father.

"What a shitty end to a good day," I said as we escaped from the hall of hell.

"Are you okay?" Dan repeated.

I repressed a sigh when I heard the quaver in his voice. I made an effort to sound upbeat. "Yeah, 'course I am. No wannabee wanker can get the best of me. Although, I've got a feeling I'm going to have a few bruises. You were right about him, Dan. He wanted to thrash me." I smiled ruefully at my brother and admitted, "And he succeeded."

Dan laughed. "You'll be alright, Sis. A deep hot bath with some of Mum's crushed herbs will help. Look. Here she comes. She's been talking to the new sensei. At least she'll be pleased with him. He pushes us a lot harder than sensei Alan did."

"Well, how does everyone feel?" Mum smiled as she opened the car door. "He certainly worked us hard tonight."

"Mum, he is like a boot camp sadist."

"Oh, Tara. He isn't that bad. He seems nice. I actually feel very invigorated."

Nice! I climbed into the back seat and leaned forward to examine my mother's face. Why she actually looked quite pretty. *Oh, no, don't tell me.*

Mum gave a soft laugh. "Bob and his son moved here from Sydney a few days ago and they hardly know anyone here. I've invited them over this Saturday for lunch. Bob was interested to hear of my theories regarding Armageddon and the future."

I'd been right to feel apprehensive. "You didn't, Mum? Oh, how could you? They're both probably laughing their arses off at us right this very minute."

"Tara, your language. Now I realize some people consider swearing is acceptable but I won't have you dropping your standards. As a future leader, you need to set an example."

"Gaaaaah." I flopped back into my seat and folded my arms.

My brother hooted.

"Bob actually had a couple of suggestions to make which have given me food for thought," my mother prattled on as the car jolted to a halt outside our house.

Dan turned off the ignition and winked over his shoulder at me.

I did the eye-roll thing at him. "That's it. I'm going to ring Dad straight away. You have to listen to him."

"Oh no, Tara. That's where you're wrong. Your father agrees with me." Mum leaned over the seat to stare at me.

My heart missed a beat at the fanatical expression on her face.

"The end is coming and you're a special one. That's why your father and I changed our identities and have remained hidden all these years."

CHAPTER 4: SECRETS

Three nights later I stood on the station platform, craning my neck to stare along the railway tracks. *Finally.*

Light from the setting sun glinted on metal in the distance and gradually I made out the front engine of the last train for the day from Canberra. Due to repairs to the line, the seven o'clock train service had been disrupted and had turned into the eight-fifteen service.

Turning aside, I tilted my water bottle and drained the contents before tossing the empty bottle into a nearby garbage bin. My stomach did a funny little flip but I steadfastly refused to look behind me to where Alex lounged on the hard timber bench.

It had been quite a jolt to discover him waiting for the train when I'd arrived earlier. And even more of a surprise when he'd captured my gaze and nodded. He'd looked as if he was about to speak but I'd hurried to the opposite end of the platform where I spent the next three-quarters of an hour pacing up and down feeling like an unsophisticated geek.

An urgent need to visit the restroom had sent me stalking back down the platform and past where he sat. And this time, I mumbled a brief, *'Hi'*, before disappearing into the *Ladies'*.

I teetered on the edge of the platform in my awesome boots, my mind full of nothing but the guy behind me.

When a hand grasped my right elbow I nearly jumped out of my skin. Startled, I lifted my eyes to meet Alex's intense stare, as he tugged me back behind the yellow line. Tingles shot up my arm from where his hand held me.

Alex said, "Best be careful."

"Right." Face hot, I pulled free and quickly stepped to the left. Out of his reach. My stomach clenched. Or did I want to remain within his reach?

He remained where he was and somehow that irritated me even more than my crazy thoughts. "Not working tonight?" he asked.

"My shift was cancelled." I shrugged. "It's no big deal. Now I get to spend more time with my friends." But it meant my finances would be tight until the next pay day rolled around.

From the speakers overhead, the station master announced the train's arrival. Before he'd finished, however, the train whooshed into the station with squeals of brakes and one final grunt from the engine.

"Waiting for someone?" Inwardly I cringed at my pitiful attempt at small talk.

"Yeah, mate of mine is coming to stay for a few weeks."

The train shuddered, doors groaned open and out spilled weary, frustrated passengers. Loaded up with two bright crimson suitcases and a bulging backpack, Em appeared in the doorway. She squealed when she spotted me and struggled onto the platform.

Alex stepped forward and held out both hands. "Need some help?"

Em giggled and immediately let go.

One case landed squarely on Alex's left foot.

"Shit!" he exploded and did a bunny hop sideways.

"Ooops." Hand covering her mouth, she hovered

giving a good impression of an intoxicated butterfly, not knowing if she should stay or fly off somewhere.

"Hey, Em." Grinning, I pulled one of my best friends into a big hug. Releasing her, I indicated the guy beside us. "This is Alex. He's new to town."

"Oh, really? So are you two like, together already?" Her baby-blue eyes as big as the rising moon, Em glanced from me to Alex then back again.

"God, no." The words burst out of me like bullets. Positive my face was as red as Em's cases, I mumbled, "He's a friend of Crystal's."

"Eeuw. What a waste." Em did a 'loser' pose with her thumb and forefinger.

The gesture served to remind me of the million times she'd done something similar over the years and how embarrassed I'd felt. It didn't look like she'd done any growing up since we'd last seen one another in January. She was still a bubbly, drama queen with a high, childish voice that could shatter glass. And completely impervious to whoever may be around whenever she voiced every single thought that entered her head.

Still I loved her and had done, ever since she and Marnie had befriended me on my first day at high school.

I hunched my shoulders as I spotted the narrow-eyed glare Alex sent Em and mumbled, "That's it, we're outa here."

Alex shifted his gaze to stare along the platform at a group of people and I sensed he was impatient to be gone from our company.

"Has Marnie arrived?" Apparently oblivious to the tension simmering like a boiling kettle between Alex and me, Em burbled on. "This is going to be totally frosty. All girls together. Let's head to the pub first. I'm dying for a drink and it'll be fabulous for us to walk in with hotty Alex in tow. I can just see Crystal's face." She snickered.

"Alex...is...not...here...with...me.   Remember?"   I whispered, carefully avoiding looking at his hotness still holding Em's luggage.

Still standing right there beside her.

Time for us to lose this guy and make tracks before I died from sheer embarrassment.

"Thanks, but we can handle it from here." Reaching out, I tugged at the closest suitcase.

"I said I've got it." Alex reefed the case backwards and knocked the passing station guard in the knee. The guard dropped his whistle.

"'Ere, mate. Watch what yer doing with that thing." Picking up his whistle, the guard hobbled past.

Biting down on the hysterical giggle bubbling in my throat, I grabbed Em's arm.

"This way." Quickly, I hustled her out of the station and into the carpark. The crunch of boots on gravel reminded me of the guy that stalked behind.

"Oh, you've got your license?" trilled Em.

Kill me now! "No, not yet." I unlocked the boot of Mum's car and directed a defiant glare at Alex.

But after stowing the bags in the boot, Alex merely gave a curt nod and strolled back to the station leaving me staring after him. I realized my gaze was glued to his backside so nicely packed inside a tight pair of faded blue jeans. What was I doing eyeing him off? But, he sure made up to one sexy package. I'd have to be blind not to realize it.

I watched as he slapped an arm around the shoulder of a dark-haired guy waiting near the entrance.

"Tara!" Em's shrill voice finally pierced my absorption.

"Sorry, I was thinking."

"Oooh and I know exactly what you were thinking about too." She tossed me a grin and opened the passenger side door. "Nice arse. And from what I can see, his mate looks just as hot."

I slid onto the driver's seat and slammed the door shut, groaning, "Frikking hell, Em." After starting the car, I turned onto the road.

"I wouldn't blame you if you were. Thinking of him that is. Alex is drop-dead souped up sex on legs." Em cranked down the protesting window, leaned her curly, white-blonde head out and waved enthusiastically calling out, "See you at the pub, Alex."

The remaining passengers waiting near the taxi rank all turned and goggled.

I put my foot down and the car leapt forward as if we were in the Bathurst 1000. I slunk lower in the seat. "Why do you do that?"

"Do what?" She batted her dyed eyelashes then busied herself amongst the many zippered pockets of her backpack. "Shit. Where's my compact?"

She plucked out a silver disc and after opening it, peered anxiously at her reflection. "Ugh, I look like hell."

"You never look anything less than perfect."

"Tara, you are the bestest. Did you say whether Marnie is here yet?"

"I didn't get a chance to say much of anything!" I grinned, my irritation vanishing. I flicked on the indicator and turned the car onto the back streets. It was the long way to the pub but there was no point in pushing my luck. The last thing I needed was a fine for driving unlicensed. "She caught a lift from Sydney earlier today with a truckie and has been caught up with her grandmother. No point in phoning her, Em. Marnie's flat was broken into two days ago and her mobile phone plus a bunch of other stuff was stolen. The cops reckon they have about zero chances of catching the thief."

"Oh no! Really?" Em turned wide eyes and open mouth to gape at me. "Is she okay?"

"Would I be sitting here as cool as ice, if she weren't?"

Em frowned. "I guess not." She whisked 'Ivory' cream foundation over her face clicked shut the compact and packed it away. "Did she ring you when it happened?"

"No."

"I wonder why? She could have easily borrowed a

phone."

I shrugged not really interested. Em was the one who had always needed to turn everything inside and out. I was the one more inclined to take people at face value. I eased off on the accelerator as the car approached the turn off to the hotel's carpark. The car bumped over the rutted driveway and rattled across the pitted gravel, its squeaking springs making Em giggle. She made a comment about bonking in the backseat and we laughed.

I parked at the far end away from the glaring lights marking the rear entrance to the beer garden and the building beyond. As soon as I turned off the engine, the cicadas' song thrummed through the hot, night air.

"I hate secrets," announced Em.

About to heave open the driver's door (which weighed as much as a tank-door), I stared hard at Em trying to interpret her shadowed expression. Sitting bolt upright, Em looked dead-ahead out the windscreen. There'd been an emphasis on her words, the way she'd uttered them as if they'd been forced out of some hidden place deep inside.

Did she mean her own secrets?

But what secrets could Em possibly hide? With her stable, well-adjusted upbringing, her classy mother with her designer clothes, her newspaper owning father with his brisk, workaholic manner, the custom built home complete with in-ground swimming pool, cabana and spa, she had the perfect family life.

A life I often envied.

I swallowed the sour taste in my mouth, feeling pretty mean and low for the bitter thoughts.

More than likely, Em referred to something else. But what?

Icy pinpricks stabbed along my spine. I shifted on the hard plastic seat and the sound jerked her gaze around to meet mine. The street light was reflected in her tear-drenched eyes and my faint foreboding was swamped by instant sympathy.

Well, whatever it was, it sure had Em upset.

"What kind of secrets?" I muttered. My mind winged to my own problems and the bombshell Mum had dropped the other night. Not that I'd taken her seriously – it was just like Mum to pluck verbal rabbits out of a hat.

So far, I'd kept that little gem to myself, not wanting to worry Dan or even Dad. Mum had never even hinted or mentioned her previous words again. It was if she'd never spoken them in the first place. For some weird reason, I'd been reluctant to question her any further. I kept telling myself it was just Mum being Mum.

And yet...

I shivered in the warm night air. I wondered whether I should share with Em. Dan had too much grief on his own plate with his impending departure from school and Dad...well, I didn't see that much of him anymore. The last thing I wanted to do was load more crap onto him while he was battling his own problem.

But before I could make up my mind, Em said, "Nothing really. Mum and Dad have been fighting a lot lately."

"Oh, is that all?"

"Well, it may be nothing to you, Tara but I don't like to see my parents unhappy."

"You're right, that was a mean thing to say. I'm sorry." Biting my lip and feeling like a total cow, I opened the car door then shot another look over my shoulder. "I wouldn't worry too much about it, Em. Your parents are rock solid."

"How would you know?"

I stumbled on, "Well, I guess I don't really. Maybe it's something to do with your dad's business? Times are tough out here in the country at the moment."

I swung out of the car and shut the door. I tossed the keys from one hand to the other. I'd intended to talk to Em about Mum and the weird messages I'd seen, but if she had troubles at home, maybe this wasn't the best time.

Em joined me and linked arms. The simple gesture reassured me our friendship was as solid as always. Together, we strolled toward the pub where laughter, the clink of glass and light spilled out into the shadows.

"That's possible, I did overhear the last time I was home, Mum telling Dad that she had changed her mind and didn't want anything more to do with some project or other," said Em.

"See? A business deal."

"Sometimes, Tara, I swear you live on another planet." She jerked open the door and stepped into the pub.

Now what did I say?

Frowning, I followed Em as she worked her way through the cluster of tables and chairs and two billiard tables to the front bar; the same bar I usually manned. Unlike the other room, this one was crowded and I recognized most of the faces including Crystal with her usual convoy of admirers and hangers-on.

Oh yee-hah.

And Alex.

My heart did an odd kind of jump in my chest. Whether it was his stance or his in-born charisma, he gave the impression of a sun circled by a plethora of planets.

A woman on a mission, Em barged through the crowd to end up beside Alex who stood next to a guy with shoulder length, straight blue-black hair. I recognized him as the guy from the railway station.

"I can't believe you got here before us," burbled Em, smiling up into Alex's face.

Standing a little beyond the rough circle, I crossed my arms. My fingernails dug into my bare skin, not liking the surge of resentment swelling inside me. Was Em flirting with him? And if she was, shouldn't I be cheering her on?

Alex shrugged. "What can I say, I drive fast." He glanced across the room and swept his cool gaze over me.

The impact of his stare hit me like a cricket bat. My stomach muscles quivered, my mouth wobbled as I managed a weak smile.

"This is my mate, Shay." Alex indicated the guy at his side. Clad in a khaki tee-shirt and faded blue jeans he stood a few centimeters shorter than Alex, with a leaner body. He had the look of a marathon runner about him. But that same, brooding sense of control and command Alex had in spades, clung to him, too.

I shifted my weight, testing the heels of my boots on the sticky tiles. What was it with me lately? I didn't normally delve that deep about other people.

His slightly slanted, almond-shaped dark eyes glinted as he smiled and greeted us.

"Where are you from, Shay? Same place as Alex?" Em transferred her wide-eye gaze from Alex to the other guy and fluffed out her shoulder-length curls.

Crystal sidled between them and cut Em a glare that should have sliced her in two. I grinned.

"They're from Sydney of course. Where else?" Crystal raised one arched eyebrow.

Probably hoping for an *I'm-so-cool-kinda-expression*. If you asked me, she looked a bit demonic.

Blithely ignoring Crystal, Em said, "Do you work? How long are you here for? Is your family moving here too?"

"Let's get a drink." I grabbed Em by the wrist and tugged. What was she playing at? For a moment there, Em had sounded like a mother interrogating a prospective boyfriend.

I hustled her to the bar where she ummed and aarhed over her choice of drink for at least five minutes before giving her order. I had my usual. Scotch and dry. I fished out some change from my pocket and paid. At my insistence, we nabbed a high table near the wall and perched on a couple of stools.

I took several gulps, half-closing my eyes, enjoying the slide of cold liquid down my throat and the hit of alcohol burning my stomach. A nice little buzz kicked in my brain.

"That's better." I eyed Em who was craning her neck to look over the crowd. "What's with you tonight? I haven't seen you act this desperate for attention in forever."

"I'm not desperate," snapped Em still peering over heads. "But I'm not dead from the waist down either. Come on, Tara! You must admit those two guys are the best thing to hit this dead-end town in years."

"Exactly." Unable to resist teasing her, I leaned close. "So what are they doing here?"

Mouth sagging open, she twisted round to stare at me. Sometimes, it was just too easy. I laughed.

I glanced over to the door then jumped to my feet, waving my arm above my head. "Look, Marnie's arrived." Gesturing wildly, I smiled while my super-thin friend weaved through the jungle of bodies and tables.

As soon as she was within hugging distance, I pulled Marnie close. "It's good to see you, Marnie. How was the trip?"

Disentangling herself, Marnie hastened round the table and hugged Em. "No problems, although it was slow. I had to swag a lift with three separate truckies. No one was doing a straight run. I wish I'd had the money for the train but the robbery cleaned me out."

"You were lucky you weren't home at the time." Em frowned as Marnie slipped onto a stool and placed her perfectly manicured hands neatly on the table. "Whoever it was might have hurt you."

"Any more word from the cops?" I asked. At a year older than Em and me, Marnie had always been the voice of common sense in our circle of three.

At least, for as long as I'd known her.

Marnie's hopes and dreams were centered on becoming a superstar model. With her tall, slim body, waist-length hair the color of burnt honey with blonde highlights and olive skin she was a natural. If anyone deserved success it was her.

"No. I doubt I'll see my laptop again." Marnie sighed, her wide mouth drooping downwards. Her milk-chocolate eyes met my anxious gaze. "I know the police think it was a couple of kids but I can't help wondering otherwise. I mean, the diamond ring Nic gave me for my eighteenth was lying in plain sight on top of my dresser and wasn't touched. I know the rock in it is only small, but still a pawn shop would have given at least fifty bucks, maybe seventy for it."

"That's weird." Nic was Marnie's dad and in all the time I'd known her, I'd never heard her call him anything else.

"I know, Tara. And it's not as if my laptop was top of the line. I'd bought it second-hand off eBay. Of all the days for a break-in, it had to be the one day I forget to take my mobile to work."

Em shuffled closer and lowered her voice. "What if there was something on your lap top they wanted?"

I chuckled. "Em, there's no conspiracy happening here."

Mouth tight, Em averted her face.

Astonished at her reaction, my jaw dropped. Em was never this touchy. She usually gave as good as she got. What was with her tonight? Unless, she was angsting over her parents. And here was me, acting the shit-stirrer.

"If the police doesn't catch them, we'll probably never know the real reason. And what's worse my phone held the contact details for a new modelling job. They'd asked for more details and I'd decided to send off my full portfolio. But after the robbery happened, I couldn't go ahead with it." Marnie sighed. "I had no way of contacting them either. I'm a bit down about the whole deal, as the job sounded sweet."

"If you found the job on-line, you could have borrowed someone's computer and searched for the ad again," Em pointed out.

"I know and I feel really weak that I didn't, but at the

time all I wanted to do was scrape up some money and head home. I had one of my feelings I was needed here." Shrugging, Marnie gave a wry smile.

"Well, I'm really happy to see you. Both of you. I've missed you guys," I said.

Em beamed and Marnie squeezed my hand before continuing, "I doubt I'll hear from them again. There's so many models out there looking for work and the competition is something fierce."

"How did you get my Facebook message if your computer was stolen?" A tiny frown wrinkled Em's smooth forehead.

"Mister Lee, from the take-away-shop out front of my apartment, let me use his computer to keep in touch with friends and my family."

"Oh."

I grinned to ease my words of any sting and said, "Now that Em's sixty questions have been answered... Isn't it time for another drink?" I raised my glass and waggled it suggestively. "Don't worry, Marnie, I'm sure another job will come along and it will be bigger and better because you deserve it. But in the meantime, best friends forever."

"Yes, best friends forever." Marnie was the only one who parroted my words.

Somehow they rang hollow when Em failed to respond. She stared like a blind man into the distance. What was she thinking about?

An awkward silence fell and lengthened between us until Marnie dug out a clunky-looking mobile from her handbag and tapped it with a pearl-colored fingernail.

She smiled. "I've got a replacement phone. It's practically out of the ark. One of Nonna's old ones she found in a drawer, but it works. Same number guys."

She slipped it back into her bag and looked serenely at both of us.

Em switched her gaze to Marnie's bag and scowled as if she suspected it held a bomb.

The silence dragged on.

This was seriously weird. I needed another drink. No one had offered to head to the bar so it looked like the next shout would fall to me. Again. Not that Marnie ever touched the stuff these days and anyway, I couldn't expect Marnie to offer to pay given the break-in.

I crunched on my last ice cube and mentally counted the dosh in my wallet.

Marnie's gaze slid past my shoulder and she gasped. Nodding she indicated the wide TV screen on the opposite wall. "Look, guys. It's a news flash. I want to hear what's happening."

As if on cue, the room quietened to a few barely audible whispers. All heads lifted and all eyes turned to the screen.

"I can't hear, what's that they're saying?" complained Em.

"If you'll keep quiet for a moment, we'll all be able to hear," I teased. "Something about a meteor shower."

The crowd shifted and Alex pushed through to stand beside my stool. His gaze bored into me and heat flooded my cheeks. His arm brushed against mine. My tummy fluttered. *Dammit.* With difficulty I kept my eyes on the screen, refusing the temptation to ogle his hotness.

Someone in the bar shouted to turn up the volume.

"....servicemen and women have been recalled. We repeat, news is at hand of a large meteor shower, which is expected to pass close to Earth's atmosphere in ten days time. Scientists are monitoring its path and the government has issued a statement advising there is no immediate threat. The recall of our service personnel has been explained as part of a long planned military maneuver to be undertaken over the next two months. More news at ten."

The image flickered and for one long minute the silence was deafening.

My beeper went off.

A music video blazed onto the screen. Music pumped from the speakers spread around the room and voices rose to compete with the noise.

One quick flick and I turned off the irritating bleeping. Talk about timing! It could only mean one thing, Mum had heard the news broadcast and wanted me home quick smart. Anger welled. I'd go home when I was good and ready. Without looking I could feel Alex's gaze now zeroed onto my belt. His curiosity positively buzzed in the air between us.

"This is Marnie." I waved a hand about in a feeble attempt to distract him.

Marnie and Alex nodded to each other.

Hands in pocket, Shay strolled over to stand a little beyond our small circle. I noticed how his dark eyes appeared to be fixed on Marnie who angled her shoulder in the opposite direction.

Em swallowed the last of her drink then raising her voice, said, "Does your Dad know anything about this, Tara?"

"He hasn't said anything." Actually, I couldn't remember the last time I'd spoken to him. I frowned and fiddled with my straw, chasing the few drops of liquid left in my glass. *Christmas?* Guilt spiked like claws and I squirmed on the stool.

"Why would her father know about meteors?" Alex leaned his elbows on the table and glanced at my friends.

Em chattered on, "He works at the observatory."

Like an evil gene Crystal popped up beside Alex and snuggled into his side, her eyes as hard as rocks. "I can only imagine what kind of information he'd have access to ... as a cleaner."

Biting down hard on my lower lip, I shoved my glass across the table before I did something really nasty.

"Since he's a scientist I'm certain he'd know a lot more than you give him credit for, Crystal." Marnie turned to me and added, "There's a bad smell in this place. Let's go and grab a coffee at your house, Tara."

"Good idea." Relief made my voice overloud. I fished the car keys from my pocket and made a beeline toward the door.

An easy smile stretching his lips, Alex stepped into my personal space, blocking my path. "I could do with a coffee."

I shook my head and met his steady gaze. "Girls night out."

The smile faded from his face leaving a sharp-eyed stare that sent a shiver creeping like a thief along my skin. He turned back to Crystal and, for a few seconds until my friends joined me, I stood alone.

***

Alex

"Not a bad command post." Shay stood in the doorway of the small bedroom we'd commandeered as a study and surveyed our equipment.

"You boys have to share a bedroom," announced my father without turning his head from where he wrote busily on a smart-board with a black marker.

Shay and I exchanged a mildly horrified look as the other two rooms only held double-beds.

"I'll take the pull-out sofa in the living room." I leaned back in the computer chair and grinned. "He's a spooner."

"You don't know what you're missing." Shay chuckled.

Dad turned around and pointed the pen at him. "What happened in Sydney?"

"I didn't find anything of interest."

At the barely disguised frustration in my mate's voice, I blocked my father and flashed Shay a message, *What gives?*

Nothing I could put my finger on, but I'm positive someone very clever erased the data before I could access the hard-drive.

I gave a soundless whistle and looked over to find my father staring at me with narrowed eyes. He knew we'd been *'flashing'*. Did he have to know every little thing about me? I shrugged off my momentary irritation and waved

Shay to a chair. The job had priorities over my yearning for a little privacy.

"Your full report please, Shay."

Shay crossed the room and sat, keeping his back stiff. "Sorry, Sir. I don't have any proof, however I suspect the data had been wiped clean."

"That could work two ways. Either you're correct in your suspicions or your mark is a lot cleverer than you've given her credit for," my father said drily.

I frowned, thinking back to my recent encounter. "I met Marnie Tolini in the pub. It could be the simple fact that she has nothing to hide."

"Everyone has something to hide." My father turned back to his board and wrote *'Marnie T'*.

"There could be another reason, Sir."

"You're talking about someone else gaining access either before you broke into her apartment. *Or* you were spotted and they uploaded a virus which activated the moment you began your search."

My father could always arrow onto the source of any problem, he was that good. But Shay was like a stealth machine. I couldn't see how he'd been made. I pondered over the implications while my father quickly jotted down the three possible conclusions we'd arrived at then stood back a pace to scan the board.

"This Ferguson family interests me," he finally said.

Yeah, he wasn't the only one. I ignored the questioning look Shay shot at me as he picked up on my confusion.

"The dynamics are correct for the marks we're searching for." Dad tapped the pen against his teeth. "Any indications of a connection yet, Alex?"

"None." But I lied. I'd already sensed the pull toward Tara and I still couldn't work out why I was so reluctant to admit she could be my mark. Sure I was attracted to her, but this felt different from the other girls I'd had in my life. It felt deeper, stronger. I wasn't certain whether the connection was lust or she really was the one I had to protect and keep alive at all cost. Or could it be something else entirely?

"Have the other Warders checked in, Sir?" asked Shay, while he logged onto the secure computer and brought up a map of Earth.

"Not yet. Eleven have not uploaded their reports."

I frowned and leaned over to scan Shay's screen where several red blinking lights had appeared all over the globe. "That's an unusually high number. Can we send out recon teams to check the missing guys' status?"

"That's a negative. We need everyone to maintain their current roles. Any deviation from our plans could be fatal."

"Do you think this is going to work?" I had to ask. I'd give anything to discover my father's real opinion on the subject.

"Considering the alternative, Alex, we don't have any choice."

As usual, my father failed to give me any inkling of what lay hidden beneath the soldier. As a commander, he had no equal. He'd led our small, secret band of soldiers for as long as I could remember. And kept us alive.

But our time was limited.

Our army scattered.

The fate of this planet was now in the hands of our marks. Our job, as well as protecting them, was to make them believe and assist them connect with our *'friends'*. Whether that would be sufficient to stop Earth from being destroyed, I had no idea. There was so much about this entire operation I didn't understand. But a good soldier never questions his orders.

"Alex."

I stirred and looked up to see my father glaring at me.

"Sorry, Sir. I was thinking about what's coming."

"That's a pointless exercise. We have to proceed with our mission. That's all there is to it."

"Don't you ever wish our lives were different?" I held

my breath, half expecting my father to shoot me down in flames with one of his legendary brush-offs.

He crossed the room to stand near the window, hands clasped behind his back. Not that he could see anything because we'd boarded it up the moment we'd moved into the house. "Yes."

One word uttered in such a low tone, the hairs on my arms bristled as coldness swept through my veins.

When my father turned around, there was no trace of any softening to his hard expression. "I don't dwell on it. Sentimentality will get you killed. And your death will mean you fail your mission." He pointed to the fine gold chain around Shay's neck, just visible above his tee-shirt.

My mate's hand closed over the tiny locket that, although hidden under his shirt, I knew hung from the chain, as if protecting the memento from my father's razor sharp gaze. "Because of my lack of diligence, my mark died."

"Brooding over it, won't change the facts," my father snapped. "Man up, Shay. Focus on the facts. Your mark failed to trust and as a direct consequence, a Mundos Novus operative was able to get close enough to take her out."

Anxious to deflect my father's attention from Shay, I said, "That's the problem, isn't it, Sir? Developing the trust factor with our marks."

"Exactly. Considering time is not on our side, every Warder must do whatever it takes to achieve the desired outcome."

I snapped straight in the chair. "Yes, Sir."

Shay squared his shoulder and echoed me, although he hadn't as yet, been assigned a new mark.

Apparently satisfied, my father crossed to the board again. "Let's go over everything we know about the people we've singled out. With luck, something will pop. Every little detail, no matter how small, must be examined. Somewhere in these reports, is the information we must find."

He had no need to state the obvious. Because if we didn't find it, we'd fail.

And failure would mean death; for all of us.

***

Tara

I switched off the car engine and headlights then opened the door. After my friends had scrambled from the car, I locked it and led the way back down the drive to the front of the house. Em and Marnie spoke in low tones, their high heels crunching on the rough gravel as they followed me.

A feeble light from the lone streetlight trickled down the road while overhead the pale light from the crescent moon made it hard to see my footing. I stepped on a rock. My awesome boots failed me. My ankle turned and pain streaked up my leg. I swore, regained my balance and limped up the three steps to the front door.

About to insert my key in the lock, a huge roar caused me to spin around to search the shadowed road. My friends squealed and covered their ears in such a girly-girl fashion, I laughed. I glanced over to see them looking up at the night sky checking for a low flying F1-11 from the air-force base located twenty kilometres east of the town.

"Don't panic," I said drily and pointed. "We're not about to be bombed. It's my father."

Amid a cloud of dust, an immense black Harley Davidson rumbled into view and rolled to a stop near the gate. The engine gunned twice before ceasing. There were two black clad figures riding pillion on the bike.

I waved a casual hand and stayed where I was, resisting the urge to dash down the path and into my father's arms. The couple dismounted and pulled off their helmets. Turning back to the door I unlocked it and pushed it wide.

Light from inside the house spilled down the steps, across the thin stretch of straggling grass and over the gate to reveal my father's slightly worn face and that of an unknown girl. Just as I suspected. A girl who surely wasn't that much older than me.

My mouth compressed as I took in the tattoo on her cheek and the possessive hand she placed on my father's arm for a moment before leaning back against the bike, her boobs poking up at the sky.

Dad had his shoulder-length, faded-red hair tied back in a pony tail at the base of his neck. As he strode toward me and my friends, his tall body cast a long shadow over the garden. Looking up and with a broad grin on his close shaven face, he mounted the steps.

"Hi, kiddo." He reached out to pull me into his arms but I shoved him aside, ignoring the way his mouth drooped downwards.

Standing back and holding the door open I peered around him at my friends. "Are you two coming in for a drink?"

"Yes, please." Em hastened forward, her bright eyes fixed on my father standing like a great shambling bear on the threshold.

"Are you sure it's okay, Tara?" Tilting her head on the side, Marnie added, "You might prefer to be alone."

I grimaced. "No, its fine. It'll be good to kick back over a hot cuppa and catch up. I guess you should come inside, Dad, since you're here. Your friend too."

Head high, I stalked down the hallway and into the kitchen. I didn't want to admit it, but damn if the sight of him hugging that chickie-babe was like a kick in the gut for me.

Once upon a time, the only girl he'd hugged like that had been me. Besides, there was Mum. I hated the thought she'd have to confront my father's girlfriend.

"Don't mind if I do," boomed Dad. "Hey, Cissy, wait here. I won't be long. Cooee, Marion? Mind if I come in?" His voice seemed to bounce around the confines of the narrow hall.

My shoulders sagged with relief as I sidled past where

Mum and Dan were seated at the table with what looked like house plans laid out in front of them. Snatching up the kettle, I filled it with water from the protesting taps, muttering over my shoulder, "Hi Mum. Dan."

"Hello, dear. Come into the kitchen, Gary," Mum said. Paper rustled as she folded the large sheet into a smaller neat square.

"How ya going, Dan? Wooah, look at the size of him. You're almost as tall as me." Dad punched Dan on the shoulder.

"He's fun," whispered Marnie walking up to stand beside me as I turned the kettle on and placed mugs on the kitchen bench.

"Yeah, he's a real barrel of laughs."

Marnie frowned and stared hard at me, obviously wanting me to explain but I opened the cupboard door and pretended to scan the contents. I really didn't want to go there, and certainly not in front of Dad. Still, I did manage an apology. "Sorry, I'm a bit on edge lately."

Em paused in the doorway, smiling as she greeted everyone.

"Hi, Dad," said Dan smiling.

"Help yourself to a beer, Gary." Mum pushed her glasses further up her nose and shot a narrowed stare across the room. "You didn't answer the beeper, Tara."

"No, Mum, I didn't." I folded my arms.

"Humph. Have you heard the news?"

Unfolding my arms, I attended to the drinks, added milk and filled them with hot water from the kettle. "It's no biggie. A couple of meteors miles from Earth, I don't see any cause for you to be worried, Mum. The government certainly isn't."

Turning around, I intercepted the quick look my parents exchanged and Dad's raised left eyebrow. What was that about?

"Recalling our armed forces back to home soil is serious." Mum's lips tightened as if she'd been sucking lemons.

I frowned, thinking about it.

"Do you really think so, Mrs Ferguson?" Still in the doorway and giving the impression she was contemplating a quick getaway, Em's eyes widened.

She looks just like a startled rabbit. I handed out mugs of fragrant dandelion tea. Dad shook his head when I offered him one. Instead he opened the fridge door and took out a can of beer which he snapped open and raised to his lips.

After chugging down several mouthfuls, he said, "At the observatory, they've had their eyes on these meteors for some time. There's been a lot of chatter twenty-four-seven between NASA and other countries. I know for a fact that a lot of time and energy has been spent on analyzing trajectory models recently."

"Are you certain, Mister Ferguson?" queried Em. "I mean…"

I knew she wanted to ask how a cleaner would have privy to this information but didn't know how to word it. It was a good question. I wouldn't mind learning the answer myself. I had to wait though, while Dad chugged down more beer.

Wiping his mouth with the back of his hand, he considered Em before saying, "Cleaners are like servants, people don't really see us. You'd be surprised at the amount of gossip we pick up."

"So it's true?" I eyed Dad, wondering whether he'd actually heard this information himself or whether he'd been utilizing his awesome computer skills to hack into the observatory's mainframe.

Dad placed his right hand over his heart in an almost theatrical gesture.

"Oh my god!" Em hugged herself. Her voice rose. "They're going to hit Earth. We have to tell everyone. We have to find shelter!"

"No need to shriek, young woman. Settle down," ordered Dad, a heavy scowl wrinkling his forehead.

"You've got a voice like a train whistle. Never heard anything like it in my life."

I couldn't help it. I laughed and Dad winked at me. If only things could go back the way they used to be; Mum and Dad together, with us.

"I don't see any reason to laugh, Tara," snapped Em, her eyes suspiciously shiny.

My happy moment snuffed out like a lit match in a thunderstorm. "Sorry, Em. I wasn't laughing at you." All I seemed to do these days was apologize. Why couldn't I learn to think before I acted or spoke?

"Hey, Astro. Hurry up in there." The yell from outside came loud and clear through the open window. And female.

"Astro?" Damn, now both Mum and Dan knew there was a chick waiting for Dad outside.

My brother ducked his head, thin shoulders hunched, his hands bunched into fists where they lay on the table. I stared down into my mug. I couldn't bear to see the hurt lining Mum's face.

"Yeah, it seemed appropriate. Loved that cartoon show." Dad swigged more beer then set the empty down. Taking a clean handkerchief from his pocket, he dried his silver ring nose, fiddling it round and round.

Was he stalling?

Dad thumped his chest and belched.

Mum sighed long and loud but her lips were curved upwards; just a tiny bit.

And for a few seconds, everything was like it used to be; Dad acting the bogan teasing Mum and Mum pretending to be the long-suffering, put-upon wife.

I blinked away stupid tears as they shared another one of those damned glances that really puzzled me. Like they knew something I didn't.

Finally Dad stuffed the cloth away and cleared his throat. "I came over as soon as I heard they were finally going to announce it. You need to know what's happening and begin preparations."

What?

That word.

My mouth dropped open. My hand shook and hot tea sloshed over the sides of the mug scalding my skin. My heart thumped filling my ears with its noisy beat. Exchanging my mug into my other hand, I shook my wet hand and tried to concentrate on what Dad was saying.

"Firstly, there's some strange magnetic impulses emanating from the meteors and they're playing havoc with our instrumentation making it hard for us to interpret the data we're retrieving. In some circles, it's believed these impulses may affect our weather patterns as the shower approaches Earth." His gaze swept the room to linger on me.

I couldn't work out what the expression in his eyes meant. But a terrible sense of dread swept over me.

Dad added, "Secondly, at the very least there will be airbursts. Of what magnitude the scientists are unable to gauge at this point."

"I don't understand," said Em.

Dan explained, "What Dad is saying is that some or all of the meteor shower will impact on our planet. It will depend on the size of the meteorites as to how much damage it will cause. Many will probably burn up in our atmosphere. Those that are really big may cause large explosions."

"Good lad." Dad ruffled my brother's hair.

"This is terrible," wailed Em. "I have to tell my father. People must be warned."

In two strides, my father reached Em's side and wagged a finger under her nose. "You can't tell anyone, got it, girlie? Another public announcement will be made soon enough but until that happens, its closed mouths."

I caught yet a third silent communication Dad exchanged with Mum.

"Is this true, Dad?" Suspicious, I examined both my

parents' bland expressions. They were keeping something from me, but what? Was this one of Mum's crack pot ideas that Dad, for heaven only knew what reason, had decided to buy into?

"If you don't believe me that's your call." Looking grumpy and somehow stern at the same time, Dad stomped to the door. One hand on the wall, he tossed a grim warning over his shoulder, "But you must be ready to act when the shit rains down."

Thirty seconds later the front door slammed.

Two minutes later, the quiet was rent with a powerful rumble that faded into the night.

CHAPTER 5: PREPARE

The next morning, I stood in the shower enjoying the beat of hot water cascading down my back. What was real? What was fantasy?

Were both my parents crazy?

Placing my palms on the tiles I leaned my forehead against their coolness fighting tears and my stupid self-pity. I needed to think through what was happening. Sort out the craziness from reality, because my every sense I possessed screamed at me something was wrong.

Prepare.

What did it mean? Why had everyone begun to mention that word?

The timer pinged.

I turned off the taps immediately, knowing how important it was not to waste what water we had left in the tanks. I remained in the shower recalling the conversation I'd had earlier that week with Mum, the moisture slowly drying on my skin.

Warder.

Mum had mentioned the sensei but that didn't explain the tat on Alex. Could he be a Warder too? How many Warders were there anyway?

Another weird coincidence?

Then there was the inference we'd spent our entire life hiding from someone or something. *Dammit. Why does everything have to be so hard?*

And what, if anything, did any of this have to do with the meteor shower?

Tapping my short nails against the tiles, I considered the ramifications. My friends had walked home soon after Dad had left last night. Marnie would hold her tongue but there was no way Em would withhold any information from her journalist father. It was only a matter of time, before the news would be all over the local paper.

Next the internet.

Afterwards, the entire country.

But if that were the case, wouldn't that force the government to either refute it or admit it? Hard to say what they'd do, it was an election year after all.

Really, it was mind boggling that something of this magnitude had remained a secret this long.

Tension built behind my eyes. Flashes of sparking white light signaled the start of a migraine. I had to unwind and quick. Rubbing the back of my neck I tried to clear my mind of the stress pressing into me.

The back screen door whined as it closed. In the distance, came the unmistakable noise of a lawn mower. The clownish screech of a flock of galahs cackled through the open window.

Just another typical Saturday.

Except this wasn't going to be a typical day.

Shivering, I grabbed a towel and wiped off the remaining drops of moisture, slapped on some moisturizing lotion in a haphazard fashion and encased in the towel, dashed for my bedroom.

Saturday. How could I have forgotten?

Any moment now, the new sensei would be knocking at the door and Mum would be smiling into his stern face.

It was enough to make any girl cringe. But I guess

Mum must have been lonely since Dad left. Lately, I'd had a dry spell too, guy wise. Maybe I should cut her some slack.

This could be exactly what she needed. A new direction in her life. I guess I could make an effort to be civil.

After perusing my rather limited wardrobe, I pulled on a white tank top and a pair of blue cotton cargo shorts that ended mid-thigh. I ran my fingers through my damp hair, hung up my wet towel and left my room.

Pointless slathering my face with makeup when I intended to work in the garden for a couple of hours.

The sound of voices drew me to the kitchen; that and the smell of brewing coffee. Yeah, I hated to admit it, but I was curious.

"Oh there you are, Tara," said Mum. "You remember our new sensei. His name is Bob Garroway, and of course his son, Alex."

Two pairs of frigid grey eyes stared at me.

I don't believe it. He's here. In our house. I should have put some make up on.

Oh crap, I should have put on a bra!

No sooner did that thought pop into my head, than Alex dropped his gaze to my chest. Face burning, boobs tingling, I mumbled something and jerked open the fridge door, longing to crawl inside. A bottle of soy sauce toppled out and rolled under the table. Now I had to scrabble on my hands and knees to find the bottle.

Why me?

Coffee could wait. There was no way I was going to so much as blink an eyelash.

Only eleven o'clock. Already the day seemed a year long. Where were my friends when I needed them? They'd said they'd be over first thing this morning but it looked as if they'd also taken the opportunity to sleep in.

I retrieved the sauce, leaned against the cupboard, shoving the bloody thing hastily out of sight behind me. I dithered wondering whether it would be too obvious to dash back to my bedroom. I decided it might be better to remain still. No one paid me any attention. Alex had shifted his gaze to the window. The others had their heads bent over some paper which was spread out over the table.

A puff of hot air lifted the net curtains slightly. The sound of a fighter-plane, high in the sky, droned outside.

I relaxed sufficiently to find my voice. "What are you looking at Mum?"

"Plans of our house." Dan looked up and smiled. At the sight of the endearing flop of light brown hair hanging over his rich brown eyes, the remainder of my embarrassment fled.

Dan was a real sweetheart. I'd do anything for him.

"Bob has suggested a couple of interesting ideas. Check it out, Sis." His excited voice made me smile.

A chair scraped along the rough vinyl floor as Alex moved further along to make room.

Curious, I edged to the table only to trip over a chair leg. Catching myself just in time, I narrowly averted falling into the sensei's lap. From the corner of my eye, I could see the smirk twitching Alex's lips. *I'm such a clutz.*

Clenching my fists over the table edge I scanned the large document, my cheeks as hot as a lit stove. It took a few moments for me to knit the lines together into recognizable images but I still didn't get it. "So? What is it?"

"We're going to build a bomb shelter!" Dan grinned.

"Seriously? Why would we need a bomb shelter?"

"It's best to be prepared for any contingency," Bob Garroway said in his firm *'no-nonsense'* voice. He stabbed a finger at the paper. "See. This is a sketch of the room itself. And this is where it can be built under the house."

I did my best to repress my shiver at the sensei's use of the word *'prepared'* and stared fixedly at Mum. This was her doing. "A bomb shelter. Honestly, Mum, this is the absolute limit."

Mum pinched her lips together and bent over the

elaborate plan.

"Please don't start again, Tara. Bob and I think it is an excellent idea especially considering the meteor shower. Of course it won't be ready in time. But if we survive, it may come in handy in the future. We can build up our own seed bank for vegetables as part of our preparations. Look this is where we'll excavate and here is where the entrance will be."

There was that word again. Swallowing, my gaze followed the line Mum drew on the paper with her finger. With difficulty I managed to identify the front of the house and then imagined the layout of the house. I snapped straight as a steel rod as realization smacked me upside the face.

"But that's my bedroom!"

"Well, we have to have the entrance somewhere."

"But why do we have to dig up my bedroom? Why can't we dig up your bedroom, Mum? And why are you discussing this idea with him?" I could feel the pressure building deep inside. Any minute now and I'd be the one exploding.

"If you will just calm down and be courteous, Tara. Bob has said he can build the shelter at a reasonable price. See, this area here which is the dining room is going to be made into your room. We don't use it anyway and it is much larger than the one you have now. Bob says it will be easy to wall it in. I was thinking we could leave the French doors as they are. They open onto the side verandah and I'm sure it will look just fine."

"Are you for real, Mum?"

"I think it's an excellent idea."

"Guess what, Mum? I don't want a bomb shelter under our house. I don't want to sleep in the dining room. I want my own room. The one I've got now." *Even better, I'd like a room in a house far away from this crazy shit.*

I stared around the table. The sensei sitting as stiff as a poker, with an expressionless face. My mother tracing the lines of the plan with her forefinger. Alex...well, his hotness was eyeing me in a speculative fashion that sent my hackles rising further. Dan, his forehead wrinkled with worry, glanced from Mum to me then back again. *Get a grip!* I was scaring him.

Summoning control, I managed, "It's your house, Mum, if this is what you want to do." And was rewarded by a smile breaking out on Dan's face.

"It'll be fun, Sis."

"I guess it will be. If you'll excuse me, I've got work to do in the garden." One brief nod and I fled.

***

I drew a deep breath sucking in the familiar scent of earth and foliage and exhaled slowly. Some of the tightness inside my head eased. I jumped over the railing and landed on the path outside the house. What I needed now was some time-out.

What I needed was a new family.

Feeling more than a little depressed, I ambled around the garden. Already my top was clinging to my back and my skin was damp with prickling sweat. I flung myself down on the grass under the shade of the old apple tree and looked at the cloudless sky. The air was heavy and sultry. I closed my eyes, wanting to drift away from the madness that existed in my life.

Our neighbor had moved on from the lawn mower to the whipper snipper, the noise loud before fading as he wandered along the boundary fence. Every few minutes, a car bumped down the gravel road.

My eyelids grew heavier, my breathing deepened.

The sound of crunching dry leaves startled me. My eyes snapped open and I propped myself up on my elbows, staring around. Wow, I'd almost fallen asleep.

"You sure have a great garden," said Alex as he sat down on the grass.

Beside me.

Not too close.

Careful not to intrude into my personal space.

Dumbfounded I nodded in response, aware that my pulse rate had kicked into overtime. I closed my mouth with a snap. What was he doing here?

"All these trees and flowers just growing anywhere. It looks restful." He linked his hands around his knees. "We didn't have a garden in the city. We lived in an apartment building. Before that, we moved around a lot, overseas mostly, depending on where Dad was posted. That's why I think this quiet town is so great. No guns. No fighting."

I said nothing, nerves clenched like a fist around my throat. So he was an army brat. Still, that didn't explain what he was doing out here in this one road town. Feel vulnerable lying there like an offering, I sat up and brushed dirt off my legs.

"Parents can be difficult at times," said Alex.

I looked at him so quickly, my hair whipped into my eyes. Impatiently I brushed it aside. He was smiling at me, his cool eyes softened like a misty grey dawn. My heart did an odd thump.

"Yeah," I muttered. Maybe I was wrong about him! Maybe he wasn't *so* bad. When I came to think about it, I rather liked the color of his eyes.

"My father's had some crazy ideas in the past."

I rolled my eyes. "Yeah, maybe, but I bet he never came up with a bomb shelter."

Alex grinned. "I wouldn't worry too much about that it. The plan might not go ahead. It'll take ages to go through Council for approval. An engineer will need to calculate first whether it's doable without your existing house collapsing. It always takes builders months to do anything. We had some guy in to renovate our bathroom once. He ripped up the tiles, yanked out the tub and loo and said he'd be back after lunch. Didn't hear from him for five weeks. Dad said he was going to rip his throat out. He was so mad." He laughed revealing straight, white teeth.

For the life of me, I couldn't think of anything

intelligent or witty to say. He was staring straight ahead, his stern profile just like his father's. He looked harder and more worldly than any of my male friends and former school mates. He looked just like my idea of a city tough.

Or an army grunt.

"Why did you move here?" The words tumbled out of me before I could bite them back. I hadn't really meant to speak my thoughts out loud. Not this time, anyway. Hardly breathing, I waited for his brush-off to my nosy question.

Alex grabbed a handful of leaves and crushed them in his fist. The glance he gave me was cold as frost. Almost calculating.

I shivered.

"Mum was killed in some botched hold-up at the local shop. We stuck it out for a while then Dad reckoned there was too much violence and drugs in our neighborhood. I guess he just wanted to find some peace. While Dad was in the Army, we've lived in some pretty bad places around the world. I'm thinking this was the furthermost place he could find and when he spotted the garage in town was up for sale, he decided to buy it. I came along to give him a hand for a few months."

"I'm sorry. I had no idea," I whispered. No wonder both of them seemed so hard and distant. I couldn't even imagine what kind of a life he had led. The things he'd seen. And lived through. It would be awful to lose one of your parents.

At least my mother and father were alive, even if they did drive me nuts.

"My parents met at University where Dad studied genetics and physics and Mum studied biology," I mumbled, sneaking a sideways peek at him. He turned and smiled so I kept talking. "When Dad was offered a position in England after they'd both graduated, they got married. They came back to Australia when Mum fell pregnant with me. We've moved around a lot, so I know what it's like starting new schools over and over. I remember the first school I attended was in Perth. Next thing I know, Dad had a new job and we were in Brisbane. " I grinned.

Funny though, I held little memory of my early years apart from a recurring dream of being trapped inside a white room. Although why I'd always felt the dream to be connected to my childhood and not some movie I'd seen, I couldn't say.

"Yeah, it can be tough but you do get to see a lot of the world. Whereabouts did you live?"

I shrugged. "Capital cities mainly. A couple of times we lived for a few months in the US. The last big city we lived in was Canberra. A few years ago, Mum and Dad decided on a tree change and we moved out west."

All those moves, never staying long in one place.

Constantly being lectured to never draw attention, to never err on the wrong side of the law.

Even a parking ticket had been the subject of an argument.

Now, for the first time, I wondered why.

Alex didn't respond. He'd plucked a blade of grass and sucked on the end, staring straight ahead as if lost in his own thoughts.

Silence stretched out between us like a rubber band.

What would happen if it snapped?

I needed to change the subject. Desperately I searched my mind then blurted, "There's a live band playing at the pub next week. My friends are home for a bit and we're gonna go. Why don't you come along with us?" *OMG! Did I just ask him out?*

"Yeah, I heard it was on. Maybe I will." He reached out and took my left hand in his turning it over to smooth his thumb across my palm. His touch spiked a flurry of goose bumps skittering up my arm.

"What's your story, Tara? Why are you here in this town?"

My throat tightened. Should I pull my hand out of his

grasp or act cool? Act as if I'm not imagining pulling him down on top of me and running my fingers all over those hard muscles.

Clearing my throat, I said, "I'm only here until I've finished my land care course, then I'm long gone."

He quirked his eyebrows as his cool gaze studied me. "Really? You seem to be very close to your mother and little brother. I can't see you up and leaving them any time soon, even if your parents do piss you off with their odd ideas."

"You know nothing about me or my family." I glared at him. It was okay for me to be annoyed, but that didn't mean I was going to let anyone else cast judgment. I remembered the bomb shelter. This guy had better not spread any rumors about Mum.

"I know more than you can possibly comprehend."

Now, what's he talking about?

I yanked free of his hold and wiped my hand against my shorts. His gaze followed my movements. The intentness of his stare made me feel all trembly inside.

"What's the story with your old man working as a cleaner? With his qualifications he could get a job anywhere in the world."

Why was Alex so interested in my family? Had he heard gossip about Dad's involvement with drugs?

"What my father does for a living is none of your business." Anxious to be rid of him, I leaned closer and almost hurled the words in his face.

"When I make a pledge, I stick to it," he drawled, his eyes ice cold.

Huh? This conversation is totally off the scale of weirdness.

Feminine voices floated towards us. The scowl on his face vanishing as if it'd never been there, Alex stood up as Marnie and Em sauntered around the side of the house. Their faces lit up like they'd spotted Liam Hemsworth and they both smiled.

Alex lifted a hand in greeting and tossed me a casual,

"I'll see you later, Tara. Dad's staying for lunch but I've got some work to do at the garage."

My friends stared after his retreating back. Their drooling over Mister *I'm-so-awesome* irritated me.

It annoyed me even more when I realized I was also staring after him. I still didn't get it though.

Why come here? Over all the places to pick and most had a far better economy, why had his father decided on our town? Why not the coast? Close to large shopping centers, malls, tourists. I sighed at the wonderful images springing to life inside my mind, then squashed them.

Then there were Alex's questions about my life, about my family. Why should they bother me? Everyone asked questions, especially when meeting for the first time.

Why am I analysing everything these days?

But shit yeah, the way he'd so smoothly rolled out that info on his past, it had sounded rehearsed and somehow evasive. As if he were holding something back. As if none of it was real. But why would Alex lie?

I rubbed a hand over my nape where my hairs stood as stiff and straight as a brand new toothbrush. *Come on girlfriend, get a grip*. I was not the one with the out-of-control imagination. I usually left that up to Mum.

Or Em.

I smiled as I looked at my friend. With her blue eyes and curly white-blonde hair, she always reminded me of a china doll I'd had when I was small.

True to form, Em flapped a hand in front of her face and cooed, "He is soooo hot. What was he saying to you, Tara?"

"Oh, nothing much but I did ask if he was going to hear the band."

"Awesome." Em fluttered her lashes and heaved another dramatic sigh.

"You're wasting your time there, Emma," said Marnie smoothing her long hair over her shoulder. "If you ask me, Alex has his eye on Tara."

"Me?" I snorted, truly astonished. Damn though if my tummy didn't quiver at the thought. "Try Crystal and she's welcome to him. Have you heard the latest crazy development in the Ferguson household?" I quickly changed the subject.

Em and Marnie exchanged glances, then laughed.

"Yes, your Mum told us when she greeted us at the front door. She showed us the plans. At least the bomb shelter looks big enough for all of us. Have you spoken to your Dad today?"

I shook my head. "Why do you want to know, Marnie?"

"Em and I were wondering whether there was any further update on the meteor shower. Emma told her parents and guess what?" Marnie pulled a handful of her hair in front of her face and critically examined it for split ends. "It's seems they already knew about it. Apparently there's been rumors flying about this town for ages. So much for secrecy."

"How come we haven't heard about this before?"

Em shrugged her shoulders. "Well, this is the first time I've been home since January. And Marnie was only here for Christmas Day before heading back to her glam life in Sydney."

Marnie playfully swotted Em's shoulder. "Glamorous, is not the word. I spend ten hours a day holding impossible poses for incredible lengths of time while some stupid photographer takes four million shots. I'm so stiff at the end of a photo shoot, I can barely move."

"It has to beat uni." Like a dog hounding a rabbit, Em turned her big eyes in my direction. "Dad didn't even tell Mum until yesterday. He'd been told to keep it quiet for as long as possible. He's even had a direct fax from the Prime Minister's office telling him to keep the story under wraps."

I said, "Wow. That sounds serious."

"Maybe," murmured Em wrinkling her forehead.

"What do you mean?"

"Oh, I got the impression that Dad knew something else that he was keeping from us. Something very newsworthy. He's been so preoccupied lately." She flicked me a quick glance as if gauging my reaction then looked down at the ground.

"What could be bigger than this?" I exclaimed, refusing to share the doubts niggling away in my mind. *I don't want to sound like an idiot. Best if I keep my mouth shut. It's all nothing anyway.*

Em jutted her chin and turned away.

"I've got more news, unfortunately, Tara. Crystal's been posting snide comments on Facebook and Twitter about your family. I'm sorry." Marnie crouched down and enclosed my hands in hers giving them a gentle squeeze.

"Maybe we should start working on that bomb shelter straight away." I plucked a dandelion weed from the grass. "Maybe, I can incarcerate Crystal in the walls or something."

Em giggled, apparently over whatever was eating her.

"I have a bad feeling, Tara." Marnie met my gaze, her brown eyes sad and serious. Her mouth drooped downwards. "I felt it first when my apartment was broken into but since then it's grown stronger every day. I think we're going to need something a lot bigger than a bomb shelter."

CHAPTER 6: THE CAMP

"I can't take any more. All this doom and gloom is giving me a headache." I jumped to my feet and brushed grass off my clothes. "Let's go quad-bike riding."

"Oooh, fabulous idea, Tara" Em clapped her hands. "With luck, there'll be bikes still available for hire at Carstairs. We could go out to the creek and see if we can find a deep enough waterhole to swim in."

"Now *that* sounds like a plan," Marnie said as we hustled toward the house.

I trotted up the back steps, saying over my shoulder, "We could drive past those acres your Dad purchased last year, Em."

"Why?"

"I wouldn't mind seeing how he intends to improve it. The soil on that land is nutrient poor and would need a lot of work before he could even run cattle on it. Any idea what he intends to do with it?"

"None, Tara. I haven't been there since he bought the place and Dad never mentions it much. I know he goes out there every so often. I guess he checks on the fencing or something."

"Weird. Why do adults have to be so secretive?" I

shook my head as I yanked open the fly-screen door.

"There's no secret!" Em snapped. "It's just a bit of dirt. My father doesn't have to tell me everything he's doing. I still don't understand why you're so interested."

Surprised, I paused in the doorway and stared at Em. "Gee, Em. Take it easy. I was talking about adults in general. And I guess I was really snipping about my own parents. They've been acting even stranger than usual. As if they're not telling me something I need to know. Besides, I'm curious because land care interests me."

"I'm sorry, Tara It's just that I'm a bit on edge at the moment. I'm thinking of dropping one of my subjects at uni as I'm struggling with my study load. I'll wait out here. I need to make a phone call."

"Sure. I'll change into a pair of jeans." I headed off to my room with Marnie following. As soon as I shut my bedroom door however, I shared a serious look with my other friend. "Sounds like Em has some serious problems at home. Has she spoken about it to you?"

"Not really. She did say it was her study that's bothering her. I got the feeling it's her parents."

I scrabbled under my bed for my boots. "Yeah, Em did mention something about that last night. It's so hard to believe though. She's got the perfect family, a great house, money. They go on holidays. Her parents are always flying somewhere."

"Sometimes things are not always what they seem," Marnie said soberly, her eyes gleaming mysteriously.

"Don't tell me you've got one of your 'bad' feelings about that as well." I shot her a quick smile while I exchanged my shorts for a pair of faded jeans, slipped on some socks then pulled on my boots. "I hope it's nothing serious. I wouldn't like Em to have to go through a divorce like my parents. We've been lucky. It can get nasty sometimes. That's it, I'm ready. I'll ask Mum if I can borrow her car. It's far too hot to do any serious walking."

Marnie produced sunblock from her handbag and

applied it to her face.

"Good idea, I don't want to get sunburnt," she murmured anxiously. "I'll need to stop at Nonna's and change, too."

***

There were plenty of quad bikes available for hire at Carstairs. And it wasn't long before we were rumbling along the dirt road which wound through the bush to the west of the town.

Adjusting my dark shades over the bridge of my nose I took a deep breath. Instantly the smells of late summer filled my nostrils.

Heat, dust and the familiar lemony scents of the Australian bush.

There was nothing like it anywhere in the world.

It reminded me how much I loved it here. Even though I bitched about wanting to ditch this town and my responsibilities, I knew no matter where I went the country would always call me back home.

I relaxed on the hard leather seat, enjoying the hot wind blowing on my face. I'd kept the face shield of my helmet up for this very reason. This was better, much better than mooching about the local pool or hanging out getting wasted at the pub.

The sparse gum-trees which grew close to the road offered at least a little shade and some relief from the relentless sun as it rode high in the sky. At first, we drove slowly down the road, but it wasn't long before we'd opened up the throttles and were racing one another, dust and pebbles flicking up from the spinning wheels of the quads. The rolling paddocks were left behind. Grevilleas, bottlebrush and tea-trees pressed close and the air was thick and heavy with the silence of the bush.

Ahead of us, the narrow road branched into two. The one to the left wound back to town, following the meandering path of the creek which due to the drought was little more than sand and rocks. The other track led deeper into bush land.

I changed down through the gears and my quad coasted to a halt. My friends drew up beside me.

"Whew! It's hard to breathe here isn't it?" Unsnapping the strap beneath my chin I pulled off my helmet and raked a hand through my flattened hair. Nothing quite like hat hair. I was glad no one was here to see me.

No one meaning his hotness.

I wriggled on the seat.

"Perhaps, the bush is warning us. That there is danger here," murmured Marnie, her gaze darting to each side of the track as she examined the dense foliage.

Em jumped, her eyes turning as big as an owls.

I laughed, not taking her seriously. "Marnie, will you stop all that physic stuff? You're scaring Em shitless."

"I can't turn it off like a tap, Tara. I'm sorry, but I can't shake this feeling crowding in on me."

Wow. She *was* serious.

"It could be a reaction from the break-in. That would have been pretty scary to find someone had entered your home so easily." I plonked my helmet back on and tried for a joke. "What you need is a hot guy to take your mind off your problems."

"I don't want or need any man in my life. Period. Are we going to sit here all day or actually do something?"

I cringed at the coldness in my friend's voice. I tried to soothe over my foot-in-mouth moment. "Sorry, I only want to see you happy."

"Happy? Oh let me think about this for a moment, as if a decent guy would even look sideways at me. I have a jail-bird for a father and the town drunk for a grandmother. Oh and don't forget the final pearler...I'm a date-rape victim who off-loaded her baby to the system." There was a world of hurt and repressed anger in her voice that cut right through to my heart.

Damn. The last thing I wanted to do was remind her of this painful taboo subject. Marnie never spoke about what had happened that night, never mentioned her little girl and out of respect Em and I had never asked any questions. I wished there was something I could do to take away her pain.

Knowing I didn't have the right words, I tried anyway. "Marnie, no one who knows you and cares for you, could ever blame you. You didn't do anything wrong. You're one of the kindest people I know!"

Marnie turned sideways, averting her face.

After eyeing my friend's hunched shoulders for a long moment, I decided it might be better if we dropped the subject. Clearing my throat, I said, "Decision time, girlfriends. The creek or we follow this road a while longer. I say we check out the acres."

Em tapped her hot-pink colored nails against the gears. "That's fine with me."

"I'm easy," responded Marnie, finally turning to face me.

My shoulders slumped in relief when I saw the smile on her face. Marnie appeared to be her usual calm, Madonna-type self again. Gone was the bitter expression that had, quite frankly, scared the pants off me. I set my quad in motion and turned onto the right-hand track.

Scrubby bush land hemmed in on both sides of the rut filled road.

As I approached a particularly large pothole, I slowed. Bending over, I examined the deep grooves which marked the passage of vehicles. Straightening, I yelled above the noise of the engines, "This road looks as if it gets used frequently. Does it lead to other properties, Em?"

Em shouted back. "I thought only Dad's place was out here. Obviously I was wrong."

We drove steadily on, moving deeper into the bush. Dappled sunlight filtered through the branches of the gum trees and tea-trees. Sweat prickled my scalp making my head itch. My top clung uncomfortably to my back and chest. I swallowed over a throat parched from the dry heat.

No one spoke and when I turned round, I caught Em casting nervous glances from side to side. The sudden raucous laugh of a kookaburra startled me and my grip tightened on the throttle. The quad leapt forward with a jerk. The right wheel came down into a deep pothole, spinning the bike round as it lost traction in the dirt.

Heart pounding, I fought to keep the quad from rolling. Standing, I attempted to re-balance the bike. I rapidly worked through the gears and gently applied the brake.

Finally, the quad stopped rocking.

My legs quaking like chocolate mousse I dropped into the seat and remembered to breathe. "Shit. That was close."

"Are you all right, Tara?" Marnie, who must have stopped her bike the moment I hit the pothole, now stood beside me and laid a hand on my shoulder.

Grateful for the show of support, I smiled. "Yeah, no worries. Thanks, Marnie." I released my strangle-hold on the handlebars and slumped in the seat.

"Hey guys. Check this out," Em called out.

Raising my head, I gaped at the sight a little beyond the next bend in the road. The trees had been cleared off to the left and the massive steel gate in front of us, glinted from reflected sunlight.

"That is some gate." I gave a low whistle. After turning off the engine, I released my helmet straps and slipped off the bike. As I walked to the gate, my gaze travelled over the ground. I frowned. "Looks like a lot of traffic goes through here. See all these tire marks?"

"The fence must be about ten feet high. Why put rolls of barbed wire on top of chain fencing this far out of town?" asked Marnie, taking off her helmet and swinging it by its strap.

In silence I stared at the heavy padlock locking the gates and effectively baring entry. The land was cleared a few meters both sides of the fence and a wide cattle grid lay under the gates as a further deterrent.

The hushed quiet of the bush pressed in on me.

We were standing out in the open. Those damn hairs on the nape of my neck stood up.

Again.

"To keep people out," I said slowly.

"Security like this, also keeps people in," muttered Marnie. Her brows knitted together and we exchanged glances.

"Uh huh." I nodded.

"Let's move off the road," Marnie suggested.

My gaze followed her pointing finger. To our right, there was a faint trail that appeared to follow the fence line. "We could follow that path and see where it leads. Or we could turn around and go back."

"This can't be the right place. We must have missed the turnoff to Dad's property," Em piped up.

"I didn't see any other roads leading off this one, so this must be it, unless it's further ahead. Maybe he's got some project going on and doesn't want trespassers. That could explain all this heavy duty security."

I laid out some logical reasoning in an attempt to beat back my rising paranoia. Grimacing, I realized I was thinking like Mum. "The tire treads could be shooters hunting roos or rabbits, possibly wild pigs. Let's follow this path for a while and see if it leads anywhere."

I needed to satisfy my curiosity so leaving the quads behind I led the way, ignoring Em's muttered objections. The path wasn't wide enough for us to walk abreast, so we walked single file. The bush was so thick my vision was limited to only a meter or so around us. At times I had to bend low to avoid overhanging branches and push my way through tangled vines. I was beginning to think we should have headed for the creek. Pausing, I lifted one foot and picked a burr off my sock and flicked it to the side.

There was nothing here. About to suggest turning back, a glint like sunlight flaring off metal, caught my eyes.

"There's something up ahead." I forged on, pushing aside a prickly branch that caught at my clothes as I passed. I felt the sting as it tore through my jeans and pricked my leg.

"Thank heavens," Marnie answered. "I feel like I'm starring in one of those horror movies. You know, the one where a hideous creature comes swinging out of the trees and disembowels the hikers." She added in a falsetto voice, "Oh save me, save me!"

Em giggled.

Grinning, I climbed over a fallen tree then stopped, my hands going to my hips. *Well! I was right. Something was going on here.* I called back to the others who had fallen behind.

"Hurry up, you guys. You have to see this. We've been climbing uphill and now we have this great view into the property."

Em and Marnie joined me.

The clearing was small and through a natural gap in the trees, looked down over the fence line and the scrub that lay beyond. A fly buzzed drowsily around my face, and I absently flapped it away. I waved a hand. "What are those buildings for, Em?"

"How would I know?"

"There's an awful lot of them. I count, what, five? Could be more behind them that we can't see." I squinted into the distance. The buildings were situated quite a pace from the perimeter fencing and were painted a dull grey-green.

"They look like military buildings to me," Marnie said. "They're obviously made out of corrugated iron and they're that funny half-tunnel shape."

"Probably bought them from the Defense Force at a fire sale," I mused. "No doubt your Dad is using them to store stuff."

"Like what?" Em's voice rose. "What could he possibly be storing in there?" Her wide eyes meet mine.

"Well," drawled Marnie. "If he's been speaking with

Tara's Mum lately, he is probably stocking up on supplies for his own bomb shelter."

We all laughed and the sudden tension that had formed between us disappeared.

"I'm sure there's nothing to worry about and there's a perfectly simple explanation," continued Marnie. "It certainly doesn't look as if anyone's about either."

"Yeah. Let's go back and head for the creek. I need a swim." I took another look out over the fenced area. No livestock, no sign of people, nothing.

Marnie dug her mobile phone from her jeans pocket and checked the screen. "No bars." She waggled it. "I don't think we've got time to get out to the creek and back to Carstairs. Sorry but I don't have enough money at the moment to pay late hire fees. My rent's due next week."

"Okay, okay. Let's go home." I held my hands up in surrender.

"What a waste of a day," grumbled Em. She swung round and marched back the way we'd come. "I told you there's nothing to see here."

I raised my eyebrows and indicated Em as she hurried back along the path. "Looks like Em has her cranky pants on."

"Everyone has problems. We're not in high school any more, Tara."

"So?"

Marnie linked her arm through mine and said, "We no longer share our secrets. There's some stuff in our lives that we'll keep to ourselves and no matter how much you poke and pry, we're not going to fess up. I bet my last dollar, you haven't told us everything that's going on in your life."

Prepare.

Warder.

Did she know? No, I had to be imagining things. Still, those words pounded deep inside my head with every step I took. Marnie was right with one thing though. Barely five months since we'd completed high school and already, I could feel the gulf widening between us. Problem was, both Marnie and Em were surging along their chosen life paths and I was still right back where we started.

And with little hope of moving forward.

Some days, life sucks.

***

"How's it going, little bro?" I asked as I flung myself down on my brother's bed. Through the window, starlight glittered as unobtainable as diamonds.

"Hey, Sis. I'm working on a project for school." Dan ducked his head and flipped a hand toward his computer screen.

Crap. Had Mum told him yet? I chewed my lip and eyed him uncertainly.

"It's okay, Tara. Mum's already explained about me leaving Wallaby Creek High. I enrolled in correspondence school yesterday. The project is for my new studies."

"Already?" I rolled my eyes. "You'll get brain strain if you're not careful." I hesitated. "About the school biz, I don't think this is a good idea and intend to keep pressing Mum."

"Leave off, Sis. I'm cool with it. This way I don't have to hang back waiting for the other kids to catch up. I'll blitz my HSC in no time, then I can complete my first degree."

"Sounds like you have it all worked out." I stared up at the ceiling.

"Yep, sure do. Speaking of work, shouldn't you be at the pub?"

"My shift doesn't start for another forty-five minutes. I only scored two hours work today. Lucky me, I get to deal with drunk farmers and sex-starved truckies," I bitched. "I need a better job. More hours or something."

"Mum says you shouldn't worry about it."

"Don't you start." I rolled onto my side, propped my head on my hand and grinned at my brother.

He tossed a scrunched up piece of paper at my head.

I ducked and laughed.

When Dan looked back at his screen, I picked up his sketchbook and flicked through the pages. I stopped.

My blood turned to ice in my veins and I shivered. For several minutes I stared at the page. Totally absorbed, I turned over the following five pages before waggling the book high in the air. "What's this?"

"Just something I've been working on."

I made an effort to sound normal. "Well, duh! Come on, give."

Dan turned shining eyes in my direction. "A theoretical diagram of a space ship engine that could take us to the edge of our solar system and back. I've been fiddling with the idea for about a year now." He laughed depreciatively. "It probably wouldn't work but it's fun."

"It's amazing." And even more amazing that I could understand it. My brain didn't tighten like it normally did when I read anything. I didn't need to concentrate and focus on individual sections of the page. It was if my brain was hardwired to comprehend every detail depicted here. I examined the book again, absorbing the information in rapid fire sequence. How weird was this? Should I say something? "It looks pretty authentic to me."

"Yeah?" He wiped a hand through the flop of hair hanging in his eyes and stared hard at me. He sucked in a sharp breath. "Can you understand it, Sis?" he said in an awed voice.

No flies on my little bro. I ran my finger over the diagram I was looking at. "For once in my life, yes. But what is really strange is these markings here."

I pointed a shaking finger at the line of squiggles at the bottom of the page. To me, they formed a sentence.

One that I'd seen before.

Heard before.

And it was enough to make my knees turn to jelly. "Have you seen them before? Where did you get them?"

"I dreamt them," he said abruptly.

My jaw dropped.

Our gazes met.

I whispered, "So did I."

In his wide eyes, I read the quick flare of fear.

Was it me, or had the room become darker? I whispered, "I know what it says; *Follow the path of Elvirathon and you will be saved.*"

"That's really freaky, Sis." Dan's voice shook.

"Too right."

We stared at each other in silence. Finally, I dropped the sketchbook back onto the bed as if it had burst into flames and burnt my fingers. I fought for reason. "There has to be a logical explanation. You know, like how twins can sense each other's pain or thoughts." I recalled the words that had accompanied that message in my dreams. *Remember or perish.*

"I thought scientists had decided that was a lot of hoohah," argued Dan.

"Well, it's some kind of psychic connection." My voice gained conviction. "Or Mum. We've both spent too much time listening to her wild imagination."

"Do you think we should tell her?" Worry creased his forehead into tiny wrinkles.

I shuddered at what a meal Mum would make out of this strange occurrence. "God, no. Besides, I don't think there's anything to tell. Was it just the once you dreamt it?"

"It's been off and on for about five years."

Like me. Although, lately I'd been reliving that dream almost every night. That, and the memory of that horrible white room. "Mum's got enough on her plate at the moment. Let's keep it between ourselves for a while."

"Okay, if you say so, Sis." He sounded relieved. "Hey, I've done a bit of digging on the net about the meteor shower and Dad's right. Seems those in the know are a bit edgy."

They weren't the only ones. Excitement blazed in my

brother's eyes and I smiled, glad we'd left that tricky subject behind us. "Okay, what have you been up to, little bro?"

"A little sneaking, a little peeking."

"Dammit, Dan. What if you get caught? Hacking is a criminal offence."

"I'm not doing any harm." My brother's mouth set into a stubborn line. One that I recognized. "Dad and I believe in freedom of information and knowledge."

I was right. *Dad.* "Shit. I should have known Dad was involved somewhere." I tugged at my hair struggling with my frustration. "Tell me."

Dan turned the screen towards me. "This site is particularly interesting. There's a lot of chatter about the strange signals from the meteors. The guys on this forum are really wired and talk a lot about state of emergencies and martial law."

"Seriously?" I sat up and whistled. "Is this a government site you're looking at?"

Dan nodded.

"That could explain the sudden withdrawal of our armed forces from overseas. Does it mention how bad they think it might be? Or the number of possible impacts? Where they'll hit?"

"Not on this site. I've been trying to crack a back door to a US site."

"One day, men in black commando suits will repel down from a chopper and you'll be carted away."

"They have to catch me first." My brother fisted his hand and raised it above his head. He grinned. "Freedom to the people."

I hooted with laughter.

The door opened and Mum entered.

I quickly shoved the sketchbook under the bed.

"Keeping an eye on the time, Tara?"

"Yes, Mum."

She crossed the room to ruffle Dan's hair. He bobbed

and weaved to dislodge her touch. "What are you two up to?" Bending over, she looked at the screen.

"Oh I see." Straightening, she turned and met my gaze. Grim lines were etched in her face making her look older and tired, as if for too long she'd been carrying a heavy burden.

My heart did this queer pang thing.

"I hope you're taking this seriously now, Tara. Once the country is locked down under martial law, events will move fast."

I plucked at the blanket. "I don't see why and besides, Mum, nothing's certain yet."

"Time is no longer on our side." Mum gestured towards the computer. "With martial law will come curfews and everyone will need to be accounted for at every hour of the day."

I swung my feet to the floor and stood. Determined not to admit to my own rising anxiety, I blustered, "That sounds so extreme."

"Both of you must be careful, now more than ever. If anyone asks too many questions, let either your father or myself know as soon as possible. Don't give them any information, especially about our past."

"Aw, Mum, not this conspiracy shit again." Throwing my hands in the air, I stormed to the door. I'd always found anger the easiest way to deal with stress.

"Tara!" Mum's sharp voice stopped me from leaving the room.

I slumped against the doorjamb, my eyes squeezed shut.

"This is vital. Keep quiet about whatever strange memories you have of your early life."

My heart skipped a beat. Immediately a vision of that sterile, white room peopled with shadowy figures popped into my mind. My stomach clenched and I folded my arms across my chest. How could she know?

Mum continued, "You must learn to consider others'

needs before your own. With the Warders appearance in town, the Mundos Novus Force won't be far behind if they haven't already infiltrated the area. Unfortunately, both your father and I believe it's too late to run. This town is where we will stand."

I spun round and gaped at her. *What the hell?*

"God, Mum." Shaking my head, I could only stand there and gape at the light of battle burning in my mother's face.

"Remember, both of you. Everyone has secrets. Even the Warders. The sensei appears a solid man but I sense he's keeping something from me. Not everyone is who they say they are, just like us."

What was this shit?

My heartbeats roared inside my head. I whispered, "Who are we, Mum?"

My fingernails dug into my palms as I gripped my hands together. This was all new, this paranoid hysteria But like a nest of red-belly black snakes, doubt slivered in the dark recesses of my mind. My hot words of protest choked in my throat while I recalled the past few days.

And the questions, that had begun to plague me.

Were we refugees from some war torn country?

"We're runners. All of us, your father, myself, both of you. We took you from an underground bunker and escaped. We've been running ever since."

CHAPTER 7: THE STORM

I stared around the aisles of the supermarket in disbelief. After Mum had dropped another one of her bombshells, she'd left the room and with my head whirling and pounding, I'd headed for work.

The pub had been busy with a truckload of Air-Force guys turning up apparently determined to run the bar dry. Too late by the time I reached home to question Mum, I'd flopped exhausted into bed and slept until mid morning. Dreams of a faceless man, dressed in a white coat bending over me had made for a restless night. I woke feeling as if I hadn't slept in a week.

My own confused thoughts hadn't helped either.

Mum had bustled into the kitchen where I was stacking the dishes after breakfast which was really brunch, and asked Dan and me to help her with the shopping. She'd yakked on and on about food rationing and stocking up on supplies. In order to stave off another conversation that was bound to send me screaming off into the bush, or turn my bones to mush, I'd agreed to come along.

Now as I stood unmoving in the grocery aisle, that niggling sensation in my mind loomed like the shadow of doom.

It was chaos.

The rumor of imminent impacts must have spread throughout the town, sparking a frenzy of shoppers. I overheard the people standing next to me talking about it. I couldn't believe my ears. In hoarse voices they whispered of the end of days and an impending invasion.

Did people really believe this stuff? What if it was true?

By the number of vacant shelves, people must have been raiding the shop since it opened that morning. Now at barely midday, stock had dwindled at an alarming rate.

There were people everywhere. Some were pushing two or three trolleys loaded to the hilt. The lines to the checkouts spread down the aisles. People were elbowing and shoving each other, grabbing anything and everything in sight.

The noise was unbelievable. I caught a brief glimpse of Marnie squeezing past a trolley loaded to the hilt. She was lugging a huge container of spring water and disappeared from sight before I could call out to her.

Someone touched my arm.

I spun around to front my grim-faced mother who said, "This isn't good, Tara. It's not going to take much for these people to start a riot. Have you got the list?"

"It's okay, Mum. I've got the list memorized. Why don't you wait out in the carpark with Dan?"

Mum reached out and brushed her knuckles along my cheek. "You're always trying to protect us. No, we'll do better if we each work our way through the list and meet up at the checkouts. I can't help wondering who spread the rumors about town. It was a very foolish thing to do."

"As long as Dad isn't involved, I don't really care. I'll catch you later, Mum." I squeezed Mum's hand before striding off down the aisle, shouldering my way through the press of people. Mum was right. The tension crackled in the air like a stick of dynamite. It wouldn't take much to set off an explosion.

At least people were still polite but determined. Mrs

Anderson from down the road, after a mumbled apology, snatched the last box of matches from beneath my fingers.

A trolley jabbed me in the back. While I was rubbing the sore spot, someone trod on my toes. I should have stayed home. Wheeling to the right, I ducked to avoid being hit on the head by the guy from the service station who barreled past balancing a sack of potatoes on his shoulders.

What a shitty weekend this had turned out to be.

I wandered the aisles and soon had the shopping bags full.

A sudden roll of thunder made me jump.

I looked out of the huge plate glass windows which made up the majority of the front of the supermarket. The day had dawned hot and sultry and still. A sure indication bad weather was on its way and by the look of the heavy, black clouds darkening what I could see of the sky, a dangerous storm was brewing.

A jagged spear of lightning slashed through the green-tinged, dark clouds. The streetlights switched on automatically, as the growing dimness registered on their sensors. Another rumble of thunder shuddered the building.

Inside the shop, the rattle and bustle of the shoppers ceased. Wary glances were cast towards the carpark were the trees doing sentinel duty along the sidewalk drooped motionless, as if exhausted from the heat.

I didn't like this; I had a feeling all hell was about to break loose.

Time for us to get out of here.

Climbing onto the first shelf facing me, I looked over the crowd searching for Dan and Mum. I found them over near the meat section. But they weren't alone. Even as I stared, a guy with short fair hair turned and glanced in my direction.

Alex.

My heart did a funny flop in my chest as our gazes met.

Mum raised her hand and beckoned. I jumped to the floor and picked up the jammed-packed calico shopping bags. Turning my back to the windows, I headed for the rear of the building.

Just in time.

From behind, came the roar of the wind as loud as a runaway freight train. The force smashed into the glass, shattering shards into the store and slammed into my back like a giant hand. I fell forward, knocking against a shelf, smacking my shin on the wheel of a trolley which at least stopped some of my momentum. With my hands full of shopping bags, I landed facedown on the floor.

Pain shot along my jaw, shooting down my neck and up the side of my head. Blood spurted hot and sickly sweet inside my mouth as my teeth bit my tongue. My gut lurched at the awful taste. For thirty seconds I saw nothing but stars. As the pain eased my vision returned.

The sound of screams intermingled with the howling of the wind and the drumming of the rain as it fell in torrents from the sky. The pounding on the roof was deafening.

Then the lights went out.

Someone kicked me in the ribs then tripped over me. The heavy weight pinned me to the vinyl floor. I wheezed, "Crap. Get off me."

Scrabbling about, I managed to wriggle out from beneath the body before staggering to my feet by hanging onto the shelf next to me. The woman, who'd fallen on top of me, still lay on the ground floundering about like a fish beached on the riverbank and wailing. My head spinning, I reached down to the woman and hauled her upright.

"Thanks." She grabbed an unattended and upright trolley and stumbled down the aisle.

I need to find Mum and Dan, make sure they're okay. With my heart pounding heavily, I spat out blood and wiped the back of my shaking hand across my mouth. Blinking away tears of pain I peered around the now dark interior. I took a few seconds to grope about the floor for the grocery bags with no luck. I doubted the contents would be intact anyway.

The wind howled. Leaves, paper and plastic blew crazily around the aisles, whipping against my legs, brushing past my face, making me squeal with fright. Rain poured through the ceiling where half the roof had been ripped off. My clothes were soon sodden. I took a hesitant step forward, my feet crunched over the remains of the shelves.

The floor was littered with broken glass, fallen food stuffs, overturned trolleys and damaged stock. I couldn't see jack-shit. Using the edge of my tee-shirt I wiped away rain, tears and blood and squinted. All around me, people cried out, some in pain, but more in fear and panic, as they jostled in the darkness trying to reach the eerily glowing green exit signs.

I groped and limped along the aisle. My shin throbbed like crazy and the pain along my jawline felt like someone had taken a knife to my brain. I hoped I hadn't lost any teeth.

"Tara! Are you okay?" yelled Alex as he appeared out of the gloom.

"I feel like my head is broken but I guess I'll live. What the hell happened?"

"Tornado."

"You're kidding me?" I shouted. "I need to find my brother and Mum."

Even though I wasn't sure whether I liked him or not, I was so thankful to see someone familiar, I had to fight the urge to throw myself onto his chest and bawl my eyes out.

"Your mum's fine. She sent me to look for you. She's helping a couple of old codgers out the back exit. They were badly hurt when some shelves landed on them. Is that blood on your face?" he lowered his head to peer at me. His fingers brushed my cheek.

"Probably." I pushed him away. "Let's get out of here."

"You look like you've been hit by a bus. Come on, you need medical attention." His hand closed strongly around my wrist making me feel safe.

How stupid.

With Alex leading, we struggled to the rear of the store. It seemed to take forever as we pushed their way through the debris. Some of the shelves had fallen to the ground, scattering cans and groceries everywhere. We had to climb over the pile, our feet slipping in the dark as we skated over the wet floor.

My ears rang from the cacophony of noise filling what remained of the building. My head ached and the rain continued to pound down from the sky. A huge tree branch hurtled through the hole in the roof. Alex quickly pulled me out of the way. The wind swept leaves, rubbish, pieces of gyprock and broken roof tiles into the shop and we battled our way forward. What remained of the ceiling rattled and groaned. Thunder rolled menacingly.

I flinched as a crack of lightning sounded frighteningly close and unconsciously edged closer to Alex, seeking reassurance.

What if the tornado swept back on its tracks?

"Almost there Tara. See? The exit's around this corner," Alex yelled.

I stumbled again, grabbed hold of his belt and leaned heavily against his side.

Sickness welled up from my stomach. Bright spots whirled in front of my eyes and my head felt funny – kinda light and floating. Blinking, I looked around at the people hurrying to and fro outside, shouting instructions to one another, the emergency vehicles with their blurred, flashing lights just visible through the driving rain. I was vaguely aware Alex now held me upright. Me knees shook, the muscles in my legs appeared to have dissolved into putty. My fringe was plastered flat to my forehead dripping water in my eyes, making it hard to see properly. My clothes felt so heavy they made my feet drag.

It was like a war zone.

The desperate need to lie down slowed my steps.

Alex said something but I couldn't seem to hear him through the noise inside my head. I stumbled.

My head spun and the ground rushed up to meet me. I was aware of strong arms lifting me and the world around me diminishing into blackness.

A dazed awareness seeped gradually into my mind.

I lay on my side on the back seat of a car, snug inside a blanket. The car rocked as a heavy gust of wind slammed into its side. My fingers clenched over the edges of the blanket and I bit back a groan. Every jolt and bump seemed to accentuate the throbbing of my body. I knew we were headed for the hospital but never had a journey lasted a lifetime.

Our tiny hospital was little more than a well-equipped medical and birthing centre situated inside a renovated store building as old as the township itself. Serious cases were either airlifted by chopper or the Flying Doctor Service to larger hospitals, depending on the type of emergency.

The centre would be swamped after this storm. Especially as the weather would be too dangerous to attempt a flight out of here.

My head felt like someone had taken an axe to it. Dizziness swamped me and I fought the surging nausea raging in my belly. The sickness ebbed leaving me limp and hot and the low murmuring of voices finally penetrated the roar inside my head.

"Have you narrowed down your list?"

I recognized the voice. Alex's father was in the car with us.

"Yeah, it's her." Alex didn't sound particularly pleased about whatever he'd found.

"You sound very certain."

"I am."

"Good. I'll proceed with the mother."

I heard movement and lifted my head. Bob Garroway had reached out and placed his right hand on the top of Alex's head. He held it steady for a while. Removing his hand, he gave a satisfied grunt.

Weird.

But maybe this was all a horrible dream.

"You're attracted to her. This will make your job easier."

Who's her?

Alex's father shifted in his seat, the leather squeaked in warning. Quickly, I snapped my eyes shut and played possum. I was positive he'd turned around to stare at me.

Heart galloping, I didn't dare move.

I had no idea why, but suddenly I was afraid.

***

Alex

Rattled more than I cared to admit, I pushed through the country hospital's screen door and, head down against the wind, I stalked across the carpark.

What the fuck was this? I've never had this problem before. I thrust my shaking hands into my jeans pockets and frowned.

"Any sign of the Mundo Novis Force?" asked my father through the open driver's side window as soon as I neared his car.

Not a 'how is she?' or for that matter a 'how am I?' An unfamiliar surge of resentment soured my mouth. It had always been like this, why should now be any different?

Setting my jaw, I reefed open the passenger door and slid inside.

"No, their trail has gone cold." I turned and stared at the man I'd thought of as my father since I'd first opened my eyes in that laboratory so far from this land of heat and sun. There'd never been any warmth, any affection between us but there'd always been respect. And on his part, an expectancy that I'd hungered all my life to meet. I examined his expression before the interior light flicked off. As usual, the man was an enigma, implacable, ruthless and completely devoid of any feeling. I wondered whether I'll ever measure up to being half as good.

"And yet all our intel indicated one of their major players operates out of this town."

"We could be wrong."

"That's a negative. My sixth sense doesn't lie." My father's voice was hard as rock.

"I'll go over the intel later tonight and check if we've missed some fact."

"Good. We need to know what we're up against before our friends arrive. Work these people, Alex. Reach out by volunteering to lend them a hand cleaning up their town. You know it's vital we show our friends that the people of Earth are worthy of life."

He spoke like he harbored no doubts whatsoever about our so-called friends' intentions with our planet.

I was more skeptical and never really bought into the lines we'd been fed. More than once, in those cold, lonely minutes between night and dawn I'd wondered whether they had another agenda. But I kept my niggling worry to myself. "I intended to do that anyway."

I felt rather than saw the sharp look he speared at me. From the corner of my eye, I noticed his hand shift slightly on the steering wheel and I tensed, thinking he was about to place it on my head again.

But no, he merely drummed his fingers.

I twitched my shoulders, remembering how the contact had felt, like it seared through to my brain and tore out my thoughts and memories.

Being a genetically modified unit sure had its downside.

My father gave a satisfied grunt and started the car. "I don't have to remind you, Alex, it's imperative we complete our mission. I cannot and will not tolerate anything less than success."

Jaw tight, I mumbled, "I know what's at stake. I won't fail."

The car pulled out onto the road while I stared out the side window, paying little attention to the destruction wrought by the storm.

'Your job'.

It had always been about the job.

Always.

In all my life I'd never thought about or wanted anything different. But now?

My skin heated as I recalled the feel of Tara's body as I'd carried her in my arms. The panic that had assailed me when I'd scrambled to reach her in time. Even now the memory caused a cold sweat to break out along my spine.

If I wasn't a Warder, if I'd been born like a regular person, if the entire planet wasn't under threat of total destruction, I could have a normal life.

Like any other guy.

My chest tightened painfully. I'd go to barbies, go to the footie, hang out with mates. I could say goodbye to fleeting, one-night stands. I could have a proper girlfriend.

And I know who I'd choose.

***

Tara

Sunday night at the pub was always quiet. And tonight was no exception with the majority of the town's people either still in shock mode or cleaning up after the storm.

Perched on the stool, my elbows resting on the bar, I poured another shot of scotch into my glass.

I shouldn't be doing this, I should be out there doing what I could to help. But for the moment, my energy was as sapped as a century old light bulb.

"The world's gone to hell," mumbled the wizened old fellow slumped beside me. From beneath bristling white eyebrows, his bleary eyes lighted on the scotch bottle and he licked his lips.

"I'll drink to that." I poured him two fingers and watched him raise the glass with a shaking hand to his lips. "Here you go."

I sculled my drink then followed it up with a chaser of beer I'd pulled from the taps. A pleasant buzz made me feel slightly lightheaded. I embraced it. Getting wasted had seemed like a fabulous idea when I'd finally been released from casualty over an hour ago.

Mum had arrived while I was completing the paperwork. After inspecting my face, she demanded to talk to the doctor. When I'd first seen her, I'd wanted nothing more than a motherly hug and the familiar scent of the lavender water she used, wrapping me in safety.

But she hadn't turned up alone.

Bob Garroway had marched in with her issuing quiet requests in his *'take charge'* voice that had people scurrying in all directions.

I'd felt like I was about three years old.

But at the time, I didn't bother arguing.

Carefully I fingered my swollen jaw. The good news was I'd suffered no broken bones and had mercifully kept all my teeth. Always a plus. Bruising, a slash on my shin now bandaged and no longer bleeding, a massive headache and a face that looked as if I'd been in a boxing ring. I guess I'd been lucky, considering some of the other patients I'd seen in the clinic. The place had been overflowing with casualties.

I stared out the pub window. Outside the rain plummeted from the night sky, the streets looked like rivers of sluggishly moving mud. The wind had finally died down, as the destructive force of the storm had moved further north. With luck it would die out before it reached the next town.

At the other end of the room, Ray Watson, the owner of the pub was busy with a mop and bucket, cleaning up the water that had flooded the carpet when the window shattered. When I'd arrived, I'd asked for a drink and he'd told me to help myself. I knew he'd take it out of my next week's wages. Although strictly speaking the pub wasn't open for business, Ray had no problems with anyone who wandered inside looking for a drink provided they left the money on the bar. I poured another shot into my glass. Footsteps muffled by the thin carpet on the floor sounded behind me and I stiffened.

Before he spoke, I knew who it was.

Alex.

He leaned against the bar, his left arm brushing against mine.

Heat chased away the coldness in my stiff body. Frowning, I wriggled on the stool. I didn't want the company.

"I see the SES has recruited you. I thought you had to undergo training before they'd take you on." Lifting my glass I indicated the bright yellow-orange of his jumpsuit that all members of the SES wore.

"The mayor asked for volunteers. It's pretty foul out there and with the fire brigade busy with the blaze at the abattoirs. I figured I could lend a hand."

"Shouldn't you be out there, being hero of the hour?" As soon as I said the words, shame swamped me.

"I was about to ask you the same question." Alex grabbed the bottle and moved it out of my reach. "What have you got to be so sorry about? There are people with their homes reduced to rubble, your people, neighbors, friends. They've lost everything and yet you sit here sinking scotch."

"I'm thinking, not that it's any of your business." *And you and your father are top of my list.* What were they up to?

"Now is not the time. You need to be seen working to help fix this mess."

"What the ...?" I slammed the glass onto the counter and glared.

Alex lifted his hands. "Hey, don't shoot me. I came into the pub looking to use the loo and spotted you at the bar. If you want to wallow, not my problem. But we could use another pair of hands. Or you could stay here enjoying your pity party."

Shoulders stiff, he turned and marched out the door leaving me gaping after him.

My glance tangled with the old timer's rheumy eyes. There was such weariness in his expression it gave me pause. I bet this fella had to deal with a lot worse than a storm in his life.

My childish resentment at Alex's interference faded.

I poured one last shot but this time, handed the glass over to the old guy. After capping the bottle and stashing it behind the bar, I wiped my sticky hands on a damp tea-towel.

Snatching up my jacket, I shrugged it on as I walked outside.

Alex was right, but I'd never tell him.

I kept to the footpath, sidestepping debris and at times climbing over fallen trees. By following the glow of light in the distance, I made my way through the dark to where the SES had set up a temporary base.

Power lines were down, some snaking across the road and others buried under debris. Remarkably there were buildings standing with barely a mark on them and others reduced to tangled piles of timber, brick and tile.

The energy workers had already swung into action and set up temporary lighting run by generators. In their orange suits they hung from power poles and scrambled about below with ladders and tools.

The townspeople were out in full force, sweeping mud, hauling rubbish into trailers, clinging to roofs hauling tarpaulins over gaping holes. Others huddled in small groups, talking and gesturing toward the damage surrounding them.

After I registered my name with the task force manning a white tent, I was given a dolphin torch and dispatched to help clear rubble off the road so emergency vehicles would have access into the worst hit areas. Hurrying off, I passed the remains of the huge, ancient Morton Bay fig tree, now lying on its side, broken and dying. Half of the massive tree spread across the road blocking it and the other half rested in the middle of what used to be the council chambers.

The Mayor gestured angrily to three men in overalls who stood, hands in pockets, staring at the damage.

A pang of loss hit me. That tree had stood proudly spreading its shady branches across the sky for over one hundred years. Rather than destroy this memory of the past, the town had been built around it.

CHAPTER 8: MISSING

"I can't believe she's gone! And without saying goodbye to me," wailed Em, sniveling into her sodden tissue.

A full thirty-two hours had passed since the tornado had pummeled the town. And I was effing exhausted having worked throughout most of the previous night and all day, assisting the SES.

The last thing I wanted was to deal with more problems. But I could never let Em down.

So now I sat on my friend's double bed with its pale pink bedspread and gauzy white netting hanging from the canopy, in her pretty pink and white bedroom and wondering whether I'd been sucked into a sadist's twisted dream.

How could she stand sleeping in such a fussy room? If it were my room, I'd suffocate.

I shifted position on the soft mattress, grimacing as I sank deeper and watched two fat tears roll down my friend's cheeks.

In the dim flickering light provided by the candles, Em's eyes were swollen and puffy. The moon peeped through the lace curtains, slender beams that lit up the room briefly before being swallowed by heavy clouds.

It was still raining.

The drops trickled slowly down the glass windowpane. From elsewhere in the house, came the distinct sound of rain thunking into buckets.

A lot of tiles had blown off the roof and the rafters above the billiard room had shattered. The SES had covered the hole with a tarp but rain still found its way through the damage.

"Yeah, it sucks," I mumbled.

Truth to tell, I was almost as bewildered as Em.

But what could I say?

What do you say to your best friend when her mother disappears into the night with no explanation?

No note.

No phone call.

The landlines were still down, but she could have called Em on the mobile.

But there'd been nothing. What could have happened to her?

Then there was the weird behavior of Em's father who apparently had appeared briefly at breakfast before leaving the house. He'd evinced no comment, no outrage, no concern about the disappearance of his wife and beyond a few curt sentences had little to say about the matter.

Em had told me that she'd first thought he'd gone out to help the SES crews but no one had seen him. There'd been no sight of his Toyota four-wheel drive anywhere around town.

I knew this for a fact, because I'd kept an eye out all day after Em's frantic text around breakfast time.

Shifting again on the mattress, I clenched my jaw then quickly relaxed it as pain shot up the side of my face. I checked my teeth again.

Just in case. Nope, all good.

As well as performing the assigned SES duties, Dan and I had to fix the damage to our home. We'd boarded up the lounge room window with timber after what looked like half a small tree had speared through it. Mum had spent the morning donating blood and helping where she could at the clinic. Then we'd all trooped to the elderly couple's home next door and did what they could to help with the damage to their roof and the mess inside their house.

After a hurried sandwich, I'd left Mum cleaning out the leaves, rubbish and mud for our neighbors that had poured through the broken glass. Dan had been picked up earlier by Alex in his father's ute and they'd taken off somewhere on a SES task.

It was only now, well into the night that I'd been able to check up on my friends. I frowned. There'd been no answer to my insistent pounding on Marnie's front door. Although I could have sworn I heard someone moving about inside. After standing back and surveying the front of Marnie's grandmother's house, I'd given up then pedalled madly to Em's home.

She was still pretty distraught and who could blame her?

Given the circumstances, I decided now was not the best time to mention I couldn't contact Marnie.

For about the hundredth time, I suggested, "Perhaps there was a family emergency and your mum was called away?"

"If there were, Dad would have told me. Oh Tara, what if something awful has happened?"

"I'm sure she's fine. Didn't you tell me that your father refused to inform the police? If that's the case then he must believe that she's fine."

Em hunted wildly for the tissue box. She plucked out the last tissue and blew her nose. "They've been fighting such a lot in the last six months. You know, really yelling and screaming at each other. You don't know how horrible it's been. Every time I come home from campus I can't wait to leave again."

I scooted across the bed and wrapped my arms around

her. Tears slid down her cheeks as she sobbed.

"I'm sorry I wasn't there for you, Em. I didn't realize you were having problems."

"That's okay." Em raised her head and gave a watery smile. "How could you have known? I kept it to myself, hoping it would all go away. I wanted us to a happy family. I pretended to everyone that we were a happy family. But it's always been like this, the arguing and cold silences, at least as long as I've known them."

What on earth was she talking about? "I don't understand."

Em took an audible deep breath. "I was adopted when I was ten years old. My real parents were killed in a car accident when I was very young. I remember very little. I can't remember their faces, the sound of the voices. Nothing. I wanted to be like everyone else and that's why I never told you."

Marnie and Mum were right. Sometimes things and people were not the way they seemed. I studied my friend as if seeing her for the first time. There was a lost, haunted expression in her blue eyes I'd never seen before and I wondered why no one was looking out for her.

"Where's your Dad, I mean Mister Andrews?"

Em sniffled into her tissue. "I have no idea. He drove off a few hours ago. I thought he might have gone to the office to clear up the damage, but he should have been back by now."

I made a snap decision. "Pack your bags." I scrambled off the bed and groped my way to the large white-paneled wardrobes lining the opposite wall, flinging the doors wide. There was no way I was going to let her stay here in this house a moment longer.

"You're coming to stay with us." I snapped my fingers when Em continued to gawk at me. "Where's your mobile? I'll ring Dan and ask him to pick us up." I turned around and rummaged inside the wardrobe and hauled her suitcases onto the thick soft carpet.

"But what if your mother won't let me stay?"

"As if! You know Mum likes you and trust me, there is no way she will let you stay here after I tell her what has been going on," I paused. "That is, of course, if you don't mind her knowing?"

Em smiled tremulously. "I don't mind. But I'd hate for this to be spread around town."

"Mmm. I see your point." I thought about it for a second then rolled my eyes. "Mum will probably tell Bob – she seems to tell him everything else these days. He'll probably tell you-know-who. But I know Mum won't mention it to anyone else. And I'll have to tell my brother. Will that be okay?"

Em nodded wordlessly, tears brimming in her eyes.

"Cheer up. It's going to be okay. How about you give me a hand here? I can't believe you have so many clothes. They certainly won't fit into these three cases. We'll just have to take the bare essentials."

Well that worked! Em jumped to her feet and began scurrying around, bleating about using garbage bags and how she couldn't possibly function unless she took *all* her clothes. I told her we didn't have time for a hundred trips back and forth.

I bit back the reminder the offer was for a few days only as I'd rather thought she'd be keen to return to campus.

Using Em's phone, I made a quick phone call to Dan and it wasn't long before a set of headlights swept up the driveway and briefly lighting up the bedroom. I left Em stuffing her belongings into huge black plastic bags. I struggled down the stairs to the front door, dolphin torch in one hand and with a bulging suitcase bouncing against my legs with every step I took. I dropped it in the foyer just as the doorbell rang. Propping the torch under one arm I wrestled with the dead lock, heaving a sigh of relief when I flung open the heavy door.

"I've brought Alex with me, Sis. Hope that's okay but

Mum didn't want me behind the wheel without a licensed driver beside me and she's with the old folks next door." Dan sent me a quick grin. Beside him in the shadows of the portico, Alex leaned casually against the doorjamb, looking so much bigger than my narrow-framed brother.

Em won't be happy. Nothing I can do about that now. I sighed. "I guess there's nothing for it. Come on in, both of you. I need some help with Em's luggage."

"I'm wearing steel-capped boots this time," drawled Alex.

Before I could catch myself, I laughed.

Dan walked past me into the dark hallway. Looking up the long sweep of stairs visible due to the tall glass window where fickle moonlight trickled inside alleviating the gloom, he said, "What's going on with Emma, Sis?"

"Everything." I hurried after him and promptly tripped over the suitcase I'd left on the tiled floor. I would have fallen to the floor if a pair of strong hands hadn't grabbed me around my waist. Warmth radiated from Alex's hands, and I shivered.

There was no mistaking that sudden surge of clamoring hormones.

"Thanks," I mumbled.

"Not a problem," his voice muttered close to my ear.

Heat spread through my body with each heavy pulse of my blood. *Dammit.* I couldn't possibly be attracted to him. Or could I? I sure didn't need this complication in my life right now.

I certainly didn't want to fall for a guy who raised every red flag I possessed.

My hair stirred from his steady breathing. Later, I wasn't sure how long I stood there, with Alex's hands firm on my waist and he standing so still behind me. I felt like I'd become lost in a spell.

"Tara," whispered Dan and I jumped in surprise. "Have you got a torch? I can't see a thing on these stairs."

"Coming." Annoyed with myself, I pushed Alex's

hands away and with the light from my torch swinging wildly, hurried up the stairs to where Dan waited on the first landing.

"I'll explain later, but in a nutshell, Em is coming to live with us until she gets some personal stuff sorted."

"Yeah?" I felt rather than saw Dan shrug. "It doesn't bother me."

"Good. Her room's up here."

Together we mounted the last flight of stairs, Alex following us. Dan paused in the doorway and whispered, "She's got a lot of bags. How long is she staying with us again?"

"I'm not sure, just until she sorts some things out."

The bedroom was now lit with burning candles. Em was standing near the window peering out into the night but turned at the sound of our voices. She gave Dan a smile but then her gaze drifted past him. Raising her hand, she fluffed out her hair. "Hi Alex. I wasn't expecting you but it's wonderful of you to help out."

"No worries." Alex, an amused smirk on his face, edged past us and picked up two enormous suitcases. His biceps bulged in a very impressive way. "Let's get moving shall we? I've got to get back to the SES."

A couple of tiring hours later, Em and I sat curled up in the comfortable couch in Mum's lounge room, sipping hot chocolate. I'd explained the situation briefly to Mum when we'd arrived earlier. She didn't let me down. With her usual generosity, she'd immediately given Em a hug and declared she could stay for as long as she wanted. She had, however, insisted on phoning Mister Andrews on her mobile and left a message advising him of Em's whereabouts. Alex and Dan had carried Em's gear into my bedroom and had then left.

The quiet murmur of Mum and Bob's voices and the comforting smell of dandelion tea wafted from the kitchen. Em, looking as woebegone as an abandoned puppy, took a sip of her hot chocolate.

I wanted to crawl into my bed and stay there for about a month. My muscles ached, my shin injury throbbed and my headache was like a vice around my forehead. But I wanted to make Em smile and forget her troubles for a while. So, I related my adventures at the supermarket, giving it a humorous slant.

"…and when I see my father I'm going to strangle him!"

Em giggled at my disgruntled tone. "You don't know that he was the one to leaked the news out."

"No, but I do know him. He's like a vigilante for the truth." I blew on my hot drink.

"But what if he's right? What if that storm were caused by the meteors? It's not as if the weather bureau had any warning it was going to form. Oh God!" Em pressed her fingers to her face and stared in horror. "What if something terrible is going to happen? Oh Tara, I don't want to be a statistic!"

"Come on, Em. It's just a storm. The weather bureau on the radio called it a super-cell thunderstorm and apparently it's not an unusual occurrence. It's just a coincidence it happened now when there's all this hype about that meteor shower."

I fielded the *'oh yeah right'* look Em shot at me. "First thing in the morning, we'll talk to the police and they'll start a proper search for your mum. I'm certain the power will be back on by then and we'll post some queries on social media."

"No, no police." Em's voice was sharp. "Dad doesn't want them involved."

Why? It was the most logical thing to do. I cast her a wary glance over the rim of my mug noting how her face had hardened chasing all the little-girl prettiness from her features. She looked older, more determined with all warmth missing from her eyes. But the corners of her mouth were turned up in a tiny smile.

"I guess it's your call," I said slowly. Fatigue slammed

into me and I yawned. If both Em and her adoptive father didn't want the police involved then perhaps the reason her adoptive mother had disappeared *was* as simple as a domestic argument. But still, I didn't understand. One minute Em acted like the woman was dead in a gutter and then she did a complete turnaround.

As if tuned into my thoughts, Em said, "It's probably nothing. I bet Mum's taken off to her favorite spa to have a break from Dad."

Her blue eyes flicked to me and back to inspect the dregs of her cup. "After this natural disaster, I know nothing will hold Dad back from running with the story about the meteor shower. I'm scared, Tara. It's like a bad dream I can't wake from and I can't help worrying about where it's all going to end."

"I know. I feel exactly the same." I grabbed the empty mugs and trudged to the kitchen. Out of sight, I palmed my mobile and texted Marnie. I waited.

And waited.

Still no response.

Where was she?

CHAPTER 9: MYSTERY MEN

At least it had stopped raining. I peered out the kitchen window as I washed the last of the dishes. The sky remained overcast with heavy grey clouds dulling the day but the storm had done little to alleviate the heat.

Water lay everywhere. Our low-lying backyard lay three centimeters under water but thankfully the chickens were all fine. Perched in their hen house on the highest shelf they'd squawked indignantly and fluttered damp feathers when I'd checked on them. I hadn't had time to suss out the vegetable garden and made a mental note to add it to my list of *'must-do's.'*

On the street out front deep potholes had formed and were full of water. Power had yet to be restored but it'd been fun cooking breakfast on the small gas stove Bob had brought over last night.

The first thing I'd done this morning was check for messages. Nothing from Marnie. I decided it was time I checked her grandmother's house again. Maybe Marnie's mobile was on the blink. If she wasn't there, maybe I could speak with her grandmother.

But I still couldn't shake the feeling of dread weighing me down. I needed answers soon or I'd go crazy.

Footsteps tramped down the side path. I glanced out the window again and spied my mother heading for the side-gate. A pile of clean, neatly folded linen lay in her arms. She kneed open the gate and disappeared round the side of their neighbor's house. Trust Mum, always thinking of others.

Looked like I'd have to wait. Tonight. It was time I stopped burying my head in the sand. I needed to work out what, if any of her wild ideas were real. "As soon as dinner is over, Mum and I are going to have a chat."

"Chat about what?"

I spun round to see Em standing in the doorway, smiling and dressed in a cotton candy-pink sundress and wearing makeup.

"Nothing, Em. I was thinking out loud."

She considered me for a moment before saying brightly, "You know what they say." She giggled.

"Are you going somewhere?" I indicated her clothes before glancing down at my faded cargo shorts, white tee-shirt and bare feet.

"I thought I'd look in on Dad." Em gave a casual shrug. "See if he's heard from Mum. It is awkward. I still find it hard to believe she left without a word to me. You know, I never felt as if they were my parents, Tara. But I did think that we were friends, Sheila and I. It's hard for me to accept she left no note. As for my so-called father – at best, we had this polite relationship. I often wondered why they ever adopted me."

Had she always thought of her adoptive mother as *Sheila* or was this something new to distance herself from the hurt she must be feeling? Just last night, she hadn't wanted to be anywhere near her adoptive father.

I didn't understand any of this so I remained silent, remembering all those times when I'd been envious of Em and her family; the same family I'd thought to be so perfect.

Nothing was as it seemed, these days.

"I'll come with you," I said quickly, thinking she might need some emotional support.

"Sure." Em sounded offhand and made me wonder whether she wanted me there or not.

"When are you heading back to uni?"

"I'm not certain." She examined her nails. "I think I'll take leave of absence for a week or two."

"Won't that put you behind?"

Em shrugged. "I'll catch up and if I don't I'll redo the course next semester. What about you, shouldn't you be heading off to your class?"

"A tree went through the roof of the admin section. All classes have been postponed for a week. Not that we had much left to do. Phil intended to hand out our results and get us to do one last essay."

"I guess you've still got another month before your trade-course begins."

I frowned. Somehow my goal of learning a trade had faded, as if it were someone else's dream.

"Hello? Are you in there?" Em did an exaggerated eye roll as I stared into the distance and worried over this latest revelation. "Let's talk about something important. Like where's Alex?"

"How should I know?" I picked up a pile of clean plates and stowed them inside a cupboard.

Em raised a brow. "Cranky pants. You have to admit, Tara, that he is seriously hot."

"Maybe. If you go for that macho, he-man of the hour routine." My tummy did a jellyroll as an image of Alex striding past with a log balanced on his shoulder flashed into my head.

"You can't fool your bestie. I know you like him."

"I barely know the guy. I'm not blind. I can see he's good looking and got a great body. So what?" No need to mention how much his smile made my knees go all gooey.

"Then you won't mind if I make a play for him." Em turned round and added over her shoulder, "I'll text him and see if he'll pick us up."

Something twisted painfully inside my chest. I forced myself to sound normal. "You have his phone number?"

"Well, duh," came Em's voice floating down the hallway.

I fingered the edge of my tee-shirt. Should I change? Heat bloomed over my face. *Stuff it.* I'd wear what I had on. What was the point in attempting to impress Alex? My best friend had staked her claim.

The thought left a sour taste in my mouth.

Shoving my hands in my pockets, I wandered out to the hall to look for a pair of canvas shoes.

Em stood on the porch, talking on her mobile. When she saw me, she smiled and ended the call. "He's on his way."

"Good."

An awkward silence fell between us. I used the time while we waited to pull on my shoes. Tying my laces, I slid a glance up at my friend who was humming and had an air of barely repressed excitement shimmering about her. I thought she'd be more worried about her adoptive mother. I guess there was nothing like a guy to make the day shine brighter.

A late model Holden V8 pulled up outside my house. I eyed the bristling array of antennas, the racing spoilers and heard the thrumming rumble of its engine. That was some car.

Alex sat in the driver's seat sporting a pair of aviator glasses that successfully masked the expression in his eyes. His friend, Shay, also wearing a pair of similar shades, sat in the passenger seat. There was someone in the back but I couldn't make out who it was.

Feeling a bit like a third wheel, I followed Em who ran down the path, giving little squeals as water sloshed over her high-heeled sandals. She leaned in through the open passenger window, giggling in her high girlish voice. Straightening, she opened the rear door and slipped inside.

I followed suit, accidentally slamming the door shut.

"Hi", I mumbled in general. Fumbling with my seat belt I looked around and found my brother squished in the corner, grinning.

"Dan? What are you doing here?"

"Just hanging," he said. "We're taking a break from working with the SES crew. We've got an hour. Alex suggested we grab a bite to eat before heading back."

"Sounds like a fabulous idea. We'll go to the café together later." Em scooted forward to the edge of the back seat to lean over the Alex's shoulder.

"Leather seats," she purred, running her hand back and forth along the top of the seat. "They look so comfortable."

"Uh huh. Sit back and belt up." Alex turned and speared me with a sharp glance over the top of his shades, nodding when he saw my seat belt was already fastened.

"I like a man who is protective." Em bounced back into the seat and snapped on her belt.

I elbowed her in the ribs and whispered, "Try controlling."

"He can hear you," she sang sweetly and I cringed.

"So where are we going?" asked Alex, changing gear and expertly dodging a fallen tree branch without slowing the car's speed.

"First stop is Dad's office. It's on the main street, you can't miss it. He owns the regional newspaper." Her voice was smug.

I hunched further into the corner. Em hadn't been kidding when she'd said she intended to make a play for Alex. My friend was giving it everything she had, flattery, lots of smiles and fluttering eyelashes every time she caught his gaze in the rear vision mirror. It was embarrassing.

And irritating.

Somehow it made me feel alone. Confused, I blurted, "Em's mum is missing."

"Say what?" Shay turned his head to stare at us.

"Tara! You promised." Em's voice was shrill with accusation.

"They have to know sometime," I defended myself. "This way we'll have more people to help with a proper search."

"It's no big deal. Mum's gone off to a spa."

"But last night..." I began, wondering whether I was hearing right.

She cut in quickly. "Last night was last night. I was upset she hadn't told me but on thinking it through, I can't see that there'd be any other possibility."

"Maybe she's got a boyfriend," said Shay. Craning his head round, he met my eyes and winked.

"No way," said Em with heavy emphasis and turning a shoulder to me she engaged Alex in a conversation that totally excluded every other person in the car, mainly drilling him about where he lived previously, what he liked to do in his spare time. Alex kept his answers short, almost brusque but nothing deterred Em when she was on a roll.

"Seriously?" she squealed. "You're a uni student like me? We have such a lot in common." She shafted me with a triumphant glance. "What are you studying?"

Sounding hunted, Alex said, "Engineering. I've taken leave from my final semister until I've sorted things out here."

"That's so sweet, helping your Dad out like this," cooed Em.

"Not really. I always keep my word."

I frowned. Hadn't Alex said something similar to me?

She bounced in her seat. "Here we are, Alex. Pull in behind that blue sedan."

"No worries."

As soon as the car stopped, I was out the door and on the pavement as if the Hound of the Baskervilles was on my tail.

A lot of shop owners were still cleaning up from the

storm. Some were busy sweeping debris, broken glass, mud and branches off the footpath. Across the road, two men maneuvered a wide plate-glass window off a truck while the butcher issued directions. Rubbish piles were stacked neatly along the street. Several men were crawling about the roof of the pub and hammering in replacement sheets of colorbond. The sound of an electric drill from further down the road indicated power had been restored.

A horn tooted.

My brother lifted a hand and waved as he joined my side. "Did you see that, Sis? Looks like the Johnsons are leaving town. I wonder why?"

I had no answer as I watched the car go past. Boxes and suitcases were lashed to the roof and the car towed an equally over-laden trailer.

"This way everyone," called Em gaily.

"What's with your friend making the moves on Alex?" Dan muttered, sending a dark glance at Em as she linked her arm through Alex's and sauntered toward the door of the newspaper office.

"She likes him."

"So? I thought...you know..." Dan shoved his hands in his pockets. "You and Alex..."

My stomach lurched. I spluttered, "What gave you that idea? I hardly know him."

"I think he likes you. He's asked a lot of questions about you."

"What kind of questions?"

"Just stuff."

I remembered the conversation I overhead in the car on the way to the medical centre and caught his arm as he went to follow the others into the building. "About us? About where we've lived? Anything about Mum and Dad?"

My brother pulled out of my grasp. "Leave off. I'm not an idiot. Jeez Sis, forget I ever said anything." He hurried off.

Could Alex really be attracted to me? His father's words blared inside my mind. Mister Garroway had said something about seeing to the mother.

My blood ran cold.

Em's adoptive mother was missing. Could he have had something to do with it?

Deeply troubled, I slouched inside to join the others. We crowded about in a small reception area which apart from a desk complete with monitor and printer held little else. The front windows were boarded up but otherwise the office appeared to have suffered very little damage from the recent storm.

"In here." Em pushed open another door and went down the hallway entering a room to the right.

This room was huge filled with desks, computers, photocopiers and rows of gun-metal filing cabinets. It was well-lit with overhead fluorescent lights and wide windows lining one wall. A few people were grouped around a desk near the rear of the room.

As I inched past empty desks, I spotted Em's adoptive father. Looking tired and anxious with dark bags under his eyes and deep lines chiseled into his sagging cheeks, he spoke with two men dressed in business suits. They certainly stood out in the small country town with their smart suits and styled hair. As I approached, Mister Andrews slipped a black USB stick into his jacket pocket.

"Hello Emma." He nodded. "I see you've brought friends with you."

"I was wondering if you've heard from Mum?" Em asked.

"No, unfortunately I haven't heard a word but I expect she'll be in contact shortly. I'll let you know as soon as I hear. I expect you to return this courtesy."

"Of course I will. By the way this is Alex Garroway and his friend Shay who's come for a visit."

"Thank you, Emma. I was wondering when you would decide to introduce us," Mister Andrews said, his voice so cold I squirmed, wondering why I'd ever thought this guy was nice. Dad would never be this rude.

Mister Andrews' keen eyes appeared to linger on Alex. "Welcome to our small town. So your father is the new mechanic? I can't imagine he'd get that much business here, seeing as old Rogers has been here for decades. Country people can be slow to change their habits."

"Dad's enjoying the quiet pace." Alex smiled easily as he leaned casually against the wall.

It was easy to see where Em got her penchant for asking questions.

Mister Andrews' eyebrows rose. "Lucky man. Not all of us are so fortunate to be able to afford to work as and when we please."

There was the faintest hint of a sneer in his tone.

Surprised, I glanced up.

The other two men laughed.

Tension filled the room.

Em stared at the strangers as if transfixed.

"Have you heard anything more about the meteor shower, Mister Andrews?" Dan asked. He and Shay were sprawled in a couple of chairs. "Dad and I believe there's a lot more going on than what we've been told."

"You're right there, Daniel" Mister Andrews turned to his friends. "I told you we had a genius in this town. This boy is going to be someone to watch out for in the future."

Now that was a weird thing to say. His hands seemed to be shaking as he fiddled with the computer screen on his desk, adjusting the angle so that it faced the wall behind him. Was he hiding something?

"We'll have to get a lead on everything the government knows about these meteors. Perhaps you can help me there, Daniel."

"Me? I don't know that I could help much."

"No? But your father must know a lot more given his connections," Mister Andrews said smoothly. "Perhaps you could give me his mobile number. He doesn't appear to be listed."

My blood ran cold. He was fishing for information. I snapped, "You're wrong. That was a long time ago."

"Really?" His eyebrows rose to his sparse hairline. "Well, if you'll excuse us. We have business to discuss."

Mister Andrews furtive behavior made me remember the strange buildings we'd found on his land. "Actually, I was wondering about that land you have down near Yerabee Creek Road. Em, Marnie and I went riding down there the other day and we're curious to know what's in those buildings."

"I don't see that's any of your business, young lady." He smiled smoothly, showing all of his teeth.

"I'm interested in land care." *See, I can smile like that too.*

His cold eyes drilled into me. "Sheila and I intend to start a hydroponics business."

"This is a waste of time. We have to leave," interrupted the taller of the two men.

I shivered as his eyes alighted on me. And stayed. The way he examined me was down-right creepy. The urge to run made my knees quake. I'd never met him before but damn his voice sounded familiar.

"We'll wait until we hear from you. I trust you won't forget," the other man said.

"You can count on me." Mister Andrews shook hands with them and ushered them towards the door.

Overhead, the lights flickered. A zapping noise.

Then Mister Andrew's monitor exploded.

CHAPTER 10: ANSWERS

What a day! I couldn't remember the last time I was this happy to reach home. With a resurgence of energy, I pushed open the gate and ran up the path, leaping over the puddles. Behind me, car doors closed and footsteps sloshed over the soggy ground as the others followed.

The clouds were finally beginning to drift away. Sunlight spread like laser beams over the land, causing the droplets of water lingering on the grass and the native bushes planted in the front yard to sparkle like clusters of diamonds. The air smelt crisp and clean, new born after the recent deluge. The humidity had finally eased.

A faint breeze rustled through the fruit trees. Overhead a flock of sulphur crested cockatoos screeched as they winged their way north.

The power surge had not only affected the newspaper office but most of the town was again without power. We'd left Mister Andrews cleaning up the remains of his computer in the dark. He'd insisted we leave and take a shaken Em with us.

"It's like a nightmare. An awful nightmare!" she had cried.

I could only agree. I didn't feel so calm myself. It was

lucky no one had been injured when we were showered with shards of plastic and splinters of glass. In fact, the whole experience had left me with a sinking feeling of dread twisting my belly. For two pins, I'd bundle Mum and Dan and my friends in the car and leave this town behind.

I swung open the screen door and headed for the living where I found Mum and Bob sitting close together on the old sofa. They looked pretty cozy. Were they holding hands?

It looked like both my parents were moving on. Maybe it was about time I accepted it.

But not with this guy.

I didn't trust him. I knew on a gut level he was up to something shady. Until I had some hard facts though, it would be pointless to share my feelings with my mother.

Instead I collapsed into an armchair, saying, "You won't believe what happened, Mum. There we were, in the back office of *The Chronicle,* when ka-boom! A computer exploded. I thought a bomb had gone off. You should have seen those suits hit the floor. I've never seen anyone move so fast."

"Suits? What suits?" asked Bob sharply, shooting a swift look at his son when Alex entered the room.

"No one important, just something to do with Dad's business." Em sighed and leaned her weight against Alex forcing him to place an arm about her or she'd tumble to the floor.

I couldn't help grinning at his resigned expression. You had to hand it to her, she sure knew all the right moves. She snuggled into his side and I had to look away. The thought that they might become a couple bothered me more than I wanted to admit.

"Was anyone hurt?" Mum's worried eyes studied me then switched to Dan.

"No, Mum. Everyone's okay. Did you have any problems here?"

"Power hasn't been returned to any of the residential

areas as yet," Bob said. "So the answer to your question is no."

Cheeks hot, I gritted my teeth. His pompous, *I'm-in-charge* attitude grated on me and I couldn't work out why Mum found him so attractive. Sure he was a buff, military type but that was the total opposite of my laid-back, *she'll-be-right* father. Maybe Mister Garroway would grow on me. I owed it to Mum to at least try to be civil.

My brother crossed the room to perch on the arm of my chair while he explained what happened.

"I see. Thank heavens, for a moment there I thought it was something quite serious." Mum smiled. "Have you heard from your mother yet Emma?"

"No and Dad hasn't heard from her either," Em responded quietly.

"I'm sure she'll contact you very soon. Try not to worry too much, dear."

Bob cleared his throat. "You mentioned that Mister Andrews had visitors with him. Business associates?"

"I guess so. I really don't know." Em ducked her head as everyone turned to look at her.

Remembering my impression I'd heard the tall man's voice before I shifted my weight and the old springs in the chair creaked. "I don't believe they're journalists. They didn't look the part for one thing."

"What exactly do journalists look like, Tara?" Alex queried, a grin spreading slowly over his face.

"They looked like high-powered business men. Ones with a lot of dosh. Ones used to wielding a lot of responsibility. Didn't they Em?"

Alex drawled, "Maybe they were here to do a business deal with your father, Emma."

"Maybe. If you'll excuse me, I don't feel very well. I think I'll go and lie down for a while." She hurried from the room.

Poor Em. She was probably thinking about her adoptive mother and here we were giving her the third degree. I glared at Alex. "Now look what you've done!"

He spread his hands wide, as if to say *Who me?*'

"Did you notice the USB stick, Sis? The one that was handed to Mister Andrews?" intruded Dan's excited voice.

"Yes, and did you notice how he turned the screen away so we couldn't see what was on it?"

Alex snorted. "Conspiracy theorists eat you hearts out. You should hear you two. You'd think there was a war going on."

"You were there, Alex," Dan pointed out. "Those guys were acting seriously weird."

"We barged in on them with no warning." Alex shrugged. "Your imagination's in overdrive."

"Remind me exactly what you're doing here?" I said sweetly, immediately on the defensive.

"Where you go, I go." Alex worked his jaw as if biting down on further words.

I rolled my eyes, not in the least sucked in with his chest beating. "Oh please. A second ago, you were all over Em."

"She was upset. You'd prefer me to let her fall?"

How to answer that when I knew full well Em had been playacting?

Mum rose to her feet and glared round the room. "That will do, all of you. No more arguing please. I can't help worrying about the real issue here."

"I agree." Bob stood. "I believe it's time we took action. We need to be prepared for any eventuality." He stated in his firm no-nonsense voice.

"Sir..." began Alex but his father shook his head.

"Not the bomb shelter idea!" I groaned, shivering inside at the mention of that bloody word again.

"We could leave town. Head out into the desert. Live off the land," said Alex who immediately shouted with laughter at the horrified look I knew must be written all over my face.

I couldn't imagine anything worse even though I knew

he was teasing me. Suppressing my answering grin, I pointed toward the door. "On your way cowboy."

"Bob, would you mind giving us some time alone? I need to talk to my children."

"Of course, Marion. Call if you need me." Bob squeezed my mother's hand. She nodded and he ushered his son and Shay from the room.

Left alone with Mum and Dan, I waited.

The click of the screen door latching shut sounded loud in the weighted silence. I could tell by the way Mum kept touching the wedding ring she still wore on her finger that she intended to have one of her *'serious talks.'*

She sank back onto the sofa and pressed her fingers to her temple. "Really, your father should be here. I wish..." She fell silent.

"Mum?" I shared a look with Dan who shrugged his shoulders. "Mum, what's going on?"

She sighed. "I know what you think of me, you especially Tara. That I'm crazy, suffering from delusions or paranoia or both!" Mum gave a wry smile and raised her head. "This is important. Vital actually, that you both accept the truth."

"What truth?" I huddled into the chair and folded my arms, feeling an icy coldness creep up my spine.

"The truth of your birth."

"What the...? Are we adopted?" I squeaked.

"For heaven's sake, Tara. Be quiet and listen." Mum glared.

"Sorry, Mum, I'm listening."

"Good." She took a deep breath and clasped her hands together in her lap. Her face took on a far-away look as if she was reliving the past while she spoke. "Your father and I met at University and we fell in love. Deeply, crazily, madly in love."

She paused, a tender smile curving her lips. Giving her head a little shake she continued. "We were both fired with the desire to change the world for what we believed to be for the better. When we were offered jobs with a multi-national research company with a facility in Germany, we leapt at the opportunity. At first, everything seemed aboveboard. We believed we were doing valuable work that would benefit mankind. But gradually over the next couple of years, we realized there was something much more sinister happening."

"Woah," whispered Dan.

"Shush. Go on, Mum."

"We thought we had it all. A perfect marriage and perfect jobs. Your father was brilliant." Warmth infused her voice. "He was tireless, always working, always searching for answers. He thought, actually we both thought, we were working on ways to eliminate disease and genetically inherited illnesses. We were wrong. The research was geared towards producing genetically manipulated human beings. Ones who were programmed before birth to have certain abilities."

Dan reached for my hand and I gripped it hard as Mum looked at us with tears shining in her eyes.

This was major and beginning to make a lot of sense.

"The corporation who ran the underground facility where we worked, wanted to create special beings. Their research was founded on technology way beyond our capabilities at that time. But we didn't question it. Not then. First it was whispers, and when we investigated it further, we found our research was based on alien technology. And the facility had one goal. In particular, they wanted people who could communicate with or understand alien language."

"Aliens? Holy shit!"

"Tara!"

"You don't really expect me to sit here and say nothing, do you? You're going to tell us that we're not your kids. That we were created in some laboratory. That we're some kind of freaks." My voice rose with the fury and hurt surging beneath my breast. I thought back on the long years of struggling to read, to fit in, of the misery of school and the deeply held belief that I was mentally defective.

That I wasn't normal.

Now, here was Mum actually telling me that yes, I wasn't like everyone else. My brain was faulty thanks to scientists tampering with genetics.

I should be thinking not another one of Mum's delusions. But this certainly explained the nomadic life we'd led until we arrived in Wallaby Creek.

And my nightmares.

"It wasn't like that, it was never like that." My mother held out her hands beseechingly.

I shook my head furiously, clinging to my anger, my sense of outrage. I knew if I let go, I'd fold. "Why should we believe you?"

"I can't make you believe. All I can say, is this is the truth."

The quiet words hit me like stones.

"What about the alien bit, Mum?" The fear in Dan's voice only fed my bitterness.

"They're coming. They needed someone who'd act as an intermediary and stop them from destroying Earth. When we discovered operatives from a secret military force had infiltrated the facility with the intention of killing....."

"Am I interrupting?"

I jumped and looked up to see Em beaming from the doorway. How much had she heard? Until I was certain this was true, I sure didn't want the rest of the world to know, not even my closest friends. I needed to check with Dad first, then think about what, if anything, I could do. But seriously?

Aliens?

Em chattered on, seemingly oblivious to the fraught tension in the room. "I'd thought we'd go to the pool."

After giving Dan a warning squeeze to his hand, I pushed to my feet. "Sorry. I've got a shift at the pub in an hour. I need to get ready."

"Tara..."

Ignoring Em, I brushed past and headed to my bedroom.

No sooner had I closed the door, than my mobile was in my hand. I found the number I needed and rang. It went straight to message bank.

"Dad, it's me. I need to see you. Like now."

***

Alex

"I'm getting a bad feeling, Alex." Shay slumped onto the lounge with a sigh.

"Yeah, I feel the same way. Wish I could pin-point the source." The past couple of days had been grueling but we'd both worked non-stop helping the SES out. In our spare time, we'd gone over every snippet of information in the reports, word by word. Sleep had not been on the agenda.

Flexing my neck muscles by rotating my head, I yawned before strolling into the kitchen where I opened the refrigerator door and scanned the contents. "Beer?"

"Sounds good. Where'd the Colonel head off too?"

"No idea." I grabbed a couple of tinnies and brought them over to where my mate sat, head back, eyes half-closed.

"What's with that Andrews guy? And those blokes?" Shay snapped open his beer and took a sip.

I followed suit before responding. The ice-cold slide and slightly bitter taste was like nectar down my throat. Like Shay, I nursed it. Neither of us were big drinkers. I'd known at least two other Warders who'd turned to alcohol to ease their troubled conscience and soothe their doubts.

They now lay rotting in their graves.

"They were definitely suss." I rolled the can between my hands. The liquid sloshed against the sides.

"I checked out Andrews the other night. Nothing popped."

129

"Maybe we missed something. He's definitely not on the up-and-up."

"Could be a simple matter of a shady deal on the wrong side of the law."

"I know, that's why we have to be certain before we make any moves. How about you keep tabs on him?"

"Sure thing. What about you? Going to keep a close eye on that Tara babe?"

I glanced over and met Shay's suggestive grin. "That's my job."

He laughed. "Somehow I think there's more to it than that, just don't let the Colonel catch on."

"Shit, yeah." Barely repressing a shudder at my father's reaction, I rasped a hand along my jaw and remembered I needed a shave.

"Must be a cool buzz to have three chicks hanging off your arm," Shay teased.

I groaned. "That's a complication I could do without."

"Emma seems a nice girl. And determined. If we had more time, I'd bet she'd have a ring on your finger before next Christmas."

Laughing, I allowed his comment about Tara's friend roll over me. I noticed he didn't mention Crystal Chambers. Like me, did he believe there was more to her than she let on?

The smile faded from my mate's face and I tensed.

Shay dug his phone out of his pocket and began to scroll through his messages. "I got a ping on my mobile, about an hour ago."

I waited until he found what he was looking for.

"Text from Johns. You know him? He's stationed in New York." Shay raised an eyebrow and I nodded.

"He's good." And he was good. One of our best but I hadn't seen him in over two years. As Warders, we spent the majority of our lives living a solitary and secret life. I'd been one of the lucky ones; I had a father and a good friend as support, even if there'd been months when I'd had to work alone.

"He reckons that according to his sources, there definitely is a MN operative in this town."

I sucked in a harsh breath. "Identity?"

"He's working on it. Will let us know if he finds anything more."

"Ask him to send us all his data. We'll go over it as well, just in case. Learning that identity must be our top priority."

"If there's an operative, then there'll be a force close by," Shay pointed out. "Are we going to send for reinforcements?"

"I asked a similar question of the Colonel, yesterday. Our sources are stretched. Several marks are having difficulty in believing, so they've been provided with extra protection. We're on our own."

Shay lowered his head.

"What happened with Lorraine wasn't your fault," I said, wanting to ease my mate's pain.

"Doesn't matter. I failed."

Shit! What to say now? Clearing my throat, I muttered, "It's a hard ask, expecting people to believe in what most think is impossible."

"Maybe we're not worthy of saving. I've seen men do terrible things to each other."

"Same." Carefully, I placed my beer onto a side table then leaning forward, resting my linked hands on my knees as I stared at the one guy I trusted above all others. If he had doubts... "It's hard to believe in something beyond comprehension. But we must have faith."

Shay snorted softly and met my gaze. "I've sensed your concern about our 'friends.'" His lips twisted.

"We'll play it as it unfolds. Keep alert."

"Always."

"Tomorrow we'll do a recon beyond the town's limits. Check for any signs of a force hidden nearby."

"Right. Tonight, I'll run another diagnostic on Marnie's

hard drive. Last time, I found a ghost."

"Yeah? That's interesting?"

"Isn't it? And get this, the chick is missing."

"What?"

"No sign of her about town since the storm."

"You've noticed?" I said slowly, wondering why Shay had thought it necessary to keep this girl in his sights.

"There's something about her." He crumpled his empty can. "A deep sadness."

That explained the empathy Shay felt toward Marnie. He'd taken the death of his mark to heart and I'd often thought there'd been more than duty in their brief relationship.

Tara's face swam before my eyes and my gut rolled over. I felt like I was plummeting from a great height.

Yeah, he wasn't the only one who'd fallen for his mark. It was more than duty for me now, too.

***

Tara

After racing around on my feet (and my superb boots) for six hours, I was beat. It seemed like everyone in town, had decided to visit the pub and discuss the recent events over copious beer schooners.

A large group of former school mates had entered about an hour ago and had kept me busy mixing cocktails. Crystal was amongst them and had for once, refrained from any snide comments. She seemed unusually subdued and determined to get wasted, if the number of drinks she'd already consumed was an indicator.

We'd never been friends. Even so, I kept an eye on her as I slapped the damp tea towel down onto the bar and served another customer demanding a beer. Crystal's shoulders were hunched as she leaned on the table, not interacting with her friends. Normally she was party-girl central. It was strange seeing her staring into space and not speaking to anyone. Whatever her problem was, I hoped it wasn't serious. I wondered whether I should go over and ask if she needed anything but the thought of getting my head snapped off made me stay behind the counter.

My dithering only added to my confusion.

Over in the corner of the main bar, a band was setting up. Every so often one of them would do a sound test and the noise felt like a drill screeching through my brain.

Any minute now, I was going to lose it.

Bracing my hands on the bar, I lowered my head and concentrated on taking deep breaths. My head pounded. Mum's words went round and round. It couldn't be true. It just couldn't be. Aliens for god's sake!

But if it were true, my *'disability'* now made sense in a kind of weird way.

If only Em hadn't interrupted us at such a crucial moment. There were so many other questions I needed answered. I knew deep in my gut, there was more my mother wanted to say. But it was hard to get her alone with Em dogging my shadow.

Prepare.

Warder.

Could all those weird messages I'd read in obscure patterns over the years actually be real? The thought turned my insides to mush.

I had to cling to the bar or my knees would give way. Why wouldn't Dad answer my messages? If I didn't hear from him soon, I'd borrow Mum's car and head over to the observatory. It would mean cutting short my work hours since it was a good forty minute drive. But I needed to see him, talk to him.

I sensed rather than heard someone approach the bar.

"Headache?" the sympathy lacing Alex's voice caused my eyes to sting.

"No," I lied, not wanting to appear weak and girly. "Just taking a moment to regroup. It's been pretty hectic." I straightened and eyed his tall figure admiring how cool and confident he appeared in his black, silk dress shirt and jeans. In the yellowy light of the bar, his blond hair glowed like sunlight and his smooth olive skin appeared a rich gold. What was it with guys who wore black? They were like chick magnets.

I could have stared at him all day.

"You're all dressed up. Going somewhere special?" What I really meant was *who are you with?* Was it Em? I picked at my short fingernails.

He shrugged; a movement that had me inwardly sighing over the width of his shoulders. "You look tired."

Oh and wasn't that just perfect. Bags under my eyes and fading bruises on my face. Reality check. Here I was with the hottest guy in town and I looked like a hag. I winced as another shooting pain spiked over the top of my head and mumbled, "I've been working."

His steady gaze unnerved me and I shifted my weight, sternly resisting the urge to smooth down my, no doubt, messy hair. "I wanted to make sure you're okay after today."

For one mind-freezing second, I thought he knew my secret. The sheer horror of that thought had me gaping at him as if he'd suddenly morphed into the devil himself.

"Tara? Are you alright? You've gone as white as a sheet."

My mouth opened and closed. All my blood seemed to leave my head and I felt all floaty.

"Fuck." He leapt over the bar, landing lightly beside me much to the amusement of the old timer seated on a stool nearby.

The old guy yelled, "Go get her, mate!"

Blinking rapidly, I attempted to hold it together, cringing as all eyes turned toward me.

"You need to take a break," said Alex grimly. "When was the last time you drank any water?"

"Dunno," I mumbled. Blackness closed in on me. I could barely hear him over the crescendo of noise rising inside my brain to fever pitch. My body shook.

"Come on." Alex took my arm and towed me,

stumbling, along behind him.

The only protest I could manage was a feeble, "Where are we going?"

"Somewhere quiet where you can take a breather. You need food too."

"Work..." I bleated.

"Forget it." He led me into the dining area where he located an empty booth and pushed me toward it. "Sit. I'll order us a meal. Don't worry, I'll square it with your boss. Ask him to take you off the clock."

Feeling overwhelmed, I perched on the seat and gripped my trembling hands together on the table. A few minutes later, Alex re-appeared, sliding along the bench until he was right up beside me. The warmth of his body and the tangy scent of his aftershave hit me simultaneously. His thigh rested against mine. My head whirled.

Whether it was from being so close to his hotness or not, I couldn't tell nor did I have the energy to try and figure it out.

"Here, drink this." He pushed a glass of water into my hand.

"Thanks." I sculled it down without pause. A little of the heaviness in my head lifted. The rush of white noise abated. My tense muscles began to relax, my shoulders slumping. "Where's Em?"

"I have no idea. Feeling any better?"

"Yes, thanks."

We fell silent. Alex re-filled my glass from the jug he'd brought with him and nudged my hand with the glass. Obediently, I chugged down more water.

Finally, my heart eased its frantic pace and my dizzy, light-headedness lifted. Sighing with relief, I fiddled with the empty glass in my hands, turning it round and round. When I snuck a peek at Alex, I saw he was staring at the table, a heavy frown puckering his forehead. "Something on your mind?"

"Yes, you."

Not knowing how to answer, I remained mute and waited. At last he moved, lifting his left arm to rest along the back of the bench. If I leaned back, his arm might drop down around my shoulders. My tummy quivered.

So, I was attracted to him. The knowledge sank deep into my soul.

Any girl in her right mind would be! But I didn't know what to do about it. My life was such a mess at the moment and with my best friend keen on this guy, how could I betray her?

No, he was off-limits, so I'd better keep it cool and just 'friends'. Or should I?

Jacey, one of the waitresses, bustled up to our table with a laden tray in her hands. She winked as she set down a bowl of potato wedges, a plate of garden salad and another plate filled with crisply fried cocktail fish pieces.

The aroma caused my stomach to rumble and, giving my belly a pat, I laughed. "I didn't realize how hungry I was, thanks, Alex."

"Any time."

We smiled at each other.

And for one insane minute, it was like there was no one else in the room.

The clatter of cutlery hitting the table broke our connection. Face hot, I tore my gaze away and nodded my thanks to Jacey who sauntered off grinning.

Keep it cool.

I picked up a fork and speared a piece of pan-fried barramundi and bit off a mouthful. "It tastes great. Aren't you going to eat?"

"Yeah, I'm starving too." He moved his left arm, draping it now around my shoulders. The weight was warm and comforting. I couldn't believe how much I longed to cuddle into his side.

He said coolly, "You don't mind do you?"

"No. I like it." Did I really say that?

But Alex didn't make any derisive remark, only smiled and picked up a fork. While we ate, Alex spoke about the work he and Shay had been doing with the SES and the damage to the town that still needed to be fixed. Gradually, I relaxed, enjoying listening to his quiet, deep voice and the feel of his arm around me.

He made me feel protected.

Safe.

"I need to get back to work," I said gruffly.

"If you're sure you're feeling better...?"

I nodded.

"Your boss said you can work out the remainder of your shift in the kitchen. Less hectic. I tried to talk him out of it, but he was adamant he needs your help. Sorry." Alex slid out from the bench and stepped aside to allow me to follow suit. When he held out his hand I took it, a buzz of electrical excitement tingling up my arm where his fingers closed strongly over mine.

Ooooh yeah. Talk about hot! This guy needed a safety warning tattooed on his chest.

"When you've finished your shift, how about we go into the bar and listen to the band? I'd like a dance with you."

"Sounds like fun." Surprisingly I meant it. I could do with some R and R after the past few days. And surely, Em wouldn't mind if I had one little dance with him? Besides, I was fairly certain now that Dan was right, I was the one Alex was interested in. A little thrill sizzled over my flesh.

I checked the time on the old railway clock. "I've got an hour and a half to go which gives us about twenty minutes before the band packs up."

"I'll hang around here. Take it easy, okay?"

I gave a quick smile and hurried off through the door that led to the kitchen and pantry areas. Away from the noise and bustle of the bar, the remainder of my headache fled while I kept busy doing some washing up and stacking the washing machine. When I'd finished I made a quick visit to the loo, brushed my hair and applied fresh lipstick. Tugging at my clothes, I found Alex where I'd left him.

His gaze locked with mine as I crossed the room to his side. I went all hot and fluttery inside at the sight of his slow smile and steady stare.

The lights were dim in the main bar. Hand-in-hand, we entered the room. A blast of sound hit me and I teetered on my heels. On the raised dais the lead singer belted out a song at the top of his lungs, competing against the blare of his band's instruments.

The room was packed with people, some dancing, some standing around watching, others laughing and yelling at each other.

Alex glanced over his shoulder at me and grinned. He wound his way through the crowd until we reached the dance area where he swung round and placed his hands on my waist. Drawing me closer until our bodies touched, he leaned his chin against the side of my forehead and began a slow swaying dance.

My body pinged into overdrive.

I wound my arms around his back and half-closed my eyes. *Heaven.* Em was right; he was sex candy on legs. Heat, hard-packed muscle and sinew, he moved with the lithe grace of a panther and the lure of a dangerous predator.

Along with that thought, came the questions.

Who was this guy?

He has the word *'Warder'* tattooed on his neck.

What did it mean, if anything?

My bestie was interested in him.

And his father could be involved in said bestie's mum's disappearance.

Jeeze, what a mess!

For the life of me, I couldn't imagine Alex hanging around in such a small community for long. He looked like a fast-paced life was more his style. For all my protestations about moving away and seeking the bright lights of the city, I knew I could never live far from my parents and little brother.

They relied on me.

And for all my raving about wanting to live elsewhere, I'd miss them. So even if Em weren't on the chase, a short-term relationship was not what I wanted.

But what was stopping me from pretending for a few minutes?

Every girl likes to dream.

Closing my eyes to shut off my turbulent thoughts and enjoy the moment, I nestled closer until I rested my head on his chest. His mouth nuzzled my forehead in a way that sent my tummy quivering as our footsteps slowed and we swayed together in a sensuous rocking movement. My hormones roared into life, squealing...*yes!....yes!...yes!* Every part of me fizzed and sizzled. With his arms round me and pressed so close, I wanted to stay in his embrace forever.

What happened to keeping it cool?

The song came to a crashing end and the band broke for a break.

Feeling more than a little guilty, I pushed out of Alex's arms and avoiding his eyes left the dance floor.

"I think I'll go home," I tossed over my shoulder, deciding it was time to retreat before I caved and dragged him off to some dark corner. That was something I could never allow to happen.

"I'll drive you." His tone was flat, hard and instinctively I knew it would be useless to protest.

Outside the hotel, the night was still and warm and rich with the aroma of the bush. Alex linked my fingers in his as we strolled to the rear of the building and the carpark. I didn't protest although in my mind's eyes, all I could see was Em's tearful face.

When we reached his car, he pressed his key lock and opened the passenger door for me.

It didn't take long to drive the few blocks to my mother's house. When Alex pulled into the curb and turned off the engine, I sat, waiting.

My conscience battled the pull I felt towards him. *Em.* What would I do if he kissed me? Should I give in and kiss him back? Push him away? Invite him inside? Make a run for the front door?

"Tara?"

Suddenly there didn't seem to be enough oxygen inside the car.

I forgot about my best friend.

Breathless, I turned toward him. "Yes?"

"What's your Dad's take on this meteor shower? Has he mentioned it to you?"

"Huh?"

With shadows painted across his face, it was hard to read his expression but there was no mistaking the grim slant to his voice. This was not about me. He was fishing for information.

Disappointment sliced into my heart and the bubbling lust frothing about inside me, cooled. This would teach me to poach on my friend's preserves. Blindly I groped for the door handle. "Thanks for the lift and for the food, Alex. If you want to ask my father questions, why don't you talk to him yourself?"

"I don't have his number. He's like a ghost, not listed anywhere."

I shrugged. "Try the observatory. See you around."

I opened the door. Alex's hand landed on my shoulder but I wriggled out from under his hold and escaped.

I couldn't reach the porch quick enough. It wasn't until I entered the house before I heard his car roar off down the road.

He'd waited until I was safe inside.

I really wanted to kiss him. Damn it. What, if anything, was I going to do?

***

Alex

I should have kissed her. Bloody hell, I wanted to do more than kiss her. The realization beat inside my skull with an insistent tune similar to that last head-banging song played by the band in the pub.

Feeling a little as if I'd been blindsided, I changed down a gear and took the next corner wide. As soon as the car straightened, I pressed my foot down, heavy to the metal. The car responded, surged forward with a power that normally thrilled me, normally sent the adrenaline crackling through my blood. Heightened every sense I possessed.

Nothing.

Fuck it. My jeans felt painfully tight, my body still tense, and stupid, dumb thoughts filled my head.

The fact I didn't experience that quick rush worried at my mind like a rodent chewing on wood.

This chick is getting under my skin.

My shoulders twitched.

I can't let it interfere with my mission.

The thought of seeing that cold disappointment etched on my father's face, effectively chilled the heat that had flooded my body when I'd been near her. But it had been more than a shit-load of lust that had sent my senses reeling like a monk in a whore house.

It had been worry.

The way her pain had split inside my head as if I was right in there with it had knocked me sideways. I hadn't expected it; heard about it but actually experiencing a sacred connection like that with another person was mind blowing.

All I could think about was my need to take it away.

What was even more amazing, was I succeeded. Her headache had eased once I was in her company. Whether that was pure luck or something else, I couldn't figure out.

I'd blown it though. The first opportunity I'd had to spend a little one-on-one with her and I blew it.

Maybe I should have started with a kiss instead of a question.

She'd withdrawn from me immediately.

Shit! I'm not getting anywhere with this mission. What if I'm wrong? What if it's not her? Fuck it. I need those answers. Fast.

Cause I could have done with her trust. That would have helped big time.

Guess that was something I had yet to earn.

I thought of Shay and his dead mark, Lorraine. Jaw clamped tight, I lowered the window.

A wash of cool night air swirled through the cabin as I sent the car roaring down the dark country road.

The intel my father had greeted me with before I'd left for the pub, pounded with urgent force inside my brain.

The seeders were coming.

Our time on this Earth had reduced to days; if not hours.

What I needed was some solitude to bring me to my senses.

Force me to remember there was more at stake than one, amazing, sweet...and hot girl.

CHAPTER 11: THE LIST

Tara

It was thirst that woke me.

Blearily, I opened my heavy eyes. I swallowed over a throat that felt like the bottom of a budgie cage. I really needed to stay better hydrated.

The faint light from the moon illuminated the face of the antique clock on my bedside table. It was after three in the morning. I cocked my head and listened, but apart from the creaks of old timber, the house was quiet. I looked over at the sleeping form of Em on the camp bed. From the sound of her regular, soft breathing she appeared to be dead to the world.

I smiled glad now I hadn't kissed his hotness.

Friendships like ours were sacred.

Sitting up, I ran a hand through my tousled hair and yawned. The events of yesterday, seemed a million miles away. Dawn might bring disaster and god only knew what new revelations about my secret past but for now, I desperately needed water.

I shuffled along to the bathroom and after emerging wandered down the hallway to the kitchen. The power still hadn't come on which made it difficult to see the interior of the refrigerator. After a bit of rummaging around, I found a two liter plastic container of water and poured a large glass full.

I drank then pressed the glass to my hot cheeks before opening the refrigerator door again. Puddles of water left from the slowly melting blocks of ice Mum had placed in the refrigerator to keep the food from spoiling had formed on the shelves. Grabbing a sponge I soaked them up and tossed the sodden sponge back into the sink.

Mum might have thought she'd given us answers but really all I had were more questions. What did it all mean? If what Mum said about Dan and me being genetically bred inside some lab was true that meant we really were in hiding.

But from what or whom?

I remembered the white room and shivered.

Pouring another glass, I slumped against the cupboard and sipped. I didn't know what to think any more. It was so hard to imagine an organization such as Mum described taking it lightly that two of their scientists had run off with the results of their research.

No, they'd move mountains to get back what they believed belonged to them.

What if they were here, in this town, looking for us?

There'd been a few newcomers to town recently, including the two suits in Mister Andrews' office and Alex and his father. My heart constricted painfully at the thought of Alex. Pushing my yearnings to the back of my mind, I concentrated on the serious stuff. What had Mum said about recognizing a Warder at the supermarket and her belief he was Bob Garroway?

That meant, both Alex *and* his father were Warders.

And what the hell was a Warder? Someone we should be worried about?

But Mum hadn't given us that impression, although she'd expressed concerns over whether they could be trusted. Rather she'd seemed more worried with a group called, the Mundos Novus Force. Could they be linked to the research organization?

Is that what we were running from?

I clutched my hair with both hands and tugged hard.

Zeeze, I'm acting like I believe this stuff.

I tried to make sense of my whirling thoughts and think logically. Those two men in Mister Andrews' office had certainly acted strange. Now, that much I did accept. I knew I'd heard that tall guy's voice somewhere before. What if he were connected to my past? It might pay to find out more information about them. Get some proof.

But how?

The USB stick.

Of course.

I sculled the remaining water then went back to my room where I stripped out of the thin tank top I wore to bed and pulled on a pair of cargo pants and a tee-shirt. After pulling on my joggers, I roughly shook Em by the shoulder. I was going to need reinforcements for this one.

"Come on, Em! Wake up."

"Huh?" mumbled Em, groggily rising to her elbows. She stared at me, blinking owlishly. "Tara is that you? What are you doing here?"

"What do you mean, what am I doing here? Don't you remember? You're at my house." I shook her again as she slumped, mumbling to herself, back down amongst her pillows. "Oh do wake up."

"Okay! Okay, I'm awake. Just stop shaking me. What's happened?" Her voice rose.

"Shush! Not so loud, Em." I perched on the edge of the camp bed. "Remember the USB stick?"

"I've got no idea what you're talking about."

"Remember those men in your father's office?"

"So?"

"One of them handed over a USB stick to your father. I need to see what's on it."

"You're kidding me right?"

"No, I'm serious." I eyed my dazed-looking friend now sitting up and yawning. *How much to tell her? Keep it simple. Give her something that's plausible.* "I think it has some details about the meteor shower."

"And?" She sounded thoroughly irritated.

"And if it does, I believe it should be made public."

"You sound like your Dad."

"I mean it, Em. Knowledge should be transparent and available to everyone." As soon as the words left my mouth, I realized I believed what I said. Guess Dad's beliefs had rubbed off on me, too.

"I suppose it wouldn't hurt to take a look." She gave another bone cracking yawn. "Can't this wait until morning? I could phone Dad and ask him."

"I don't want him to know."

"You're acting really strange these days, Tara. What's got into you?"

Only that apparently I'm some kind of mutant who can talk to aliens.

"Did I hear the sound of Alex's car? Did he bring you home from the pub?" Sharp suspicion was rife in Em's voice.

"It was a lift, okay. He's not into me." I spread my hands wide. "Nothing happened." Should I tell her I danced with him? Better not. I rubbed my damp palms over my pants feeling the bite of guilt snap at my conscience. My secrets were piling up.

"Humph. Alright, what do you want me to do?"

I said gruffly, "I knew you wouldn't let me down. We break into the office, grab the stick, copy it and put it back before anyone knows it's missing."

"I shouldn't have asked," groaned Em. "If the stick is important, Dad wouldn't leave it at the office. He'd put it in the study safe at home. But we've got a problem. Dad texted me today and told me he's changed the locks and I haven't seen him to get the new key. I don't see how we are going to get inside."

"We'll go up the trellis and through your bedroom window, just like we used to do when we were in high school."

Em threw the cotton blanket off, and scrambled to her feet. "I can't believe I'm letting you talk me into breaking into my own home!"

"Think of it as a learning experience." I grinned while she dithered over her clothes before finally settling on pale pink track pants with matching tee, and then pulling on her shoes. "We'll go in Mum's car."

It didn't take long before we pulled up in front of Em's house. For two minutes we sat without moving, both looking out into the darkness. The street appeared deserted. Not even a dog barked. It was once again, hot and humid. No breeze stirred the leaves of the remaining trees lining both sides of the street.

We either did this now or hauled our butts back to bed.

"Come on." I grabbed my satchel where I'd placed my Acer notebook and slipped the straps over my shoulder then opened the car door, closing it as quietly as possible. With Em leading the way, we hurried down the path to the back of the building.

Feeling like I was a kid again, I grasped the trellis and began to climb. Em was close behind. The window was opened wide. I had to fight my way through those bloody lace curtains, and then scramble over the chest of drawers. Ornaments tumbled to the ground thumping dully on the carpet. Heart pounding I waited in the centre of Em's bedroom. A thud and a muffled yelp singled her arrival.

In spite of our intentions to be as quiet as possible, we couldn't help giggling when I tripped over the cat just outside Em's bedroom door. Bartholomew hissed and swiped at my ankle. Righting myself, I switched on my mobile and using the glowing screen like a torch, we tiptoed down the stairs.

The cat raced ahead of us and disappeared into a dark room off the side of the front foyer.

Outside the study, we hesitated before entering, listening intently. But no sound broke the stillness of the night. I took a deep gasp of air to try and still my rapid heartbeats.

It didn't work.

A faint light glowed down the hall from where an old oil lantern burned steadily on a side table.

"Maybe this isn't such a good idea," She whispered anxiously. "Dad will kill me if he finds out."

"We can't chicken out now." I turned the knob.

As soon as we entered the room, Em hurried over to the bookcase, her fingers drifting across the binders. With the curtains pulled wide over a large window, light from the street lamps outside and the fitful moon made it fairly easy for me to see what she was doing.

She hooked her finger into the binder of a particularly thick book and pulled. A line of mock books swung out and behind was the pale gleam of metal.

"I hope he hasn't changed the combination," she said as she twisted the handle.

I crowded close behind her and heard the faint tumbles of the lock disengaging. She yanked open the metal door and rummaged inside. Smiling triumphantly, she turned around and waved a USB stick in front of my nose.

"Got it."

I tugged my mini laptop from my satchel. It fired up immediately and I plugged the USB stick into the connection on the side.

Em sighed. "This is going to get us into trouble, Tara. I just know it is. But you're right. It's odd how those two guys came all this way to give it to Dad. I mean they could have emailed it."

"What is all this stuff?" I squinted. Pain slashed across my forehead, my vision blurred, darkened. Crazy glowing glyphs danced in front of my eyes.

"Looks like a list of different types of equipment. Probably for the hydroponics business. See? Here it mentions seeds and over here an excavator."

"That doesn't sound important." I had to force out the words. Should I tell her I saw something quite different?

"I agree, plus there was no password to unlock it," she pointed out.

Chewing my lip, I sent her a sideways glance. The light glowing off the small screen revealed a look of utter boredom on her face. Maybe, I'd better keep this to myself for a while longer. I made an attempt to sound like everything was hunkey dorey. "I was so sure I'd find something on it to explain those two guys."

"They're business acquaintances of Dad's. There's no big deal."

It couldn't be that simple. I'd met or heard one of them before. I knew it.

I continued to open files. And in each one, I saw strange symbols amongst what I knew were normal words. Symbols that I understood.

It was true. My chest constricted and I found it hard to breathe without sounding like I was desperate for air.

"Let's get out of here." Em heaved an impatient sigh.

I spotted something else. "Wait. What's this? Looks like numbers to me."

She leaned over. "It's a bunch of dates against what looks like random numbers. So what?"

"Well, that could be important."

"Duh! Delivery dates," snapped Em. "Can we go now?"

"Shush. Not so loud."

"Dad won't hear us. He's a heavy sleeper."

"Still, I think we should keep it down a little."

"Whatever. Can't you hurry up?"

"Give me a sec. I'll just open this last file," I lied.

"Honestly." She strolled off to peer outside the window.

Quickly, I opened Outlook, copied the files from the disk and sent the email to Dad just as Em walked back where I had perched on the settee.

"Done. You're right. This was a waste of time." My hands shaking, I handed the stick back to Em who tossed it back into the safe while I shut down my computer. "Let's go."

"Finally. I'm going back to bed." Em stomped out of the room and out the front door.

I couldn't believe I'd lied to my best friend. What was happening to me? Surely, of all people, I could trust her? Confused, I followed as she marched to the car. Nausea swirled in my gut.

Em slammed the car door shut and sat, with her arms folded over her chest.

After starting the car, I pulled out onto the road and increased speed. The silence inside the car thickened. I wanted to say something but had no idea what so I kept my mouth shut.

When we reached the next intersection I slowed down and stopped. I checked the road for any oncoming traffic then gaped in amazement.

Forgetting my guilt, I pointed. "Bloody hell! Look at that."

We watched as a convoy of what looked like army trucks rumbled down the main street.

Once they'd rolled past, I turned and met Em's wide eyes. "What do you think they're doing here?"

But for once my chatterbox friend had nothing to say.

***

I rose at six am and headed for the garden where I spent the next two hours working hard wanting to free my mind of the craziness that had recently taken up residence.

Sweat beaded on my forehead and upper lip. I lifted the bottom of my tee and wiped my face before bending again to my task. Already small shoots of green were forcing their way through the turned earth. Satisfaction swelled at this obvious result of my labors: late lettuce; potatoes; carrots; leeks; broccoli and zucchini. I carefully examined the plants for signs of disease and removed a couple of bugs.

This was what I loved, working the earth, smelling the richness of dirt, manure and the sight of new life blooming.

The first stanza of a popular heavy rock song blared from my mobile.

Finally.

Wiping my dirty fingers over my shorts, I fished my mobile from my pocket and answered. "Dad."

"Hey kiddo."

"Did you get my text and the email I sent you?"

"Yep. Where'd that info come from?"

I looked around checking to see if I was alone, then felt stupid. Still I lowered my voice. "I copied it from a USB stick some guys gave Mister Andrews yesterday. Is it important?"

"Yep. Has your mother spoken to you yet?"

I sucked in a deep breath. "Do you mean about you and her and your jobs?"

"Exactly. How much did she tell you?"

I knew it! "You mean there's more?" My voice rose as my blood pressure spiked. I attempted to focus. "I guessed there may be, we were interrupted. According to Mum, we're on the run because you snitched us when we were babies. Oh and the final pearler? We're freaks," I added bitterly.

My father's laughter boomed out.

I flinched, shifting the mobile away from my ear. The tightness in my chest lessened and unexpected tears stung my eyes.

"Never, kiddo. Never refer to yourself or your brother like that, do you hear?"

"Yes, Dad." His endearment for me, made me smile.

"That's my girl. Listen. Does anyone else know about this info?"

I shrugged. "Emma. She was with me when we broke

into her adoptive father's house last night."

"Adoptive father?"

"Long story."

"Mmm."

"Oh, and have you heard her adoptive mother is missing? Em and Mister Andrews seem to think she's off to some spa but I don't think that's true. You see Dad, last night at Em's house the cat was there. Mrs Andrews never leaves him. She's always taken him with her when she goes to that resort because it has some up-market pet accommodation there too."

"What are they doing about her disappearance?"

"Nothing. I guess that's why I didn't mention to Em what I saw in those files."

"What?"

I hesitated, raising my gaze from the ground to stare round at the garden, taking in the way the sunlight dappled the ground, the rustle of grass as a little gecko lizard darted out and scurried into the garden, the heat beating down on my shoulders and hair. Everything was familiar, I'd seen it a million times before and yet, it was if now I saw it for the first time.

Or the last.

"It's something I've always seen. Stuff that isn't or shouldn't be there, messages or diagrams hidden in ordinary words that no one else can see. I read the word *'Warder'* in a tattoo Alex has on the back of his neck and yet it looks like a pattern of squiggles. Is this..." I gulped. "Dad, is this what I was bred to do?" Yeah, bred in a laboratory like a rodent.

"Aw sweetie. I'm so sorry." He sighed. "But this is bigger than any of us and I can't explain over the phone. Can you remember any of it?"

"I've never forgotten anything I've seen." My voice shook.

"Thank God. Tara, don't mention this to anyone, do you hear? Be careful who you trust. As soon as I learned about the meteors I reached out to the Warders and I'm bloody glad I did."

"And they're the good guys?"

"They're here to protect you and your brother."

Then Alex and his father were on our side, whatever that meant. I couldn't believe how relieved I felt. But it still didn't answer all the questions I had, especially about Alex's dad. And I hadn't Dad's warning. "This sounds...shit, I don't know what this sounds like. Like our lives are in danger!"

"That's right, kiddo. Don't go taking any chances."

"But now that the army is in town, we'll be fine."

"What army?" The sudden tension in his voice vibrated through the phone.

"Army trucks came through the town last night, Dad. Em and I both saw them."

"Are you sure they were the army?"

"Who else would they be?" I said.

"I don't like the sound of this, Tara. I'll call you soon." The next moment, he was gone.

Dammit. I'd forgotten to tell him I couldn't contact Marnie. And I never mentioned Mum had a thing for Bob. If he was a Warder then how much of that was real or just part of a protection plan? But what if he were a phony? Both Alex and his dad could be pretending to be Warders in an attempt to do what exactly?

I still couldn't get past that conversation in the car.

Could he be responsible for Mrs Andrews' disappearance? Or was the *'mother'* he'd mentioned, my mum not Em's?

I shivered, remembering the feel of Alex's arms around me.

What a pity the one guy I was interested in had a totally different agenda.

And was off limits.

Go figure.

Shaking my head I went inside to shower and change.

The sound of sobbing coming from my bedroom had me backtracking. I pushed open the door and peeped round to find Em lying face down on the camp bed crying.

Immediately, I rushed over to sit beside her.

"Bad news?" I asked, hoping it had nothing to do with the dance.

Em sat up, scrubbing at her face with the backs of her hands. "No, I just felt overwhelmed, what with everything that has happened."

I rose from the bed, found the tissue box and handed it over. "Is there anything I can do?"

"Not really. I'm so glad you're my best friend," whispered Em, plucking a handful of tissues from the box and blowing her nose.

"Best friends forever," I quipped. "I've got a great idea. As it's so stinking hot, why don't we spend the afternoon at the pool?"

We could worry about the end of the world later.

"Count me in. Although I don't really feel like walking all that way in this heat."

"Mmm, your right." The sound of a car pulling up outside drifted in through the open window. "Someone's here. Let's go and take a look."

We linked arms and walked outside to the front porch.

"Umph! He's back again. I wish…" I shoved hair out of my eyes with a grimy hand.

Shoulders back, head high, Bob Garroway stood as if on parade next to the front gate. His stern face looked grimmer than normal as he spoke to my mother who looked at the house and waved us over.

My stomach muscles tightened into a million knots. There was a stark expression in Mum's eyes that told me louder than words, shit was about to hit the fan.

"Hi, Mum, Bob."

Mum clasped Bob's hand.

Looked like Mum had it bad. I hoped this guy was on the up and up.

"We were thinking of heading to the pool," I said, wanting desperately to stave off whatever crap was heading my way.

Another sedan sped down the road and pulled up with a shower of gravel. Alex swung out from behind the wheel and his friend, Shay emerged from the passenger side. Beyond a curt nod in my direction, Alex didn't speak as he strode round his car to lean against the side, arms folded.

"Alex." She pushed past me like a bullet and hastened out the gate to snuggle up against his side. Her sad face of a few seconds ago, gone.

Alex didn't move. Didn't encourage her but sure as hell didn't reject her either.

Remembering how close I'd come to kissing him last night had me clenching my jaw and glad that I hadn't made any moves on him. I jerked my gaze from his intense stare.

"There's no time for that now, Tara." Mum turned to look up into the sky. "The meteorites have picked up speed. Impact could be a matter of hours away."

My gut turned to mush.

"Shit! How is that even possible?"

"I don't know." Mum wrung her hands.

"I thought the government said we had ten days. It's only been six." I snapped my gaze upwards, scanning the bright blue sky. "I see them. There's so many!"

I clung to the gate to keep myself on my feet.

The sky was speckled with thousands, possibly hundreds of thousands, of brilliant orbs of light trailing tails of fire.

Death heading towards us.

Bob Garroway stated, "Time is no longer on our side. I understand you obtained certain information off Mister Andrews and sent this to your father."

How did he know? Maybe Dad was keeping him in the loop since he was supposedly here to protect us. Irritation warred with suspicion. I didn't like his interference. My hands went to my hips. "So?"

Over by Alex's car, Em gasped, holding her hands over her mouth in a theatrical gesture. "Tara, how could you?"

Both Garroway and I ignored her as we stared each other down. The ice in the man's eyes could have frozen the Sahara Desert.

I remained unmoved. Hell, I was genetically modified. Who knew what I could do. He didn't scare me. "I don't see how anything I do is any of your business."

"They were my father's private files, Tara," wailed Em.

Words of apology trembled on my lips as I glanced over at Em only to shrivel and die as she buried her face against Alex's chest. His arm came around her.

Act cool.

Friends only.

I jerked my gaze away to war with Bob's commanding stare again.

"It was burglary," bit out Alex. "Not to mention theft. Em's father has the right to have you charged."

"Whatever. It was a list of farm equipment," I lied, sending the couple by the car another peek. "There's no need for everyone to get so excited."

"I'm not excited," Alex drawled and I had to agree that the hard look on his face was anything but excited. I suppressed a shiver as his cold grey eyes met mine. He was seriously pissed off.

"What you and Emma did was extremely foolish and reckless. What if Mister Andrews had caught you? What if you had run into those two guys again?"

"They'd left town."

"You don't know that for certain. They looked like pretty tough customers. They would probably eat little girls like you for breakfast."

Okay. That did it! I almost choked over my tongue as I struggled to articulate the words seething through my brain. Little girls like me! I could take care of myself.

"You think you know everything! Well you don't. You're conceited, arrogant..." I spluttered feeling even more enraged when Alex patted Em's back.

I wrenched my gaze away.

My mother sighed. "Tara, please, try for a little decorum. We need to initiate our preparations."

"Agreed," inserted Bob in his authoritative *'don't mess with me'* tone. "At twenty o hundred hours, we leave."

"Leave?"

"Yes." Bob's stern gaze swept over me impassively.

My insides shook. There was something dispassionate in the way he looked at me, as if I wasn't a person, as if I was a tool he intended to use or exploit.

He knew I was some kind of freak.

"I'm not going anywhere," I announced. Certainly not with him or his son until I was certain they really were these *'Warders'* sent to protect us. "We'll be safe here. The army rolled into town last night."

"What army?"

Alex's quick question reminded me of how Dad had reacted. What other army was there?

I shrugged. "Ours, of course. I thought they might be here to give us a hand with the cleanup after the storm or they could have been headed to the Air Force base."

Alex traded glances with his father who nodded and snapped, "Look into it, Alex".

"Yes, Sir." Alex straightened, dislodged a clinging Em and dug out his mobile.

Em pouted and stalked toward me. "Come on, Tara. Let's go inside. I want to see if I've got any messages from my mother on my computer."

For some weird reason, those strange buildings on Mister Andrews' land popped into my head. I whispered to her, "I wonder if those trucks have anything to do with the buildings on your father's land."

"Like what?" Em shrieked.

I grimaced as Alex snapped his head round to stare at us. So much for trying to be quiet.

In three steps he was by my side and grabbing my wrist

as I turned to hurry back to the house. My scalp prickled so tight I wondered whether every hair on my head had just stood on end.

Alex said, "Wait. What's going on?"

"Tara thinks there's something sinister going on with my father's land." Em rolled her eyes.

Feeling compelled to explain in the face of Alex's heavy frown and the sudden waiting silence from Mum and Mister Garroway, I muttered, "It's nothing really. We found military type buildings on some land Mister Andrews owns. I just thought, this might be where the army is headed. They might be using it as a base or something."

I mused, "I wouldn't mind taking another look. You know, to check it out."

"Frikking hell. You need a leash." Alex glared down flaring nostrils at me. "You will not go anywhere near that place. Stay here and don't move until I get back. I've got work to do."

He dropped my arm, stalked back to his car and as soon as Shay shut his door, the car roared off down the road. Like some kind of stuffed chook, I stood gaping and staring after him.

A hand patted my shoulder, reminding me of the present. I looked into Mum's worried face. "Promise me, Tara, you'll do as Alex suggested. We don't have time anyway. You must be ready to leave tonight."

"I can be ready in fifteen minutes. You've trained us often enough." My former irritation surfaced. "Since when did we agree to Alex and his father giving us orders?" I shrugged off Mum's hand and lowered my voice. "Mum, we don't know for sure they're Warders. What if they're not?"

"Who else would they be?"

"Really, Mum?" I raised my eyebrows.

Mum leaned close and whispered, "I know, I know. Perhaps, it's because I want so desperately for you and your brother to be safe that I believe them."

"Oh, Mum." I swallowed over the lump in my throat. "I thought you weren't that certain."

"Tara. We need them. There's no one else we can turn to."

Fear sheared into my heart at the glistening tears in my mother's eyes. "What else aren't you telling me, Mum?"

Mum hesitated. Her gaze darted toward Bob Garroway. I couldn't work out if she sought permission to speak or was afraid he'd overhear.

Either way wasn't good.

I hurried into the house and into my bedroom where I flung myself onto the bed, burying my face in the pillow. Wanting to hide from the world until it was all over.

My mobile pinged. Sighing, I rolled onto my side. Three unread messages.

All from Marnie.

One by one I read the short texts.

OMG! I re-read the texts three times to make sure I wasn't dreaming. Marnie needed my help. Her dad had escaped from jail and was on the run from the law. At the moment, they were camped outside of town and intended to head to her grandmother's house to pick up supplies.

But what could *I* do to help?

My gaze focused on the last message. Only part of it had come through which suggested Marnie's battery had died. All I could make out was something about Marnie's daughter and the end of days. It had to be serious. Marnie never mentioned the baby she'd given up for adoption when we were at school.

Heart pounding, I leapt to my feet and paced my room for several minutes, thinking hard. I sent a short text in reply although I had no idea whether she'd receive it or not.

Whatever Marnie wanted, I had no intention of turning her down.

Next I made a call.

"Dad. Turn on your GPS and meet me at these co-ordinates in one hour." For five minutes, I stared blindly out the window and thought.

I was a genetically modified freak and I was on the run from whackos.

I was surrounded by people I didn't know if I could trust.

My family's lives were at stake.

It was time I found out the truth for myself.

CHAPTER 12: DON'T LOOK BACK

"I hope Dad's still there," I shouted as I pushed the quad to go faster over the rough track that wound through the bush.

Riding beside me, Em shouted back, "Must we go so fast? We're already late. Your Dad has probably given up on us and gone home."

Mum had bailed me up at the door and spent a good half hour arguing with me before throwing her hands in the air and allowing me to leave. The encounter had left a sour taste in my mouth, like I was letting her down. I didn't want to be some kind of hero or savior of the world. I just wanted to be like everyone else.

But I wasn't like everyone else and I needed to know why.

I had jumped into Mum's car only to have Em scoot into the passenger seat. Annoyed and more than a little anxious at the amount of time wasted arguing with everyone, I had given in and driven off to the hire shop.

Em had spent the entire ride there, peppering me with questions interjected with wails and moaning about the need to pack for our impending departure to God-only-knew-where. No matter how many objections I put forward, she'd insisted on coming with me although I would have preferred to go alone.

I clenched my jaw, my head throbbing. "Dad will be there. You didn't have to come with me."

"I couldn't let you do this by yourself." Em increased speed until her quad was beside me as we tore down the road. "Look, the gates should be just around that bend. Where did you say we'd meet up with him?"

"A bit further along the side track. I asked Dad to bring some wire cutters and high-powered binoculars." I worked down the gears and the quad rolled to a halt. Em pulled up beside me and wrestled off her helmet.

The heavy silence of the bush enfolded me. The heat of the sun was muted by the dense shadows cast by the tall trees. I took off my helmet and hung it by its straps over the handlebars.

"Are we still going to do this?" Em's voice sounded small.

"I am. You don't have to come any further." After swinging off my quad, I pushed it to the side of the road where a sprawling low-growing grevillea bush screened it from view.

"I said I'd come with you. Anyway, I want to know what's going on too," she said as she followed me. She gave a nervous giggle. "Alex is going to be furious when he finds out what we've done."

"Who cares?" Now who's bull shitting? I wished I knew whether I could trust him. But honestly? That dumb explanation of his father wanting to settle down in a quiet country town was crap whether they were really here to protect us or not. Both of them knew more than what they were letting on about what was happening or about to happen. They were holding back and it didn't help that every time I looked at his father, my skin crawled.

I smiled at Em suddenly glad she was with me. At least I could always count on my friends. "Let's go."

I led the way through the scrub following what looked

like a rabbit trail as it wound round and between bushes and trees and long razor sharp grasses.

Grabbing her arm, I stopped. "Listen. Can you hear that?"

"Trucks," said Em, her round eyes practically starting from her head.

"I bet it's those army trucks we saw last night."

"Do you think? Could they be using Dad's land as a base camp?"

"Maybe, but I want to make sure." Plus, I needed to get a closer look at the insignia on their uniforms. I needed to make sure they were our troops and not the people who were hunting my family and me.

Em flapped a hand in front of her face to shoo away a fly.

"Let's cut through the bush here. I'm fairly sure this will bring us out to that clearing we found the other day." I pushed a thorny branch aside.

I fought my way through another thick bottlebrush and several bush rosemary shrubs. A needle-like leaf off a Callistemon Brachyandrus pierced my finger and I sucked the spot of blood off my hand. Tendrils of the red brushes with the tiny yellow tips clung to my tee-shirt. It was hot and still and I caught my breath when I heard the steady thrum of engines.

A gap appeared in the scrub. We'd reached the clearing. There was no sign of Dad.

Looking about me, I caught my breath. "Shit! Someone's installed security cameras on the fence." Like multiple evil red eyes scanning for prey, the cameras swiveled slowly from side to side from where they'd been attached to each post.

"Get down!" I grabbed Em's hand and we quickly scrunched lower as the camera shifted in their direction.

She giggled nervously. "Do you think it saw us?"

I chewed my bottom lip, still holding tightly to Em warning her to keep still while we waited, breathless, for the camera to turn away. "No, I think we're okay. Let's go."

"I can't see your Dad, Tara. I guess he must have got tired of waiting."

"Maybe." But it wasn't like Dad to let me down. I tried my mobile phone. Nothing. No bars, no messages.

I looked at my friend. Her blonde hair had darkened with sweat and even her curls seemed to wilt in the heat. I shouldn't have brought her with me. We should turn back.

"Now what?" asked Em.

On the other hand, we'd come this far, what could it hurt to take a closer look? I couldn't give up now. Not when I was so close to finding some answers. I took another look at all that high tech security cameras and unease swept a sudden chill down my spine.

"I think you should wait here for me. I won't be long."

"No way. We're in this together, remember? So come on. You're wasting time."

After taking one look at the mulish tilt to her chin, I decided it was pointless arguing any further. Besides, Em was right. We were wasting time. We had some packing to do, if we were leaving town later today.

The reminder made my head ache.

I counted while the cameras performed another sweep. As soon as I thought I had the timing right, I scrambled over some large boulders, dropped to the ground, and crawling on all fours, scrabbled over to the edge of the tree line.

With a thump and a gasp Em arrived breathless beside me. Speechless and panting loudly, I stared at the scene spread before us.

Beyond the fence, three black vans with blackened out windows were parked near the buildings and men scurried about loading boxes into the opened rear doors of the vans. Beyond the buildings the trucks we'd seen the other night were lined up. Uniformed men stood in regimented rows in front of each truck.

I squinted. Unfortunately they were too far away for me to make out the insignia on the uniforms. The angle at which the trucks were parked made it difficult to see what if anything was written on the sides. I'd have to get closer.

"Get a load of those antenna! Enough to call up Mars," I whispered as I mentally counted the antenna sprouting from the vans.

We exchanged worried glances.

"Shit, Tara, those guys are armed," Em squeaked.

A line of men jogged in parade ground precision from behind the closest building to the fence line where we lay belly down in the dirt. The men were dressed in fatigues with helmets covering their heads; all held rifles close to their chests and their faces were marked with black camouflage.

Please, please be our military.

A flash of light caught my attention. My breathing seized for a moment. Metal glinted in the strong sunlight, reflecting off a pair of wire-cutters thrown carelessly to one side.

"OMG! Dad's been here." Ice seemed to settle in lumps in the bottom of my belly. Cold sweat formed on my back making me itch. "He's cut through the wire fence over there, where it dips down into a small ditch. But I can't see him anywhere can you?"

"He must have left," Em's voice quavered. "I think it's time for us to go too." She inched cautiously backwards.

I took one last look around the clearing.

"Look! It's his bike! It's Dad's bike." Hunched over, I raced across the clearing. There, behind a thick shrub, stood Dad's dirt-bike.

"The keys are in the ignition. He must still be here." I whirled around and ran towards the fence.

"Tara wait! What are you doing?"

"I've got to find him. You wait here. He can't be too far away." I reached the fence where Dad had cut through the wire and pulled it upwards sufficiently to allow a body to pass through. My legs feeling like jelly, I dropped onto my belly and crawled forward. Gingerly I hauled at the wire and wriggled through to the other side.

Em scrambled to the fence line, her fingers danced frantically over the numbers on her mobile. "I can't pick up a signal." Her voice was shrill with panic. She thrust the phone into her jean pocket and crouched on her knees in the grass.

I stared at her, the wire of the fence separating us. "Go home."

"No way. I'm not leaving you here alone."

"Hurry up, before someone sees us." I lifted the wire further apart, so she could wiggle through without getting her clothes caught on the jagged edges. We lay on our stomachs and peered carefully over the edge of the ditch.

"I think we need to get closer to those buildings. I bet Dad must be hiding somewhere close by, maybe trying to get a look inside," I whispered, gesturing with my index finger.

Em nodded.

"What if we get closer, take a look around and if we can't see Dad, we'll head back to the clearing. We may be able to pick up a signal further down the road."

"Sounds good to me."

"Alright." I examined the terrain in front of us. "There's enough cover for us to get fairly close to that building there. The good news is those guys are over on the other side of this compound. So hopefully, we won't be spotted. Ready?"

She gave me the thumbs up.

Placing a finger over my lips, I slunk into a crouch and ran to the closest shrub where Em soon joined me. Then off I dashed to the next clump of bushes. Feeling as if I was stuck in a B-grade movie, I fought the urge to snigger knowing it came from panic. I scrambled from bush to bush until open ground stood between me and the building.

So far, so good.

I gestured for her to join me. Still in a crouch, I scurried across the open ground where I plastered myself against the metal wall of the building. Gulping air I willed my galloping pulse to steady, as a breathless Em reached my side.

Slowly, I took a peek around the corner. No windows or vents on this side. I squeezed her hand then released it motioning for her to stay where she was while I inched along the building and snuck my head out for a look around the other side.

Bingo!

About one third of the way along the side of the building a small window was propped open by a thin strip of metal. I whispered, "There's a window open. It's fairly high up, but I think if I stand on tip-toes, I may be able to see inside."

"Any sign of your Dad?" Em whispered back and I shook my head. "Be careful Tara. I'll wait here and keep a look-out."

I crept along the side of the building. My eyes straining as I constantly searched the grounds, expecting to hear shouts at any moment, but there was no-one in sight. The engines had died down to a steady reverberation and in the distance I could hear a man yelling orders.

It seemed to take forever to reach the small window. Another quick look around to ensure the coast was clear and I stood on tiptoe, my fingers gripping the hot metal of the sill.

The low murmur of voices came from inside.

"I told you. I came alone. No one else knows about you or your cause."

Listening, I frowned. *That's Dad's voice!* I bit down hard on my bottom lip to keep from calling him.

I distinctly heard the dull thudding sound of fists connecting with another body. Then the crack of bones.

Dad! What the hell are they doing to him? Desperate to see what was happening, I raised myself higher.

The interior was dimly lit and it took me a moment for my vision to adjust. I blinked several times as if that would alter the scene I knew would be burned into my mind for all time.

Dad was bound to a metal chair that looked as if it was bolted to the ground. His hands were tied behind his back with thick rope and metal shackles encased his ankles to the chair legs. His jeans were ripped and blood seeped through near his right knee. Blood trickled down his forehead from an open wound and also from his nose, over his mouth and chin. Already one side of his face was swelling but he held his head defiantly as he stared back at the two uniformed men standing in front of him. One of the men slapped a thick cosh into the palm of his hand. Bile rose in my throat. I recognized his face as belonging to the stranger from the newspaper office. Gone were the slick suits, replaced by combat fatigues and flak jackets.

The patches on their arms revealed a capital 'M' with 'N' superimposed over the top.

The Mundos Novus.

It was true.

I squeezed my eyes shut wishing this were all a terrible dream. *Think.* I took another quick look around inside the building and spotted another man sitting in a chair over on the far side of the room.

Mister Andrews.

Em's adoptive father.

Holy shit balls.

He was hunched over a desk, his gaze fixed on the screen of a tablet and apparently ignoring the interrogation.

It was also apparent, he was no prisoner.

One of the men spun towards the window.

Quickly, I ducked down out of sight. I waited, huddled against the hot wall of the building, my heart in my mouth, hardly daring to breathe, my hands clenched into fists.

Someone laughed. There was no sound of footsteps rushing to the window. I was still safe.

My knees gave way. I squatted in the dirt on my haunches. My mind replayed the scene as I wiped sweaty hands over my cargo pants. What was Em's dad doing there? How deep in dog shit was he?

He could be under some kind of duress; forced to work for them.

My head pounded.

There'd been no one else inside that building. It sure hadn't looked as if a gun was being held to Mister Andrews' head. He sure as hell, wasn't making any objections to that arsehole beating the crap out of my dad.

I wanted to throw up. I didn't know what to think. All I knew was I had to free Dad before they hurt him anymore. If I could create some kind of diversion, maybe I could get inside unseen. I remembered the crates being loaded.

Could they be readying to move out? And if so, where were they going?

And what, if anything, did this have to do with the pending meteorite strikes?

I straightened and snuck along the side of the building then came to a complete halt.

A soldier stepped out. A black balaclava covered his face. His legs were braced apart. One hand held an open blade to Em's throat and the other clamped across her chest.

"Don't move."

Very slowly, I put my hands in the air.

Mister Andrews and his cohorts appeared behind the soldier.

We'd been made. Now what did we do?

"I should have known you wouldn't be too far behind your father. Dear me, Emma," Mister Andrews chided coldly. "Where is your gratitude? I fed you, clothed you. Gave you a home and you betray me." He cast a narrow glance around the quiet countryside. "Bring them inside."

"Dad? What's going on? What are you doing here?" Em squeaked, her eyes bugging out of her head.

"Ask your friend here. She holds all the answers. Get a move on." He stared up at the sky then back at me. *He knows what's coming.* "We need to be in position before the first impact."

The soldier holding Em released her. She staggered forward, landing in my arms. The guard gestured with his knife for us to move forward.

We moved.

We didn't have any other choice.

At the doorway, I took a last look around. The sky was a brilliant blue. The fiery meteor shower competed in brightness with the sun; so much closer than the last time I'd looked that terror gripped my insides in a savage twist.

A hawk flew lazily overhead. Gum trees stood listless in the heat, no breeze rustled the leaves or rippled waves across the sea of grass stretching to the fence.

Rough hands pushed us inside. Em fell to her knees, covering her face in her hands and sobbed.

The door slammed shut.

"Tara. Emma. Oh no. I hoped you wouldn't follow me," wheezed Dad.

I rushed to him and flung myself down at his side. I burrowed my face against his chest, my arms clutching just like I used to do when I was a little girl. "Dad."

"You have to get out of here, kiddo. You realize what's going on, don't you?"

Drawing back, I blinked away tears. "I'm not sure. How badly are you hurt?"

He coughed, wheezed and spat blood from his mouth. "Broken ribs I think, coupla broken fingers, teeth, one of my knees is shattered. My kidneys took a pounding and it's getter harder to breathe. Think I'm bleeding internally."

My heart stopped beating for a moment while I digested those horrifying words. I started working on the ropes binding his hands. It wasn't easy. My trembling fingers slipped in his blood.

"Think, kiddo. They're here for you and Dan." Dad closed his eyes for a moment as he breathed through a wave of pain. When he opened them again, the defeat shining there almost sent me back to my knees. "We tried. Your mother and I, we tried so hard to keep you safe."

"You did, Dad. You kept us safe."

Em asked, her tremulous voice revealing she was at breaking point, "Please. What are you talking about, Mister Ferguson? I don't understand. Why is my adoptive father doing this to us?"

"Good questions. But there's no time to explain. Tara. You have to leave."

"This is my fault, Dad."

"No, never think that for a moment." He grunted. Pain rippled over his face. Gathering himself, he mumbled through the blood dripping from his mouth. "Your mother and I knew what we were taking on all those years ago." He took a deep breath that rattled in his throat in a way that terrified me.

This was my fault my dad was suffering.

"What are we going to do?" I pulled the rope from Dad's left hand and hurried to his other side. A few minutes and I had the ropes off him.

Dad moved his legs in a feeble movement, making the chains on his feet rattle. "I need to be rid of all this crap."

Anger ripped white hot and hard through me. If I had a gun, I would have used it.

I leapt to my feet and paced the barracks. The only window was too small to climb through and it was certain, a guard would be stationed outside the only door. I looked over to find Em cleaning the blood from Dad's face. My heart contracted. How far could he run when he'd been beaten by that ape?

Our eyes met. His steady gaze, the love I saw shining there for me, shredded me deep inside. I knew what he intended to ask me to do, but how could I leave him? Fear clawed at my throat, as rabid as a wild dog.

"Okay Dad?" I scanned the grey hue of his face, wondering how much time he had left. I sensed if he didn't reach medical help soon, it might be too late.

"I've had better days," he managed. "Clever friend you've got here, Tara."

"Huh?" Consumed with fears for Dad, I'd paid no attention to Em. Now I saw she was bent over Dad's legs, apparently having put her tears on hold. "What are you doing?"

"Picking the lock," she said quietly. "There. I've got it." Metal scraped against metal, there was a clicking noise and Em looked up. Her mouth wobbled. "My adoptive mother taught me and she gave me my own set of lock picks for my last birthday."

She quickly replaced the picks into her pack and turned her face away.

What kind of mother or adoptive mother teaches her daughter how to pick locks? Had she suspected her husband was involved in terrorist activities and wanted to give her some survival skills?

I pulled the shackles off my father's ankles and gently rubbed his legs to help with the circulation. When I lifted his trouser hem, I sucked back my rage at the mottling skin that was revealed.

Dad bent down and took hold of both my hands in his. His clasp was weak, his fingers ice cold.

I began to shake my head. "No, Dad. Please. We can all make it."

He just looked at me, his chest rising and falling deeply as he tried to fill his airways. "I'm done for…This is where I make my stand."

So this was it.

This was what I'd subconsciously dreaded ever since I'd seen the abandoned bike and the gaping hole in the fence.

The light of battle blazed in his eyes.

"I'm not leaving without you. This is my fault we're in this mess. You wouldn't be here, if I hadn't involved you. If I had listened and stayed at home." Words poured from me. Dry sobs racked my body causing me to shudder where I stood.

He released my hands to pull me into a hug I wanted to last for eternity.

He let me go.

I'd never felt so alone in my life.

"Listen, kiddo. This is not your fault. You didn't start this and I didn't raise kids that hide in the dark, cover their eyes and don't step up to the mark. Whatever happens, I'll always be proud of you. Both of you and please tell my boy that too." He spoke slowly, each sentence an effort that I saw cost him dearly.

"Help me to stand, kiddo."

Slipping my arms around him, I eased him carefully onto his feet.

He stood there swaying, sucking in the pain of his broken body. My heart swelled with the love and pride I felt for him.

"Gotta move quick." He took a deep wheezing breath, as if bracing himself, rolled his shoulders and winked. "Got surprise on our side…it'll be a piece of cake. I'll rush them. Keep them busy. Head straight for the fence…Don't look back. Keep going."

He grabbed my shoulders with shaking hands and whispered close to my ear, "No regrets, kiddo. Everything we did, your Mum and I, every part we played, even our divorce, it was all done to keep you and your brother safe. You have an important role to play in our world's future."

He paused, his eyes wet. "Remember, my baby girl…no matter what happens, no matter who you are, your mother and I always loved you. You're ours, our own little girl who's grown into a woman we're both so proud of and we wouldn't have wanted it any other way."

Straightening, he held me at arms' length, gave me a little shake. "Now stop those tears. Pull yourself together, kiddo. We knew it would come down to this moment. You have to be strong and step up…I need you to do this for me."

I scrubbed my face with grimy hands, gulped and nodded. Inside, I was dying. With burning eyes, I stared at my father, imprinting his face on my memory and in my heart.

I'll never forget.

Never.

"I'm ready, Dad," I said. "I won't forget."

Em touched my arm. "What's really going on, Tara? Who are you?"

"Not now."

I helped Dad shuffle to the door, one arm held tightly against his stomach. I heard the hitch in his breathing, knew he was battling intense pain, but not one groan or protest did he make – not my dad. He listened for a few moments, shrugged out of my hold, then wrenched the door open.

A guard stood with his back to the building. He pivoted at the noise, his hand reaching for his side-arm, but he was too slow.

I didn't know where he found the strength but Dad's arm snaked around the guard's throat, crushing against the bloke's windpipe. Dad released him to slam his fist into the guard's left kidney. The soldier dropped to the ground.

His breathing coming in short, frantic gasps, Dad leant heavily against the wall, his face as grey as old bones. He waved us forward in the direction of the gate. "Go, kiddo. Don't look back."

Shouts and yells erupted.

Doors slammed.

I grabbed Em's hand and ran. My feet pounded over the ground but the sound was muffled by the furious cracking of my heart. I saw nothing in front of me, only

Dad's face. Hear nothing but the words he'd whispered. I could smell his spicy aftershave, feel the imprint of his arms surrounding me, protecting me.

No more.

The sound of heavy boots pounding the ground penetrated the white noise inside my head, telling me the soldiers had spotted us. Far ahead freedom beckoned beyond the wire fence.

I heard Dad's familiar voice raised in a wild yell. I risked a quick glance over my shoulder desperate to see him following behind us.

A gang of three or four soldiers stood over something or someone lying on the ground. Bayonets were in their hands. They raised them over their heads and slashed downwards.

Repeatedly.

DAD!

I stumbled. I let go of Em's hand. I pitched forward, hitting the dirt hard. She tugged at my clothes, screaming at me to get to my feet.

I took another look behind.

Sunlight glinted off rifle barrels.

Heaving to my feet, I took off in a sprint. "Duck and weave," I shouted as bullets whizzed past the side of my head, so close I felt the wind from their passage flick my hair. I ran in a drunken pattern towards the gap in the fence.

It was close.

So close.

My ears rang from the firing rifles. The stink of cordite hung heavily in the hot air.

Em reached the ditch first, slithered down and crawled through the gap in the wire. Gasping, my lungs burning, I followed. The jagged edges caught on my clothes. A straggling strand of wire sliced through my pants and down the back of my thigh as Em grabbed my shoulders and hauled me through.

I collapsed panting, in the dirt.

Em's face was whiter than snow and her lips were moving wordlessly as she helped me to my feet again.

Don't look back.

I looked back, hoping against hope to see Dad's familiar figure but saw nothing except a pack of armed soldiers running in our direction.

I remembered the motionless body lying on the ground surrounded by soldiers. I bent over retching helplessly into the grass.

Dad. Dad.

CHAPTER 13: ESCAPE

"They're chasing us! They've got jeeps."

Em's voice cut through my misery as I huddled in the dirt. Feeling as if my heart had split wide open and there was nothing left, I staggered upright.

The soldiers had turned back and were now running towards their vehicles. One of the trucks was on the move, heading to the gates.

"We better get a move on," I forced out through numb lips. I wanted to fling myself onto the ground and scream and pummel the earth until I had no strength left. I wanted to beg God for a miracle, for another chance.

But there was no time for that now.

We were in big trouble.

If we could make it to Dad's motorbike, we might escape. A dirt-bike could go a lot of places where trucks or jeeps wouldn't be able to follow.

"I can't ...." Em wrung her hands.

I turned slowly, my body feeling as heavy as if I carried lead in my veins and met my friend's wide eyes. She was filthy, scratches and bruises marred her tanned skin. I bet I didn't look a great deal better – we were like refugees from a war zone. I trembled, willing myself to think past the thick pea soup clouding my mind.

The screeching of metal and the spit of gravel alerted me that we'd better hustle. The jeep had passed through the gates. We only had a few minutes before the guards came crashing through the bush and were on top of us.

"This way!" I shouted. I led her into the dense underbrush, pushing my way deeper into the scrub by sheer will power. I ignored the cuts and welts stinging my bare skin, I was totally focused on reaching that bike. I thought I heard men shouting behind us, but this time, I didn't look back.

With a final burst of energy I ducked under the low branches of a wattle tree and emerged near Dad's bike.

"Hop on. It's okay. We're going to be okay." We had to escape. We just had to. I took a moment to quickly hug my friend before swinging my leg over the leather seat.

"Come on," I urged through chattering teeth. I could hear the jeep's engine again and it sounded closer.

Em scrambled onto the bike.

"Now hang on and don't let go." I kicked the stand up and turned the key. The throb of the engine was reassuring. Putting the bike into gear, I released the brake and with a sudden burst of power we roared across the clearing.

At that same moment, the jeep burst through the trees.

A soldier shouted.

The bike skidded and wobbled, but I kept it upright. Down the narrow track we bounced before we shot out onto the road. I notched up another gear. With a shower of stones and gravel, the bike sped towards home and safety.

"They're catching up!" shrieked Em.

I risked a glance behind. She was right. The jeep was so close I could see the grim expressions of its three occupants. The heat of the engine warmed my back. The sickening stench of diesel fumes mingled with the rising dust that clogged my nostrils. With a swift jerk of the steering wheel the driver sent the jeep swerving sideways.

"They're trying to get alongside us," I yelled. "Hang on."

The bike bounced over a pothole.

Em shrieked.

I gritted my teeth, busy trying to remember my far too brief lesson on how to ride a motorbike. How proud Dad had been of his new toy, the day he'd arrived to show it off. And how off-hand I'd been at his enthusiasm. It had been fun though, with him riding pillion behind me. The wind in my face and Dad shouting instructions as we'd circled a paddock.

Tears burned like a fireball of misery. I shook them away. If I wasn't careful I'd be joining my father, face down in the dirt.

A movement out of the corner of my eye caught my attention.

The jeep had sped up and now travelled alongside us. I opened up the throttle as far as it would go.

Em screamed and dug her fingers into my skin making me twitch away from her.

The man behind the wheel suddenly wrenched it sideways and the jeep's bumper bar nicked the rear wheel of the bike. The bike surged forward, hit another pothole and I lost control.

The bike wobbled.

Tipped over.

"Jump!" I leapt free as the bike fell toward the ground. I tumbled and slid across the gravel, knees burning, landing in a heap at the side of the road. The bike flipped over and with a terrifying screech of rending metal, was ground to a mangled mess by the jeep.

Em! Where was she? Rolling onto my hands and knees I frantically stared about me and spotted her lying still, curled up in the fetal position. Dimly, I was aware of the jeep braking to a halt, the shouts of the men as they

179

scrambled out of the vehicle.

My skin on fire, I scrabbled across the rough ground. Rocks cut into my palms and knees. Upon reaching Em's side I touched her gently on the shoulder. *Oh God, what if she's dead? What if I've killed her too?*

Em moaned, hiccupped then stared at me blinking like crazy. One of her false eyelashes hung half off her eye-lid.

"We can't stay here. Come on, get up."

"I can't." She looked like she intended to lie on the ground and never move.

Shouting and the pounding of booted feet coming closer spurred me on. I grabbed her under the armpits and heaved her onto her feet.

"Fuck it, Em. Move." Slipping her right arm over my shoulders and my arm around her waist, I dragged her towards the dense foliage. If we could make the shelter of the trees...

"Halt!"

I kept going.

"One more step, and we shoot."

Clenching my jaw, I spun around and found guns pointing in our direction. Every muscle I possessed trembled like melting jelly. My cuts and the gravel rash on my legs stung.

My sense of failure outweighed all of it.

"Hands in the air," one soldier barked.

Slowly, I released Em and raised my hands.

"Turn around."

We were going to be executed in the back. *Let them look me in the eye when they fired.*

"Fuck you," I said, tossing my head.

Shots rang out.

Blood flooded over the chest of one soldier. His legs buckled. His gun dropped from suddenly lifeless hands as he crumpled.

I hit the ground, grabbing Em by the wrist and taking her down with me as a gun battle blazed above our heads.

I didn't know who the Calvary was, but I would have kissed the devil himself if he saved us.

I held my breath, not daring to breathe, trying to squish myself into as small a target as possible while bullets whizzed past and men shouted and swore.

As the noise died away, I cautiously raised my head. Through the haze of shifting blue smoke two guys moved about, checking the bodies of the guards and removing their weapons. One of them strode over to me, while the other held his rifle at the ready and scanned the surrounds for any further activity.

I knew them.

I knew him.

Air whooshed out of me as relief had my shoulders sag. I struggled to sit.

"Alex. What are you doing here?" I mumbled.

Hands patted me down, checking for broken bones.

"Here."

Dumbly I stared at the hand hovering in front of my face. I gripped it and Alex pulled me to my feet. We stared at each other for sixty seconds.

He looked pretty pissed off.

Finally, I said, "Em."

Without speaking, Alex performed the same routine check of Em then helped her upright.

Em rolled her eyes back into her head and sagged against him.

"For fuck's sake," he muttered, catching hold of her in his left arm, leaving his right hand still holding his rifle.

I glanced over at Shay who had a tiny smile lifting the corners of his mouth. He winked and resumed his pacing of the area speaking occassionally into his collar.

"I guess this is where we thank you," I said.

Alex released Em abruptly and stalked to my side.

She snapped her eyes open.

And before Alex blocked my vision, a funny expression passed over Em's face. What was that? Jealousy? Rage?

Alex nudged my chin up with his knuckle. "I thought I told you stay away from here, Tara."

I looked him over taking in the full camouflage outfit he wore complete with kevlar vest and helmet. In this getup he appeared older, a stranger, a soldier who'd seen war first-hand. His face was marked with black face paint, sweat and dirt but the cold, grey eyes were familiar as he stared back at me just as intently. He held his rifle pointed away from my body. There was no insignia on his combat uniform.

I had to fight the urge to throw myself into his arms and bawl my eyes out.

Suddenly, he pulled me close as if sensing my need.

I could feel it welling inside of me, a huge dam about to burst its banks and drown me in an ocean of guilt and misery. I stayed stiff, knowing if I didn't, I'd lose it.

He hugged me tight before setting me away from him.

I wiped a hand over my face. It came away wet with tears. I mumbled, "If you're supposed to be looking after me, you're not doing a very good job. You're a bit late to the party."

Alex thrust his face so close to mine, I saw the fascinating rim of black that edged his clear silver-grey eyes. Through gritted teeth, he said, "You're not making it easy for me. Of all the stupid things to do..."

"I don't need you to remind me of the consequences of what I've done." I blinked furiously to ward off the flood of weak tears.

"Oh fuck." His face softened. Worry creased frown lines along his forehead and he rubbed his cheek against mine, whispering, "I'm so very sorry. That was dumb of me, saying that stuff. I didn't mean it."

My gut twisted. "You know what happened?"

"Yeah. We went to the camp first, then heard the sound of a jeep in a fucking hurry and followed."

Please. Please. "Dad. Did you see him?"

Alex drew in a sharp breath.

I braced myself.

"He didn't make it."

There was nothing left to say.

***

The jeep rolled to a stop out the front of my mother's house. I sat slumped in the back seat, my body throbbing with pain from the tumble off the bike and everything else that had happened. But I sucked it deep inside.

I deserved it.

I deserved to feel every ache, every twinge, every slice of hurt.

I deserved every shitty thing life threw at me.

The porch screen door slammed wide and my mum appeared.

Oh God, I didn't know what to say, how to tell her.

Mum raced down the steps and across the grass.

Stricken I could do nothing but stare into her white face, hating the grief I read clearly etched into the new lines like trenches around her eyes and mouth.

I had done this to her.

"Tara. Thank heavens, you're alright." Mum reached the jeep. She held out her arms.

No recrimination in her eyes, nothing but sadness and love, fear and relief.

Choking down a sob, I stumbled from the jeep. My eyes squeezed shut when Mum enfolded me in a tight embrace. I sucked in the familiar floral scent of the shampoo Mum always used. I longed for a return to my childhood where responsibility was someone else's problem.

My mother soothed my hair while I clung to her and the long minutes ticked slowly by.

Gently, I disentangled myself from her arms. Mouth trembling, I looked at her. I had to say it.

"I'm okay, Mum. Do you know...," I hesitated, searching for the words, the right way to tell her I'd killed my father.

"Yes, honey, Alex phoned me."

I gulped. "It was my fault. I'm the one responsible for Dad..." I couldn't go on, couldn't say that dreadful word.

Through the tears dribbling down her cheeks, my mother smiled her familiar sweet smile, the same one that had encouraged me, comforted me and had made everything right in my little world.

My heart cracked open again.

She chided me gently, "Rubbish, Tara. Your father and I both knew the risks. We made our decision long ago. Nothing ever really mattered except keeping you and Dan safe. You didn't place a gun in those men's hands. You didn't incite them to murder. Don't forget this started a long time ago and by people who want nothing but power."

Nowhere in the universe were there parents as wonderful as mine.

If only I'd realized this sooner.

"We can't leave him there," I mumbled, heedless of the tears flowing down my face. I sniveled.

"I know." Mum passed me a fresh handkerchief and I blew my nose.

"I'm sorry, but the Mundos Novus will be here at any moment. They know where you live. We don't have any time to lose. We've got to move fast," inserted Alex. He stood soldier straight watching us, one hand resting on the butt of the pistol in the holster on his hip, the keys to the jeep dangling from his other.

His eyes were shadowed, his jaw tense.

Shay drove up in Alex's car and parked behind the jeep. He got out and strode over to the passenger side where he opened the door for Em who hurried to my side.

Talking as she walked. "What's going on? I wish someone would explain. Who were those people? Who are you really? Where did you get those outfits?" She cut her eyes from me to Alex and back again.

"Later, Emma. I've packed a few suitcases." Mum

indicated the house behind her.

Alex nodded. "I'll get them." He and Shay strode over to the pile of bags and began to load the cars.

"Where's Dan?" I asked Mum quietly.

"He's in his room."

"Wait..." began Em.

"Sorry, Em. I need to talk to him. By the way, there's something I haven't told you. It's about Marnie. Her father has escaped from jail and she's camping out in the bush with him." I decided not to mention Marnie's little girl until I'd had a chance to speak with her. It was possible I'd read that last message wrong.

Em clapped her hands over her mouth, her eyes wide with shock. Blinking, she squeaked, "That's awful. Is she okay?"

"I hope so. I'll talk to you later." Shaking my head, I ignored her restraining hand and raced into the house.

I found my brother huddled on his bed. "Dan."

He looked up and at the sight of his blotchy red face and swollen eyes, guilt and grief clutched me with vice like fingers. "Dan, I'm sorry."

He scrubbed at his face with the back of his hands and sat up, nodding.

"We have to leave straight away," I said. What I really wanted to say, roared inside my mind. My stupidity had cost us our father's life. I'd left him to die alone like an animal. Making a tremendous effort, I held it together. The clock was ticking. "Get your gear together."

"Already done." Dan wriggled off the bed and shoved his laptop into a leather satchel. Zipping the case shut, he pushed the straps over his shoulder. "Where are we going?"

"No idea but I'm sure Alex has it all organized."

A high-pitched alarm splintered the quiet of the street. I jumped. At the same moment both our mobile phones buzzed.

"Shit." I pressed a hand to my racing heart and reefed

out my mobile to stare at the screen. I flicked it around and showed Dan.

"It's an emergency broadcast. It says...*impact event imminent. Five minutes. Stay inside or shelter in school and community halls.* Holy fuck. It's really happening."

"Hurry." I picked up a bulging gym bag. "Is this everything?"

"Just my backpack and laptop." Dan scooped up his gear.

"Time to go, little bro." I hustled him out the door. Snatching one minute to myself, I raced into my bedroom, changed into jeans, fresh tee-shirt and socks and pulled on my volleys. My precious boots lay discarded on the floor. I had no idea where I was heading, but I did know wherever it was, I wouldn't need my boots.

Joining the others outside the house, I searched the sky. "OMG! Look!"

Overhead, burning balls of fire and rock hurtled toward the Earth, growing larger by the second.

"Move. Get into the jeep," shouted Alex, coming up and pushing us on our backs much in the manner of a dog rounding up sheep.

Mum and Em were already seated inside Alex's car with Shay stashing the last suitcase in the boot. He took Dan's gym bag off me and stuffed it inside. Slamming the boot shut, he raced to the driver's side.

After exchanging a glance with Alex across the hood, he jerked open the car door.

I took a couple of steps towards the car only to be halted by Alex who pointed to the jeep. "You stay with me. Dan, you're with me too. Get in the back seat."

Alex swung behind the wheel of the jeep while I scrambled in beside him, asking, "Where are we going?"

Alex yelled, "The only place where we'll be safe from impact. The garage. It's got a strong roof with steel beams. We can shelter in the concrete pit of the workshop."

"Do your belt up." I turned around to ensure my

brother was safely in the seat.

He did the thumbs up gesture.

The jeep shot down the road.

"Impact in twenty seconds to the west of town," yelled Dan.

I slewed around to find Dan had his laptop open and was typing on the keyboard.

"I'm on a weather station site," he said.

Feeling as if I was trapped in a never-ending nightmare, I stared at my panic stricken neighbors running about the streets with suitcases and cardboard boxes as our small world was torn apart. The alarm continued to blare its message. I knew once it stopped...well, that was obvious.

Rubble from the recent super storm still lined the streets. Frantic families piled belongings into cars; crying, shouting, stuffing kids and pets inside and slamming doors, obviously heading for the halls. Those choosing to stay in their homes raced round boarding shutters over windows or rounding up their family and pets inside. Some people pushing laden supermarket trolleys ran along the footpaths crying or in a daze casting terrified glances up at the sky.

So this was what the end of the world looked like.

Alex yelled information into some type of communication device inserted in his collar. Words like state of emergency, the Mundos Novus force, fall-out from the strikes and the jeep's precise whereabouts reverberated inside my head like out of control ping pong balls.

I clung to the side door as Alex took the next corner like a racing pro. The jeep hurtled down the main street, sweeping round the slower vehicles. Alex applied the brakes and worked down the gears then turned into the workshop yard to come to a jolting halt.

"That's it," shrilled Dan, slamming his laptop shut as he struggled with his seat belt.

I reached over and unclipped him before attend to my

own but Alex was already at my side, yanking open the door, wrestling with my belt.

"Inside," he roared at Dan who took off like a racehorse. "Quick." Alex pulled me out of the car.

Boom!

His gaze whipped to the horizon. "We won't make it."

Huh?

Instead of racing to the workshop where Dan was being grabbed by Shay and hustled inside, Alex pushed me to the ground, wrapped his arms around my chest, protecting me with his body.

Through the concrete beneath my palms, the ground shuddered and rippled.

A mighty energy force punched into us, scraping us across the yard where we slammed into the railings of the perimeter fence. The scream of the wind generated by the impact deafened me. It sounded like a freight train about to crush us to the tracks.

We lay there huddled together until the pressure eased.

Alex rolled off me, heaving me to my feet where I swayed while the world around me swam in crazy dips. Not giving me any time to orientate myself, he pulled me toward the workshop.

Breath wheezing as I gulped in large lungfuls of air, I stumbled after him too battered to do anything other than obey.

Alex hammered on the closed door with his fist.

The steel door slid open and Shay dragged us inside.

I took one last look around.

To the west, a massive plume of smoke and dust interwoven with flames of fire billowed into the air. A group of screaming people hobbled down the middle of the road, caked in red dust, their arms full of possessions, blood and smoke staining their clothes. Even as I watched I heard it first; a roar like a dragon, a whizzing sound then saw the dazzling glitter of light as a small meteorite flashed over the roof to explode in the building across the street.

The door slammed shut blocking my view.

With Alex gripping my arm like he'd never let go, I raced to the pit where eager hands helped me down. Alex jumped down. Together with Shay, he pulled a steel lid on rollers across the top of the pit effectively sealing us inside.

The shock wave hit the workshop.

The iron roof rattled, the thick concrete walls creaked and groaned.

Shaking, I clamped my hands over my ears and squatted, my back against the wall. A kerosene lantern glowed in the corner giving a feeble light to see by. Mum smiled at me from where she cradled a terrified Em wrapped in a blanket. Bob Garroway sat quietly amidst six ten-liter containers of water and a pile of boxes which I suspected contained ammunition. Shay sat on his butt looking into middle space, his rifle resting like a baby in his arms.

Beside me, Alex stared at the floor, a deep frown on his face. And my brother... As our eyes met, Dan scrambled over and pressed against me shivering violently. I hugged him close.

"It's okay, little bro." My reassurance sounded hollow but I had to say something.

Outside, chaos erupted.

Noise louder than anything I'd ever heard assaulted my eardrums. Explosions like cannons, the screaming of ripping metal, the clangs and thuds as objects hurtled against the walls, the constant barrage of whistling as the meteorites rocketed from the sky, crackling sounds like gunshots, thunderclaps and the hissing sound of escaping steam...it was madness.

It sounded like the end of the world.

At least my family was safe for the moment. But what about everyone else?

What about Marnie, somewhere out there in the bush?

Squeezing my eyes shut, I thought about the message I'd read in my brother's drawings.

Where were those fucking aliens when you needed them?

CHAPTER 14: SEEDERS

The impact strikes lasted for a little over two hours but it could have been as long as a hundred years so slowly did the time pass.

Outside I knew night was falling. Shadows were thick and dark where we waited. We'd been lucky to escape a direct hit to the building. The steel roof of the pit might be strong but I was glad we hadn't cause to test its might against a meteorite impact. I knew nothing about engineering but I doubted we would have escaped alive. But our chances were better here than being inside a house.

"Do you think it's over?" I asked through a throat as dry as sand paper.

Bob Garroway tossed me a six hundred milliliter water bottle, saying, "Make it last."

What a charmer. I unscrewed the top and with my hand shaking like I was a ninety-year-old woman, chugged down four, blessedly cool, mountain stream smooth, mouthfuls. When I finished I offered it to my brother who took it with a mumbled, 'Thanks'.

"Alex, check it out," ordered Garroway.

Warder or not, the guy was an arsehole.

Shay and Alex rolled back the pit lid before Alex crossed to my side to retrieve his rifle.

I laid a hand on his arm. "Be careful."

The startled surprise on his face both delighted and troubled me. *Had no one voiced any concern for his safety before?* His cheeks reddened. His gaze flittered from mine as he picked up his rifle. Frowning, I watched him climb the rungs to the top of the pit then disappear from view.

The heat of the day had ebbed but now the air was acrid with the stench of smoke and fire. It made my lungs hurt with each breath I took.

With my ears still buzzing from the noise I blew my nose on a scrap of tissue I found in my pocket, not at all surprised when it came away spotted with blood.

Every part of me either throbbed or burned. My shin pulsed with a heavy dull pain that felt bone deep and I wiggled my toes inside my boots experimentally. Not too bad. Bearable.

Which hopefully meant I could still run.

It was nothing compared with the pain of my broken heart.

Dan wriggled out from under my arm. Did he blame me? Could he ever forgive me? I wouldn't blame him if he did. I could barely manage to think Dad's name. It was like I was all raw inside.

He said quietly, "You didn't kill him, Sis."

My eyes stung. He was so much like Dad, it broke my heart. "Thanks. That means a lot to me Dan," I finally managed.

I knew it would be a long time if ever, before I forgave myself. One thing I did know was if I ever got the chance I'd make those bastards pay.

Anger stirred deep in the pit of my belly as I stared into my brother's face taking in the haunted expression in his brown eyes. Dan was growing up fast.

The hard way.

"We didn't ask to be hunted." I folded my arms over

my chest.

"What are we going to do now?"

"We're going to do what we were born to do. Or, at least, I am."

"Talk to some aliens?" His sad expression lightened a little.

I smiled at the sparkle reappearing in his eyes. "Yeah, little bro. I am going to talk those suckers out of the sky."

Somewhere over the course of the day, I'd made a decision.

If this was my fate, my responsibility, then I was damn well going to get the job done. All I needed was some direction and a lot more information.

I rotated my shoulders, working out the kinks. Fatigue sank heavily into my bones. *Crap, I'm tired.*

"Tara." But Mum's admonition lacked bite. She looked as worn out as I felt so I mumbled an apology. Mum rewarded me with a smile and a little bit of my grief eased.

Em had pulled the blanket up over her head as if hiding from the world. Shay was studiously examining his rifle and Bob Garroway stared at me.

I raised my eyebrows and looked back. *Yeah, check me out arsehole.* I could see I wasn't a person to him. I was a tool, to be used and discarded once I'd passed my use-by date. The knowledge ate into my soul.

Did Alex see me the same way?

It shouldn't hurt so much but it did.

Placing my hand against the concrete wall to steady myself and stood testing my weight on my aching leg. Backwards and forwards, I walked, gritting my teeth, working out the stiffness in my muscles, feeling them strengthen as I continued to pace. My pulse steadied while I thought.

Would Alex stand up for me when I was thrown to the wolves? Did he care for me? Even a little?

'You can do this, kiddo.' As if I could hear him standing right beside me, Dad's voice echoed inside my mind.

Squaring my shoulders, I stopped in front of my brother. "Dan, check if there's any local news on your computer." I pulled out my mobile.

"Turn that thing off," snapped Bob Garroway, springing to his feet. "That's how they've been tracking you."

"I don't see how, this isn't a smart phone."

"Nevertheless, you will obey orders. They knew your father was going to the camp. They knew you would follow."

Yeah, I'd already worked that one out for myself.

"Tara, turn it off, please," interrupted Mum. I heard the warning note in her voice.

"Okay, Mum." That sick feeling was lodged in my gut again.

It wasn't my phone that had been tracked. Dad had encrypted all our mobiles and computers so nothing could be hacked. At the time, he'd given the excuse of on-line predators. Now, I realized he'd been covering our tracks even back then.

The only way those murdering bastards could have known about what we were doing had to be from something else. Or more to the point someone else.

But who? Who was working with them?

One of my family?

A friend?

A Warder?

On the pretence of turning my mobile off, I took a split second to scan the last message, recognizing the avatar that popped up beside the text. *Marnie*. I noted the time; sent ten minutes ago which meant my friend was, so far, alive. No time to decipher the message with Garroway's beady eyes boring into my back. After pocketing my mobile, I resumed my pacing.

The sound of the workshop door sliding open made me flinch. A few seconds later, Alex leaned over the side of the pit. His gaze swept around until he located me.

Despite my reservations about his intentions, my heart pitter-pattered as I was held immobile by his clear eyes.

He'd looked for me first.

I smiled, feeling giddy, enjoying the warmth heating my cold body as the seconds passed and our connection remained unbroken.

"Well," demanded his father.

Poof! His dad sure had his timing down pat.

Alex looked over at his father. "It's not good out there, Sir. A fair bit of panic. Water and power are down. There are a lot of houses destroyed and several fires burning out of control. I thought we should lend a hand."

"Out of the question. You and Shay secure this building. None must be allowed to enter." Bob pushed his sleeve up and checked his watch. "We stay here for the next twenty four hours."

"Hold on a minute. People out there need our help." I planted my hands on my hips.

"Everyone stays here and by everyone, I particularly mean you." Garroway pointed at me. "The Mundos Novus have immunity and the moment these strikes are over, they'll tear this town apart searching for you. The chaos and panic will work to our advantage. We sit and wait."

"Wait for what?" asked my mother.

"Immunity? From what?" I asked in unison with Mum.

"There's no time for chit-chat." Lips thin, Garroway rose to his feet. "Alex, you've been given your orders. Get rid of that jeep while you're at it. Take it to the other side of town as soon as this building has been secured."

"But that's dangerous. Those soldiers might spot him," I cried.

"It's his job."

Alex straightened. "Sir. Shay."

Nodding, Shay slung his rifle over his shoulder and climbed the rungs of the pit.

In the sudden quiet that settled inside the shadowy pit, I felt it; the prickling spider sense of danger that told me more positively than words, someone here was my enemy.

But who?

***

Alex

I snatched a few moments to have a brief confab with Shay as soon as we'd put sufficient distance between us and the workshop. And my father. This past day, I'd sensed his telepathic ability strengthening. How soon would it be before I'd no longer be able to block him from my thoughts?

"How did we miss spotting that force? They must be, what? A thousand strong?" I asked but I was really questioning myself and my failure. We'd only just arrived at the camp in time. Mere seconds later and I would have had to bury my mark.

My mark.

Tara.

She was more than my mark and it was about time I accepted that fact.

Bile rose, scorching my throat. I swallowed the sourness down, wondering how the mission had become so complicated.

Shay said, "This unit must have a good leader. From what I've seen so far, they appear to be well-trained and motivated. Devoted to their cause."

"Is it really Andrews, Shay? If that's the case, I can't believe we've been so blind." I could have punched my fist into the dashboard, so frustrated did I feel. Instead, I pressed my foot heavy on the metal and the jeep responded with a surge of power, hurtling down the road. "Look at this mess. Look at what our so-called friends are doing to us." I flung a hand out to encompass the horror that surrounded us.

Rifle cradled in his arms but ready and aimed, with the muzzle resting on the door, Shay continued to scan for any sign of the Mundos Novus force. But they must have gone to ground until the all-clear sounded. Or they could be busy elsewhere. It made my gut clench wondering what havoc they'd inflict on the town in their search for Tara and her family. Above our heads, a few stray meteorites plunged like the murderous fire-balls they were towards Earth's surface.

"I don't see that we have any choice but to continue with our mission plan," said Shay flatly.

"Yeah, me neither. They've got us over a barrel. I bet they're up there right now," I jerked my chin skyward. "Up there and enjoying the sight of us dying like flies in a firestorm."

"I wish I knew whether it was our lot or the other alien race responsible for the strikes. This comes off as being way over the top. If we're all dead, what the heck do they hope to achieve?"

"No idea. My father believes they have some weird alliance going on even though they're enemies. So, the strikes could be coming from both of them."

"The Colonel could be wrong. This could be some type of war-game with Earth as the prize."

Trust Shay to voice the thoughts swirling about my mind. I turned off the road and the jeep bumped over the rough ground until we reached an old, abandoned produce store. I drove through the rotting timber doors inside. Switching off the engine, I opened the door and jumped out. "Let's get moving. I don't want to leave Tara alone for too long."

"The Colonel's there."

I didn't answer, instead I broke into a jog and headed back to the workshop.

Shay ran up beside me. "I found evidence of corruption on Chambers. And he's got this huge cattle property about forty kilometers west of here."

"The Mayor?"

Shay nodded.

"I guess that would make him an easy target to persuade to work with the MN forces. They could have been hiding on his property for weeks. Still, Andrews doesn't strike me as a man of vision, capable of inspiring or leading that many soldiers. What about a woman?"

The same thought must have struck us at the same time.

Our startled gazes met.

I damn well nearly fell over the charred and still smoking body of some poor soul before catching my balance.

My eyebrows feeling as if they'd reached my hairline, I exclaimed, "The missing Mrs Andrews!"

***

Tara

I woke a little after dawn from a sleep where my mind continually repeated my actions at the camp. If I'd acted differently, done something... The hollow feeling inside my chest reminded me of what I'd lost and would never find again. If I'd had more time...what I wouldn't give to tell Dad everything I'd never bothered to say before...now, it was too late.

I had my chance and I blew it.

I rolled over and shifted into a sitting position, my body stiff but one good thing, at least the pain from my various injuries had dulled to a mild ache. The smoke had cleared from inside the workshop and breathing was no longer an effort.

Pushing my fringe from my eyes, I locked away my tormenting memories. My stomach rumbled. I'd eaten little food the previous night. Garroway had doled out one military protein bar to each person and one bottle of water.

I wondered how long we could survive on such piddly rations.

If the entire country had suffered devastation from the strikes, food and clean water would soon become the new gold; rare and valuable enough to fight to the death. The thought made me shudder as nightmarish images of the days to come flashed through my mind.

"How are you feeling, honey?"

I looked up to find Mum bending over me, her face lined with concern and fear.

Fear for me, for my safety.

I'd lost Dad, I couldn't lose anyone else.

Emotions choked and burned inside but I managed to respond, "I'm good. Don't worry about me. You need to start thinking of yourself."

I hesitated, wondering whether it would do any good to voice my suspicions about the Warders.

But before I could decide, my mother said, "Oh, sweetheart, I'm so proud of you. Your father and I raised a strong, young woman."

"Mum, about Dad..."

Her gaze slid from mine and she stared into the distance. "I keep expecting to hear his voice or feel his touch," she murmured almost absently. "I don't think it's sunk in, that he's gone. Even after the divorce, it didn't feel like he'd left me."

"I wish..."

"I know, sweetheart." Turning back to me, she touched my cheek. "I know when all this is over, I'll remember. And I'll grieve. But not now."

I gently enfolded Mum's hand in both of mine. "I'll do whatever it takes, Mum, to keep you, Dan and everyone I possibly can, safe."

I snuck a look at the other members of our group. The Warders were sleeping or at least, gave that impression. Em and Dan were curled up on the hard floor and covered in blankets. I lowered my voice. "But I don't know how to do it, Mum. How do I make contact with the aliens?"

My mother shook her head. "I'm not sure. Perhaps if we can get to a military installation, we could use satellite communications."

"We don't even know where they are or if they're within contact distance." Frowning, I muttered,

"Somehow I don't think using our technology is the answer. I'm certain that we're missing something important here and it's to do with me. Are there others out there like Dan and me?"

"Probably." Mum smoothed strands of my fringe from my eyes. "I should imagine they'll be under the control of the Mundos Novus Force by now, perhaps imprisoned. Or dead unless they've changed their agenda. When we left the facility in Germany, all we knew about this force was that they wanted Earth to fall and that they'd do everything possible to make it happen."

"Do you think anyone else may have escaped? They could be here, like us, lying low."

"What are you talking about, Tara?" Mum frowned.

I admitted, "I saw a message for a GM Batch #9, telling him or her or whatever to prepare."

Mum wrung her hands together. "Oh dear, if that's the case, it could be anyone. And we have no way of knowing whether they can be trusted." Mum's eyes met mine.

"What about the Warders, Mum? Are there other Warders running about?"

"Yes. Your father and I understood they've also been charged with protecting all GMU's."

"So some did escape?" I pressed.

Mum nodded. "A few. I don't know how many or who they are or where they could be. Your father and I always assumed the research at the facility continued after we ran. If that's the case, those born afterwards could well have amazing abilities."

"Number nine could be on our side."

"True, but we have no way of knowing for certain. I believe we should remain on our guard."

I had to ask. I had to. The question was eating me alive. "Am I a clone? Is that what I am?"

"No, not a clone." Mum bit her lip and hesitated before saying, "You and your brother are more like test tube babies. You were taken from batch number three and your brother from batch number five."

"Wonderful," I said drily. "So my real parents could be anybody. A serial killer, an axe murderer, a monkey, maybe even some kind of rodent."

"Nonsense, Tara. The researchers chose only the best DNA and manipulated it. And remember, your father and I were part of that team."

"Then there's bits of you and Dad inside me?"

"Yes."

Well, that was something. I hugged that comforting thought close. "Number nine would be someone a lot younger than me."

"Not necessarily." Mum hesitated before adding, "Before we left, we worked on accelerated growth DNA cells."

Whoever number nine was, could be anywhere between ten years old and fifty! Or even more. No, that wouldn't work, what would the aliens want with a geriatric?

I chewed my lip for a second. "What's this immunity business Garroway mentioned last night?"

"I wish I knew. We've had no contact with anyone from our previous lives for such a long time. So much could have happened since we left. There's a lot we don't know." I could hear the stress in her high-pitched voice. Normally, Mum had the kind of voice that soothed even when she was cross.

Inside my pocket, my mobile vibrated. Before I could check it out, a pair of boots appeared in my vision. Glancing up I clashed with Bob Garroway impassive stare.

"Good morning." I smiled, hoping my suspicions about this guy weren't written all over my face. I'd never been a good liar.

Garroway placed a hand on my mother's shoulder. "Marion, here have something to eat." He handed over more protein bars.

Mum smiled outwardly as friendly as ever but I noticed

a certain reserve in her expression. That plus the way she instantly stood, effectively dislodging Garroway's hand and walked over to check on Dan.

"What were you discussing?" His gimlet eyes bored into me.

"What do you think? You need to be more open about what's going on. For instance explain what you meant about immunity."

"Very well." Garroway placed his hands behind his back, his stance all military officer.

Here it comes. I scrambled to my feet aware the others were staring and listening.

"Strictly speaking the meteorites are seeders."

I opened my mouth to speak.

"Don't interrupt when I'm speaking." He held up at hand and I snapped my mouth shut. "Made of part rock, part metal and the remainder an alien compound of which we have little knowledge. What we do know, is each meteorite jettisons microscopic debris the moment it hits our atmosphere and begins to break apart. Within each minuscule fragment are seeders for an air-borne virus manufactured to affect both humans and animals."

The day just gets better and better. I folded my arms and slumped against the wall. Em gave a frightened squeal and picking up her blanket scurried over to Alex where she hunkered down beside him.

Since it didn't look as if Garroway intended to continue, I asked, my voice hoarse from my mounting tension, "And?"

"The virus affects different people in different ways. We understand it's primarily to ensure compliance with the new world order but those who are genetically inclined to rebel or unable to be controlled will eventually die. It's highly contagious."

"It sounds terrible. Will everyone catch it?" I prodded when he fell silent. "What are the symptoms?"

He frowned, suddenly looking a little paler. "I've been

led to believe it's highly contagious and there is an incubation period of twelve to eighteen hours. That's the sum total of my knowledge."

Or was it more along the need to know basis?

"Let me get this straight," I said, battling the panic screaming like a banshee inside my head and attempting to focus on his words. What I really wanted to do was run, run and find a bunker and hide. "What you're telling us is the majority of the world's population is going to die. And you really don't know how and what we can do to stop it."

My fingernails stabbed into my palms as I waited for his response.

Boots crunched over the scattering of pebbles on the floor and Alex stood beside me. I spared him a quick glance, also taking in the dagger look Em directed at his back. She rubbed a hand over her face. A twinge of sympathy plucked at my heart at my friend's drooping mouth and sad eyes.

Em turned her back.

I'm sorry, Em, I'm sorry.

"Yes. That's about the sum of it," said Garroway, matter-of-factly.

"This doesn't bother you?" Maybe this guy was an alien. Emotion certainly wasn't his strong suit.

His grey eyes drilled into me. "Our planet has a history of survival of the strongest."

Fuck! The end of the world. No. I don't believe it. It can't end this way. "But this is not through a natural event, this is through someone or something's deliberate actions. Someone orchestrated this strike."

"You're clever, but not clever enough."

That sounded ominous. What was this guy up to? "Who has immunity? You, the Warders? The Mundos Novus Forces? Us?"

"All genetically modified units will be safe. That is, those like yourself and your brother."

Horror hit me, as the implication of his words

registered. "What about Mum? My friends? Is there some kind of vaccine?"

"The probability is high the Mundos Novus Forces will have access to a vaccine. Only time will tell who will fall and who will rise."

"How do we know you're telling the truth?"

"As the leader of the Warders of Earth, I'm privy to certain information."

"Someone could be feeding you a pack of lies," I pointed out. "Or you could be lying."

"If that's the case, none of us will survive. Logic dictates this to be otherwise." Garroway angled his body away from me. Apparently, debriefing session was over. "Alex and Shay. I need an update on the situation outside. Rendezvous back here in three hours." He produced a map from his pants pocket and after unfolding it, jabbed at particular landmarks.

Head reeling, I stared at his stiff back. These aliens sure meant business. A hostile takeover of our planet so they could claim our resources for themselves. At least, that's what I assumed they were after. But I still didn't understand; where did the initial alien technology to manipulate human DNA come from? Could it have come from the aliens themselves? But why give us the knowledge to breed people to communicate with them if they intended to either kill or subjugate us?

What was I missing?

And where did the Warders come into it? Who did they work for? Our governments, the aliens, or someone else?

I rubbed my aching forehead before shoving my hands in my pockets.

Garroway appeared occupied with issuing orders. From the tense set of his jaw, I suspected he had no intention of answering any more questions, so I walked over to where my brother was huddled under his blanket. I crouched down beside him.

"Dan," I murmured softly. "Have you got your

computer on?"

"Sure thing, Sis."

I smirked. *That's my bro.* As soon as Garroway had started talking about the composition of the meteorites which weren't really meteorites, I'd notice Dan had pulled the blanket back over his head. A second later I'd seen a faint tell-tale blue glow under the cover. "Is he telling the truth?"

"I think so. The government has changed their tune and the latest press release advises Earth is under attack. They're saying this was only the first strike and that military installations and service suppliers like power stations were targeted. I guess with the Air Force not far from us, that's why we were hit too."

"Makes sense." I rubbed my gritty eyes, tired to the bone. "Anything else?"

Dan popped out from under the blanket, tousled haired and with white-rimmed frightened eyes. I wanted to pull him into my arms and tell him everything was going to be okay. Somehow I knew he wouldn't believe me.

Dan said, "They're telling everyone to stay inside their houses and lock their doors or remain in the public shelters until the all-clear is given. They're saying another strike is anticipated within forty eight to seventy two hours."

"He's telling the truth. Or most of the truth. If there are aliens out there, Dan, we need to make contact before the next round of those pseudo meteors. We need to find out their agenda. It also sounds to me like an invasion could be imminent. Any ideas?"

My brother shook his head.

"I can't think of anything either." I sighed. "Better turn your computer off and save your battery life. Let's keep this news to ourselves for a bit, huh?"

"Sure, Sis."

"I need you to stay here and look after Mum." Giving his shoulder a quick squeeze, I straightened and headed for the rungs. Alex was hauling himself over the top of the pit when I reached the side wall.

"Where do you think you're going?" barked Garroway.

"I need to pee. Or are you going to suggest I use a bucket?" I asked sweetly.

"I'll come with you," Em said quickly, flinging off her blanket.

"I want some time alone." What I really wanted was some privacy to check my messages. Taking no notice of Garroway's muttered growl and Em's sagging mouth, I climbed the ladder.

Once on top of the workshop floor, I scanned the area. Shay and Alex were about to open the front door. Maybe Alex heard me, I don't know but he spun around and swept his narrow-eyed gaze over me. I gave an airy wave of my hand and headed for the restroom located at the far end of the workshop.

I used the facilities then washed my face, grimacing at my reflected image in the mirror. I didn't think anything would ever be able to save my lank-looking hair and the shadows beneath my eyes made me look totally gothic.

After a peak under the stalls to make certain I was alone, I dug out my mobile. My head throbbed as I concentrated on the words until they made sense.

My hands shook. My phone clattered to the floor.

I scooped it up and re-read the text.

Urgent. Need your help. At Nonnas.

I pocketed my mobile and paced the small room. The last time I'd gone against everyone's wishes my father had died. If I ducked out now…

Jeeze.

I tugged at my hair.

Air-borne virus

Highly contagious.

What to do.

'Need your help.'

Garroway had seemed pretty damn positive I'd be

immune. It made sense in a far-reaching kind of way. The research lab could have had access to a shitload of alien technology, not just genetics. And they would have wanted to give us every chance possible of staying alive.

Still, it was a huge risk. I could be clutching at straws.

But if I was quick, Alex, Mum, Garroway…they'd barely realize I was gone before I was back again.

I couldn't see how what I intended to do would hurt anyone. No one would be with me. My family were safe in the workshop for the moment. All I had to do was get over to the other side of town and bring Marnie and her family back here before the next strike.

Before they caught the disease.

I'd leave them quarantined inside this workshop while I headed off to do whatever my thing was with those aliens. I'd bargain to keep my family and friends safe. Hell, I'd bargain with the devil if it would keep *everyone* safe.

On the one quick trip to the bathroom Garroway had allowed everyone last night, I'd noticed the manhole above the toilet cubicle. This was the only way out of the workshop if you discounted the front door and sure as eggs were eggs, Alex would wait outside for at least ten minutes to check I hadn't followed him.

The manhole was my only option.

I knew this idea wouldn't go down well, especially after what happened the last time I charged off on my own agenda. But I couldn't abandon my friend.

Closing the toilet seat, I stepped onto it and stood on tip-toe. My palms pressed against the gyprock and shoved. It lifted. Carefully and as quietly as possible, I slid the square panel over to the side revealing the darkness of the roof cavity highlighted by the sunlight slicing through the cracks in the tiles. This part of the building which housed the office, workers' small lunchroom and the restrooms was part of the original service station that used to stand on this site. That meant, this section of the roof was covered in old tiles unlike the new workshop which had solid colorbond sheeting.

A perfect escape route.

My fingers closed over the edge of the hole. I paused and willed the sickness churning in my belly to abate. By placing my right foot onto the cistern, I used it to lever myself through the gap and up into the roof.

A quick glance showed the rafters and I took care to balance my weight on the closest one so I wouldn't fall through the ceiling. The roof sloped in a steep angle to meet the outside wall.

It was hot inside the roof cavity, the air thick with dust that tickled my nose. With every breath I inhaled the distinctive musty stench of mice droppings. Scared I'd sneeze and alert Garroway, I breathed through my mouth while I pulled aside a sufficient number of old tiles to make a wide enough space for me to crawl through. Three of my fingertips were bleeding by the time I finished. *How long have I been here?* My imagination took flight, thinking any moment Garroway would storm inside and haul me back to the pit.

Teeth clenched, I wriggled through the space I'd created and landed on my belly on the tiles. My weight and gravity took control.

I slid.

Scrabbling with my fingers I desperately sought a finger hold.

My legs slipped over the edge of the roof, my body followed. About to do a nose dive to the ground I found the gutter and grabbed.

That was close.

Heart pumping, my momentum stopped, I peered at what lay underneath me.

Dirt.

Roughly a six to eight foot drop.

I can do this.

Holding my breath, I let go and fell.

Legs bent at the knees I landed on my feet and

stumbled forward a few paces until I regained my balance. I let out a noisy gust of air and bounded forward, racing round the side of the building to stop near the front and check the street for any sign of danger.

All clear.

No shouting or yelling. Now to make good my escape.

I broke into a ground-eating jog, pacing my breathing, mentally thanking Mum for all those countless hours of training. As I ran, I took in the destruction wrought by the meteorite strikes. The industrial buildings on both sides of the street were mounds of rubble, a few were burning, spewing black smoke into the sky. Some had disappeared entirely leaving nothing behind but craters in the earth. Broken bricks, sheets of iron, split timber, paper and rubbish formed a blanket over the tarmac. Melted and mangled metal had re-formed into un-recognizable shapes. An iron pylon stood on its end, embedded in the cabin of a bull-dozer. *Jeeze I hope there hadn't been anyone inside.* At the next intersection I took the road to the left past residential homes or what remained of them.

Everywhere I looked, it was if I'd been transplanted into an apocalypse movie.

As soon as I thought I'd put enough distance between me, the workshop and Alex should he decide to scout around for me, I stopped and examined the houses surrounding me. I realized I was in the street where Em lived. The pavements were empty of people apart from one cat that sat in the middle of the road about three hundred meters ahead. As far as I could tell, the townsfolk had obeyed the government's instructions and had locked themselves inside their homes.

Wise move.

Curtains twitched and faces appeared in windows checking out what I was up to. Many windows had pieces of wide timber planks hammered across them. A few houses wore blue tarps like lop-sided hats over the holes in their roofs yet to be fixed. Upended garden furniture was strewn in broken pieces here and there in front yards. The twisted remains of a kid's trampoline were jammed up beside the side of another house.

Fallen trees and branches and other debris had been piled in mounds on the footpath, ready to be cleared away by the Council trucks I now knew would never arrive.

No sound of modern technology.

No televisions, no music blared, no car horns or engines.

No galahs or cockatoos screeched from the almost leafless gum trees.

No dogs barked.

It was downright creepy.

A door to the house opposite from where I stood opened and a man appeared, a shotgun in his hands.

"Move along," he bellowed. "We've got nothing for ya." From behind him came the sound of a crying baby.

I lifted my hand in acknowledgement and walked quickly down the road. Over to the east the sun had risen well above the horizon and shone down through the thin layer of grey haze blanketing that part of the sky.

Over to the west of town, smoke lay low and black indicating buildings still burned.

And the west of town was where Marnie's grandmother lived.

CHAPTER 15: AFTERMATH

As I neared the tabby and white cat, it meowed. Startled I veered onto the road and stopped in front of it.

"Bartholomew, is that you?" I tried to pick it up but the terrified cat took off and disappeared into a nearby garden.

Thinking that Em would be happy to be reunited with her mother's pet, I raced after it. I crouched down and pushed aside a crimson fuchsia bush and spotted the animal scrunched against the paling fence.

"Oh, please, please. Help me, please."

The quavery voice coming out of nowhere made me jump. The cat hissed and fled. I pushed branches aside and stood up. Mrs Wilson, who'd lived in this town since she was born eighty years ago, stood clad in her rose patterned nightie within the confines of her walker. She held her hands out in a beseeching manner. Blood oozed brightly from a deep gash on her left cheek and there were raw scratches along her arms.

"Mrs Wilson?"

Tears tracked down her wrinkled, bloodied face.

"Oh, it's you Tara dear." A sob and a hiccup escaped. With swimming rheumy faded eyes, the old lady gazed at me and said, "It's Henry. He's trapped. I can't get him out. I couldn't bear it, if he left me alone."

My phone vibrated; reminding me that time was slipping past.

I looked toward the west and the smoke. Then back at the old woman who was nearing her century. Time was not on my side but I couldn't leave her. I had to help.

"Come on, I'll see what I can do and then I'll clean up your injuries."

Taking hold of one side of the walker, I helped her turn around and walk haltingly up the garden path and down the side of the house into the back yard.

"He's under that tin and heap of branches." The old lady pointed. Sure enough, after she spoke we both heard a rustling movement.

"You wait here, Mrs Wilson." Leaving the old woman on the path, I crossed the yard and squatted down near a large pile of debris. I heaved aside the uppermost fig tree branch, which felt like it weighed a ton. Lifting the sheet of iron beneath, I dragged it off then stared in dismay at the large stone birdbath that had been blown over and lay on top of another pile of branches. This could take me all day.

"Need some help?" piped, of all people, Crystal.

I couldn't help but gape at her while I wiped sweat from my upper lip with my forefinger. "What are you doing here?"

"Friendly as always, I see, Tara." Crystal sighed loudly and walked over in her five-inch, scarlet-red stilettos. Immaculately dressed as if about to address a board meeting or attend a public meeting, in her navy-blue sleeveless linen dress, she raised her perfectly plucked eyebrows. "What I always do, looking out for the people of my town."

"Your father's town, you mean."

Crystal waved aside the correction. "What's the problem?"

"Henry's trapped." We both knew who Henry was and

how much he meant to Mrs Wilson, so I didn't need to explain anything more.

"I see." Crystal gazed down at the mound. "We better hurry. Henry's almost as old as Mrs Wilson." She gave a strained smile. Amazing. Bending down, she slipped off her shoes and handed them to the old lady.

I wondered whether Crystal had been substituted for a different person sometime during the night. I was thinking along the lines of that old move *'The Body Snatches'*. Still staring at her with ripe suspicion, I muttered, "If you take this end and I grab the other, between the two of us, I'm certain we can lift this thing."

Without responding, Crystal followed my instructions.

"Ready?"

Crystal nodded.

"On three. One, two, three." Knees bent, back straight, I pulled. Arms straining, together we crab-walked the birdbath out of the way.

"Wow, that was heavy."

"You're telling me." Crystal rubbed her arms.

We quickly grabbed the remaining branches and tossed them aside to finally reveal a quivering, brown mass of dog curled up in a ball under a make-shift cave of broken bricks and tin. Two, terrified brown eyes peered up at us through a tangle of hair. Henry lifted his head and whimpered.

"Careful."

"What do you think I'm doing?" protested Crystal as she felt his limbs, spine and around his head. "I can't see any blood and he's not flinching when I touch him." She looked at me and nodded. "I think he's okay." She scooped her hands under his belly and gently lifted him to his feet.

I grinned, feeling a bit choked at this piece of good news. "You seem to know what you're doing," I offered by way of an olive branch.

"I run a rescue centre for animals out on the family

farm."

"Seriously?" *Yeah, she definitely must have had some kind of personality implant.*

"Surprised, huh? I keep it quiet. I don't want to taint my image."

I snorted. "What? The image of a stuck-up snob?"

"Exactly." Crystal stood up, a panting, happy dog in her arms.

"Oh, Henry, Henry," cried Mrs Wilson. "Is my boy all right?"

"I think so, Mrs Wilson." Crystal crossed over to the old lady who passed trembling hands over the dog's head. Henry, licking madly, wagged his tail.

Hands in pocket, I followed, still bemused by this new side of Crystal. Who knew that she was a decent sort under all that bitchiness? "Let's get you inside, Mrs Wilson and we'll clean you up."

"No, she can't stay here alone, Tara. I'll take her and Henry back to my place." Leaning close, Crystal whispered, "We have a fully provisioned bomb shelter underground. They'll be safe enough there."

"Seriously?" My mouth dropped open.

"Catching flies?" she drawled before rolling her eyes. "Yes and if you mention it to anyone, like those bastard soldiers, I'll make you wish you'd never been born. Come on, help me get these two into my car then you'd better be on your way."

"Crystal." I hesitated while I searched her face. "What do you know?"

"Not a great deal." Crystal's thin face tightened. "My parents are neck deep in gambling debts. They turned a blind eye and even assisted members of some terrorist group to infiltrate the town one by one over the past few years. That's why Dad had the shelter built. We've known something bad was coming but didn't know that it would take this form." She gazed up at the sky for a moment. Her mouth twisted bitterly. "I don't know what or who you are, but I do know they're searching for people like you. You know, ones with mysterious pasts and who don't quite fit in. Soldiers are patrolling the streets using loudspeakers to urge anyone with knowledge of anyone acting suspiciously to come forward. They said some rubbish about being spared if we ratted."

I nodded slowly. "Thanks for the tip. I'll run inside and pack a few things for Mrs Wilson."

"Good idea. I'll meet you at my car."

Five minutes later, I was buckling a grateful Mrs Wilson into the passenger seat of Crystal's hot-pink coupe and settling Henry on her lap.

"Tara. I know you're in the centre of this shit." Leaning across the old lady, Crystal stared through the open window. "This is why I've never liked you. I was afraid of the trouble you'd bring this town."

"How…?"

Crystal interjected swiftly, "No time to explain. It looks like we could be facing the end of the world. But these people are my people. There's been Chambers here since the soil was first turned and I intend to keep it that way. And you…if you are one of those mutants the soldiers are looking for, you do whatever you can to fix this mess."

"I intend to."

A faint smile lightened Crystal's drawn features. "Good luck. I have a feeling you're going to need it. Oh, and give Alex a French kiss for me."

As if that would ever happen! When I kissed him, it would be for me. One last wave of bright emerald-green nails and Crystal drove off.

It wasn't until her car turned the corner and disappeared from view, that I shook myself out of my dazed funk.

You think you know someone, then wham! They turn inside out. I smiled, feeling lighter, at the knowledge that in the coming days the people of Wallaby Creek wouldn't be alone.

My gaze fixed toward the west, I ran.

***

The muscles in my thighs and calves were burning by the time I jogged down the street where Marnie's grandmother lived. My eyes stung and watered from the low hanging smoke. Ash and embers covered the ground reinforcing the aura of a post-apocalyptic setting.

This was where the yobos, considered to be the dregs of our town, lived, evident by the number of cars in various stages of repair or in the act of being dismantled in front yards. Also by the fibro cladding and rusting tin roofs of the much smaller sized homes. Like the street where I lived, the house blocks were big and the roadway wide with no concrete curbs or guttering to deal with run-off water. The fencing was composed of barbed wire running between waist-high, metal star posts. A small group of stringy-looking sheep with muddy wool huddled together, their heads drooping toward the ground as if worn out by fear.

Poor things. A vision of a land where nothing walked, crawled or flew rose in my mind. And where overhead a metallic, strange-shaped spacecraft hovered.

It made my skin crawl.

Not if I could help it.

I slowed down and approached the front of the house with caution. Breathing deeply, I sucked in smoke filled air, wincing as my lungs struggled to find the oxygen in the filth I'd inhaled. I broke into a fit of coughing and wheezing.

The smoke came from a furniture warehouse set toward the back of the wide block to my right, where flames ate away at what was left of the two storey building. A discarded fire hose lay on the cement like a long, winding snakeskin. There were no signs of any emergency vehicles.

Or anyone else for that matter.

A low rumble of an engine in the distance broke the

216

tense silence. By the sound of it, a truck, possibly two.

The Mundos Novus Force?

A car roared round the corner.

Still hacking up my lungs, I raced towards the house.

I fled down the path to pound on the front door. Behind me, the car braked with a hail of pebbles and dirt.

I pounded again.

Car doors slammed.

Booted footsteps smacked against cement.

I spun round and raised my chin as Alex stopped about six centimeters from my nose.

"What do you think you're doing?" he snarled through clenched teeth.

"Helping my friends."

His hand closed around my upper arm and he jerked me forward until I was mashed up right and close against the long, toned hardness of his body. Instantly, my tummy muscles dissolved and my blood thrummed slow and sweet through my veins. Looking up into his furious face, I moistened my lips. Given the situation we were in, what I was thinking about was pretty crazy. What would he do if I kissed him?

As if he'd read my thoughts, heat blazed in his eyes turning the cold fog into hot steam.

The door behind me jerked open smacking me in the back.

"Tara!"

Uncertain whether I was disappointed or relieved the moment had been interrupted, I pulled out of Alex's grasp and turned to Marnie. I practically fell into her arms. "Marnie. Thank heavens you're okay. I've been so worried."

We hugged.

When Marnie stepped back to allow us entrance into the house, I looked her over carefully. No signs of obvious trauma, no injuries and although her jeans and white tee-shirt were wrinkled they looked clean. Marnie's burnt honey-blonde hair was pulled back into a ponytail, the expression in her eyes serious as she looked past Tara at Alex and beyond to Shay leaning against the car.

"Thank you so much for coming here. But why did you bring these guys? Do you have any idea what's going on? We saw soldiers on our way into town."

I shooed her inside. "I'll bring you up to speed but first, I'd kill for some water."

"Sure. Come into the kitchen. Everyone's there anyway." Marnie led the way down the narrow, threadbare carpeted hall and into the shabby but spotlessly clean room at the end. Grabbing a bottle of water off the counter she handed it to me. "You know my father, Nic, and Nonna. Luis here, is Nic's mate. This is Tara and Alex."

I nodded in general and unscrewed the cap. "Hi, Nic. Hi, Mrs Tolini. Luis." Tipping the bottle up, I drank.

"Ma'am." Alex gave a tight-lipped smile to the older woman with Marnie's strong features then held out his hand and shook with both men who'd risen to their feet at their entrance into the kitchen.

Nic sat down in a sprawling posture and tipped his chair back on its legs only to have his mother slap his shoulders with a tee-towel.

"Be respectful," she snapped.

"Yes, Mamma." Grinning, Nic obediently settled his chair on its four legs.

"Tara?" Marnie crossed the room to stand behind her father.

I wiped my mouth with the back of my hand. I gave a quick summary of everything that had happened the last few days and the brief amount of information Bob Garroway had advised. My voice faltered when I spoke of that terrible day at the camp but Alex squeezed my hand and somehow I stumbled on.

Marnie gasped and pressed her hands over her mouth. "Oh, Tara, this is terrible. I'm so sorry."

Of course, I didn't tell them everything.

I still wasn't certain who I could trust.

No one spoke.

Luis, who'd been eyeing me off like I was made out of gold bullion, drawled, "Ain't this something, Nic. This here is one of them mutants. I've heard there's a hefty reward for bringing one of these things in." He waggled his mobile in the air.

Alex slapped his hand onto the butt of his revolver in his holster, the movement loud enough to garner everyone's attention.

"Put that away, *giovane*," said Nic. "Luis's got a foolish mouth on him an' I have no intention of harming yer *tesoro*."

Heat scalded my face.

Marnie wriggled her eyebrows in a suggestive manner as she looked from me to Alex then back again. I ignored the questions in her eyes. This wasn't the time for heart-to-hearts.

Mrs Tolini uttered a long sigh. "*Che palle!* To think I have lived to see such things." She sighed again and shook her head. "Well, speak, Marlina, tell them your need."

"Nic and Luis have busted out of prison because they'd heard whispers on the inside about what was up. I know, the connections some of them have is unbelievable. Nic wanted to be with me when...," Marnie waved her thin hands expressively, "...when the world ends. And I, Tara, I need to see my little girl. I must know she's okay, if she needs me. So I thought of your brother and how good he is with computers. I thought he'd be able to find where she's living."

"He's a pretty good hacker, I don't see how it'll be a problem for him," I said instantly. "There's the issue of this virus, too." I snuck a side-long glance at Alex, dragged in a deep breath and blurted, "We have a place you may be safe for a while. Come back with us."

"Tara!"

"Sorry, Alex, but I've got to do what I think is right."

"Yeah, I get that." Alex gave a short laugh. "Dad's not going to be happy but, sure, why not? There's safety in numbers and we could do with a few more guns." He jerked his chin at the three rifles lying on the kitchen counter.

"We'll take you up on your offer." Nic rose to his feet and hooked his thumbs into the loops on his jeans. "Soldiers have cordoned off the town at the city limits. Probably this military force you were talking about. We were lucky to slip by them as they were first setting up. Otherwise, I'm not certain we would have gotten through. We've got weapons but nothing like the fire power these guys are packing."

Alex said, "He's right. They're searching houses, hauling people out onto the streets and interrogating them. It wasn't a pretty sight. Shay and I spotted a group doing this a few blocks away."

I had a feeling I knew what, *or who,* they were looking for.

"We want to locate my *piccolina di papà's bambina* and get the *cazzo* out of this town."

"I think you're making the right decision. But it's not going to be easy." Alex's gaze cut to the other escaped prisoner.

"*Merda!* Nothing worthwhile is ever easy." Snapping his fingers, Nic gave a crooked smile. "I figure we band together and make tracks fast."

"Yes, especially as you're both wanted fugitives," said Marnie wryly. But she patted her father's arm gently. "Sorry about the Italian everyone. Nic loves nothing more than hamming up his heritage."

The smile they shared sent shafts of bittersweet longing through me. Dad used to smile at me in much the same way.

Blindly I turned to the door, saying gruffly over my shoulder, "Are you ready to leave?"

"Been ready and waiting for your arrival for quite a bit

now, girlie," said that creepy guy, Luis.

"Grab your gear and follow my car," said Alex, placing his hand on my lower back and giving me a gentle push.

Nic responded, "Let's go."

I made a beeline for the front door.

Behind me, Shay muttered, "The General isn't going to like more people on his watch."

"I know. Let me worry about him. I'm not leaving you behind," Alex growled.

"You picked up on that?"

Alex snorted. "Of course I did. And if she's your new mark, you must fulfil your purpose."

"What are you two talking about?" I yanked open the front door only to have it taken out of my hands.

Alex poked his head out a fraction, scanned the streets before stepping onto the porch. "It's possible Marnie is under Shay's protection."

I goggled. "Then she's...?"

"I have no idea." He shrugged. "He's just got a sense of something connecting them, that's all. Hurry up and get in the car, Tara."

"So, he won't leave her and Marnie won't leave her family. And you won't leave Shay," I said slowly. "This is why you're not ranting and raving at me, isn't it?"

"You should have talked to me. I would have brought you here."

"Would you?"

I turned around and searched his face. His eyes shone with sincerity. But could I believe it? I said, "We need to source more food and water supplies, now there's more of us. Especially if we're going to escape from the town."

"I hope you're not thinking of going with your friend. You have a role to play, Tara. One that I believe you're not too keen on."

I whirled around and poked Alex in the chest. "Of course I'm not bloody keen. Who would be? I've got no idea how to do what, apparently..." I made finger exclamation marks in the air. "Apparently, what I've been bred to do."

I hiccupped. "Oh, and what exactly do I say if I somehow manage to confront these jerkoffs? Huh? Like, oh hi there Mister Alien, please don't kill us."

"Shit." Alex gripped my waist and pushed me against the fence, leaning in and trapping me with his rock-hard body. "Get a grip, Tara. This is bigger than you or me. You need to focus."

"Don't tell me how important this shit is, because I already know it. First hand. Don't ever tell me I don't know."

His touch gentled, his thumbs moving in a caressing motion over my waist as he rested his forehead on mine. "I'm sorry, I'm sorry," he whispered. "I know you're hurting but so are others."

The regret in his voice rang true and my anger deflated as if shot by an arrow leaving nothing but hollow fatigue that weighed down my soul.

"I know. I know it's down to me. But, Alex, I don't know what I'm supposed to do. How do we know it will even work?" I closed my eyes, sinking into the heat and strength of him. I drank in this one moment.

"None of us know but we have to try. I can't imagine how hard this must be for you. Remember, Tara, I will always stand by your side." Alex pressed a kiss as soft as a butterfly's wings to my brow.

What if my side isn't the same as yours? I recalled every word he'd spoken and despaired if I'd ever know what the truth was.

"Alex!" called Shay. "We need to move. They're coming."

***

Alex

I stopped the car at the next intersection, checking in both directions for any sign of the Mundos Novus force.

Clear, no sign of those nut jobs. I turned left and drove

along the road. I speared a quick look at Tara sitting quietly in the passenger seat and wondered what she was thinking. She'd done her share of *'wailing, why me?'* these past few days but I couldn't blame her. It wasn't every day a girl learns she was made from alien technology.

What really pissed me off, was her lack of trust. I'd hoped we'd moved forward sufficiently for her to confide in me. My father wasn't going to be happy about this latest escapade.

I changed down a gear for the corner coming up.

The problem was, she had my full empathy.

She'd lost her dad in pretty tough circumstances. It was enough to make any soldier lose his shit let alone a girl barely out of high school. But no, not this chickee babe, she kept on. You had to respect a chick who could handle a ton of crap without turning on the water works and wearing a man down with weeping and wailing.

It made me proud I'd been chosen to be her Warder.

It made me wish for a far different future than the one knocking on Earth's door.

"Any sign of those military guys?" Luis' swarmy voice made my shoulders twitch.

Something about this guy didn't ring true. If only I could put my finger on it. Maybe it had more to do with my gut; thinking he had a big part still to be played. One that could prove a major headache for me.

It'd made sense to split up which was why I'd ended up with this guy in my car. Marnie and her grandma remained with Nic and the dog in the ute. Their gear had been stashed in the back tray concealed by a leather tarp. I suspected from the shapes and weight of at least two of those bags they'd put in there, Nic travelled with a shit-load of weapons. Considering the circumstances, the older bloke's decision was probably a savvy one. Although how he'd managed to secure so much weaponry at such short notice was a mystery. I could only assume Nic had more than one mate on the shady side of the law.

"Nothing so far," I finally responded. My eyes met those of Shay in the rear-vision mirror and although I'd been cautioned against using my telepathic ability so close to my mark, I flashed a message. Short and sweet. *Watch him.*

Yeah, he presses my buttons too, Shay flashed back.

Glad I wasn't the only one suspicious of the escaped prisoner, I increased speed. I knew Shay had my back. He always did.

"Wait! Stop!" cried Tara suddenly.

Instantly, I applied the clutch and brakes, shifting the gears into neutral and the car jerked to a halt. While Nic's ute pulled up behind us, motor running, my gaze hunted both sides of the quiet street.

Looking for danger.

Looking for what had caused her to yell out like that.

Nothing. That is, if you didn't count a cat sitting on the footpath staring at the car with unblinking eerie green eyes.

Tara scrabbled out, leaving her door open.

"What the...? Tara get back in here," I yelled out my window.

"The cat. I'm not leaving him."

The cat?

Shay laughed.

Momentarily struck dumb, I watched her walk up to the cat and scoop the fur ball into her arms. She hurried back, a broad grin lighting up her face. The impact was like a sucker punch. All air left my lungs and something shifted inside me.

I would give anything to save her from her future.

The car door shut as she slid back inside, the cat clutched under one arm. Smiling, she clipped on her seat belt.

I swallowed, did a shit pile of throat clearing and still my voice came out hoarse as sandpaper.

"Dad's going to be pissed off a cat's joining our merry band, especially since Marnie is bringing along her father's dog." I tapped a beat on the steering wheel, conjuring up the scene that would surely greet us when we got back to the workshop. I sent the car in motion, checking the ute followed.

"He'll have to suck it up. This is Mrs Andrews' cat. I'm not leaving it here to fend for itself."

One glance at the stubborn tilt of her chin and I caved. I knew how to pick my battles and this wasn't one of them. Besides, I'd spent quite a few sleepless hours myself thinking about this same crappy deal. People weren't the only ones with their lives on the line. *If only I knew more about what's about to happen.*

The fur ball settled down on Tara's lap and purred under her petting hand.

I'd be bloody purring too, if she stroked me like that. I shifted on the seat, my body tightening with a hungry need.

From the back seat, Shay snuffled a snort.

Aw crap, I'd forgotten to sever our connection. I rolled my eyes knowing my mate would give me curry later.

"Why does Marnie call her father by his first name?" asked Shay.

"He says it makes him feel too old." Tara turned around and grinned at my mate. "I got the impression he wasn't there that much when she was growing up."

Shay grunted and returned to scanning for danger.

"What do you know about these so-called aliens? Do you know what they want with us?" Tara looked at me.

Those gorgeous soft-brown eyes of hers, made me want to move mountains. "I'm not certain, Tara." I shrugged and changed into third gear, sending the car roaring down the street.

"I only know what I've been told." *Do I tell her I suspect something quite different?*

"That's not much help," she muttered.

In my peripherals, I saw her hand tremble. What could it hurt to spill what I did know?

"There's two different races and once, a long time ago,

they were deadly enemies."

Tara smiled and placed her hand on my thigh.

I immediately covered it with mine. "They were both powerful and battled for centuries for supremacy in their galaxy. Neither won. But they brought their people to the brink of extinction. So they devised a different type of war; one which wouldn't see any harm coming to either race."

"They could have called a truce," Tara said drily.

"Yeah, there is that." I did an eye roll in her direction. "Whatever their reasons, they remained enemies and sent out exploratory spaceships, in packs of two, into the universe. One ship for each race. They would suss out solar systems with life forms and send out small, forward-scout shuttles to prepare for their arrival."

"And that's how we got the alien technology!" Tara exclaimed. "The scout ships."

"Got it in one."

"But what are they after? Our resources? Our land so they can live here?"

"I'm not sure. One race I believe has more peaceful intentions whilst the other is more aggressive. The Mundos Novus force supposedly answers to the latter. I can't help but wonder whether they're going off on their own agenda these days."

"Do you mean the Warders are with the more peaceful race?"

"Yes." I felt rather than saw her gaze switch to the passing scenery. About to mention my doubts, I paused.

A red light blinked on the dashboard.

The same instant my mind sensed danger.

I checked the mirrors.

From a yard further down the road, a Wrangler jeep tore out of a drive way, crashing through the timber gate and swinging out onto the road. Five soldiers were crammed inside, the one sitting in the rear was perched behind a PKM general-purpose machine gun mounted in the back.

"It's them!" shouted Tara, swiveling around and staring at the rapidly approaching vehicle.

I floored it. "Turn round and keep that seat belt on."

She turned around and pointed. "Take a left here."

I swung the wheel. The car swept wide, its tires gripping the rough surface and spraying dust and dirt into the air obscuring my vision for a few seconds.

"Good. Nic's turned to the right. Let's see who these guys follow." Another residential street but this one with a group of people standing about on someone's front lawn. Looters by the amount of household gear they held. One even had a shopping trolley piled high with pilfered goods. They turned and stared as our car shot toward them.

"They're behind us," said Shay.

I glanced in the mirror. My mate had palmed his 9mm Glock and wound down his window.

A burst of automatic gunfire drummed into the rear of the car. The group of people on the lawn screamed and scattered in all directions.

The cat hissed then let out a hideous yowl as its hairs stood on end.

Tara gasped, her eyes were big with fear as she spun around to stare at me, one hand clutching her throat.

"Stay down." I yanked her lower with my left hand. "Don't worry. The car is armored plated and has bullet proof glass."

"Awesome," she whispered. "Good kitty," she crooned to the terrified animal. Tara had doubled over so far, her nose was all but buried in the cat's fur. All color had leeched from her face but she didn't cry, didn't scream, didn't blister my ears with inane blabbering.

A girl in a million.

Clenching my jaw, I focused on the job; keeping her and us alive.

Shay let loose with an answering volley of shots that boomed deafeningly loud in the close confines of the car.

The jeep veered to the right then the left but in a burst

of speed came up faster. *Shit.* "We have to lose these guys."

"One's on the radio. We're going to have more company very soon." Shay leaned out the window and hit their pursuers with another round of bullets.

"Wonderful," I said, spinning the wheel and sending the car careening into another street.

"One down," Shay added coolly. "Stay nice and steady, Alex, so I can get a clear shot at that dickhead manning the machine gun."

"I'm trying but this road is a shocker. Too many ruts. Tara, unclip that rifle will you and hand it over to Shay."

Bullets punched into the car and instinctively we all ducked.

"No, I'll do it." Tara released her seat belt, placed the cat on the floor where it did its best to hide under the seat. Leaning forward, she unclipped the rifle bracketed under the dash. "Shay can distract them while I'm readying for the shot."

"Fucking hell! This isn't a game."

"I know! It makes sense for more of us to return fire. Dad made me practice on rabbits. I hated every moment of it but he said I needed to learn. Now I know why."

She was right. We needed more guns.

"Expose as little of your body as possible," I said, feeling cold to my marrow.

"I will." She pressed the button and the window slid down.

I rattled off instructions. "Right. Take a good look at her. She's a prototype with guided firearm technology, tracking ability and digital zoom plus locking-on-target ability. Basically, slick off the safety switch, turn it on, point it and pull the damn trigger."

Tara wriggled about until she crouched on her feet on the seat. Angling her body to the rear she raised the rifle and leaned her upper torso out the window.

The car hit a deep rut with a loud bang.

Shuddered.

Spun sideways.

Fuck!

Tara squealed. I saw her body jolt, begin to slide forward out the window.

Hanging on to the steering wheel with one hand, I grabbed a fistful of Tara's jeans with the other to keep her from falling onto the road.

True soldier that she was, she kept hold of the gun.

"Jeeze, Alex," muttered Shay. "Nearly broke my arm."

"Sorry." I straightened the car, glanced in the rear-vision mirror. The following jeep hit the same ditch, bouncing the soldiers high in the seats and jerking the machine gun butt skyward.

Shay let fly with another volley of shots.

"Now, Tara!"

Three sharp blasts exploded from her rifle.

Shay whistled. "He's down. I got another one." He snapped in a fresh clip then fired off yet another round with his Glock. "They're braking away. Slowing down."

Tara flopped back onto the seat, the rifle cradled in her arms. I met her sherry-brown eyes, dismayed at the sheen of tears glistening there and felt like a total douse bag for putting her in this situation. That damn cat lashed out from under the seat and took a swipe at her ankles. Tara barely flinched. She sat there, staring out the window and I knew whatever she saw, was not the view.

"We'll lose them, throw them off our trail by heading to the opposite side of town before making our way back to the workshop," I said.

Tara nodded.

I muttered, "You did the right thing. They would have killed all of us."

"I know." Her lips twisted. "Doesn't really help though."

"I'm sorry, babe."

"Not your fault."

Wasn't it? I should have been more diligent. I should have done a snatch and grab when I first saw her instead of following her to her friend's house.

She'd already be safe at the workshop.

And she'd never have had to pull that bloody trigger.

CHAPTER 16: THE VIRUS

Tara

The silence inside the car was deafening. The air stank with that horrible stench of cordite that burned at the back of my throat. I wanted to spew my guts up but I breathed through my teeth fighting for control. After slipping the safety back on, I'd replaced the rifle then huddled in my seat, my eyes squeezed shut. Horror cringed deep in my belly. Everything inside me shook and I didn't know how to stop it.

I'd killed a man.

Granted, he'd been doing his damn best to kill us but still... The image of blood exploding over his uniformed chest formed behind my eyelids. He'd flopped backwards like a puppet with no strings.

Another shitty memory that would haunt me for a long time. They sure were mounting up. Exhausted, I opened my eyes and looked at Alex, sitting all stern and calm in the driver's seat as he took us on a round-about tour of the town. I knew he was ensuring we weren't being followed.

He'd been concerned for me; I'd read it clearly in his crystal eyes, the tight lines that had pinched his mouth deleting their normal curves and the tense set of his body.

The knowledge glowed inside my heart like a welcoming fire on a frosty winter night. It flared out, warming the cold hollows my father's death had created.

My conscience twinged when I remembered Em and how much she liked this guy. Too hard to think about now.

Opening my eyes, I dug out a handkerchief and blew my nose.

"They wanted to kill us," I said thickly.

Alex flicked me a glance. "Yes."

"You said you'd seen the soldiers rounding people up and questioning them. Do you think..." I swallowed. "Do you think they'll hurt anyone?"

"Fanaticism is a strong motivator."

I frowned. "Like a religion?"

"Kinda. They believe in their cause."

"Which is...? Come on, Alex, you can do it." I managed a weak grin and was rewarded by his flashing smile.

"Sorry, habit. Okay, what I believe is the leaders or instigators of the Mundos Novus force see this *'happening'* as an opportunity to grab power for themselves. So they're doing a juggling act. I think they're pretending to align with the Skeetishas, the more aggressive of the alien races heading our way and are doing some of their bidding. But on the other hand, I think they're setting themselves up for a total takeover once the aliens leave our solar system."

"*What?* The aliens aren't staying?"

Alex heaved a sigh. "I really don't know for certain. I'm hoping they'll end up leaving us alone."

"If they do, it sounds like we may end up having to fight the Mundos Novus force. Won't our armies deal with them?"

"Not if they've been taken out by the meteorite strikes or the virus."

"Jeeze." I stared blankly out the window, my head whirling.

Shay added, "I've heard a lot of Mundos Novus foot

soldiers think they're wiping out corruption and will be building a better world."

"Amen to that," said Luis.

I spun around to glare at him. The creep scrambled up off the floor where he'd flattened himself during the shooting. "You sound like you're on their side."

"I'm on the side that means I live." Luis folded his hands over his paunchy stomach and gave a crocodile smile.

Deciding the ex-con wasn't worth the time of day, I went to pick up the trembling cat. Bartholomew spat and slashed at me.

"Ouch." I rubbed the scratch mark on the back of my hand.

"Use this." Shay shoved a thin towel over the seat. Murmuring soothing noises, I managed to wrap the towel around the cat and secured him in my arms. A glance out the window, had me expelling a relieved whoosh of air. "We're back, thank God."

The car slowed and turned into the carpark to stop, engine running, in front of the workshop bay doors.

Shay leapt out and raced over to pound on the door. As soon as the door was heaved open, Alex reversed inside ensuring the car faced outwards.

Still holding the cat covered in the towel, I climbed out of the car and walked toward the pit where Garroway stood waiting, hands clenched at his sides. As I approached him, Nic's ute drove inside.

The scowl on Garroway' face was positively ferocious as he took in the number of people now milling about inside the workshop.

"This isn't a refugee camp. You could have compromised our position," he bit out.

"They're friends and needed help," Alex said. "They won't be here for long."

Garroway's eyes fell on the cat and his face reddened. For a moment I thought steam would hiss from his ears.

"I would have thought you'd have learned your lesson from the last time you ran off by yourself."

I clamped my mouth shut, unwilling to try and justify my actions to him. The entrance door slammed shut, the heavy bolt clicked into place and shadows painted Garroway's face in a grotesque mask.

I took a step back so I was out of his reach.

Just in case.

"Do not leave the workshop again."

"Or what? The way I see it, is you need me," I pointed out.

"Don't push your luck. Everyone is expendable," Garroway said coldly. "You will be responsible for cleaning up the animal crap." He jabbed his finger in Alex's direction. "Alex. I want a full report. You had no business bringing these people back here."

"Sir. I had my reasons which I will explain in private." Alex strode over and rubbed the curve of my back in soothing circles. "The force has dug in and surrounded the town. It's going to be difficult to slip through when it's time to leave."

"Where are we going?" I looked into Alex's face.

He lowered his voice, "A rendezvous with our 'friends.'"

I swallowed.

"Is there a problem? Perhaps we shouldn't have come here," Marnie said, interrupting us.

I glanced at Marnie who until now had held back from approaching where we stood talking. Nic was by her side, a rifle slung over his shoulder by its strap and a hefty hold all in his left hand. A pale-faced Mrs Tolini tossed something from a hip flask down her throat. I suspected it wasn't spring water.

I said, "All good. Come on, Mum, Dan and Em are here, too."

A relieved smile spread over Marnie's strained face. Clicking her fingers to the dog who was growling, his eyes fixed on the cat in my arms, she hastened back to the ute saying over her shoulder, "We've brought food."

The dog trotted at her heels.

"Great. I'm starving," Alex said easily.

And just like that, the tension dissipated.

Mum called me over and I ran, anxious to be close to her. She fussed over the cat until it settled sufficiently to be placed on the ground. Bartholomew immediately wound his body around my legs and Mum said how I'd made a new friend.

With Marnie and her grandmother handing out plastic containers of food, which when opened filled the air with the rich aroma of Italian pasta, Bolognese and lasagna, the atmosphere quickly became more settled.

Thank God, those awful ration bars weren't on the menu today.

Chairs were unfolded and closed eskies were used as extra seats as everyone sat around eating and talking quietly. Even Bob Garroway appeared to have shed his *'I'm the man in charge'* persona and tucked into the pasta Mrs Tolini handed him with the air of a man on a serious mission. The knowledge we had the stout walls of the workshop surrounding us, I think gave us a sense of protection.

For the moment.

As the hours passed, I learned how Marnie had received a message from her father on the day of the super-storm and immediately left to find him. A burst tyre had delayed their return. I suspected though Nic had wanted to wait until the search for him and his jail mate had moved further afield.

We chatted.

We even laughed.

What was strange was how Em treated Alex as soon as we'd arrived back with Marnie and her family. It was if he no longer existed for her. Instead, she had inserted herself in between Marnie and my mother and begun her usual rapid-fire sixty questions.

Had she given up on him? Had she sensed his focus was me?

And if that was the case, had she decided to give me an open field?

I had to talk to her. The last thing I ever wanted to do, was hurt my friend.

Under Em's determined interrogation, Mum gave a carefully edited outline of our short history. When she admitted that both Dan and I were the results of a particular research, Em appeared to lose the power of speech. She stared at me as if I'd grown horns on the top of my head.

Or sprouted tentacles.

It was downright uncomfortable.

I felt a shift in the air, a coldness as my friends and Marnie's family continued to eye me off.

This was what I'd dreaded ever since Mum had confirmed my deepest fear that I was *'different'*. Mum always said *'special'* but I knew otherwise. Being *'different'* had made for a difficult childhood.

Now it looked as if it was directing my future too.

I counted down the seconds while no one spoke. The Warders kept their attention on their food. Generous, strong Marnie was the first to act. She jumped down from where she'd been sitting on the ute's tailgate and raced across to pull me into a big hug.

"You're still the best friend I've ever had," she said. "It's not like I've got the perfect past."

I had to work hard to keep from blubbering like a baby.

Em piped up, "Hey what about me?" She rushed over and gave me a quick hug and a radiant smile as if she'd won the Lotto. She whispered in my ear, "He's all yours. Go for it."

There was nothing like true friendship.

The day drifted into late afternoon and it gradually

became darker inside the workshop. I guessed we were waiting for the dead of night or even early morning before we made our move.

And so the day wore on.

Mrs Tolini and Mum passed out more food. For a while everyone talked and conjectured and wondered while we ate.

Picking over my cold lasagna with a fork, I gazed at my friends and family. Their familiar faces settled me on some profound level. Marnie, her sleeping bag wrapped about her shoulders, had curled up in the corner furthermost from anyone. Bluey, her father's dog lay by her feet. Her energy had flagged during the afternoon, not surprising after that scary car chase.

Em was leaning back in a fold-up camping chair, eyes closed, buds in her ears as she listened to her iPod. A tiny smile played about her lips.

My mother and Mrs Tolini busied themselves counting and re-counting our food supplies and discussed in low voices how best to ration what we had over the coming days.

Lying near my feet, Bartholomew swatted playfully at my shoelace.

Em had smiled when I presented the cat to her but refrained from taking him, saying that he really was her mother's pet not hers. It sure looked like he'd chosen me as his new owner.

I didn't mind. With a childhood spent always on the move, my parents had vetoed the idea of pets. Reaching down I scratched Bartholomew behind his ear, grinning at his purrs.

Soft footsteps heralded Alex's approach.

Our gazes snagged and my heart skipped a beat at the heat in his eyes.

Smiling, I placed my plate on the ground and stood up. Bartholomew pounced on the leftovers and began to scoff it down.

Alex took my hand and I linked my fingers through his, enjoying the tingle and warmth racing through my veins. If there was one thing I'd learned these past few days, it was make the most of every second. I intended to do just that; and hopefully he'd come to the same decision.

Besides I needed to talk to him.

"Going to check the doors are all locked?" Sexual tension shimmered in the air between us and I held my breath, waiting for his reply.

"Yeah. Want to come with me?"

"Yes." One word, so simple and yet it resonated with hope, dreams, a need for love, for reassurance that life would go on.

His hand tightened over mine and I knew we were on the same page. He tugged me closer, fitting me snugly into his side as we strolled off, our bodies brushing against each other with every step.

As soon as we were out of earshot, I asked the question that had been burning inside my brain for a while now, "All that stuff you told me about your life before you came here was bullshit wasn't it?"

"Yeah. I'm sorry. I had to keep to my cover story."

"What about your Mum?"

He sucked in a harsh breath. "I never knew her. I don't even remember her, the perfume she used, the touch of her hand. It's possible she never existed."

"That's so sad." I didn't blame him for dishing me a pile of crap. I understood he needed to maintain his secret but it must have been hard; all those years never being about to relax and be yourself.

I mulled over his words. "What do you mean by never existed?"

Alex stopped. We were on the other side of the workshop and standing in front of two doors. One said 'Office' and the other 'Storeroom'.

"Let's try the storeroom." He turned the handle and we stepped inside. The room was pitch black. Closing the door behind us, Alex switched on a mini torch and swept it around revealing lines of shelves nailed to the three walls, one boarded up window and nothing on the lino covered ground.

"It's not the Ritz."

I laughed. "Definitely. But who cares?"

The torch clattered to the ground and turned off. The light flickered then died. It was dark in here with only a faint light trickling through the boards over the window. Alex took hold of both my hands. I gripped tight, enjoying the tingle and warmth racing through my veins.

"Keep talking."

"You know what I mean."

"You're like me and Dan. Made for a purpose."

"In a way. I'm a Warder, part human..." He hesitated. "Part alien. We have one objective; to protect and serve our marks."

I gasped, my heart skipping a beat. Wow. That I'd never expected. "Seriously? Alien? How is that possible?"

"When one of the scout ships arrived here about twenty six years ago, they studied our way of life and made contact with those they considered to be most useful. This is when the research laboratories were built and using their technology we were created. The scientists began on GMB's, genetically modified batches of humans."

"So that's me and Dan and probably a lot of others like us." Tugging my hands free, I splayed my palms on his chest. "Maybe I'm part alien, too."

"You could be."

I recalled what Alex had said earlier about there being scout ships from both races. "When did the other scout ship arrive?"

"Not long after the first one. Apparently, they made contact with people who held positions of power in our governments. They infiltrated defense forces, corporations, research facilities."

My breath caught. "Where Mum and Dad worked."

"Yeah. The Warders were initially meant to be watchers only but our education became more intense, more focused on military training. Our mission was re-defined. We became protectors instead. And when the Mundos Novus force grew in strength and numbers, the Warders were forced to work undercover. Mostly alone."

"My hero." I grinned. "Exactly how alien are you?"

"I'm not certain but one thing I do know, here and now I'm definitely human."

Heat warmed my cool flesh. The contact sizzled like a river of fire through my thrumming blood, right through my body to centre in the very heart of my core.

I wanted him.

I wanted to sink into him and block out the world.

If only for a few brief hours.

I whispered, "I know what I was made for, but what about you?"

"A Warder protects his mark. At your birth, you were assigned to me. Your brother to my father. When your parents disappeared with both of you, we spent years searching the globe for your whereabouts."

"Now you've found me. What exactly do you intend to do with me?" I slid my arms up around his neck and threading one hand through his hair pulled his head downwards.

His warm breath feathered over my face.

His lips were so close.

So close.

Voice rough, he said, "Protect you. Stand beside you. Do everything possible to assist you achieve your destiny."

"Is that all? What are you doing after lunch?"

He dragged his lips down the side of my face, spiking my pulse rate and heating my hormones to fusion point. "*That* is a Warder's role. But the man in me intends to love you until his very last breath."

Our lips met, fused together, as he pulled me hard up against his body and locked me in his embrace. His mouth, hot, moist, devoured me in a demanding kiss I meet with equal hunger.

Through my thin tee-shirt, I felt every muscle, every ridge but it wasn't enough. I wanted skin against skin, wanted to glide my hands over every part of him, feel the silky power of his sex throb under my fingers and, oh heaven, I wanted more.

Heart pounding, my head full of the roaring of my blood, I pressed closer. His cock was rigid against my belly when I rubbed against him.

Gasping for air I pulled away and tried to discern his expression but it was too dark.

His fingers dug into my waist belying his words as he said hoarsely, "It's fine if you've changed your mind."

"I haven't, I want you."

He moved his hands to cup my face. His thumbs gently stroked the corners of my mouth, so tenderly I wanted to cry. "I want you too."

"Is this allowed...you know...um...a relationship between a Warder and what did you call me? Your mark?"

"I am supposed to use whatever means necessary to achieve my mission. To gain your trust," he admitted slowly.

"You shit!" I yanked at his hands, hurt and disappointment souring the moment.

"Listen, please, Tara. I don't work that way. I don't and won't use people no matter the cause." His voice rang with sincerity. His knuckles brushed my cheek. "I'll understand if you don't believe me."

I hesitated. It had only been a few days and yet in some way, I felt he'd been a part of me for a lifetime. Shaking my head, I ran my forefinger along the curve of his lips. "I believe you. I feel some kind of connection to you, deep inside and it's telling me to trust you."

His lips found mine.

Finally.

I could have yelled with jubilation but I was too busy.

The kiss was tender and sweet and full of promises that caused my heart to expand.

He rested his forehead on mine. "Do you love me?"

Effing hell. What kind of question is that to ask a girl? "I don't know," I answered honestly. I had no room, and definitely no time for pretence in my life. "I feel I could. I like you a lot and I know I want you." I grinned.

He laughed softly.

"But what I do know is I want your clothes off. Now." Giggling, I grabbed hold of his shirt, my fingers fumbling with the buttons while he tugged at the edges of my tee and tried for another kiss.

He chuckled and we kissed and pulled at each other's clothing, our hands greedily wandering over any exposed flesh. We got tangled amongst our clothes which only made us laugh harder.

He's fun.

And kind.

And oh, so hot.

I was glad he was my Warder, I thought and flung a bunch of clothes over my shoulder.

Breathing heavily, Alex held me at arms' length. "Wait. My boots. I'm dammed if I'm going to make love to you with them on."

A few seconds his boots hit the ground while I toed off my shoes. It seemed too much effort to worry about my socks as we came together in a desperate clutch.

I was full with a frantic desperation, a need to have this one time with him before it was all snatched away.

By the sound of his rapid breathing, the racing beat of his under my hand, I guessed he felt the same.

"Am I going too fast?" he panted as he sucked and nipped at my ear. I shivered with delight, my flesh puckering all over. He'd filled his hands with my breasts and they swelled, growing fuller, heavier, my nipples shrinking into tight buds that ached for his mouth.

"No." My nether lips moistened, my muscles softening

as my body hummed for him. Pulse drumming, I swept my tongue down the column of his throat enjoying the faint tang of salty sweat. My hands were busily roaming his shoulders, down his back sneaking around his flat stomach and inching lower.

I trembled, knowing whatever time we did have was going to be too short.

We could be interrupted at any second.

It was enough to make a girl want to cry.

As if the same thought had entered our heads instantaneously, we knelt down on the hard ground.

"Wait." Alex moved about in the dark.

Without his hands and body keeping me warm, my skin cooled quickly. I shivered even though the night wasn't cold. When he reached for me again and pulled me down before rolling on top of me, I realized he'd positioned his clothes to insulate me from the concrete.

A small act but one that raised him higher in my eyes.

"I hope this isn't too uncomfortable. We'll go with you on top next time when we're somewhere safer."

I scoffed, "What makes you think there'll be a next time?"

"I don't make promises I won't keep."

This guy was a protector, through and through. He was special. God, I was lucky he was mine. I wound my arms around his back and hugged him tight, hiding my face in the curve of his neck and shoulder.

"Hey," he said softly and gently tilted my chin. "Is everything okay?"

It wasn't my style to inflate a guy's ego, so I said, "Yeah. I was thinking."

"Too much thinking and your brain will explode."

I laughed. "Is that right?"

"Scouts honor. I'm sure I read it on the Net."

"Then it must be true." Grinning, I nuzzled his ear and whispered, "I'm not going to think anymore."

"Neither will I." His mouth came down on mine.

Hell yeah. This guy could kiss.

His touch seared into me. All I could feel was him, all I could think of was him. I wanted more.

Our tongues danced while his hands cupped my breasts, slid down over my tummy, explored my butt so thoroughly my entire body sizzled and tingled. Back arching, I offered myself to him. Every part of me throbbed, especially that certain place between my legs. Any moment and I was going to burst into flames. Or turn into a nerveless puddle of lust.

I heard the crackling sound of plastic being ripped.

"What?" At this point, my hazy brain was beyond thinking. I was so into him.

"Shush," Alex panted, his weight crushing down on me as he shifted. "Sorry, hope I'm not squashing you. Just slipping on protection."

"Good idea," I said not really giving a hoot. As long as this pulsing throb wracking my body was satisfied, I'd agreed to anything. I ran my tongue up and down the little valleys of his ear then sank my teeth nipping his lobe. Hoping he'd get the hint and get a move on.

He hissed and I smiled.

"Done." His weight eased. His fingers found my curls at the junction of my legs.

Yes, please. I wiggled them wide, raising my lower body, my eyes squeezing shut as he slipped his fingers through my damp folds.

I gasped. Or was it a groan?

His thumb found my nub and he rubbed. Slowly at first then faster and faster. The sound of his heavy breathing was like music. The heat of his body enfolded me. The touch of his hands, so tender and yet demanding spoke to me on a primeval level that made me feel all woman.

Powerful.

Glory waited just over the threshold.

"Quick!" I said clutching his buttocks and pulling him down.

He moved. His sex prodded my opening. I locked my legs over his backside, lifting, clenching, rocking, urging him on.

Alex thrust. "I hope you've done this before," he grunted and filled me to the hilt.

My breathing seized. "Once or twice." I clenched my inner muscles, loving how he dragged in a strangled breath. "Okay, maybe a few times. What about you? You seem a little out of practice."

Alex guffawed. "What do you think?"

Withdrawing a bit, Alex thrust again.

We settled into a hungry rhythm. I forgot to breathe as my world shrank to this one precious moment. Pleasure rippled through me as Alex's mouth settled over my breast and sucked.

"Tara," Alex mumbled, his voice strained as he thrust into me.

I squirmed, rubbing my nub against his groin. Lights danced behind my eyes. Ecstasy exploded like a million firecrackers. My body one mass of quivering convulsion that pounded through me with every fierce thrust. For one full minute I lost the ability to think, given over to the moment.

Alex stiffened. His breathing hitched then he grunted as he gave three rapid thrusts, joining me in a haze of lust and love.

I came back to Earth slowly and realized my nails were still dug into his back. *Sorry.* I didn't speak the words.

He chuckled but my ears heard no sound. *That's okay. I'm glad you enjoyed it.*

Holy crap! Did I imagine that? I snapped my eyes open, not that I could see anything. Tentatively I reached out with my mind and found Alex; there, right there, inside my head.

Easy. Don't freak out. I wasn't certain it would work.

What would work?

Mind melding.

It's how you'll communicate with the aliens — through me. You're the voice, I'm the vessel.

Then this...us... Sudden tears pricked my eyes. My silly fantasy imploding before me.

"No!" He shifted suddenly, pulled out of me and rolled onto his back, pulling me with him so I lay on top of him. His hands gripped my face. I knew he was straining to read my expression in the darkness. I could sense the intensity of his stare.

"Mind melding can be done without any physical connection. This, what we did, is something different. Something special."

When I didn't speak, he asked hesitantly, "Tara?"

Something special he'd said. He was right. Whatever it was between us was special, fragile even and I had no intention of shattering one of the best moments of my life. *I'll take my chances with this guy. I've got my big girl panties on now.*

I sifted my fingers through his hair, smiling. "I'm good. We're good."

The tenseness in his body evaporated. He rolled onto his side and spooning against him, I snuggled closer. His arms wrapped round my back hugging me tight in a way that brought those bloody tears back into my eyes.

"Thank you for your faith in me. I won't let you down," he vowed.

"I know."

When he went to move, I stopped him. "Just a little bit longer." *I could lie here forever.*

Yeah, me too.

Closing my eyes, I sighed feeling sated and content. He stroked my back in slow, long movements that evoked a well of tenderness in my heart. We lay there in the dark for some time until a single gunshot cracked through the night.

His hand stopped moving and I knew he was straining his senses seeking the source of any danger. I stirred and lifted my head from where I'd been listening to the steady beat of his heart and day-dreaming of happy-ever-afters in another time.

Another place.

The sound faded away, leaving bleakness in its wake.

Alex had tensed, readying his body for battle. His mind severed its link with mine and the loss was bittersweet when I felt his conscious thoughts focus on the intruding cold reality.

One gentle push but it was all the hint I needed. I never had to be told twice. I wriggled away from him, hunting about for my clothes, my fingers scrabbling over the concrete floor. Finally, I located everything and pulled them on. From the rustling noises beside me, I knew Alex followed suit.

"Dressed?" His voice velvet soft was like the brushstrokes of an artist, discerning and loving. My chest swelled while I railed inwardly at all I was going to lose.

"Yes," I finally croaked.

His hand found mine unerringly and he helped me to my feet.

"Do you think when we get back to the others, they'll ...um...you know...know what we've been doing?"

His snuffled laugh loosened a little of my anxiety. "Yeah. Will that bother you?"

"I guess not."

"Lets make a quick dash to the bathroom first."

"Okay."

We walked the few metres to the restrooms in silence with Alex holding my hand and leading the way. When he pushed open the door, I blinked to adjust my sight to the moon lit room. Heat burned over my face and throat as I caught sight of our images in the mirror. Swollen lips mouths, mussed hair, a faint rash on my cheeks from his day-old stubble. I dropped his hand and scuttled off to use the facilities.

After washing my hands, I stared at my dim reflection and poked at my hair. I looked the same as always, apart from my love-fest. Why did I feel so different?

CHAPTER 17: CONVERSATIONS

Alex emerged from the stall, zipping up his pants. He used the taps then dried his hands on the back of his pants.

"Ready?" His steady gaze settled the galloping fear clomping about inside me.

Hand in hand, we left the bathroom and hurried across the workshop floor.

Three oil lamps had been lit to alleviate the gloom and their meagre, yellowy light revealed Garroway pacing in a tight circle.

"Where have you been?" His lips curled downwards as he examined us.

"Busy."

Garroway sighed. "With me, Alex." He marched off.

"Later, okay?" Alex brushed my cheek with his knuckles before following.

I stood there, thinking and still glowing inside. I was glad I'd taken a leap of faith straight into his arms.

"Sis? I need to talk to you." Dan touched my arm.

When I opened my mouth to speak, he cut in quickly, "Not here."

"Okay. Let's head to the bathroom."

As soon as I moved, Alex looked over.

Our gazes tangled together.

I read the question in his gaze as if he was speaking right beside me and shook my head. *No, I'm not making another escape through the roof.*

Satisfied he resumed his conversation with his father.

The encounter, the way our minds had meshed, tilted my soul on its axis. My knees wobbled as I walked across the workshop floor. I hardly knew what to make of this mind-melding thing but it was pretty awesome.

As soon as we entered the bathroom, my brother closed the door in an exaggerated manner that made me smile. He grinned as he inspected the hole in the ceiling plasterboard.

"Did you really climb out through the roof?"

"Yes and I don't recommend it. I nearly lost it. The tiles were so slippery I almost slid off."

"Good one, Sis." He joined me at the basins and we stared at each other in the spotted mirror. "Do you think we're aliens?"

I shook my head. "No, Mum would have said so. I did ask if we had monkeys or rats in us." And as I'd hoped, Dan laughed.

His shoulders straightened. "A tail would have been cool."

"What's up?" I jerked my chin in the direction of the door. "Someone's bound to come looking if we're in here too long."

"This whole setup worries me." He peered at me through his flop of soft brown hair.

My fingers twitched. I wanted badly to soothe it back out of his eyes but knew he'd outgrown my big sister habits. It was time I stopped treating him like a little boy. *If I don't make it, it'll be down to him.*

Instead I said, "Me, too."

"I feel like we're trapped in here."

"Agree. I can't work out whether we're being protected or imprisoned." I turned on the tap and splashed cool water over my face. How long before the water tank ran dry? I made sure I only used the bare minimum, subconsciously adhering to Garroway's ultimatum about one basin-full of water per person per day for cleaning purposes. Plus, Mum and Dad had always made us conserve water, no matter where we were living at the time.

"I checked my laptop a few minutes ago. The government is broadcasting emergency warnings and instructions. About this virus?"

My gut churned. In the mirror, my little bro's face was pale and serious.

"There are reports coming in on various international forums. It turns people mad, makes them attack each other."

The breath froze in my chest, turned leaden. Hoarsely I asked, "Attack? As in...kill?"

Dan nodded.

Air whooshed out from my lungs. Every horror movie I'd ever watched flashed across my mind. I blurted, "That's the perfect way to get rid of your enemy. Have him kill his own people, then stroll in and mop up the few that remain. Bloody hell. This is awful. Does anyone else know?"

"I haven't said anything but that doesn't mean no one else has used their mobile. I saw Emma using hers behind the ute about an hour ago."

I sighed. "There's no way Em would be able to keep something as mind-boggling as that to herself. My guess is she was trying to contact one of her adoptive parents. Let them know she was okay." Gripping the edge of the basin I leaned forward and rested my aching forehead on the cool glass.

"According to Mister Garroway, this virus spreads fast. How much time before the next strike?"

"Um." Dan checked his watch. "Tomorrow morning sometime, I think."

That didn't give us much time. What could we do?

Nausea churned in my belly. I pushed away and paced up and down. "The observatory. Is there anything there we could use to contact these sons-of-bitches and try to negotiate a kind of truce?"

"It's a possibility." Dan's face brightened.

"I can't think of any other way. We'll have to hurry. We're not going to achieve anything by skulking about here. At least, I'm not."

"I'm going with you this time."

"Dan..."

"We were made, *made Sis*, specifically to these aliens' requirements. Both of us. You for communication and I suspect, I'm for inventing engines capable of flying beyond this solar system."

"I knew about me but you? Wow. Not that I'm surprised, that drawing I found in your room was amazing." I enclosed his hand gently in mine. "We can't remain together. If we're both caught, it's over. Not just for us but for Earth."

Releasing him, I swung away to pace the room. "I can't believe I'm saying all this stuff. It's like I'm stuck inside a sci fi movie."

"I know. What are we going to do?"

Drawing a deep breath, I looked at Dan. "I have to get to the observatory, it's the only place I can think that may be of some use to us. You stay with Mum and the others. You should be safe here. And don't worry about me. I'll have a Warder watching my back."

Upon returning to the others, I found some leftovers which Bartholomew happily demolished and gave him a fresh bowl of water. Lurid and nightmarish visions of what was happening outside these walls and the sight of congealed meat made my stomach turnover.

I remained close to Mum, helping her pack food stuffs back into the eskies, saying little but soaking up the familiarity of her presence, storing all the little things deep inside my memory banks.

Who knew if I'd ever see her again? The terrifying possibility that Mum and my friends might contract the illness striking down the world's population spewed poison into my soul.

"Tara? Can I talk to you for a second?"

Deep in thought, I hadn't noticed Marnie approach until she'd spoken. She cast a quick glance around the workshop as if noting everyone's position. An action that sent my eyebrows shooting to my hairline. Maybe, paranoia was catching on, like a new phase.

"Sure. I can't believe how popular I am today." I grinned glad of a diversion from my depressing thoughts. "I'll be back in a minute, Mum."

She nodded and reaching for a blanket began to fold it neatly.

Linking her arm in mine Marnie steered me over to the side wall where we sat on large cans with red lettering proclaiming they contained, Grease.

"How's it going? Has Dan found that address for you?"

"He's working on it whenever Mister Garroway isn't looking." She looked over to her family. "I'm scared."

"Me too."

She gripped my hand and I squeezed back.

"It's more than that, Tara," she whispered, her voice thick as if she held back tears.

I tensed. My skin prickled in the sudden graveyard chill that crept along my spine.

"I think I'm sick."

"What?" I gasped.

"I think I've caught the virus." The words poured from her. "I'm so hot I feel like I'm burning up inside. My head pounds and I have visions of ripping into people's flesh. All I can see is blood."

"Jeeze. Fuck. Marnie."

"You have to help me get out of here. I can't stay, I might infect Nic, Nonna, your mum. I couldn't bear it if I caused someone's death."

253

"Oh, Marnie." Hot tears boiled behind my eyes.

"Please say you'll help me."

"What about…?"

She finished the question I couldn't force out of my mouth. "My daughter? Dad will find her for me and keep her safe." She began to weep. Silent tears that shuddered through her body and that tore at my heart.

I bounded to my feet and tugged at my hair. "When? How? Do you have any idea?"

"Yeah, some." She sounded exhausted, like even the simple act of speaking was a huge effort and my stomach clenched. She blew her nose with a tissue taken from her pocket. "When you guys split so we could lose the soldiers, we stopped to fill up our spare jerry cans with petrol. I needed some tampons so I ran into the servo. Inside was an attendant. He was lying on the floor and I went over to see if I could help. There was blood seeping from his mouth and nose. And when I touched his hand, he tried to sit up and started coughing. Suddenly there's all this shit flying everywhere. I know some got on my face. My father came in and pulled me away from him, saying there was nothing we could do for the poor man."

Shoulders hunched, she stared at her hands busy shredding the tissue into tiny pieces. "I cleaned up in the restroom and we piled back into the car. Found Alex's car and followed."

What to do? How could I help her?

I thought of the soldiers who'd chased us down earlier that day. They didn't act as if they were the least bit concerned about a virus. None had worn masks. They could have been vaccinated against the virus or possibly be carrying vaccines with them. If so, what if I could steal a few vials?

Images flashed into my mind.

The camp.

The trucks.

Dad on the ground.

Don't go there. I concentrated on freeing my mind from bits and pieces of clogging crap that wasn't important. I pushed aside the bitter memories I didn't have the luxury of indulging in, deliberately relaxed my clenched hands, thinking hard. And the more I thought, the more positive I became that Garroway was right; the soldiers had vaccines.

And if they had vaccines, they could well have antidotes. I hoped.

"How long have you felt sick?"

"A couple of hours."

"Then there's still time."

"Time for what?"

I hesitated then said, "I'm not sure yet, so I'd rather not say. Come on, you need to rest."

"I was going to leave." The purpose in her voice rang like cold steel.

"Wait a bit, let me talk to Alex."

"I don't see why."

"Trust me. Give me a little time."

"I guess but I'll quarantine myself."

I remembered how she'd kept to herself during the afternoon. "Fine, you do that, let's go back to the others." I tugged her upright and we walked over to the pit. Grabbing a bottle of water, I settled Marnie over in the corner with her father's dog for company.

Hands in pocket, I chewed my lip.

What to do first: flee to the observatory and hope to make contact or go for the medicine? But if I got caught, it was over. Not just for me, but for everyone.

But Marnie needed help now.

Every second I delayed, meant her chance to live diminished.

Of course there was nothing to say I'd even find the vaccines, let alone anything to treat the symptoms. Logic told me though, it made good sense to have both.

Round and round went my thoughts until I thought my head would split wide open.

What if I did both?

If I could successfully bring back vaccines for those I loved, I could then take off to the observatory. If I didn't make it back from my robbery attempt, Dan could step into my shoes.

It wasn't going to be easy to steal away without being observed.

Every second, every movement I made while I helped Mum tidy the area, I sensed Alex keeping tabs on me from where he sat inspecting his rifle.

He knew I was up to something. Had he heard my thoughts? I hoped not, I'd concentrated on walling off my mind while I worked over various scenarios.

But his constant surveillance wasn't uncomfortable, it didn't make me feel on edge. Rather I felt protected.

Warder. How far would he go to keep me safe?

Garroway marched up and cleared his throat. "Rack time people. We need to preserve our oil lamps for emergencies, so I suggest we get some sleep."

He strode about issuing orders for the area to be cleared and tidied away. We leapt into action.

"I'm going to sleep in the pit again," said Mum, appearing at my side and smiling.

"Okay, Mum. I'm not certain if I want to go back down there. I think I'll stay up here for a while longer. Take Bartholomew with you, will you?" *I still haven't decided what to do. Come on Tara, think.*

"Of course, love." Mum picked up the cat and kissed my cheek. "Make sure you get some sleep. Don't stay up too late talking."

"I will." My chest constricted painfully as Mum walked over and gave Dan a kiss before she and Mrs Tolini crossed to the ladder. Yawning widely and lugging a blanket under her arm, Em followed. She gave a cheery wave and disappeared over the side.

After spearing me with a cold glare, Garroway stalked off as well.

Sitting on an upended esky in a patch of moonlight afforded by the large skylight, Dan was playing cards with Nic and Shay.

Luis was a hunched shadow propped against the wall. He'd been a mainly silent spectator throughout the day, keeping his opinions to himself.

I was glad. The less I had to do with that slime-ball, the better.

Several more shots rang out followed by the rapid fire of automatic weapons. Everyone stopped what we were doing and froze.

It had sounded too close for comfort.

Alex, Garroway and Nic bounded forward.

"What's going on?" cried Em, popping her head up over the side of the pit.

"Quiet. Shay, check it out," ordered Garroway.

No one spoke.

The minutes ticked by like the countdown to a detonation.

Shay re-appeared and addressed Alex and Garroway, "I got a good look out the back window. It's not good. We've got some infected out there attacking anything that moves."

"And the automatic weapons?" asked Alex.

Shay shook his head. "Yeah, you got it. The Mundos Novus Force is out front. I saw two armored vehicles and a company of men."

Something rammed against the front door. The building shook under the force.

Shay unclipped his holster. "I'd say we're surrounded."

CHAPTER 18: VACCINES

Alex

"We need to get out of here," I said, crossing to Tara's side and taking her hand. Her cold fingers trembled in my light clasp, making me want to hug her tight and tell her everything was going to be all right.

But I'd never been good at lying.

"What is it? What's happening?" Mrs Ferguson climbed up from the pit, a leather jacket in her hand which she handed to Tara.

Within seconds everyone had gathered round the oil lamp where my father took centre stage. I noticed how Marnie hung back in the shadows, her hand on the dog's collar and I signaled a warning to Shay, *something's up with Marnie.*

I'll see what I can find out, he flashed back.

Tight lipped, my father said, "They know we're in here."

"But how?" Tara's mother sucked in her breath sharply. She clutched at her throat. "We've been betrayed. Someone amongst us is a traitor."

Everyone spoke at once with Mrs Tolini yelling in Italian.

Looking from face to face, I knew Mrs Ferguson was

right. The MN force had found us too quickly. But who'd betrayed us?

Not my father or Shay.

I considered the newcomers. Marnie, still standing in the shadows. That girl was an enigma, she was so contained I found it difficult to gain a sense of what made her tick. I found it hard to believe it could be Nic or Mrs Tolini. Luis was off, definitely a coward, and the guy was a crim. Emma was staring at Tara's and my linked hands.

I felt bad about that. I hadn't encouraged Emma but I knew I hadn't brushed her off either which I should have instead of using her to get closer to Tara. I also knew I'd do it all over again. I'd do anything to keep Tara safe.

Still, a cool sweat broke out along my spine as I wondered whether Emma had sussed I'd been making out with Tara. Facing a girl's tears wasn't something I enjoyed doing.

Emma's head jerked up. There was a curious lack of expression in her blue eyes. But then she shrugged and smiled.

I relaxed, glad to know she wouldn't hold it against me or her friend. Obviously, she hadn't been as keen on me as I'd thought.

Bloody hell, who could it be?

Another thud on the door. How long before it shattered beneath the onslaught?

I held up my free hand and the others stopped arguing.

"We'll worry about who's been feeding info later. For now we need to put some distance between us and those soldiers. I propose a diversion. I'll go out through the roof in the bathroom. I'll use a grenade to blow up one of their vehicles. At that same moment, you lot drive out of here."

"Not a bad plan," said my father in a grudging tone.

"Wait," cried Tara. "If we go out there, some of us might get infected too."

Nic growled, "Too right, but staying in here is akin to suicide."

"It's our only option." I looked around the group of people. "We take only what is necessary. Emergency rations, water and ammunition. Shay, you take my car with Tara, Daniel, Mrs Ferguson and Mrs Tolini. Nic you're in charge of the ute. We'll need to put the majority of our supplies in the tray."

"Gotcha." Nic did a mock salute and swung away with Marnie followed him to the pile of boxes and eskies.

"Just a minute..." Dad began.

But I over-rode him, saying loudly, "Shay, you're responsible for Tara's safety until we meet up. We'll work out a rendezvous point. If I'm not there in two hours, don't wait. Get them out of this town." If I didn't make it, I knew Shay would take her on as his new mark, regardless of his connection with Marnie.

Face red, my father strode forward and grabbed me by the upper arm. Pushing his face right up in my personal space, he growled, "I don't share command boy."

"Sorry, Sir, but we don't have time for a pissing contest." Heart thumping, I stared back, dead-pan, knowing I was right.

We had to move.

Now.

"We'll discuss this later." My father turned around and began giving directions.

Everyone leapt into action.

I released my pent-up breath at the very moment, Tara darted in front of me.

"I'm going with you," she whispered.

"No, way."

"I feel safer with you. Plus, if it's me they're more interested in, the others will have a better chance of getting away."

"You know they must never capture you."

"You'll keep me safe. I trust you." She gazed into my face and I thought my heart would explode in my chest, so painfully did it swell.

I traced the line of her lips with a shaking finger. "Dammit, Tara."

She kissed my fingertip before saying, "We need to get our hands on some vaccines."

"No way," I said in a strangled voice. "We have to get you to a safe place so we can make contact."

Her gaze locked onto mine and she placed her free hand on my cheek. The grim acceptance I read in her brown eyes sent a fresh shaft of heartache piercing through my body.

I knew there was nothing I wouldn't do to protect her.

"I don't believe there is a safe place. And if I don't make it, Dan will step into my shoes. I'm positive I saw boxes marked with a red cross at the camp. These guys would never leave something so valuable behind. They'd have it with them wherever their new base camp is located."

She took a deep breath. "Alex, there's more."

And I braced myself.

She linked with me and allowing me access to her thoughts.

I stiffened, my blood turning to ice. That explained how Marnie had kept herself apart from everyone the past few hours. "Bloody hell!"

"I think Marnie's infected." Obviously needing to spell it out anyway, she ran through everything her friend had told her thirty minutes ago and her belief the soldiers would have more than vaccines with them.

I let her rattle on while I thought. When she stopped, I ran a hand through my hair. My lips flattened. "Your safety is paramount."

"He's right and our orders are clear. You must complete your mission," said my father, appearing beside us.

How much had he heard? I knew my father. If he believed someone would jeopardize the mission, he'd have no hesitation in pulling the trigger and putting a bullet in their brain.

If it came down to it, should I stop him?

Could I stop him?

I didn't know but I prayed I'd never be put to the test.

***

Tara

Garroway pulled Alex away from me, saying "I've decided on the rendezvous point."

My hands curled involuntarily into fists while Alex and his father huddled over a map and muttered together. I thought of Marnie, the vaccines. What was I going to do?

Marnie's life, my mother's, all these people here…I couldn't allow them to die so horribly. And what about Alex? What if he needed the antidote?

There, decision made. I had to take the risk.

But would Alex help me? It was obvious a little subterfuge would be needed if I intended to escape from Garroway and his eagle eyes.

I hurried off to help toss supplies into the trunk of the car then scooped Bartholomew off the ground. After giving him a big hug, I handed him to Mum.

"Tara," Mum hesitated before continuing. "You're going after the vaccines."

No flies on my mum. "I have to Mum. I've got a good reason."

She juggled the cat in her arms, then gently pushed aside hair from my eyes. "I know."

Our gazes met and I knew she'd sussed something was up with Marnie.

"Be safe," choked out Mum.

"I'll try." The tightness in my chest was like a band of steel so hard did it press into me. I blinked away tears.

The garage door splintered.

"Quick!" bellowed Garroway, grabbing me by the upper arm and hustling me toward the ute, He picked up his rifle off a crate as he passed. "Everyone into the cars. Alex. Do what you have to do."

Heart hammering, I shot frantic glances around at my friends and family.

Things were happening too fast.

How was I going to get away?

Another horrendous smash. The front bay doors buckled under the onslaught. I spun around and saw Alex running for the bathroom, his boots slapping hard against the concrete.

He flashed, *Be careful. I'll catch up with you. Try the courthouse.*

A little of my anxiety eased. Not only did he have my back, the sweet guy was going to help.

Garroway practically threw me into the front passenger seat and slammed the door on me before taking shot-gun position in the back of the ute. Mum with the cat squirming inside the towel she'd wrapped him in, Dan and Mrs Tolini crammed into the back.

I wrestled into my jacket and did up the zip with a snap.

"Seat belts on," ordered Shay in a quiet undertone.

Clicks resounded as we obeyed.

Then in silence we sat waiting.

Our eyes were glued to the garage door.

Slits of bright light glared through the cracks in the heavy timber planks. It was down to seconds.

Would Alex make it in time to set off the grenade before the door collapsed?

Another thud resounded through the workshop.

The walls creaked and shook.

In the backseat, someone pumped a shotgun readying it for firing. I spun around. My mother had wound down the side window and now rested the gun on the pane, her finger steady on the trigger. Dan, clutching the cat, gazed at me sadly.

"Mum?" I said, gaping at her.

"Get ready, Tara," Mum said calmly and I knew she wasn't talking about our forthcoming escape attempt from the garage. She intended to give me the chance I needed.

Another slam against the door.

Wood fragmented and a hole appeared.

Garroway doused the oil lamps leaving the only source of light coming from outside. The soldiers must have several spotlights aimed at the building judging by the glare flooding inside.

In the distance a massive explosion rent the air.

Alex.

Shouts erupted from the soldiers. Engines rumbled into life.

"Here we go, people," said Shay as he turned the ignition and rammed his foot down on the accelerator.

The car leapt forward.

We smashed through the already weakened garage door and roared across the carpark scattering soldiers in all directions as they leapt out of the way.

From the backseat, my mother let loose with a volley of shots. The car cleared the spread of jeeps and Shay spun the wheel, turning left onto Wattletree Drive. Bullets pinged into the rear. Mrs Tolini produced a hand gun and, cursing in Italian, fired back through her open window at the soldier-filled jeeps chasing us.

My gaze fixed on the road ahead; waiting. Stealthily, I released my seat belt, shrugging it off my shoulders. *Wait for it*. As the car sped toward the T-intersection ahead I reached for the door handle.

This was my only chance.

As I'd hoped, Shay braked for the sharp corner.

The car slowed its rush.

Turned.

I opened the door. "Don't follow me."

Shay sent a startled glance in my direction. Flung out a hand.

My mother leaned forward and pressed her rifle muzzle against Shay's head. "Let her go."

I leapt out.

Curled into a tight ball I slammed onto the roadway and tumbled.

Heaving to my feet, I ran across the footpath and jumped the fence. I crept along the fence-line, hiding in the shadows. My blood pumped furiously through my veins in unison with my pounding heart. My breathing was way too loud. A deaf man would hear me, if I didn't calm down. Concentrating I focused on controlling my adrenaline rush and strained my senses as sounds of vehicles, shooting and furious men faded into the night.

No one had stopped to give chase.

A quick look around and I recognized my location. I jumped back over the front fence, crossed the road and began to circumnavigate my way toward where both Alex and I suspected the Mundos Novos Force had made their headquarters.

***

Outside the seventy-year old courthouse built from convict bricks and surrounded by almost equally old elm trees, I crouched behind an overflowing skip bin. I breathed through my mouth, one hand pressed against my protesting stomach.

The stench was unbelievable.

The sight of nine trucks lining the street confirmed Alex's guess. This had to be where the command unit was holed up. Somewhere inside, the vaccines and hopefully, the antidotes, should be stored.

So far, so good. By clambering over residential fences, I'd managed to avoid being spotted. But how much longer my luck would hold, I had no idea.

Now that I'd stopped moving, my skinned elbows and various bruises and cuts were making themselves known. The leather jacket my mother had given me had been a good idea. It had cushioned my fall from the car and limited the gravel rash to one side of my thighs where my jeans had ripped.

I took another peek around the side of the skip.

The moonlight revealed that apart from two guards standing on the front porch of the building, the road was empty of soldiers. At least what I could see. The shadows were fairly impenetrable beneath the old trees and around the far sides of the trucks. But I couldn't hear the murmur of any voices either. In the distance came the crack of rifle fire.

Where was Alex?

Were the soldiers still chasing my family? *Mum, Dan. Be safe.*

Paper rustled.

My heart seized in my chest for a moment before skittering on.

A little gecko scurried out from beneath the skip bin, paused, its tiny nose sniffing the air then skittered across the cracked pavement to disappear under a straggling grevillea bush.

Straightening, I prepared to step forward only to have someone grab a fistful of my jacket and jerk me backwards. An arm locked me in place, while a hand stifled my sharp intake of breath.

"Jeeze, Tara. Quiet or they'll hear us," whispered Alex close to my ear.

My sudden terror settled and despite the situation, I couldn't help leaning into his warmth and enjoying the feel of his hard, virile body pressing against me.

"Okay?"

I nodded and Alex slowly removed his hand from my mouth. Turning me around by the shoulders to face him, he bit out, "You could be jeopardizing the safety of millions if you're caught."

"I know but I'm not prepared for people I know to be written off as collateral damage."

Alex shifted and moonlight bathed his set face. "This won't be easy."

"I know the risks, Alex. My family and friends are not going to catch this disease. I won't lose them," I said firmly and keeping my gaze glued to his. "Even if I manage to speak with the aliens what guarantees do we have they will cease the attack? None."

"I know it's a leap of faith for you, me, all of us."

"It doesn't mean I'm not going to try. But first I intend to make sure my family and my friends have the best possible chance for survival."

"I'll go for the vaccines while you wait here."

I shook my head.

"Shit." He rasped a hand along his jaw, looking suddenly older. "Okay, we do this together. I'll be able to keep an eye on you this way. But you have to promise to obey me without question. Is that a deal?"

"Yes." I touched his bottom lip with a trembling finger. "Alex, I abandoned my father. I did nothing to save him. I can't and I won't run when I may be able to help what's left of my family. Do you understand? I don't want to put you in danger but I'm so glad you're here with me."

"Where else where I be?" he muttered. Then rolling his shoulders he smiled, his teeth glinting palely in the moonlight. "Yeah, I get it. I didn't want to leave our friends and your family behind with no insurance either. Come on, let's do this. Marnie must be close to running out of time."

"Thank you." I pressed a soft kiss to his lips.

As if he couldn't help himself he kissed me back until breathless, I slid my lips from his. "What are we going to do? Another diversion?"

"No. My guess there'll be limited guards here anyway and the security will be lax. I think these guys have underestimated us. They're devoted to their cause but blind to the motivation of others. From the amount of weapon fire we can hear about the town, I figure they're busy clearing the streets of any infected. We'll go in the back. Follow me and keep your head down."

Turning around, he slipped past the skip bin and after a quick glance behind him to ensure I followed, Alex ran along the side of the building.

As soon as he reached the back, he paused and took a moment to scan the paved courtyard that spread as far as the rear fence.

"All clear," he murmured over his shoulder.

As silent as a ghost he slipped around the side of the building and trod toward a narrow porch. I was as close as his shadow.

The first step Alex took onto the old timbers, had them creaking loudly. He froze but no shouts were heard from inside the building.

Wouldn't it be a stroke of luck if this place were empty? We could do with something going our way for a change.

Alex tried the handle but it was locked. About to force the door with his shoulder, I squeezed his hand quickly. I whispered, "Wait. I think someone's coming."

Alex grabbed my wrist and jumped off the porch, pulling me along behind him. We raced across the paved courtyard to press ourselves in the deepest shadows behind a garden shed. I half expected to feel the slam of a bullet in my back.

Footsteps tramped along the side of the building, coming closer.

My nerves taut, sickness churning in my belly, I longed for invisibility. *Hey, that would have been a nifty trick to have, instead of an ability to talk the talk with aliens.* Not daring to move in case I dislodged pebbles and betrayed our presence I plastered myself against the shed wall.

Alex released my hand. His arm brushed against mine and I heard the infinitesimal slide of metal against leather as he gently eased his gun from its holster.

Tramp.

Tramp.

Closer.

My heart became thunderclaps in my ears. I waited.

They were close, mere feet away. One complained about the food he'd been given that night. The footsteps stopped.

I held my breath.

With a rusty grind, the door to the shed rumbled open. The men grunted as if lifting something or moving something heavy. A dull thud as a box hit the ground.

The door rattled shut. Footsteps and voices faded as the men disappeared down the driveway of the courthouse.

"Stay here." Alex edged past me and checked the soldiers had gone. "I've got a hunch." His teeth gleamed as he grinned then strode quickly to the shed door.

I tiptoed to his side, straining my eyes searching the darkness but as far as I could tell, we were alone in the courtyard. When I turned around, Alex had already begun to slide the door along its tracks. Inch by careful inch, excruciatingly slowly, the door slid open wide enough to enable one of us to enter.

Alex flicked on a penlight he'd fished from his shirt pocket. Its thin beam swept over the interior revealing stacks of metal boxes of varying sizes.

Bingo.

"That's them. The vaccines, I mean. At least, they look like the same boxes," I squeaked excitedly, my fingers digging into Alex's arm.

"We have to make sure." Alex handed over the torch. "Here, hold this please."

While I kept the light shining on the closest box, he used his knife to break the flimsy lock. Sweat beaded on my forehead. Any second now and those soldiers could come marching back and we'd be trapped inside the shed.

"Got it." Alex replaced his knife into its sheath and opened the lid.

Inside were numerous tiny vials of a clear liquid. Taped to the inside of the lid were packets of syringes. The vials all had either a small green or red sticker.

"This has to be it."

"If all these boxes contain the vaccines, there'd be

enough to vaccinate an entire city. I'm going with green for vaccine and red for antidote," I said.

Alex snorted. "That's a bit of leap."

"Not really. It says it here. And it mentions deadline when the antidote won't work. Nine hours. We've got fifty minutes to get this to Marnie." I waved the sheet of paper that had fallen from the case when Alex opened the lid.

"Good one. You know, Tara, maybe that's their plan. Hold a city to ransom and gain control of the populace by offering salvation from the virus."

"We have to take as many as we can carry."

"That's not going to be very many. I have a better idea." Alex hefted up the closest box and handed it to me. "Not too heavy?"

"I can manage." I beat back my gasp as the weight dragged at my arms.

Alex indicated the door. "Go across the courtyard, along the side of the building and place the box behind the skip bin. I'll be right behind you."

"Okay." I stepped over the door track, checked the coast was clear and hurried back the way we'd come until I reached the bin where I lowered the box to the ground. Alex was right behind me. He placed two larger containers next to mine.

"Now we do it all over again," Alex said.

Two super-fast trips later we had nine boxes and I felt as if my arms had been wrenched from their sockets.

"Now what?" Rubbing my aching muscles, I looked up and down the dark street.

"We wait."

"But Marnie…"

"Don't worry, Shay will be here soon."

Alex pulled me back against his chest and wrapped his arms around me. Sagging, I closed my eyes, nestling in, glad to be given a moment's rest.

I don't understand.

I've sent for him. He'll park a block away and meet us here.

But Mum, Dan, Mrs Tolini? They may get caught.

Don't worry. He's left them somewhere safe. He hugged me closer and I snuggled into his warmth.

A long ten minutes later, Alex stiffened and stared down the road to the left.

He's here.

Shay stepped out of the shadows beside us. Without speaking he lifted two containers and set off into the night.

I stared after him. *He's telepathic too. This is so cool.*

Yeah.

I had a horrifying thought. *Wonderful. Someone else that can look inside my mind.*

No, Tara. You and I are linked and I'm linked separately with Shay.

Whew. That's a relief. I certainly didn't want anyone else privy to my secret fantasies where Alex was concerned. I looked around to find Alex had picked up two containers. Sighing, I crouched down to scoop up a box before hurrying off behind him.

Further down the street came a low muttering and shuffling feet.

What the hell is that?

Shit. Hurry, Tara. Alex broke into a jog.

I bit down on my protest and did my best to keep pace stumbling over a crack in the pavement. Just when I thought the box would fall from my numb hands, I spotted Alex's car parked outside the schoolyard.

My legs shaking like a mousse gone wrong, I tottered to where Shay was bent over the open boot. Alex strode over and took my box and stacked it on top of the others.

He took my hand and towed me to the passenger side door.

"Get inside and keep the door locked until we get back."

Before I could say anything, he was gone.

Thank heavens! I ached all over. Huddling down against the leather until my head barely topped the dashboard, I waited out the long minutes until the boys return. We were running out of time. Every so often I popped my head up and scanned both directions of the road, remembering those blood-curdling noises I'd heard. What if it was the infected roaming the streets? What if they attacked Alex?

One more look.

I peeked over the dashboard.

From a blotchy, slack-jawed face, green-filmed burning eyes stared at me. I almost had heart failure.

OMG!

An infected!

CHAPTER 19: INFECTED

Could that dribbling creature really be my boss from the pub, Ray Watson?

It had to be – the mop of salt and pepper, shoulder-length hair and his sagging pouch of a belly, gave him away. Squishing back up against the seat in an attempt to put as much space as possible between me and the windscreen, I gulped. My gaze flicked round the cabin like an insane dragonfly, then zeroed onto the rifle bolted under the dash.

If it came down to it, I'd have to put a bullet in my boss.

I remembered the soldier I'd killed earlier that day. The food I'd eaten earlier rushed up my throat. Blindly, without thinking, I yanked open the door and leaning out, vomited onto the ground. Stomach still heaving, I suddenly realized what I'd done.

Shit!

Bare feet shuffled into view.

Grimy fingers curved around the edge of the car door.

Shit! Shit! Shit!

Scrabbling about I somehow twisted my body back inside the car. I yanked on the door handle, desperate to close it. Ill as he was, Ray was surprisingly strong. His other hand wrapped around the top of the window. He wrenched the door backwards.

I had no choice, I let go.

The door flung wide.

Ray lurched back on his bare heels, arms wind milling.

I bent down, unclipped the rifle.

A snarl rumbled from Ray's throat as he regained his balance and rushed toward me.

No time to release the safety and aim.

Grabbing the muzzle I slammed the butt down onto the top of Ray's head. Still coming. He reached for me. Fingers hooked onto my shirt, pulling me forward. His mouth was open. Foam frothed from his mouth.

Limited by the confined space of the car, I smashed him again on the forehead with the gun.

And again.

Blood spurted.

He was so close, I could see the hairs growing from his nostrils, smell his fetid breath from his gaping mouth. He leaned inside the car, crowding me, forcing me back. My legs were bent under me, my back arched. I couldn't kick him. On my knees, I attempted to wriggle out of his reach.

But the gearstick stopped me, trapping me.

Using the rifle now as a lever to put distance between our two bodies, I wrestled to escape.

He snapped his teeth.

Greenish-tinged blood dripped down his face, distorting his features.

"Tara!" A pale-faced Alex appeared behind Ray.

Locking an arm around the infected's throat Alex hauled him out of the car. Ray released his grip on my shirt to claw at Alex's head.

Panting, I scrambled from the car, the rifle still in my hands.

Alex and what used to be my boss, were on the ground, rolling over and over, grunting, pounding into one another. A fight to the death.

Shay ran up, Glock in hand. His gun wavered as he moved it about to get a bead on the infected. But the men moved too fast.

Alex threw the infected sideways.

A single shot rang out.

Ray Watson flopped onto his back, arms outspread.

The top of his head blown off.

Shay holstered his Glock and stepping forward extended a hand which Alex gripped and hauled himself upright.

"We have to move now before someone investigates." Alex nodded his thanks and swept an arm about me, pushing me back inside the car. "What happened?"

"I made a mistake," I mumbled. Tremors shook me from head to toe. "I didn't think. I was sick." *I was stupid.*

I was grateful when Alex refrained from commenting and merely removed the rifle from my stiff fingers.

Alex stuffed me into the passenger seat, left my side for a moment only to return and tuck a blanket around my ice-cold body. He cuddled me, pressed a kiss to the top of my head, before snapping on my seat belt.

I snuggled into the blanket, my teeth chattering. Car doors snicked shut as Alex and Shay slid inside. Alex started the car and we sped down the street. Wandering down the side of the road was a group of five or six infected. They broke into a stumbling run and veered toward the car.

I shuddered, stifled my instinctive cry, and buried my face in my shaking hands as the car swept around them and passed them by.

"Are you okay?" asked Alex.

Raising my head, I met his frown and lied, "I'm fine." I knew by the way he worked his jaw, he didn't believe me but we both knew this wasn't the time for blubbering or hugging.

Stay strong, babe. "We've got the medicine. Thanks to

you, we'll be able to save quite a few people."

And Marnie…oh, please let us be in time. My voice was a bit wobbly but at least I could still speak. "Where's Mum and Dan, the others?"

"You won't believe it but Shay left them at Crystal's place. She's got some bunker thing and has been rounding up people and pets."

"I was wrong about her. I always thought she was a stuck up bitch," I admitted slowly. I was getting my mojo back.

"She still is," said Alex. "But she's got good leadership skills and a strong sense of community."

To the east along the horizon, a faint leavening of the darkness heralded the rising moon. I leaned forward, craned my neck and looked up at the sky where faint trails of bright light revealed another shower of so-called 'meteorites' heading towards Earth.

I threw off the blanket. "After we deliver these boxes, we have to leave. I need to make contact before this second wave enters our atmosphere."

"Yeah, you do." Alex spared me a quick glance. He nodded, a tiny smile curving his lips like he was proud of me before turning his attention back to the road. "The aliens will be close behind their seeders. It won't be long before they take out our satellites and radio transmitting stations. Once we're unable to communicate with our armed forces we'll be plunged into chaos. We'll be easy pickings."

We turned into another street.

The houses here were set on large allotments, usually with pristine gardens and sweeping driveways. Now, lawns were littered with debris from the storm, papers and discarded clothes. Alex pulled up in front of a massive, white two-storied mansion with a pillared portico protecting the front entrance.

Crystal stepped into view from the shine of the car's headlights and when Alex lowered the window, she motioned her hand to the side. "Drive around the back and straight into the garage."

Alex said *'cheers'* and set the car into gear.

No sooner had the car passed inside, then the roller door closed behind us with a loud clang. Light flooded the room.

Crystal's coupe, a confiscated army jeep, Nic's ute and the mayor's silver Mercedes filled the space.

I straightened and wrestled with my seatbelt which had become stuck.

My car door opened and there stood Crystal looking like a stranger in black cargo pants, a buttoned up grey shirt and low-heeled boots. Her hair was pulled back from her unsmiling face into a tight ponytail.

"Are you going to get out or sit there all day?"

She may have undergone a transformation in her manner of dress but underneath, Crystal was still Crystal. Nice to know *some* things never change!

"This way." With a snap of her fingers, she stalked off and out a side door.

"Come on. Let's hustle." Alex released the boot and swung out of the car.

I joined Shay and Alex and had a box placed into my arms. The guys carried two containers each as we hurried from the garage into a small room where another door hung open revealing a steep flight of well-lit stairs.

Down we tramped and by the time, I reached the bottom, I could have burst into tears, my arms were burning with the pain from my muscles. But I couldn't stop. I had to get the antidote to Marnie. I staggered through another doorway that opened out into a massive room built from reinforced concrete. At the far end a large group of people were gathered around a rectangle table, conversing. As I struggled down the long length of the bunker, my wide-eyed gaze swiveled from side to side taking it all in; this was some bunker.

At various intervals, metal doors indicated even more

rooms lay beyond. Open storage racks lined both sides and appeared to be well-stocked with boxes of non-perishable foodstuffs, even medicines and stacks of bottled water. Neat towers of plastic chairs were positioned along the right-hand side. I even saw boxes clearly labelled cat dry food and dog dry food.

Amazing. Crystal had thought of everything. Who would have thought? It looked as if she had sufficient supplies down here to last months if necessary.

"Oh Tara, thank heavens." And there was Mum, rushing toward me, a big relieved smile on her face.

"Where's Marnie?"

"She isn't looking well, Tara. She's resting in a small room by herself. On her insistence."

Nic hurried forward. His face asked the question he couldn't speak.

I nodded. "We've got it."

He placed his hand over his eyes and stumbled away to lean against the wall.

"You took too many risks." Garroway rocked back on his heels and considered me through slitted eyes as I wavered to a halt, wondering when on earth someone would take this bloody box off my hands.

Alex plucked the container from my shaking arms and placed it on the ground. He opened it and withdrew a red stickered vial and a syringe.

"Let me do this, Alex." Mum took the antidote from his hand. "I'm quite familiar with giving people injections."

I followed Mum into the room which looked little bigger than a broom closet. Marnie was huddled in the corner, shivering. She raised her eyes when we entered and I bit back my gasp as I took in her bloodshot eyes and the stark white of her face.

"It's going to be okay, Marnie." I crouched beside her and patted her leg. "We've brought a whole pile of vaccines and antidotes."

Mum pushed back the blanket covering my friend and

competently administered the dose.

"Thanks." Marnie's voice was hoarse and her smile more of a grimace.

Refusing to allow my tears to fall, I sat with her and Mum while we waited to see if the antidote would work. Mum placed her arm around my shoulders and rubbed one of my stiff arms with gentle fingers. I fought hard not to lose it. But that was nothing compared to the battle Marnie had to fight.

"You're exhausted, you need to rest, honey," she whispered before pressing a soft kiss on my cheek.

"I can't Mum. There isn't time." I picked up the plastic bottle near Marnie and unscrewed the lid before placing it gently against her cracked lips.

Marnie took a few swallows.

"I'm just going outside for a few minutes, Marnie. I'll send your dad in."

She shook her head.

"Listen, don't worry. We have the vaccines now, remember? Mum will vaccinate him before he comes in."

"Alright." She gave a weary smile.

I led Mum outside where Nic waited near the door.

"How is she?"

Mum said, "She's a fighter, Nic. All we can do now is wait."

"I want to be with her."

"Mum, vaccinate yourself first then Nic. Can you start on the others? How many people do we have here? We need to record every vaccination so we don't miss anyone."

"I've got it all under control, Tara," said Crystal coolly as materialized and waggled a clipboard under my nose.

Mum took Nic by the arm and walked to a table where Alex had set one of the boxes. Crystal and I joined them.

"Good." I looked around, spotting my brother and Em sitting on camp chairs close by. A cat carrier sat on the ground next to them. My gaze lingered when they looked up and smiled, then swept over the people next to them. "Is everyone here?"

"Yes." Garroway placed a hand on an unopened container. "Since we have the vaccinations, we may as well use them. Alex, ensure our group receives the first batch."

"Yes, Sir. I'll round them up." Alex walked off.

About to follow, I was halted by Garroway digging his fingers into my wrist.

Hard. What was his problem?

He leaned down. "If you've lost us this one chance, you won't have to worry about the Mundos Novus forces. I'll kill you myself."

And as if contact with me had contaminated him, he flicked my hand aside, his expression twisting into disgust.

***

An hour went by which I spent in a daze slumped against the wall while everyone in the bunker was vaccinated. Pain splintered like lightning strikes inside my brain, one after the other. My entire body throbbed. What I wouldn't give to lie down and sleep for a century.

But rest was not an option.

Not for me.

There was no time. I had to make contact. But how? Where? Biting my lip my blurry vision took in the faces of everyone I loved so much it hurt.

It was time for me to leave.

Me and Alex, that was.

As if I'd called his name, he was there, before me.

"Ready?" He rubbed his thumb in tiny circles on my temple, his worried eyes examining me.

A little of the pain eased even as bile formed into a ball in the pit of my belly. I knew what he was asking. My nails dug sharply into my palms when a wild rush of panic temporarily blinded me.

Faces of everyone I loved flashed through my mind. Images of the places where I'd lived while on the run unfolded like a power point presentation of the wonders of Earth then stopped on a vision of my vegetable garden. Closing my eyes, I could almost smell the rich scent of freshly dug earth, the tang of horse manure, hear the contented clucking of hens, the cackle of the kookaburra that lived in the tallest gum tree just outside our fence, feel the life-giving beat of heat from the sun on my skin.

My fate lay elsewhere. Not here. Not where I belonged. If I could save my family, my friends, my people, the land that I loved so much by facing some hideous alien, then nothing, nothing was going to stand in my way.

Opening my eyes to meet Alex's intent gaze, I nodded. "I'm ready."

And just like that, my migraine vanished, the sickness clogging my throat settled. A sense of peace settled in my heart. "I can do this. Don't worry, I won't let anyone down."

Alex released a noisy breath, stood taller, his shoulders a rigid straight line. "I'll be with you."

"Thank you." I smiled into his face, recognizing the vow in his deep voice. I looked up to see my family and friends watching us.

Dan swung his backpack to and fro in one hand and winked.

"No way." I held my hands up.

"I'm coming with you, Sis."

I ruffled his hair one last time. "No, you have to be my back-up plan. You know that don't you?"

"I guess." Dan sniveled and looked away. Wiping his nose with the back of his hand, he mumbled, "Will I see you again?"

"I don't know." Did that confident, calm voice really belong to me? "Be safe, be strong. I love you little brother."

"Right back at you, Sis." We hugged.

And my heart broke all over again.

Nic, with his arm around Marnie, came out of the broom closet. Relief had me clutching at Alex to say upright. Slowly, they crossed to my side.

"It's working. I can feel it." Marnie grinned.

Her eyes were clear and color had returned to her face. "I'm going to make it, Tara. Thank you. Now, I can go and find my little girl."

I thought Marnie's smile the most beautiful thing I'd ever seen.

"*Grazie*, Tara, *grazie*." Nic kissed my cheek.

I frowned. "I guess I can't talk you into staying here where it's safe."

"I feel my daughter needs me, Tara. Dan found an address. Nonna will stay here and do what she can to help but Nic and I are leaving too."

Em joined us.

"You're not leaving too?" I said.

"Don't worry. I have no intention of facing whatever's out there." Em jerked her thumb towards the ceiling, rolling her eyes. "I'll do my best to look out for your Mum and Dan, Tara. You just..." She blinked mistily. "You just come back to us. Okay?"

"I'll try." Opening my arms wide, I embraced my friends in a group hug.

Stepping away, I brushed the tears from my cheeks then found Mum beside me. I fell into her arms. Words rushed to my throat and were lost in the well of grief constricting my chest. I rather thought Mum had the same problem for she seemed unable to speak. Merely held me tight as if she never wanted to let me go.

The feeling was mutual.

I drank in her warmth, the comforting familiarity of her lavender scent and wondered whether this would be the last time I'd ever see her.

Alex cleared his throat. In a low voice he said, "I'm sorry, Mrs Ferguson but we have to leave."

Reluctantly, Mum gave a shuddering sob and changed her hug to gripping my hands in hers. Leaning closer she pressed her forehead against mine and whispered, "Your father would be so proud. We never stopped loving each other or either of you. The divorce, the living of separate lives was a plan we dreamt up to keep you and Dan safe. Another smoke screen."

"But the drugs and Dad's depression?" I mumbled, feeling dazed. Who would have thought they'd be such good actors?

Mum smiled. "Another smokescreen."

"Then you and Bob Garroway..."

"It would never happen. I love your father now and always. There could never be another man for me." She gave a sudden roguish smile. "We used to meet out by the creek, just the two of us."

"Mum!" Tears welled even as I cringed at the thought of my parents making out like a couple of teenagers. But it was so typical of them.

"Now don't be sad for us. We made the most of every day we had and neither your father nor I ever entertained any regrets. Be careful sweetpea. Remember everything we've taught you." A warning gleamed in Mum's steady blue gaze and I nodded.

Be careful who you trust.

***

It was a considerably smaller group that left the Chamber's property as dawn peeped over the horizon and bathed the land with golden light.

Garroway had decreed we take the jeep and leave Alex's car for use by the refugees in the bunker. With its armor plating, it would make the perfect means of transport around town, either looking for other townsfolk to retrieve and bring to safety or in the search for further supplies.

Nic and Marnie followed in Nic's ute as the jeep sped along the main road leading out of town. They'd left the dog behind with Marnie's grandmother.

Alex drove with his father seated beside him. Shay and I sat in the back. The guys were all armed to the teeth, rifles slung by straps over their shoulders, guns in holsters and grenades hanging from their belts.

It should have made me feel safer, instead, the further away from the town centre we drove the vulnerable I felt.

Grief weighed me down like I had rocks in my pockets.

I sat slumped in the seat, staring out at the passing scenery, my mind numb. I stirred. "I thought, Bob, you were supposed to be looking out for my brother."

Garroway didn't bother to turn his head. "He'll be safe enough for the moment. What's imperative is to ensure neither you nor Alex screw up this mission."

The censure in his voice told me louder than any words, he was still stewing over our racing off in search of the medicine. I bet he'd torn strips of Alex, once he'd gotten him alone.

He didn't trust either of us to get the job done.

I turned to Shay and lowered my voice. "I thought you and Marnie…"

His face tightened. "Orders. When this is over, I'll find her."

Nodding, I picked at the ragged edge of a fingernail while I looked out the window. The residential streets gave way to hobby farms, a car wrecking allotment and before long we approached the showground with its white timber fencing surrounding three acres of browning paddocks, two rickety grandstands and an assortment of tin sheds.

"What's that smell?" I took a deep breath and wrinkled my nose as the pungent stink hit the back of my nostrils. Waving a hand in front of my face, I peered across Shay to stare out his window as the showground came closer.

Clouds of smoke billowed from four large mounds of…*burning clothes*?

The jeep sped along the narrow tarred road.

Horror froze my mind. *Surely….? OMG!* I averted my gaze, jerked back into my seat.

Bodies.

Human bodies.

Alex twisted round to look at me. "The infected. If the antidote isn't given in time, there's no cure but death. It makes sense to burn the remains."

Nodding like a Noddy on steroids, I slunk lower. That's it. I wasn't looking out any window ever again.

"We're coming up to the edge of town fast," Garroway warned his son.

"I know."

This was where we'd part ways. Marnie and Nic would stay on the main road then turn onto the highway that led to the coast. They intended to bribe the soldiers stationed at the roadblock with a small container of vaccines. As the disease spread over the country, the world even, the price of one vaccine would soon be immeasurable.

And I would stay with the Warders while they sought a more covert route past the Mundos Novus Forces.

I looked behind me, leaning my arm over the back seat.

Through the grimy rear window and the short expanse of space separating the two vehicles, my gaze met Marnie's.

I smiled a little as Marnie waved a frantic hand out the window.

Alex swung the wheel and the jeep careened off the road, bounced as it flew over a narrow ditch and picked up speed as he sent it down a narrow dirt track that wound through a field of sunflowers.

I kept watching until Marnie, Nic and the ute could no longer be seen.

Feeling as if I'd been gutted, I turned slowly to face the front.

"This track doesn't look as if it goes anywhere." Garroway flapped a map in the air.

"I know what I'm doing Sir. I spoke to the owner myself. This road should turn to the left up here a bit. We follow it to the edge of the field where it ends near the house. Then we cut through another paddock and we should join up with the highway about five kilometers away."

"Let's hope the Mundos Novus Force has failed to secure private roads."

Alex shrugged. "I'm banking even if they do have a patrol here, it will only be a small one. Their unit must be spread pretty thin by now what with mopping up duties in the town."

"Horrible." I muttered, still dealing with the knowledge I'd said goodbye, like forever, to another friend.

"Perhaps, but it's for the greater good," decreed Garroway coldly.

"Once we've got past the soldiers, what do we do?"

Garroway flicked down his visor. His flat grey eyes met mine in the mirror's reflection. "We secure a site on open ground and you fulfil your mission."

"How much longer do we have? Those meteorites look awfully close."

Alex didn't respond, instead he pressed down harder on the accelerator. Gripping the jeep's side handle, I closed my eyes. *This is it. I can't believe the fate of the world is on me. What if I blow it?*

You won't, you'll do just fine. Remember, I'll be with you.

Oh, Alex, I wish we'd had more time together.

His inward sigh filled with yearning feathered across my mind.

Yeah, me too, he flashed.

The jeep cleared the last row of sunflowers and Alex shifted down a gear.

A flock of sulphur-crested cockatoos flew, screeching, across the rapidly lightening sky capturing my attention and momentarily lifting my heavy spirits. I'd always loved dawn.

Early morning sunlight glowed over the farmhouse with its cottage garden filled with colorful flowers and where a rubber-tire swing dangled from a shady oak tree. A thin ribbon of smoke fluttered from the chimneystack.

It would have made a tranquil picture straight from a

storybook, if not for the army truck squatting dead ahead.

And the soldiers peering down rifle sights aimed squarely in our direction.

CHAPTER 20: BETRAYAL

"Take them out," ordered Garroway, palming his pistol and leaning out the side window. He fired.

Shay let loose a volley of shots and I clapped my hands over my ringing ears.

The soldiers facing them returned the attack.

"Get down on the floor, Tara," snapped Alex. *You can't take any chances.*

I know. Snapping off my seatbelt, I crouched on the floor of the jeep, hanging onto the seat in front of me as we hurtled forward.

Shots pinged into the jeep's bonnet.

Silence.

"All clear," announced Garroway.

Hands closed over my shoulders. Turning, I met Shay's calm, smiling face. I allowed him help me up off the floor. But I kept my gaze on my hands, bunched in my lap until we'd left the dead soldiers behind.

Shay reloaded his Glock before re-holstering it. Finally, I raised my head to stare unseeingly out the window at the passing scenery.

When would it all end? Until not one human being remained alive?

Cold anger fused like steel inside my soul.

They started this, all this killing and grief. And what for? Resources? Domination over another planet?

"Are you okay?" asked Alex.

Garroway snapped, "Of course she's okay. Concentrate on your job, soldier. We're through their containment line, if you could call it that, bunch of ill-trained monkeys."

The engine hiccupped as the jeep rattled across the rough paddock and began to lose speed. Steam hissed from under the bonnet and dissipated into the air.

"What the devil is wrong now?"

"It looks as if a bullet's gone through the radiator, Sir. She's done." Shuddering the jeep rolled to a halt. Alex turned around. "We'll have to walk from here."

Garroway swore and wrenched open his door.

Wordlessly, I picked up my backpack from the seat beside me and exited the jeep. I should have known it wouldn't be easy.

The cool morning air filled my lungs. A light breeze lifted my hair. Over in the far paddock, three cows mooed over the fence.

"Wait, while I double check the directions." Garroway unfolded his map and after consulting it and his compass, jabbed a finger north-east. "This way."

He motioned Shay first and fell in behind.

We marched off. The men constantly scanned the landscape. I trudged along, head down not wanting to see how the meteorites now seemed to fill the sky.

It wasn't long before I lagged. Little sleep, a battered and bruised body, high stress and emotional overload had finally taken its toll.

Casting me a concerned glance, Alex looped his left arm around my waist. "Lean on me."

"I'm good. Don't worry, Alex...."

"Make sure she keeps up," barked Garroway without turning his head.

Alex lowered his voice. "He's concerned we won't get

to a suitable clearing in time."

"It's okay. You don't have to make excuses for him. I get it." *I get that he doesn't like me, considers me to be a necessary evil.*

Don't.

I'm sorry. I know he's your father but it's true.

He's doing what he perceives to be his job.

Up ahead, Garroway and Shay had slipped through the barb-wired fence and stopped to converse for a few moments before Shay darted ahead and disappeared into a thick clump of trees and bushes. Alex's father beckoned us forward.

"We're nearly there. I've sent Shay ahead on scout duties. Let's move out. No talking. And you." Garroway pointed at me. "You walk by yourself. Alex needs his hands on his weapons, not on your body."

Be nice. He was Alex's dad. Clamping my lips together so I didn't say something I'd regret, I straightened out of Alex's hold and stalked off.

Silently, Alex held the wires apart so I could climb through and I repeated the action for him. We joined Alex's father, who strode off compass in hand. *Why doesn't he use his phone? Surely he has GPS?*

Phones can be tracked.

Oh. I'd forgotten. I shivered. It was cooler here in the shadow of the trees, a reminder that soon the land would be covered in frost and the nights would be crisp and clean. I'd always have my memories.

Twigs and leaves crackled underfoot. The ground here was uneven, dipping and rising and the bush pressed in on all sides making it difficult to see what was ahead.

Or if anything or anyone watched us.

Ducking beneath a low-hanging branch, I tripped over a knotted tree root. I swore as I slid down a leaf-littered slope on my belly. I rolled onto my side and sat up, brushing who-knew-what-kind-of-crap off my jeans. About to push to my feet, I froze.

*Was that...*what was that glitter? At the other side of the gully, light glittered where the early morning sun dappled through the thick branches of a bush. I sniffed. Gagged as I recognized the sickly stench of decaying flesh.

"Tara. Let me help you up." A hand appeared in front of my face.

"No, Alex, over there. Look." Pinching my nostrils together so I couldn't suck down any more of that terrible smell, I scrambled across to the shrub and dragged aside the branches to reveal a familiar-looking rug rolled into a bulky roll.

Please don't tell me, that's what I think it is!

Alex bent down and pulled.

The rug unraveled.

A scream travelled up from my belly and shrieked inside my mind as I clamped my hand over my mouth to trap the noise inside.

There was no mistaking that red-gold hair. Or the 20 carat gold earrings.

Mrs Andrews.

And with a bullet hole in the centre of her forehead.

"There's nothing we can do for her." Garroway shooed flies aside, lifted the edge of the carpet and covered Mrs Andrews' lifeless stare. "An execution style killing. Whoever did this to the poor woman, is a trained killer. Struth, maybe we're not worth saving."

The lines bracketing both sides of his mouth had deepened, his shoulders rounded as if his burden had tripled in the past hour.

"I was wrong. I thought she was the MN force's leader. I guess it has to be Andrews after all." Alex gripped his father's arm. Quietly he added, "We need to keep moving, Sir."

"After this senseless death..." Grey-faced, Garroway glanced up at the sky. "How can we believe they'll stop their invasion?"

"I don't understand." I staggered several feet upwind

and away from the body and looked from father to son. "I thought once we'd made contact, they'll call a cease fire. What is it you're not telling me?"

"You tell her. I've had a gutful of this shit," said Garroway, shaking off Alex's hold and tramping off.

Alex took both of my hands in his warm clasp. "Unfortunately, Tara, our intel is limited as to their true purpose. But we've been told, they prize honor above everything. Apparently we have to show we're worthy of being allowed to live."

I snorted. "How's that supposed to work? They're up there, miles away and no one apart from me can speak to them."

"They've been watching us for some time." Alex hesitated. "Through me, through my father, through all the Warders. Everything we see and hear is transmitted telepathically to someone here on Earth. Someone who we assume was a member of the initial scout ship. I guess, he or she, sends off this information once the mother ship is within communication distance."

He smiled wryly. "We have no control over this process, its automatic. I did tell you, I'm part alien."

"You should have told me this earlier. What other secrets are you hiding?" Hurt and confused, I tugged free.

"Would you have listened?" Sighing, he ran a hand over his jaw. "Meeting you changed everything. The job, this mission means little to me now. All I want is to keep you safe. Please believe that I wanted to tell you the little that I know but I also had to hold true to my orders."

"So they've seen us killing each other, stealing, fighting." Overwhelmed, I covered my face in my hands. What chance did I have of making the aliens leave us alone?

Alex pulled me into his arms and hugged me close, mumbling into my hair, "We're not all bad. You know that."

"Yeah, but is that going to be enough?" For sixty

seconds I hid in the folds of his shirt, his heartbeat strong and sure beneath my cheek. I leaned back to look into his face. "I'm not giving up. I'm going to make them hear us, realize that what they're doing is much, much worse. Its murder on a grand scale and they have no right to play God."

"You're amazing," he said softly.

"No. I'm just human. A little bit good, a little bit bad but mostly somewhere in between." I grinned. "We're wasting time."

Hands half-curled into fists, I staggered up the slight incline and strode off in the general direction Garroway had been leading us earlier. "Bob! Where to now? "

***

Head whirling, partly through lack of food and sleep and partly through the sight that had burned into my brain, I jogged behind Garroway as he tore through the forest. I knew that terrible sight would remain with me forever. At every crunch of leaves and crack of twigs I flinched.

My parents were wrong. I was no hero. Inside I was a blubbering mess.

I could barely think straight.

Had Mrs Andrews decided she wanted no part of her nutso husband's acts of terrorism? Had he decided she knew too much and had to be silenced?

Shit...killing your wife...that was cold.

A bullet whizzed into a tree, inches from me. A scream tore from my throat. I hit the dirt only to be hauled onto my feet by Alex and hustled forward until we hunkered behind a wide tree trunk.

"Come out! You're surrounded," bellowed a harsh voice.

From my crouching position behind Alex, I glanced over at Bob Garroway who'd positioned himself behind another tree. Pistol in hand, he fired off two shots.

A burst of semi-automatic fire shredded the bushes and trees around us into confetti.

I clapped my hands over my ears and flattened myself to the ground.

"It's over. Surrender."

Raising myself onto my elbows, I peered through the leaves. Undergrowth crackled and rustled as soldiers pushed into view. I spotted Em's father standing behind two burly, unshaven soldiers. *Coward.*

"All of you," Mister Andrews shouted.

Alex motioned with his gun toward the ground. "Don't move, Tara."

"We only want the girl. Leave her and we'll let you go."

Garroway answered by firing off a shot, hitting one of Andrews' men in the shoulder. The impact spun him round. His buddies answered by peppering the trees with more gunfire.

I hugged the ground again as pieces of bark snapped through the air above my head.

When the racket finally ceased, acrid blue smoke singed the air. Coughing, my eyes stinging, I managed a hoarse, "We need to make a run for it."

"Not yet." Alex jerked his head to the left. "Shay's on his way back to us. We need to give him time to get into position and distract them."

"Come on out, girl. I've got someone here you'll want to meet."

At Andrews' smug voice, ice trickled like buckshot pellets down my spine. "What's he talking about? Can you see, Alex?" I whispered.

Alex took a quick look then slumped back against the tree trunk. His grim face said it all. "Oh fuck. Marnie and Nic have been captured."

"What?" My heart thumping like a death knell, I risked another peek.

"Let go of me!" cried a familiar voice.

A disheveled Marnie with blood stains on her shirt was wrestled into view by a grinning soldier. Two other men dragged a semi conscious Nic under the armpits then let go. He sagged to the ground. He must have put up one effing fight. His hair was matted with blood. His right eye swollen shut and already purpling with bruises. A long gash had slashed through his left sleeve. Blood had drenched his shirt, back and chest and appeared to come from his right shoulder. On his knees, head bent, breathing hoarsely, he clutched his right arm protectively.

"Arseholes!" screeched Marnie who elbowed her captor in the face and when he loosened his grip, wrenched free to rush to her father's side. Scooping her arms around his back she cradled him to her chest.

A little of my anxiety lessened when I realized the source of the blood on Marnie must have come from her father. But how badly was Nic hurt?

"It's simple, Tara Ferguson," called Andrews. "You show yourself, your friends throw down their weapons and I'll spare these two. If not...?"

One of his men marched to Marnie's side and pressed a pistol to her head.

I clutched my throat. "Frikking hell! He's going to kill her." I stared at the scene my mind flashing back to my father's murder.

"Stay where you are!" ordered Garroway, gesturing furiously with his gun.

"Don't do it, Tara!" yelled Marnie. "Run. Nic and I'll take our chances. Forget about us!"

The soldier smacked her in the face, slamming her sideways. She flopped like a broken doll onto the dirt. Nic swore and made a clumsy attempt at attacking the man who laughed and punched his gun into the back of Nic's head. He kicked Nic repeatedly in the stomach.

"Stop it!" Hot tears built behind my eyes.

Tara. No.

Oh Alex, I'm sorry. I can't let her die because of me.

And what about everyone else?

You don't really need me. You can do it, all you need to know are the right words and that's where I come in.

Don't do this, Tara. I can't and I won't leave you here to die.

You have to. Through the long, yellowing grass separating us, our eyes met. *Remember these words.*

And I made him flash back three times the strange sounding alien symbols that I was positive was the message that needed to be told.

No need to make this any harder than it already was, so I kept my mouth shut. I wouldn't tell him *'goodbye'*.

I couldn't.

My muscles tensed as I tore my gaze away.

"Tell your soldier to back off," I yelled.

Andrews gestured and the man kicking the shit out of Nic stopped. "Come on out."

His face, pale and drawn, Alex straightened, held out a hand to help me stand. His rifle muzzle was pointed down.

Is this it? Is it all over? Stomach cramping as angst ripped through me, I stood on legs as wimpy as wet noodles and raised my hands toward the sky. The blue had all but vanished behind the brilliant white light shining through the branches above my head. *Alex, I told you to leave me.*

I can't, no matter what happens. Love must always be worth more than greed or war. Otherwise, what's the point of living?

Oh, Alex.

Tara, listen. They're not far away. I can sense it. If we can get away, we still have a chance.

I sucked in a shaky breath. Love. He'd mentioned love; again. His words burrowed deep into my soul and filled me with light.

With Alex by my side, I stepped out into plain view of the enemy.

"What the fuck do you think you're doing? Get the hell down. Alex." Garroway pointed his gun at me.

Terror and bile churned in my gut.

Alex pushed me in front and presented his back to his father, protecting me from him. I couldn't help the rush of emotions swelling inside my chest at his actions. He'd chosen me. Over his father. I knew that must have been one effing tough decision.

"Get out of the way, soldier," ordered Garroway.

"Sorry, Sir, but you need to put your weapon down or shoot me instead."

"You'd best do as your boy says, Garroway or my men will cut you both down where you stand. I have no truck with you and give you my word, you can leave as soon as I have that girl," said Andrews.

Cursing and still clasping his pistol, Garroway slowly raised his hands in the air.

"Well, here I am. Now, you hold your end of the deal." I raised my chin, curling my hands into fists at my sides. I didn't dare allow my gaze to linger on my friend's bruised face as Marnie scrambled to her battered father curled on the ground. I didn't want to draw any more attention to them.

"Let them go," Andrews said as he advanced toward me, a broad smile stretching over his face.

"Marnie, can you get Nic to his feet?"

"What about you?" Marnie glanced at me wildly through her tangled hair.

I shook my head and made urgent shooing motions. "Get out of here."

Nic groaned when Marnie slipped an arm around his chest and hauled him upright. Locked together, they took three staggering steps towards freedom.

A high, shrill voice rang out. "Stop them. That's an order."

Safeties clicked off, as the surrounding soldiers snapped to instant attention and levelled their weapons directly at us.

CHAPTER 21: DEADLY GAME

"Em?" Feeling my world rock on its axis, I stared at my other best friend, unable and unwilling to believe the evidence of my eyes. "What are you doing here?"

"Well, duh! I rather thought that was obvious." Dressed in a lacey pink cami and pale blue cargo pants and with combat boots on her feet, Em strolled over. She smiled. "Surprise."

Through my constricted throat, I squeezed out, "I don't believe it."

Em sighed while she took the pistol a soldier held out. Waving it idly in the air, she said, "It's quite simple. I'm from batch number nine."

Desperately wanting to block my ears to the reality hammering into me like death blows, I mumbled, "You're with them. You're the one that's been feeding them information about us."

I remembered all those furtive mobile phone calls, the lack of interest in her adoptive father's activities...and...*oh God;* the lack of caring about her missing adoptive mother. How could I have missed those clues? "Did you know your mother is dead?"

"Of course." Appearing unconcerned, Em raised one

shoulder. "Sheila got cold feet. She became a liability."

I shuddered as betrayal burned like hell-fire through my soul. Who was this person? Walking, talking, her appearance, her mannerisms...everything told me that here in front of me was my best friend.

But no longer.

She was a stranger.

My worst enemy.

"We took you into our home. I thought we were friends. And Dad...Dad..." I choked off the sob tearing at my heart. "You warned them he was going to the camp that day. You're responsible for his death."

"So?"

I struggled to remain where I was and not rush over and plough my fist into her lying face. "Why did you help me escape? Why didn't you kill me too?"

"We still weren't certain you were the one. For a while we thought it might have been Marnie. It was decided to continue with our charade while we looked for the answers we needed. We didn't want the Warders breathing down our backs until we were absolutely certain." She sighed. "We also hadn't decided whether you'd be of more use to us alive or dead."

"You were our friend. All these years."

Em blinked rapidly. "We *were* friends. Then, I was activated."

My gaze caught Marnie's shocked stare and she shook her head violently.

"I knew nothing about this, I swear, Tara," said Marnie. Tears dripped down her white face. "I can't believe it. Emma, please, think about what you're doing."

"You're both too dumb to live." Em clicked off the safety and levelled the gun at Marnie.

"Em! Don't! Your father gave his word Marnie and Nic could leave unharmed."

"You still don't get it, do you, Tara?" The gun lowered. "I'm the one in charge."

"You?"

Em smiled.

From somewhere deep inside me, cold rage replaced the betrayal. *She knows where Mum and Dan and all the others are hiding. I've got to protect them. But how?*

Keep her talking. You're doing fine flashed Alex.

"It's a game. Haven't you realized that by now, Tara?" The whites of her eyes showed as she waved her hands wildly in the air. "This ... the destruction of our planet all for a game."

"You can't possibly know that for certain."

"Honestly. Do you really think you're the only one that's been programmed before birth?" spat Emma. "I have their filthy genes inside me. If I could, I would rip them from my mind and body. But it looks like I have to make the best of the situation."

Drawing a deep breath, I managed to keep my voice steady. I'd be damned if I was going to show how totally shit scared I was to *her*. "Going on a murderous rampage is not what I'd call dealing with a shitty life."

Emma rushed forward to thrust her face inches from me. The expression I read in her eyes had my blood curdling in my veins.

Someone or rather something else stared back at me; flatly and with a total lack of human empathy.

"What do you think it's been like, living with this other thing inside me? Each hour, each minute feeling it claim more and more of me. I had to choose or lose myself completely. In the end, I compromised."

"I don't understand..." I began, not wanting to believe, not wanting to accept the evidence standing right in front of me. Her betrayal cut me deep inside, made me hollow as if something precious had been destroyed forever.

Emma, or whoever she was, interrupted, "Of course you don't. That's because you're from the early batches, primitive, limited intelligence. You should have been destroyed along with the other feeble mutants. How you've managed to live this long is a true miracle."

"This has gone on long enough. Emma, let's leave the girlish spats to some other time." Mister Andrews strode forward and took his daughter's elbow and pulled her aside. Turning to his men, he said, "Take the men out of my sight and shoot them."

Five soldiers with their weapons raised, tramped towards Alex and his father.

Terror clawed inside my mind.

"Wait!" I shouted and the soldiers paused.

As if surprised I dared issue orders and even more surprised his men had obeyed, Andrews stared at me too.

"Killing each other is not the answer. And killing Warders... is... not... a good... idea," I said with slow emphasis. My heart beat so heavy and loud it was a wonder no one else could hear it. We *must* get the upper hand.

"I don't see why. They have meddled in our plans too long." Andrews frowned.

Suspicion eliminated the little-girl prettiness when Emma scowled at Alex.

I rushed into speech. "You need them alive. Every single thing you're doing here now, everything you've said is being recorded and transmitted to the aliens by these guys; aka Warders. If we continue to act without mercy, with no compassion, like rabid animals, we'll all be destroyed. There'll be nothing left for you to rule over. Nothing but ash and bone."

"What is she talking about?" Andrews turned to his daughter who rolled her eyes.

Sounding achingly so much like the Emma I thought I knew so well, she said, "Who cares?" She lowered her voice, adding, "We've always known it would come down to a war between us and *them*. Our followers are strong, Dad, and growing stronger by the day. Many of the military have already joined us. They believe in the New Order. None have any desire to live under the yoke of

301

some alien freak."

"But that's the whole point," I said loudly, feeling a glimmer of confidence rise as several soldiers exchanged wary glances. "If we prove ourselves to be worthy of saving, they'll break off the attack. They'll leave us alone."

"Bullshit! This is a game!" Centre stage, Emma spread her arms wide and walked in a tight circle, staring down each and every one of her soldiers. Under the impact of her glare, they straightened, re-tightened their grips on their weapons.

"A game played by their rules. They're not interested in resources, in our land or even in us. They sail through the galaxy playing out some twisted game on planets inhabited by intelligent species and gamble on the outcome."

"They place bets on the winner, is that it? One of them or us?" *Come on, Shay. What's taking him so long?*

Almost in position flashed Alex.

Emma crossed her arms over her chest. "They have no intention of whoever inhabits these planets to win. It's either one of them or our destruction."

But what about proving our worth to live? Was Emma lying? Alex? Or was it another step sideways in this devious game the aliens played? I shot a frowning glance at Alex who shook his head.

She's got it wrong, Tara. I swear.

Gathering my thoughts I returned to the attack, hoping to plant doubts in the soldiers' minds.

"That's not what I heard. And remember, I've got alien genes inside me." I waggled my fingers. "Do you mind? My arms are killing me."

"Fine." Emma nodded.

Slowly, I lowered my hands and hooked my thumbs over the edge of my belt. *Act calm, casual, maybe these guys will relax a little.*

As soon as they do, we'll act, flashed Alex.

Cold sweat chilled my flesh. But I clamped down on my protest. We'd need every tiny slice of advantage if we were to escape.

"If you ask me, you're the ones been brainwashed into believing propaganda. Who do you really work for? I mean, seriously? Emma? There is no way your father is the leader of the Mundos Novus Force. Who's the puppet master? What's your real objective? To save us from the aliens? Or to carve out power for yourselves?"

"This isn't about power or greed. It's about eradicating the sinners and leading the way into a new era," Emma snapped. "Here and now is where the voice of the masses will finally be heard, when we rise up and say 'no' to the corruption that's been suffocating our souls for decades."

Who really gave a shit about this conspiracy stuff? I shrugged. "I dunno. To me, it still sounds like exchanging elected governments with some religious despot. Who decides who will live in this new world you think you can create?"

"Only those who follow the new path, of course."

Path. Weird that she chose that word. Could there be any connection to the alien's message?

"And I guess anyone who objects will be killed." In my peripherals I noted frowns appearing on several soldiers' faces. A couple of men shifted their feet, definitely uneasy with the words spilling from Emma's mouth.

Drive it home. "Who's your boss? Who's waiting in the wings to take control and about to issue death notices?"

"You still don't get it, do you, Tara?" Clearly bewildered, Emma exchanged a wide-eyed glance with her father standing by her side, a smirk spreading over his features.

"It's me. I'm the chosen one. The one who'll lead the faithful into a new era."

"Now, that is strange. Mum always called me the chosen one."

Emma shrieked and flung herself on top of me. Her weight slight as it was, felled me. I landed awkwardly, my right foot tangled behind my left leg and with Emma on top.

Hands fisted she pummeled my sides, my head, my face, connecting hard. For a second the sheer shock of what was happening froze my brain then all that training Mum insisted I did, kicked in.

I fought back.

This was no longer my friend.

This was a murderer determined to kill me.

Two shots rang out.

Someone sucked in a sharp breath.

"Stay down," yelled Alex.

Punching, kicking, arms and limbs flailing, I battled what used to be my best friend for the right to live while above my head a fire battle erupted.

I landed a punch to Emma's ribs, temporarily winding her. Gasping for breath, Emma ceased her pounding and I scrambled away from her prone body.

This way, Tara.

In a crouch, I crab-scuttled sideways, edged past a fallen soldier and picked up the rifle lying on the ground. Holding the gun in trembling hands, I took in the scene as Alex bounded toward me, shooting at anything that moved.

Mister Andrews lay on his back, arms spread-eagled.

Somehow Nic had rallied and was brawling with a soldier. Swearing in Italian, Marnie danced around them, thumping the other guy with a branch whenever she got the chance.

A splash of pink and blue revealed Emma running through the trees. Four soldiers turned and crashed through the bushes after her.

Alex landed next to me, on his knees. "Get behind me." He jerked his head as he fired off another shot.

"Cease fire," bellowed Garroway from his position behind a tree.

Another bullet whizzed past me. I cringed.

Spinning around I saw the soldier with his hands

around Nic's neck reel backwards as the bullet ploughed into him. The guy stiffened, his knees buckled. Nic pushed him aside as he folded with a dull thump like a bag of dry cement.

Silence reigned.

Head throbbing, my body pulsing in one slow throb of pain, I peered around Alex as Garroway strode across the small clearing, gun in hand. Shay shoved past a thickly leaved bush, squinting down the length of his sniper rifle as he held it steadily in the direction of the enemy.

Garroway halted a few feet from me. His gaze fixed on the remaining soldiers, he barked, "Put your weapons down. Slowly."

One by one the men tossed their guns onto the ground.

"Hands in the air."

They raised their hands.

"Alex."

"Sir." Gripping my elbow, Alex helped me up, making sure I wouldn't crumple to the ground, before he looked over at his father.

"You need to go." Beneath the dirt and sweat Garroway's face gleamed pale.

"We've got this covered," inserted Shay in his quiet voice. He kept his rifle trained on the soldiers.

"Nic needs help..." I cried, knowing as soon as the words left my mouth I wouldn't be the one giving the help.

Garroway glanced at me and shook his head. "We'll look after him."

"Okay." My gaze zipped to where Marnie sat on the ground beside her fallen father. Lifting her head, Marnie met my eyes and smiled.

"Best friends forever," she quipped.

Even from where I stood, I could see how Marnie's mouth trembled as she spoke. Her eyes glistened with tears and the stark knowledge; this was our last goodbye.

I repeated, "Best friends forever."

Feeling as if my heart was being ripped apart, piece by

tiny piece, I turned away, gripping Alex's hand so hard my nails dug into his skin. But he didn't complain. Instead he holstered his pistol, slung an arm around my shoulders and encouraged me to run.

"I'm proud of you son," shouted Garroway.

Alex hissed in a sharp breath. I knew without looking, he was dealing with his own grief as with every step we took we increased the distance between ourselves and the ones we loved.

And now had to leave behind.

What about Mum? Dan? The others in the bunker?

Dad and Shay will help them.

We continued our mad dash. Gradually, the forest gave way to widely-spaced trees then we emerged onto the edge of a massive field.

The light from the approaching meteorites was glaringly bright, defying the glow of the sun. How much time did we have left?

Minutes?

Seconds?

"Come on. A little bit further." Alex urged me onwards.

Muscles burning, legs as weak as a new-born calf, I struggled to keep up. First in English and then in the alien language I'd read in my brother's drawings and dreamt about, I started to chant: *Follow the path of Elvirathon and you will be saved.*

"They're coming!" said Alex.

A shot rang out.

He crumpled.

His pain ripped through my body. Screaming Alex's name, I fell to my knees. This mind meld shit sure had its downside.

Clenching my jaw, I attempted to block the connection while I tugged at his shoulders. We couldn't stay here, we had to keep moving. I glanced wildly around, seeking help. But instead, my eyes followed the glint of metal.

Standing beside her remaining loyal soldiers was Emma. One of the men had a sniper rifle aimed directly at us.

"Emma! Please stop this, it doesn't have to be this way!" I yelled, my heart jack-hammering like crazy.

"Go." Alex raised pain-glazed eyes. Blood soaked his shirt from where the bullet had entered his back, near his right shoulder-blade. "Leave me, Tara. Please."

Gently, I stroked a strand of damp, blonde hair from his face. "I'm never leaving you. Now, get on your feet, lover."

Placing my hands under his armpits, I pulled.

Alex grunted but staggered upright, his weight leaning heavily on me. I widened my stance and took it.

Took his agony from his wound deep inside, lessening his burden, opening our connection until nothing on this Earth could shatter it. I shared my hope, my faith in him, giving him my strength to carry on. "Keep walking."

Entwined together, we staggered drunkenly forward.

One step.

Two.

Three.

A bullet whistled past my cheek.

I flinched.

I feel their link, flashed Alex. *They're here.*

About time.

Something icy and alien slithered into my mind and I shuddered.

I could feel it, rummaging about like a possum in a garbage bin, stealing my thoughts, my emotions, pondering over my memories.

Right. You want to know about us, then know this. I poured all my anger, resentment, my disgust at their dirty tactics and horrific competition into the link. I let them experience my love and anguish over my family's fate, the faces of friends and the people of my town and my horror over the destruction of the beautiful land I loved so much.

Would it be enough?

"Tara! Don't move! Don't make me shoot you!" screeched Emma, her voice now a faint cry that echoed over the empty landscape.

You know what, Alex?

What? His response was weak. My heart did a nose dive as the paleness of his features registered, the life dulling in his eyes.

I flashed, *Now would be a good time for these aliens to finish their stupid, senseless game.*

The ground rumbled beneath my feet.

A thunderous roar filled my ears making it hard to think.

Wrenching my gaze from Alex, I looked up just as a massive metallic-grey, space ship like nothing I could ever imagine, cut through the thin clouds.

Terror eroded my shaky courage. My eyes tracked to Alex.

He smiled.

His image wavered, like a bad transmission.

A zillion electrical sparks pricked my body.

The earth fell away from under my feet.

Blue sky flashed past.

A bright white light blinded me and I felt myself splinter into millions of particles. Deep inside, I screamed from the pain crashing through my body.

Was this death?

Three seconds later, the agony receded and I fell into darkness.

***

When I opened my eyes I found myself staring out from inside a transparent tube. Standing beside me, was Alex, whole and hot, if still covered in dried blood. With a wide grin on his face, he said, "We made it."

"Alex! Are you okay? You've stopped bleeding? What happened? Where are we?"

"They fixed me, pulled out the bullet and repaired my

body. We're on board their ship."

I burst into tears. Alex pulled me into his arms and hugged me tight.

After sniveling into his shirt for a few minutes, I leaned back and studied him. "How long have we been here?"

He shrugged. "No idea, but I think several hours. There's no way of checking the time, my phone has been shut down. Part of their security precautions, I should imagine."

"OMG! Mum! Dan! Shit, we have to stop them bombarding Earth." Wrenching out of his hold, I pounded on the tube with my fists. "Let us out of here!"

"That is not going to work."

When I looked at him, he spread his hands wide and said, "I tried."

"Dammit. Where do you think they are? What's taking them so long? I would have thought they'd be in here wanting to question us."

"They're watching us." Alex jerked his chin toward the corner of the room where an orb rather like a massive eyeball protruded from the end of a flexible-looking cable.

I crooked my forefinger hoping the aliens would understand and finally front us. Slowly, I examined the rest of the room. Oyster-colored, on three walls of the room, multi-colored equations and data scrolled down in a continuous stream of information.

Data that I could read.

I caught my brief, fascinated and leaned closer to Alex. "It's a history of their world."

The lights dimmed.

Alex squeezed my hand. *I'll never leave you.*

Across the room, a door slid open.

And my smile faded.

Five aliens glided in as eerily as ghosts. With their soft grey complexions and billowing cream robes that fell to their bare feet, they could have passed as spirits from some horror movie. They all stood a good thirty centimeters above Alex and were so thin, they looked like stretched rubber bands. I was relieved to see they were humanoid and not some hideous creatures with tentacles. Their eyes were big, dark ovals and unblinking as they examined me.

Welcome, Tara Ferguson, intoned a disembodied voice inside my head. *You have been judged worthy to be an ally of the Elvirathon race. We are impressed by the strength of your concern for others.*

I tried a mind connection thing with the aliens and shuddered when I felt their cold presence, *Good, then does that mean you've decided we're worthy to live?*

Not all are worthy.

True but when people are scared they sometimes do stupid things. That doesn't make them bad. Please stop the destruction on my planet.

We have ceased our attack while we discuss the next tactic.

One of them stepped forward and clasped his hands in front of him. Inclining his head, he said, *We have watched you for some time.*

I tried not to feel creeped out and nodded.

When the lead guy glanced back at his buddies, Alex tightened his grip on my hand. *Something's wrong.*

Had they lied to us? Did they even now, continue to destroy my home? "You promised." The words shot from me like bullets.

They stared back impassively.

"They're not capable of communicating like us, Tara. Only telepathically," Alex advised.

"Right." I drew a breath and concentrated. *Will you leave Earth alone?*

We, the elder council of the Elvirathon race, have discussed this matter in depth. It is our opinion your race shows several traits which are interesting and are worthy of further study. It is possible, your people may reach a level of worthiness we judge similar to ours.

So, it's a ceasefire?

Alas, the attack has not stopped. The Skeetishas have decided the competition is far from over.

You said we'd be saved. My body shook with a combination of fury at this betrayal and fear for those I'd left behind.

This is true. However, the choice is not ours.

That's bullshit! What you're doing is bullshit! What gives you the right to kill people and animals for some stupid game?

The leader held up his hand and I shut my mouth.

Ranting and raving was not going to get me anywhere. I needed to think, negotiate, search for a weakness in their so-called logic. *Tell me about this competition?*

The leader lifted his hand.

Light streamed from the ceiling to a single point about midway toward the floor. The particles formed into a 3D image of a solar system.

Both the Elvirathons and the Skeetishas are ancient races. Many cycles ago, we ascended to such a logical lifeform that physical pleasure and emotions devolved until they were mere whispers in our past. All that was left, was supremacy. The war began. When we realized we could not destroy each other, we decided there was only one way to prove which of us held supremacy over the other. The challenge of conquering other planets. Since that time, the competition has changed.

You send out scout ships, make contact and sit back to watch what happens. Is that it? I raised my eyebrows.

Only the worthy can live.

I bit down on the hot denial springing to my lips. Turning to Alex, I whispered, "We're their entertainment."

The way he clenched his jaw, told me he agreed.

I flashed, *This isn't about resources or a new planet to live on, is it?*

Negative. It is about winning.

You must really hate each other. I shook my head. *What can we do to change the other aliens' minds?*

We do not believe this to be possible. The leader made a slashing motion with his hand and the image disappeared.

I looked at Alex. In his gaze I read a steadfast determination and trust; trust in me. I had no idea whether

311

what I intended to propose would work or how to go about it, but I had to try. If I didn't, the outcome was too horrible to contemplate. *Can they be stopped? What if you form an alliance with us, with Earth?*

The leader stepped back and the five formed a tight huddle. They conferred with each other for several minutes before breaking apart. The group as a whole walked forward to stand before the tank which contained Alex and I.

Realizing my nails were digging into Alex's palm, I relaxed my grip. Heart thudding, my gut shuddering in sickening spasms I waited for the verdict.

The leader flashed, *This sounds like a worthy challenge. We agree. But be warned, Tara Ferguson. It will not be easy. The Skeetishas have proposed a different set of rules. The winner will take all.*

~The End~

Thank you for reading ***Don't Look Back*** – the first book in my apocalyptic, science fiction New Adult series, **Warders of Earth.** I hope you enjoyed it.

Look out for Book 2 – **Marnie's War**.

Books by S. E. Gilchrist

Darkon Warriors series: *Legend Beyond the Stars*
The Portal
Awakening the Warriors
Star Pirate's Justice
When Stars Collide
Bargain with the Enemy
Touring the Stars
The Slave Trap
The Mars Academy series: *Stranded*
Cosmic Fire
Apocalyptic: *Paying the Forfeit*
Storm of Fire
Bound Series: *Bound by Love*
Bound by Lies
Contemporary: *Dance in the Outback*
Cowboy under the Mistletoe
Bindarra Creek Makeover

BIO

S.E. Gilchrist can't remember a time when she didn't have a book in her hand. Now she dreams up stories where her favourite words are…'what if' and 'where'? SE lives in the Hunter Valley, Australia with her family and is the author of over eleven books. Her stories are set in the exciting worlds of science fiction, ancient worlds, apocalyptic settings and contemporary small towns. SE takes a keen interest in the environment and animal welfare and loves bushwalking and Zumba.
SE is published by Escape Publishing and Momentum Books and is an indie author.

*

If you'd like to know more about SE and her books or to connect online, please visit the following links:
Website | Facebook

SE's twitter handle is: @segilchrist1